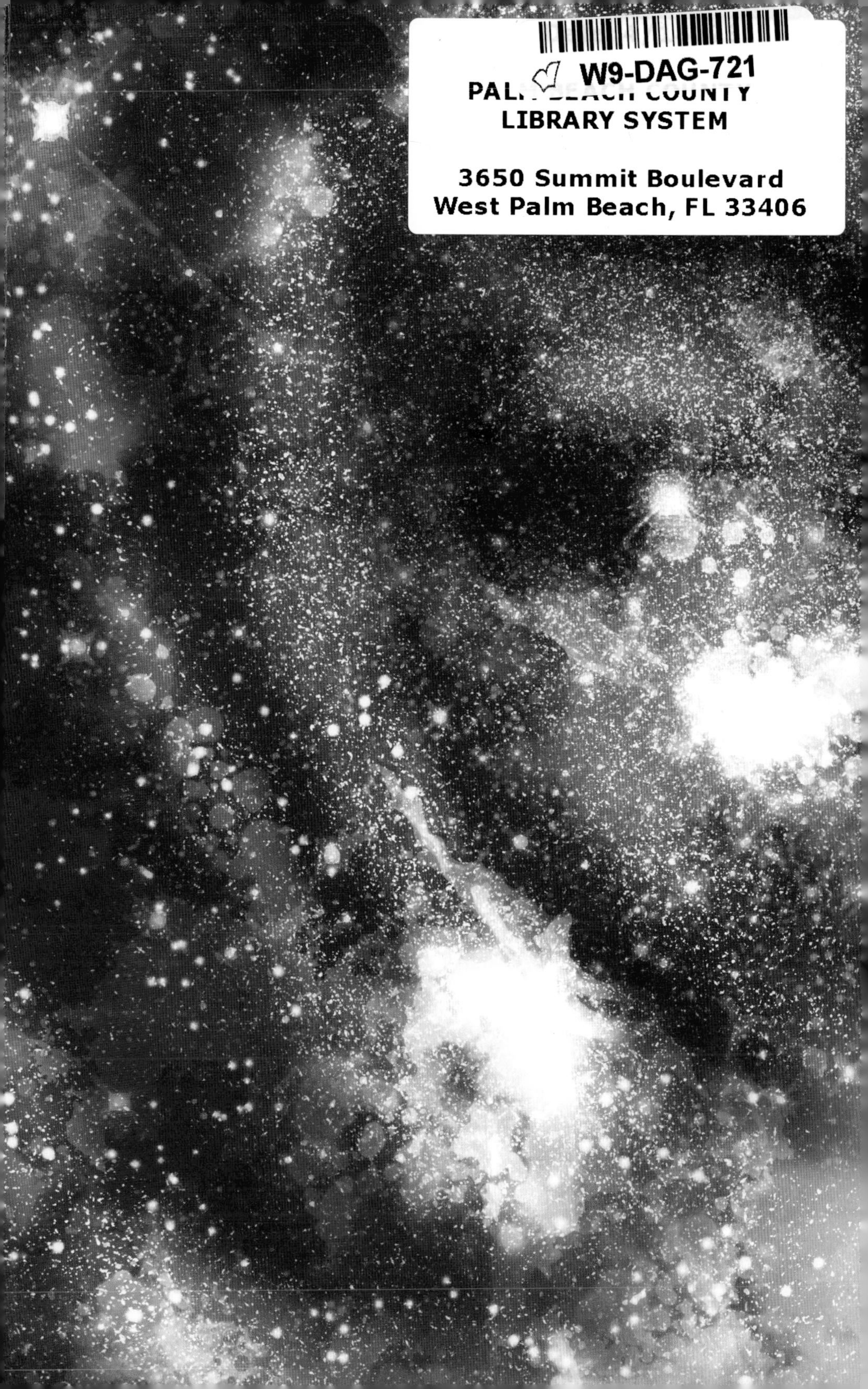

# PEANUTS® GRAPHIC NOVELS

# Snoopy Soars to Space

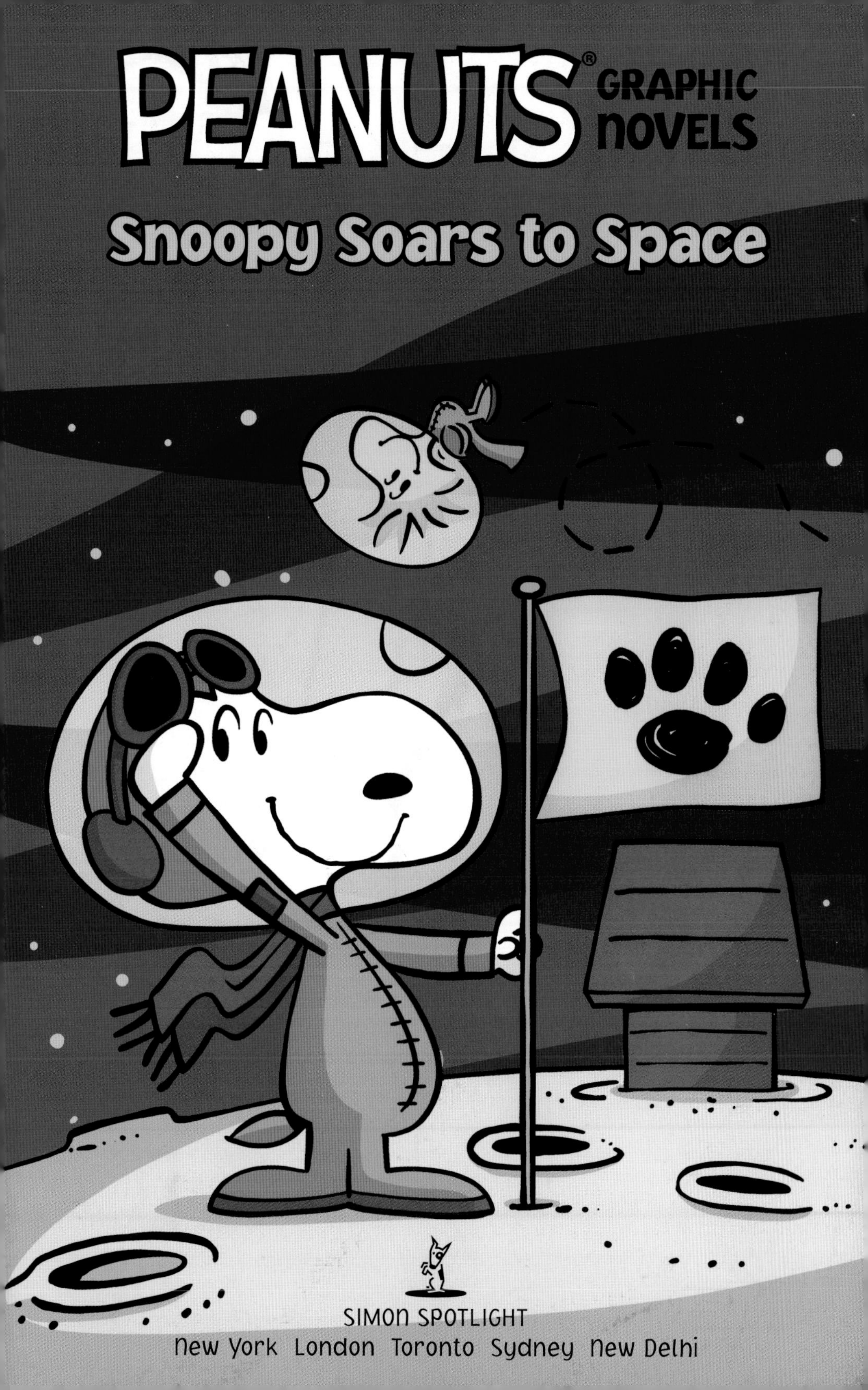

SIMON SPOTLIGHT
New York London Toronto Sydney New Delhi

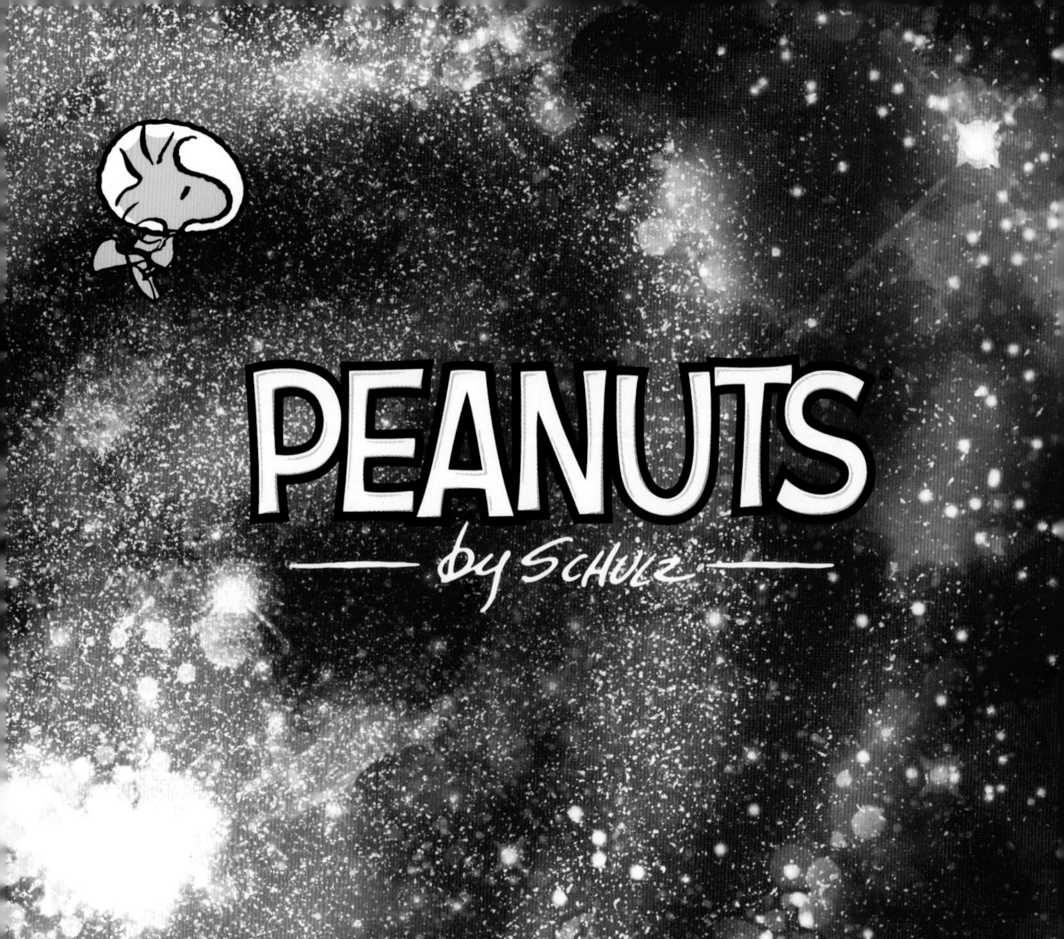

# PEANUTS

## by SCHULZ

SIMON SPOTLIGHT
An imprint of Simon & Schuster Children's Publishing Division
1230 Avenue of the Americas, New York, New York 10020
This Simon Spotlight edition January 2023
Peanuts and all related titles, logos, and characters are trademarks of Peanuts Worldwide
LLC © 2023 Peanuts Worldwide LLC.
"Plane and Simple," "Food for Fraught" © 2013 Peanuts Worldwide LLC.
"Have Dish Will Travel," "The Beagle Has Landed, Charlie Brown!,"
"Twinkle Thinkle" © 2014 Peanuts Worldwide LLC.
"From the Drawing Board" © 2015 Peanuts Worldwide LLC.
"Charlie Brown's Star," "Sunny Disposition" © 2016 Peanuts Worldwide LLC.
"Kickoff to the Moon" © 2023 Peanuts Worldwide LLC.
Most stories in this volume were originally published in the PEANUTS comic
series by Boom Studios 2010–2021.
All rights reserved, including the right of reproduction in whole or in part in any form.
SIMON SPOTLIGHT and colophon are registered trademarks of Simon & Schuster, Inc.
For information about special discounts for bulk purchases, please contact
Simon & Schuster Special Sales at 1-866-506-1949 or business@simonandschuster.com.
Manufactured in China 0922 SCP
2 4 6 8 10 9 7 5 3 1
ISBN 978-1-6659-2848-9 (hardcover)
ISBN 978-1-6659-2847-2 (paperback)
ISBN 978-1-6659-2849-6 (ebook)

# Contents

**Cover art by Vicki Scott**

# THE BEAGLE HAS LANDED, CHARLIE BROWN!

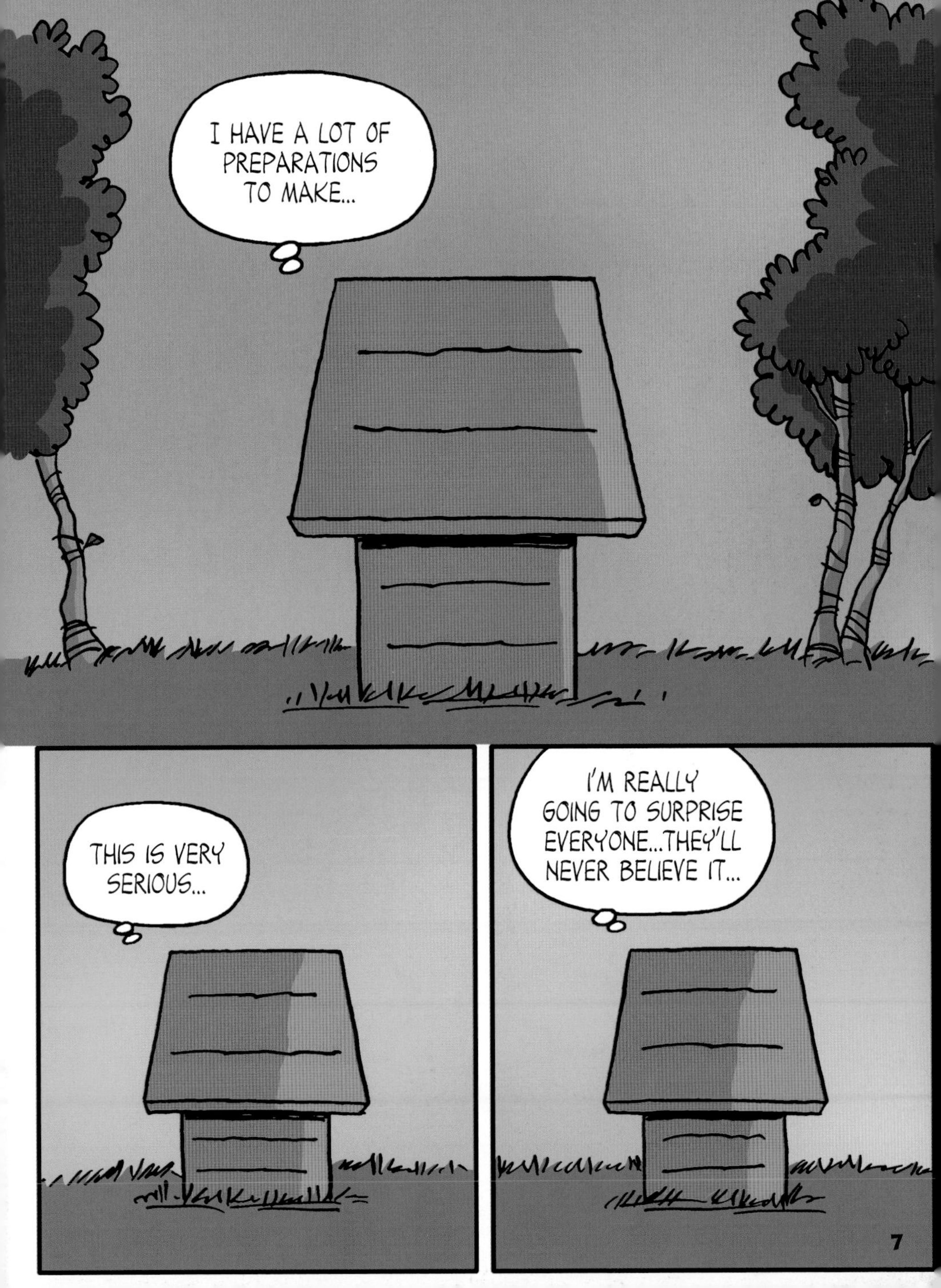

I HAVE A LOT OF PREPARATIONS TO MAKE...
THIS IS VERY SERIOUS...
I'M REALLY GOING TO SURPRISE EVERYONE...THEY'LL NEVER BELIEVE IT...

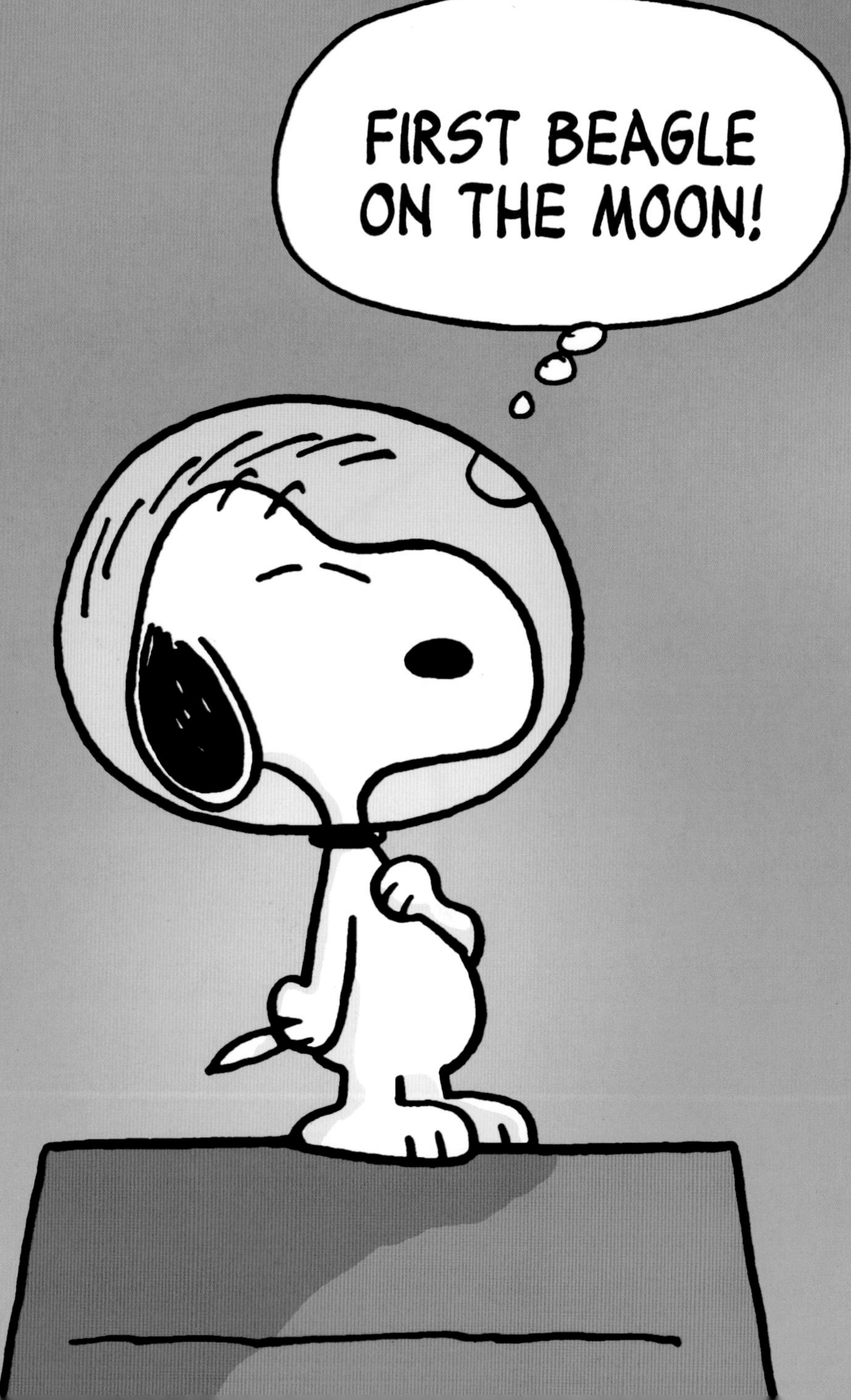
FIRST BEAGLE
ON THE MOON!

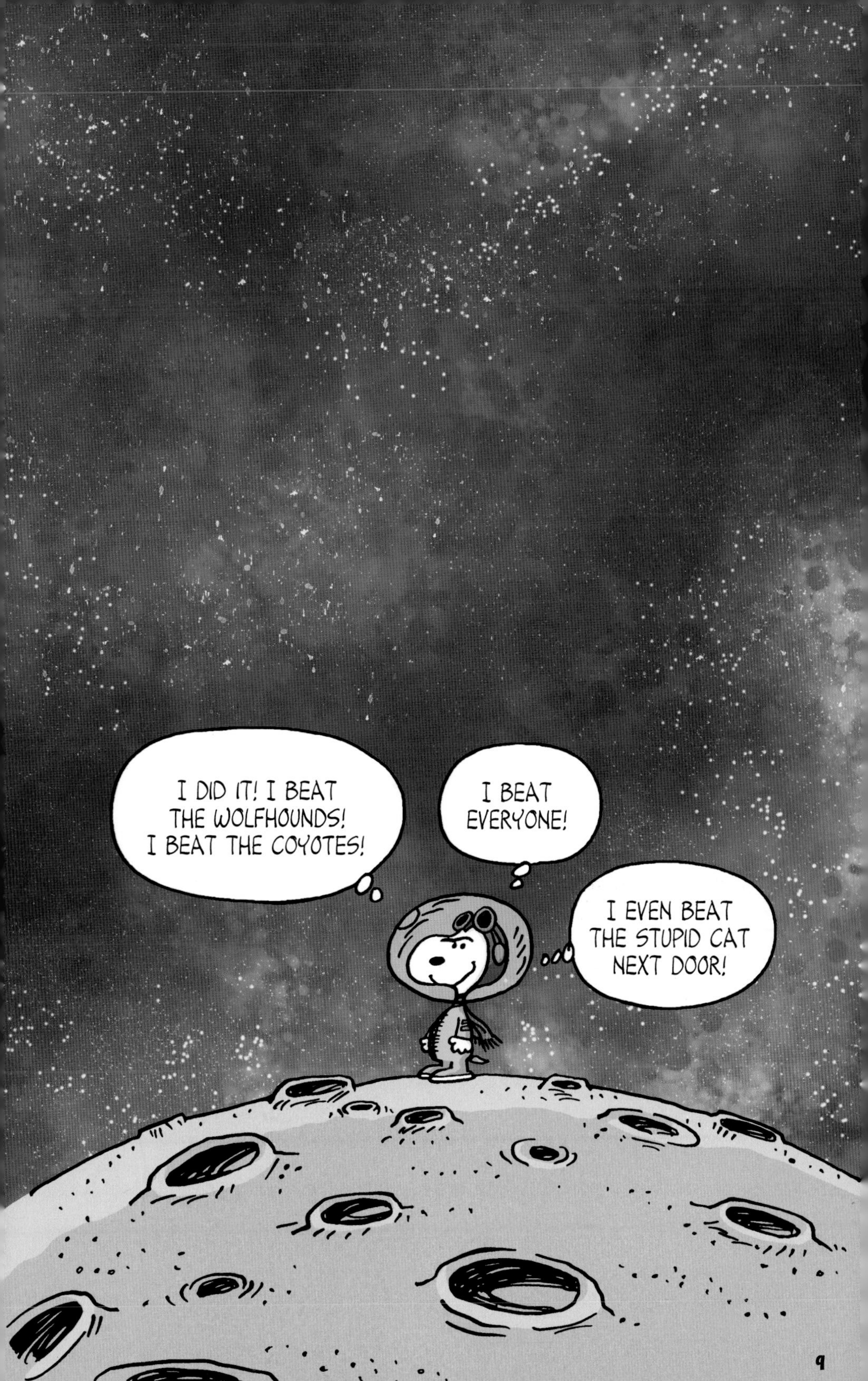
I DID IT! I BEAT THE WOLFHOUNDS! I BEAT THE COYOTES!
I BEAT EVERYONE!
I EVEN BEAT THE STUPID CAT NEXT DOOR!

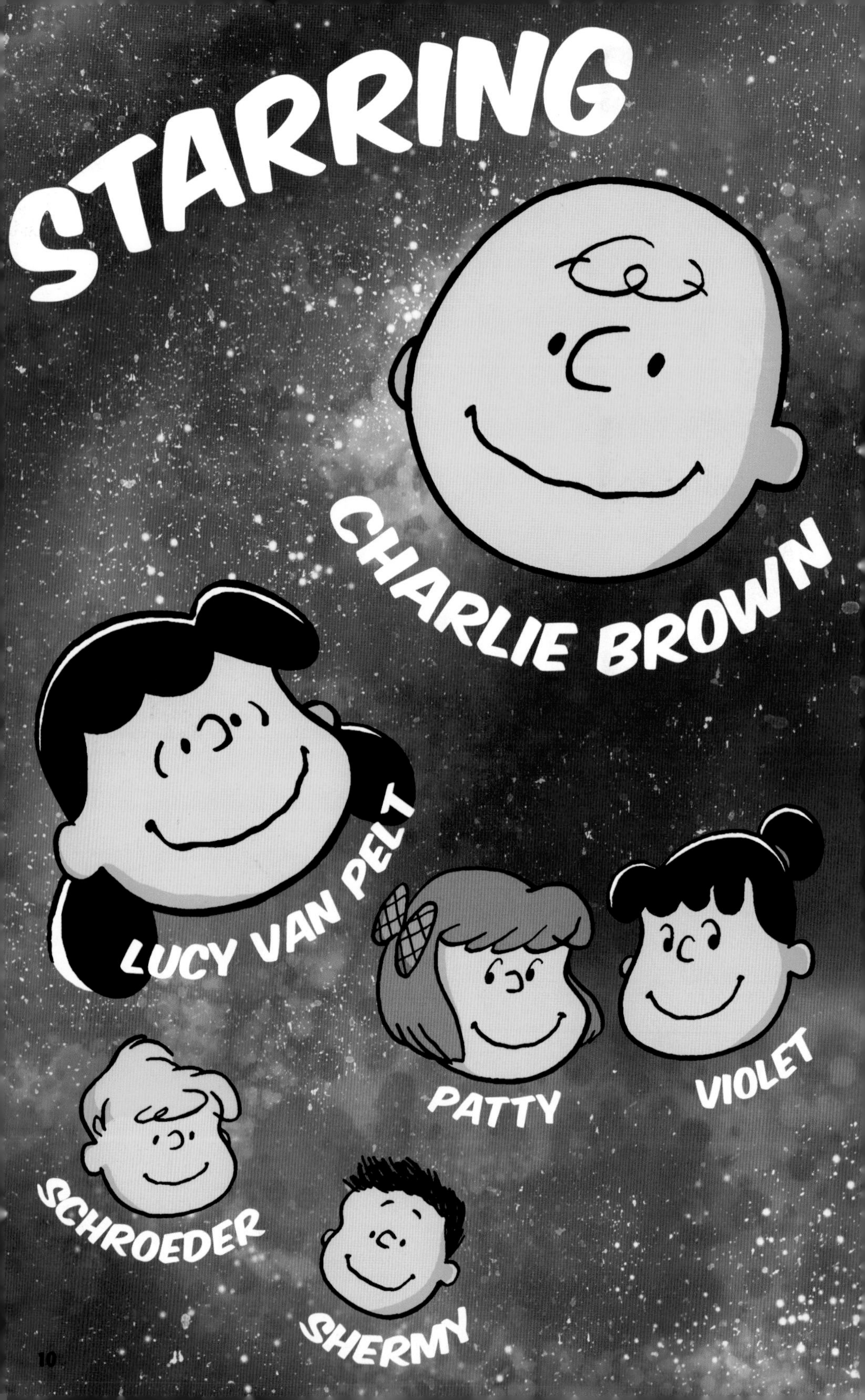
STARRING
CHARLIE BROWN
LUCY VAN PELT
PATTY
VIOLET
SCHROEDER
SHERMY

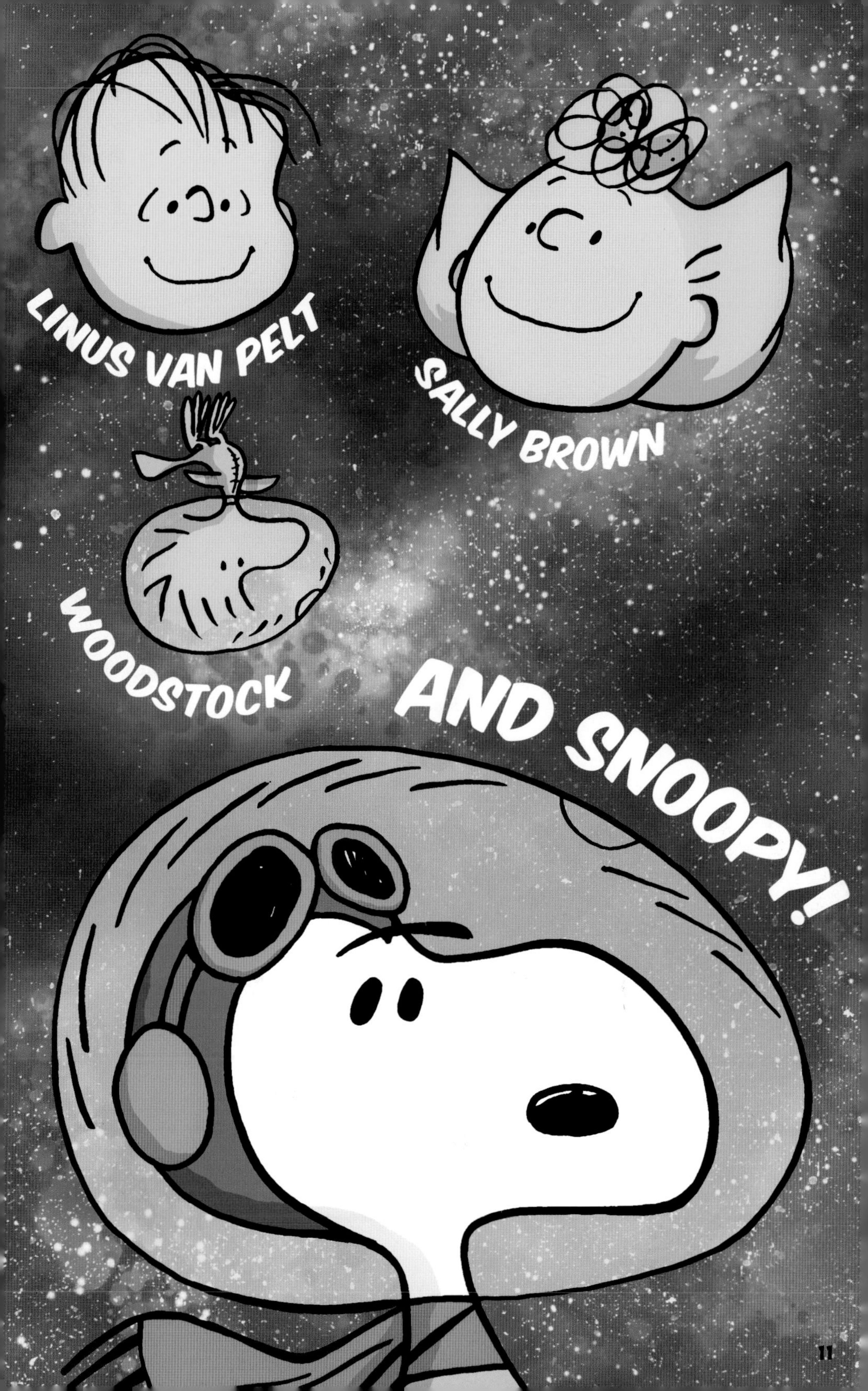
LINUS VAN PELT
SALLY BROWN
WOODSTOCK
AND SNOOPY!

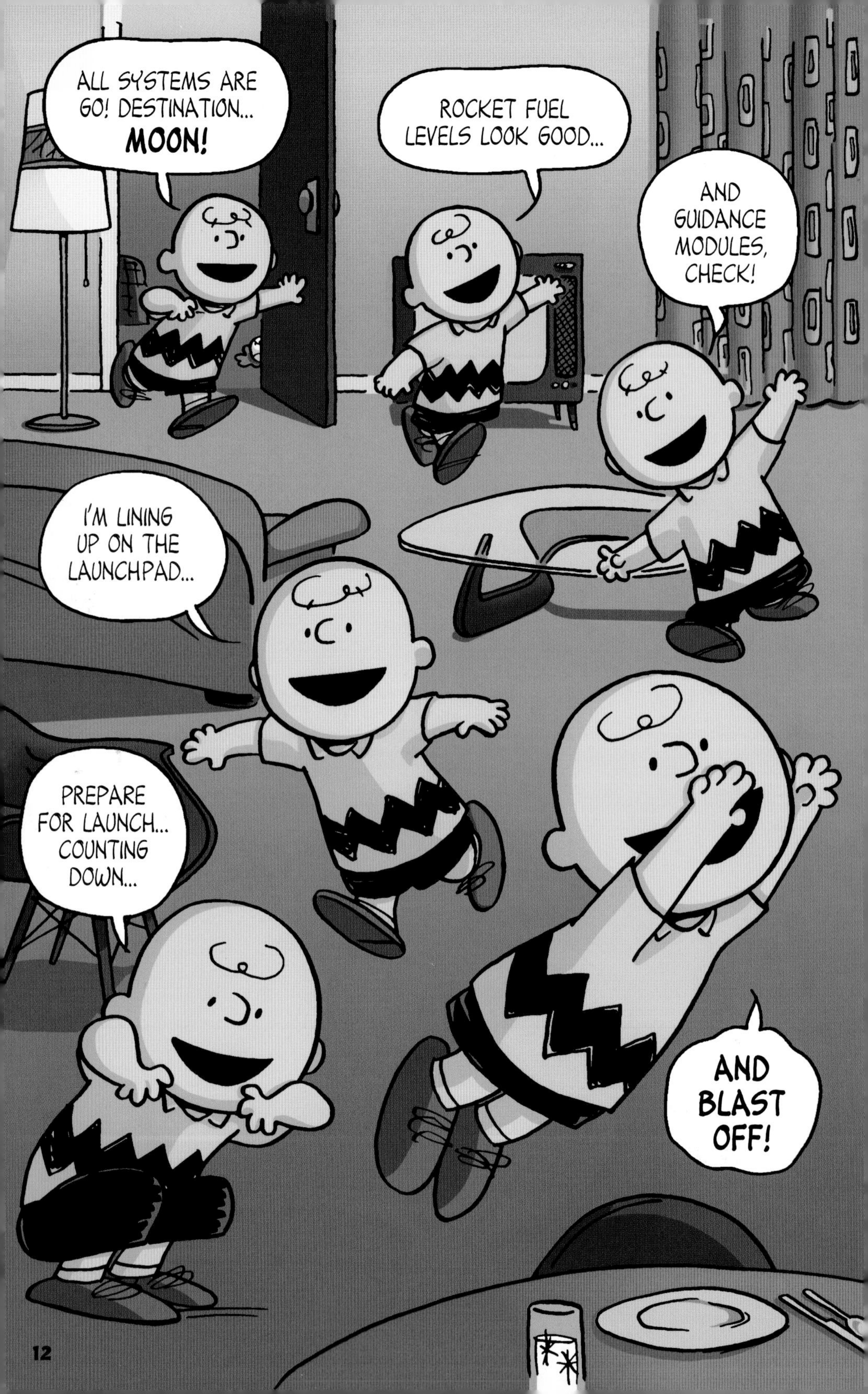
ALL SYSTEMS ARE GO! DESTINATION... **MOON!**
ROCKET FUEL LEVELS LOOK GOOD...
AND GUIDANCE MODULES, CHECK!
I'M LINING UP ON THE LAUNCHPAD...
PREPARE FOR LAUNCH... COUNTING DOWN...
**AND BLAST OFF!**

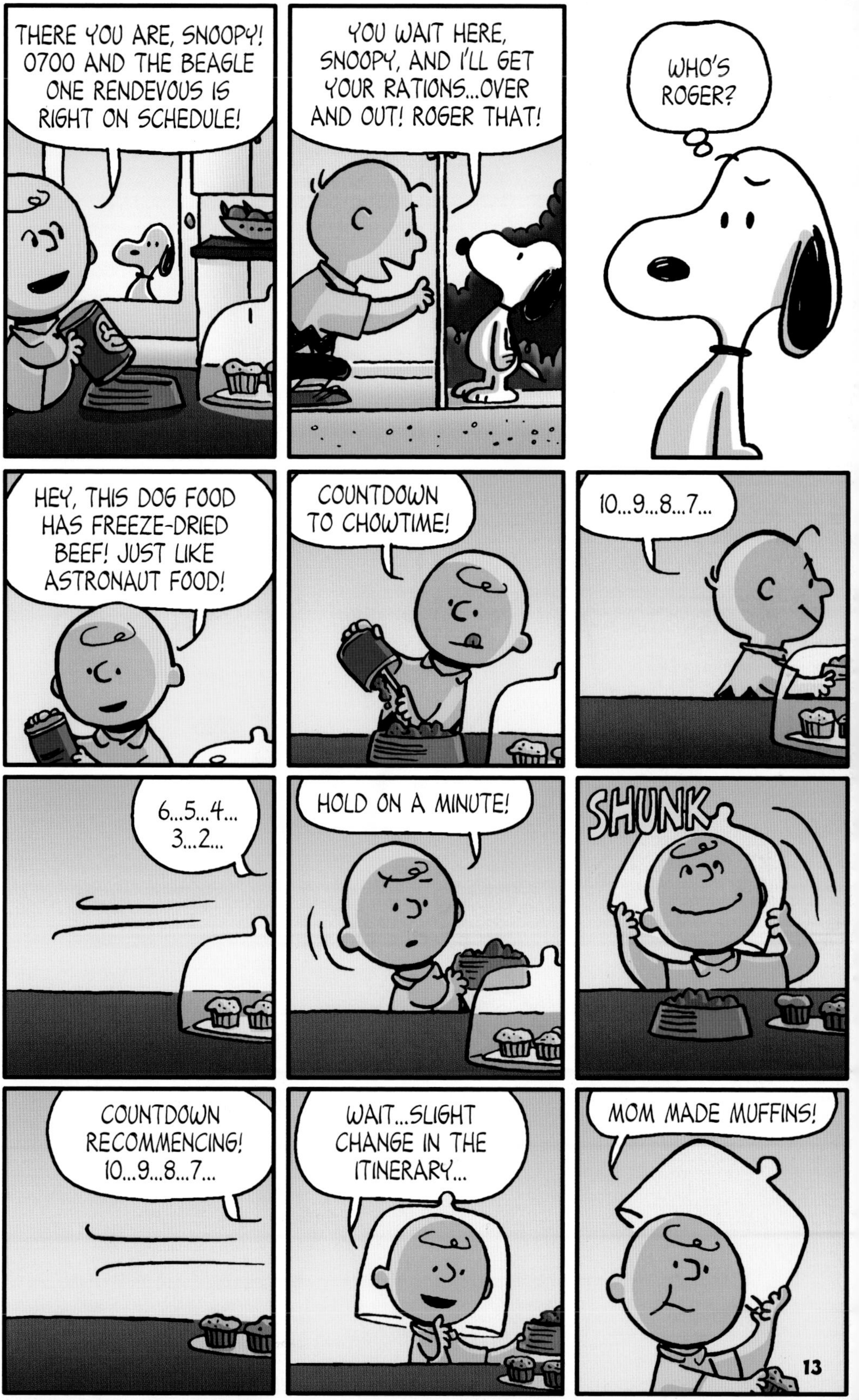
THERE YOU ARE, SNOOPY! 0700 AND THE BEAGLE ONE RENDEVOUS IS RIGHT ON SCHEDULE!
YOU WAIT HERE, SNOOPY, AND I'LL GET YOUR RATIONS...OVER AND OUT! ROGER THAT!
WHO'S ROGER?
HEY, THIS DOG FOOD HAS FREEZE-DRIED BEEF! JUST LIKE ASTRONAUT FOOD!
COUNTDOWN TO CHOWTIME!
10...9...8...7...
6...5...4... 3...2...
HOLD ON A MINUTE!
SHUNK
COUNTDOWN RECOMMENCING! 10...9...8...7...
WAIT...SLIGHT CHANGE IN THE ITINERARY...
MOM MADE MUFFINS!

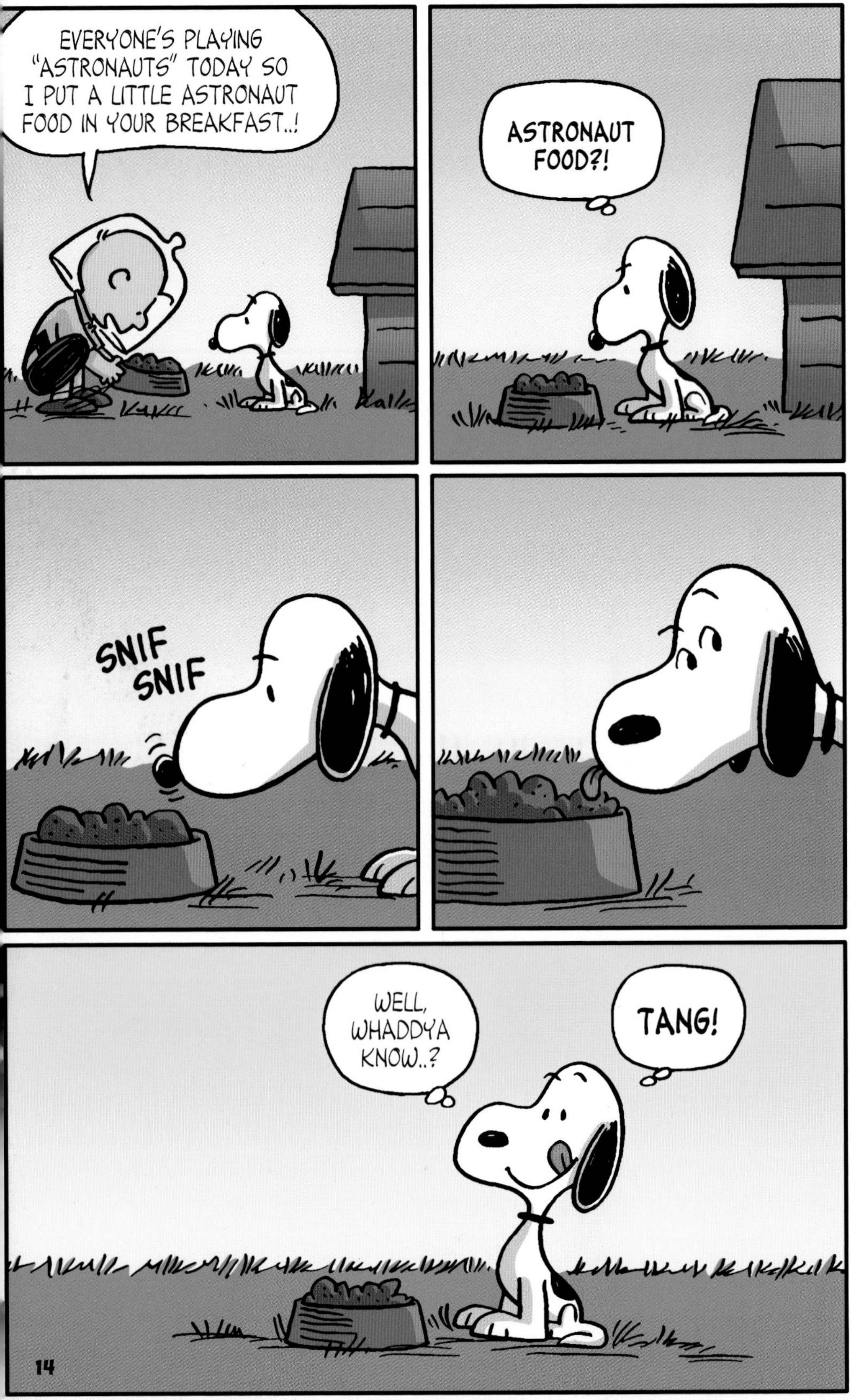
EVERYONE'S PLAYING "ASTRONAUTS" TODAY SO I PUT A LITTLE ASTRONAUT FOOD IN YOUR BREAKFAST..!
ASTRONAUT FOOD?!
SNIF SNIF
WELL, WHADDYA KNOW..?
TANG!

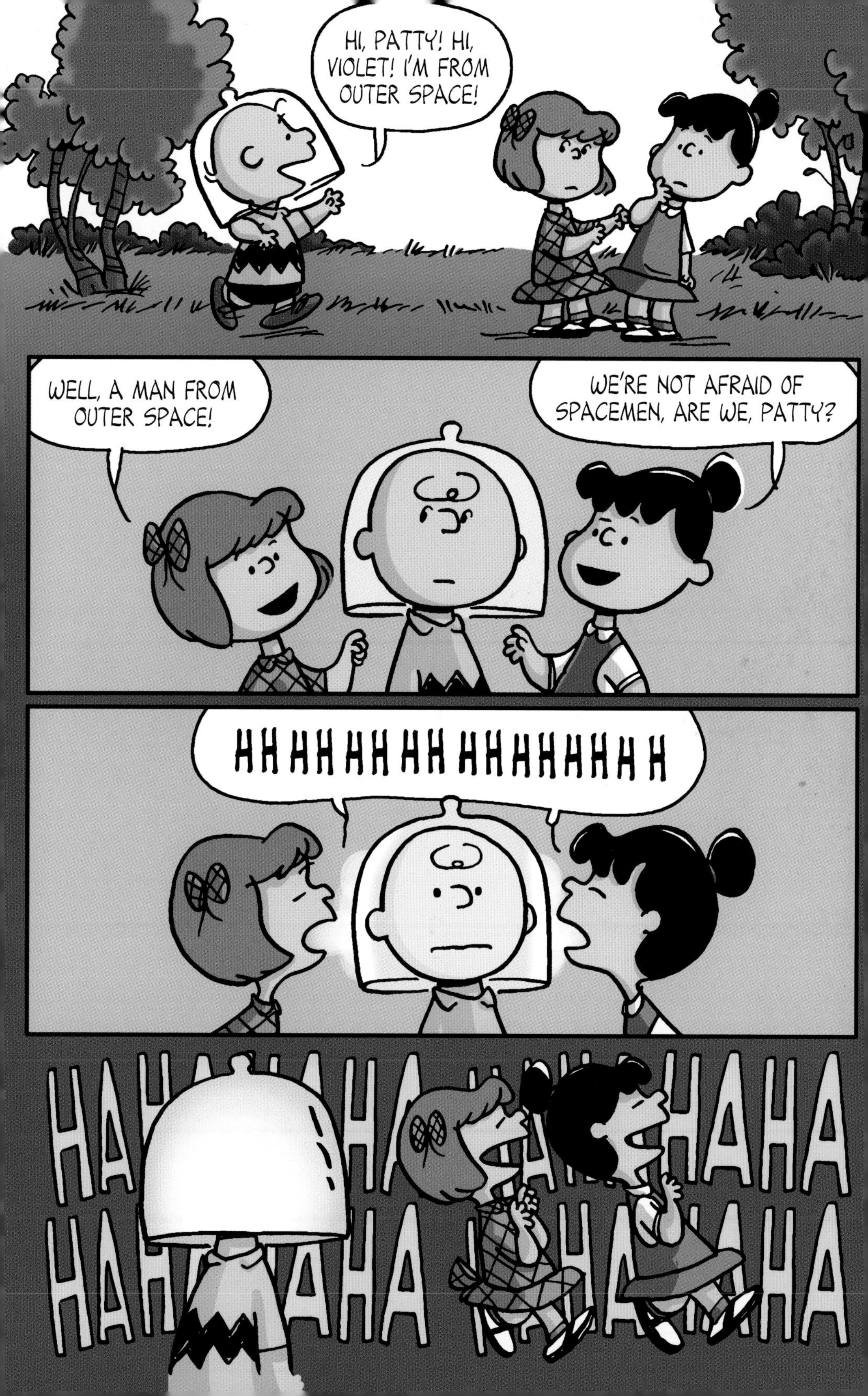
HI, PATTY! HI, VIOLET! I'M FROM OUTER SPACE!
WELL, A MAN FROM OUTER SPACE!
WE'RE NOT AFRAID OF SPACEMEN, ARE WE, PATTY?
HHHHHHHHHHHHHHHH
HAHAHAHA
HAHAHAHA

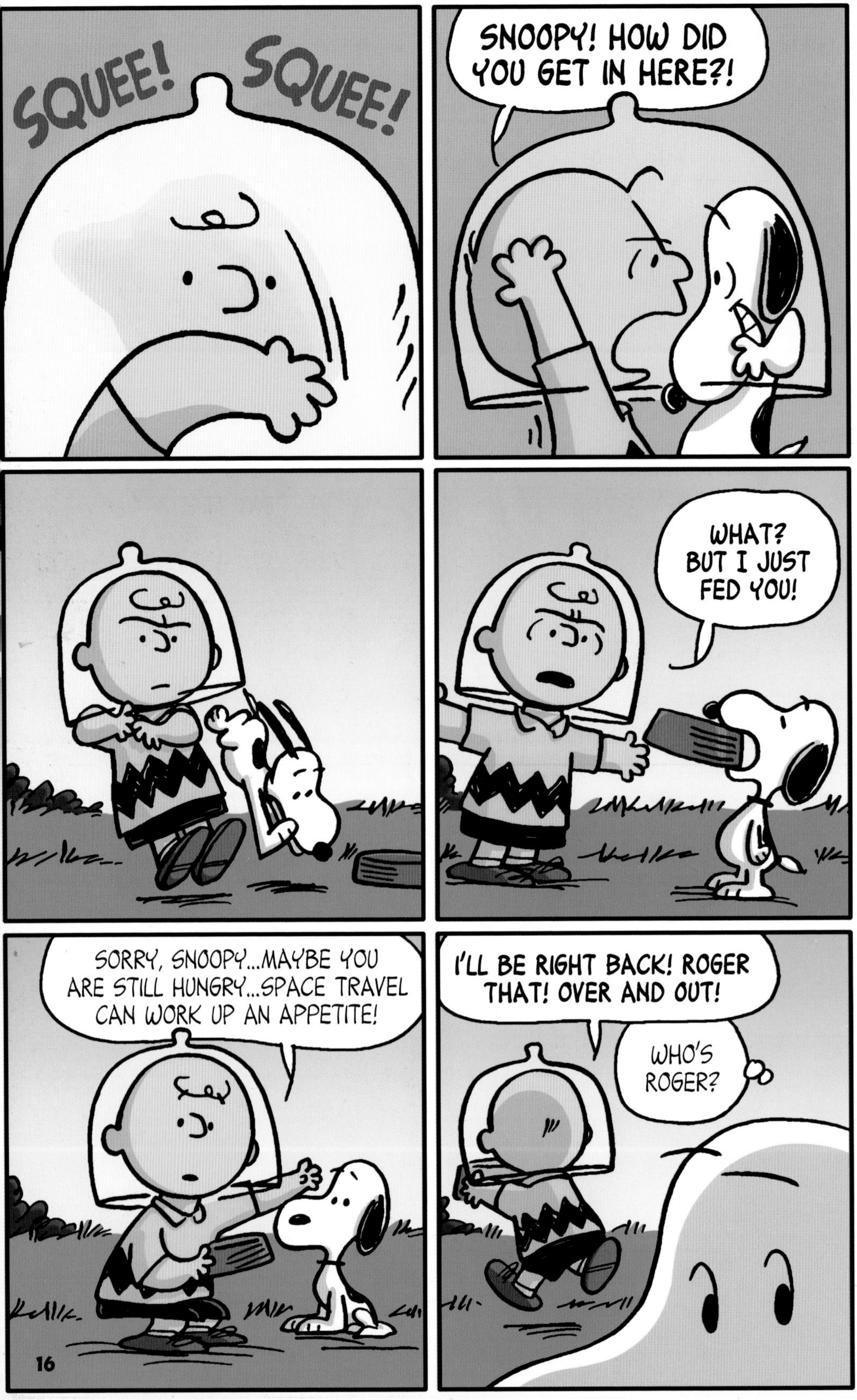
SQUEE! SQUEE!
SNOOPY! HOW DID YOU GET IN HERE?!
WHAT? BUT I JUST FED YOU!
SORRY, SNOOPY...MAYBE YOU ARE STILL HUNGRY...SPACE TRAVEL CAN WORK UP AN APPETITE!
I'LL BE RIGHT BACK! ROGER THAT! OVER AND OUT!
WHO'S ROGER?

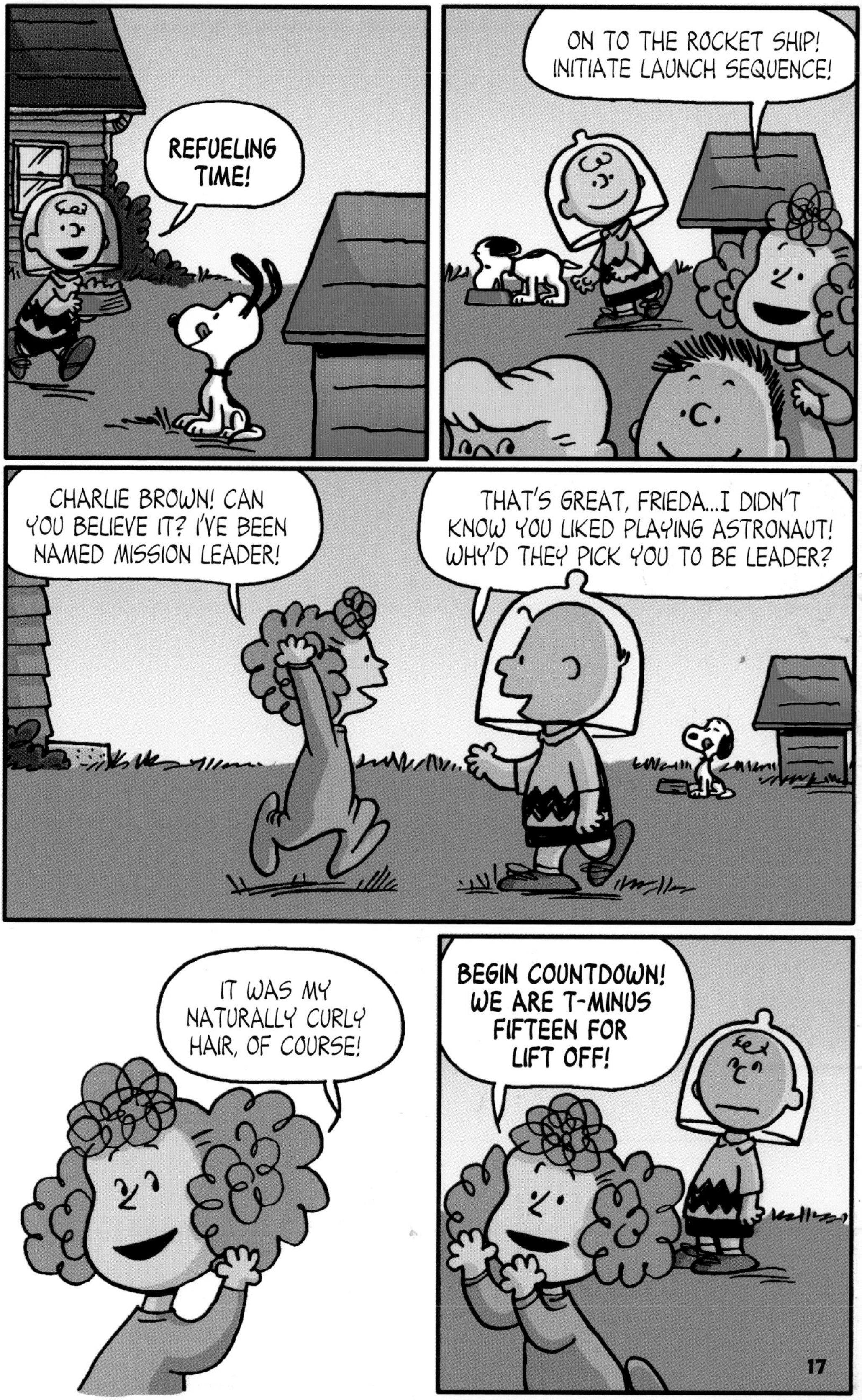
REFUELING TIME!
ON TO THE ROCKET SHIP! INITIATE LAUNCH SEQUENCE!
CHARLIE BROWN! CAN YOU BELIEVE IT? I'VE BEEN NAMED MISSION LEADER!
THAT'S GREAT, FRIEDA...I DIDN'T KNOW YOU LIKED PLAYING ASTRONAUT! WHY'D THEY PICK YOU TO BE LEADER?
IT WAS MY NATURALLY CURLY HAIR, OF COURSE!
BEGIN COUNTDOWN! WE ARE T-MINUS FIFTEEN FOR LIFT OFF!

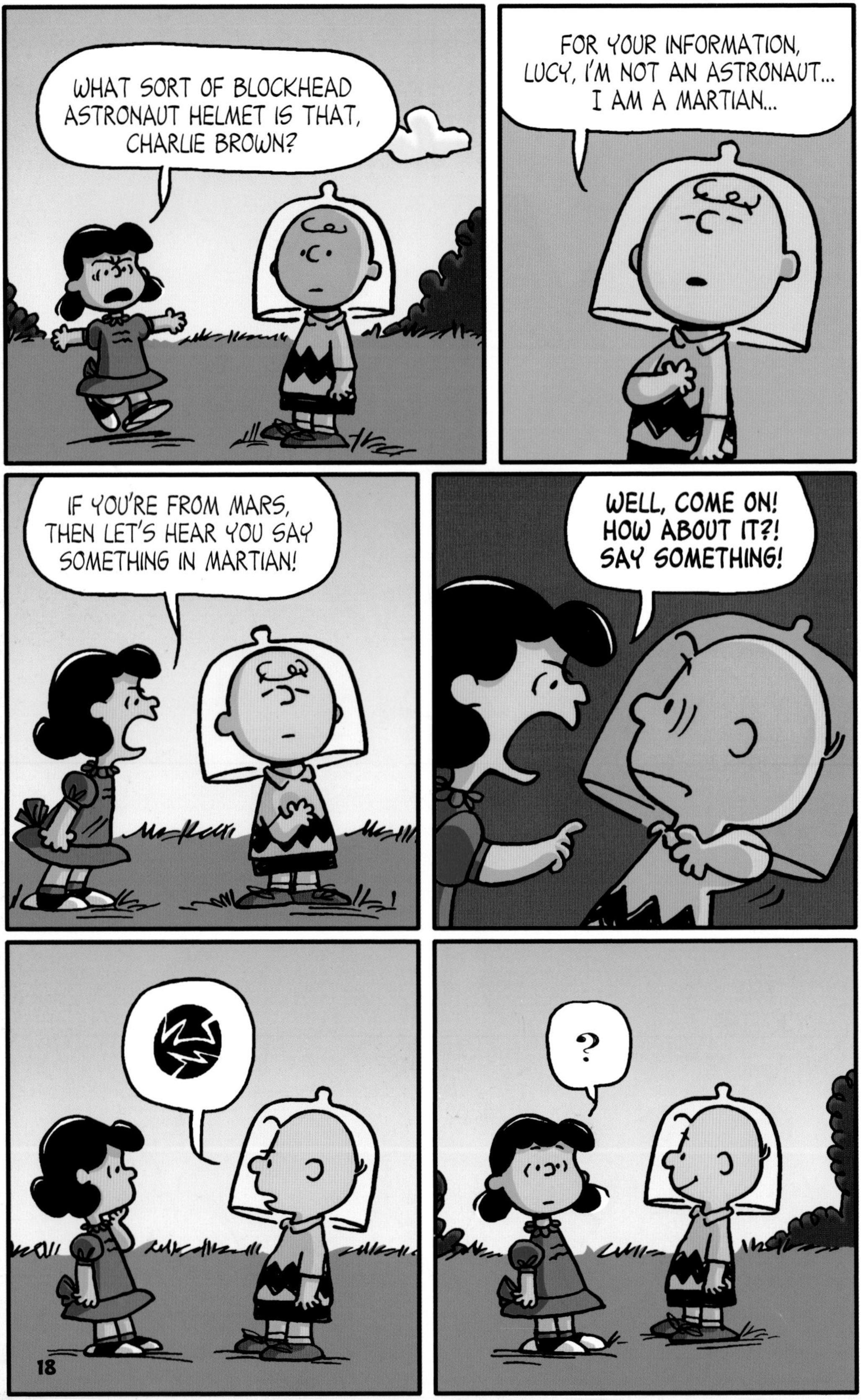
WHAT SORT OF BLOCKHEAD ASTRONAUT HELMET IS THAT, CHARLIE BROWN?
FOR YOUR INFORMATION, LUCY, I'M NOT AN ASTRONAUT... I AM A MARTIAN...
IF YOU'RE FROM MARS, THEN LET'S HEAR YOU SAY SOMETHING IN MARTIAN!
WELL, COME ON! HOW ABOUT IT?! SAY SOMETHING!
?

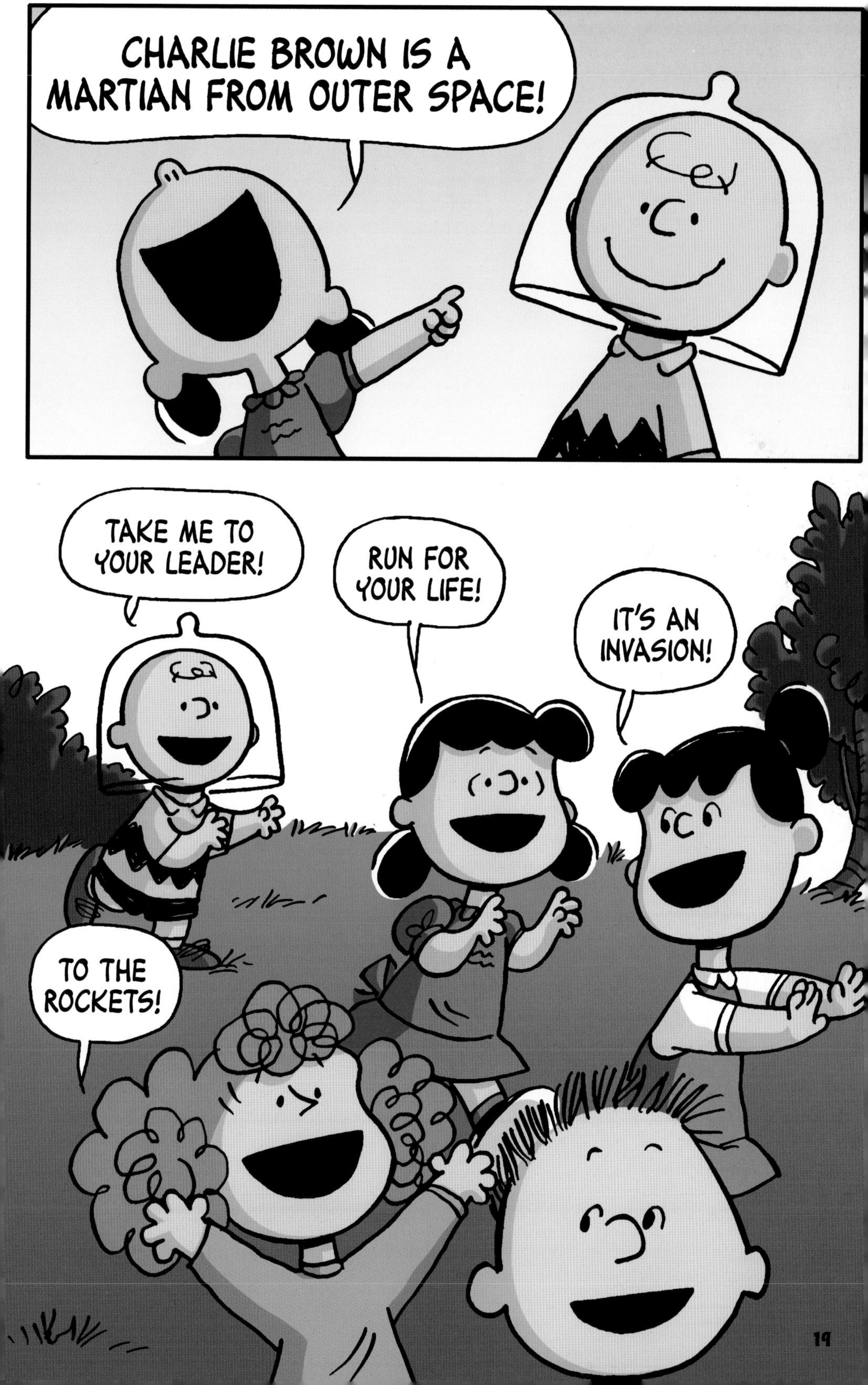
CHARLIE BROWN IS A MARTIAN FROM OUTER SPACE!
TAKE ME TO YOUR LEADER!
RUN FOR YOUR LIFE!
IT'S AN INVASION!
TO THE ROCKETS!

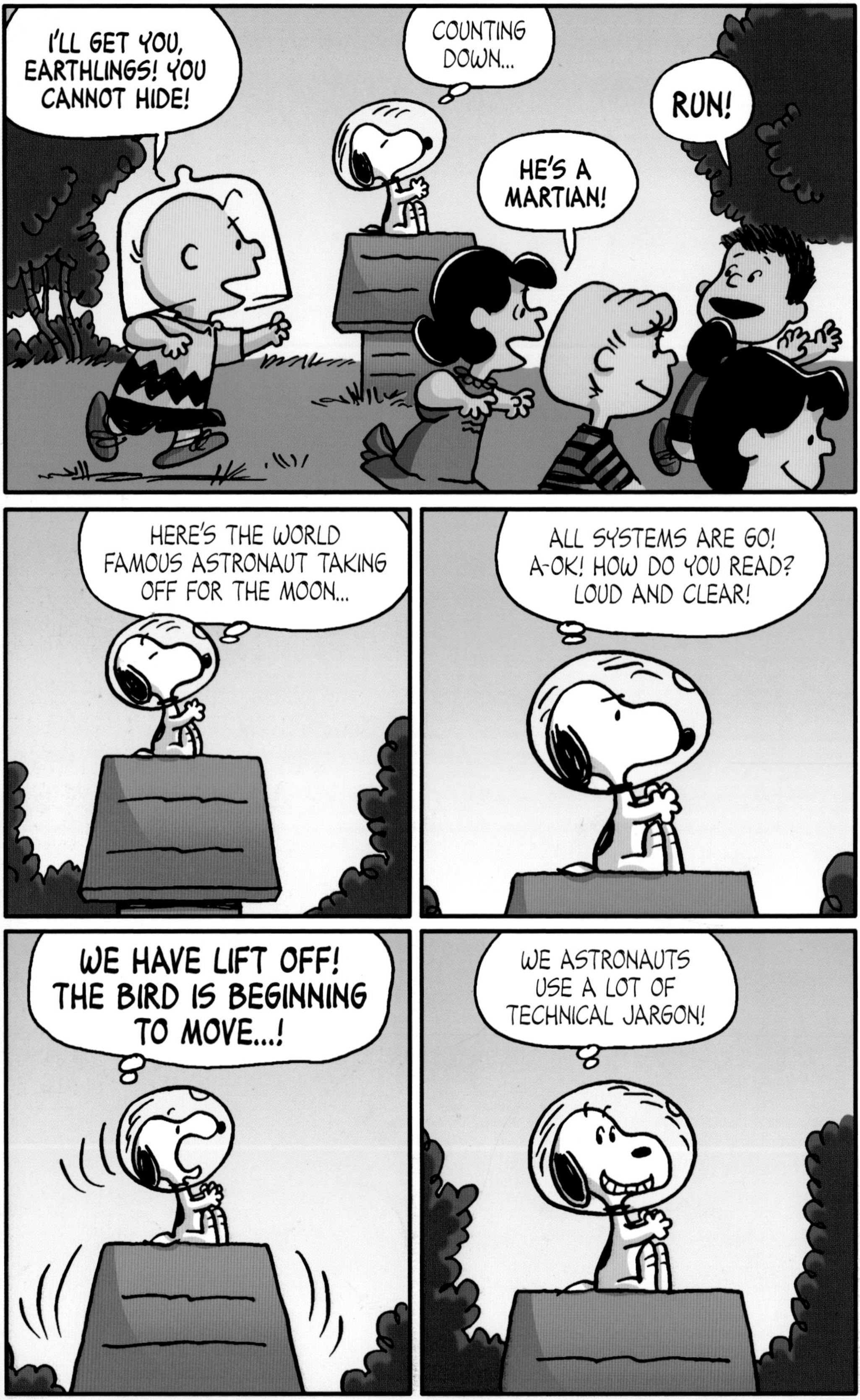
I'LL GET YOU, EARTHLINGS! YOU CANNOT HIDE!
COUNTING DOWN...
RUN!
HE'S A MARTIAN!
HERE'S THE WORLD FAMOUS ASTRONAUT TAKING OFF FOR THE MOON...
ALL SYSTEMS ARE GO! A-OK! HOW DO YOU READ? LOUD AND CLEAR!
WE HAVE LIFT OFF! THE BIRD IS BEGINNING TO MOVE...!
WE ASTRONAUTS USE A LOT OF TECHNICAL JARGON!

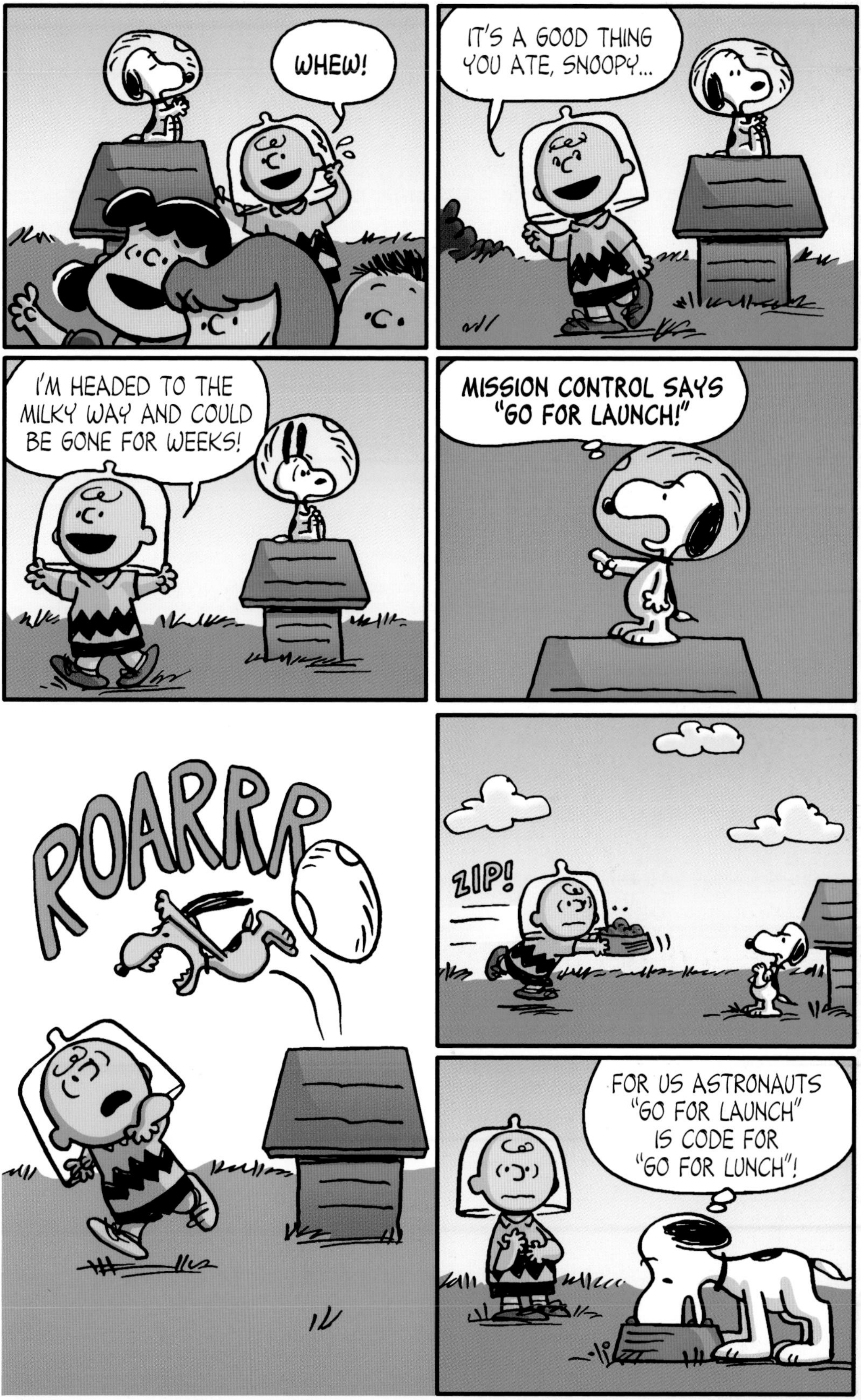

WHEW!
IT'S A GOOD THING YOU ATE, SNOOPY...
I'M HEADED TO THE MILKY WAY AND COULD BE GONE FOR WEEKS!
MISSION CONTROL SAYS "GO FOR LAUNCH!"
ROARRR
ZIP!
FOR US ASTRONAUTS "GO FOR LAUNCH" IS CODE FOR "GO FOR LUNCH"!

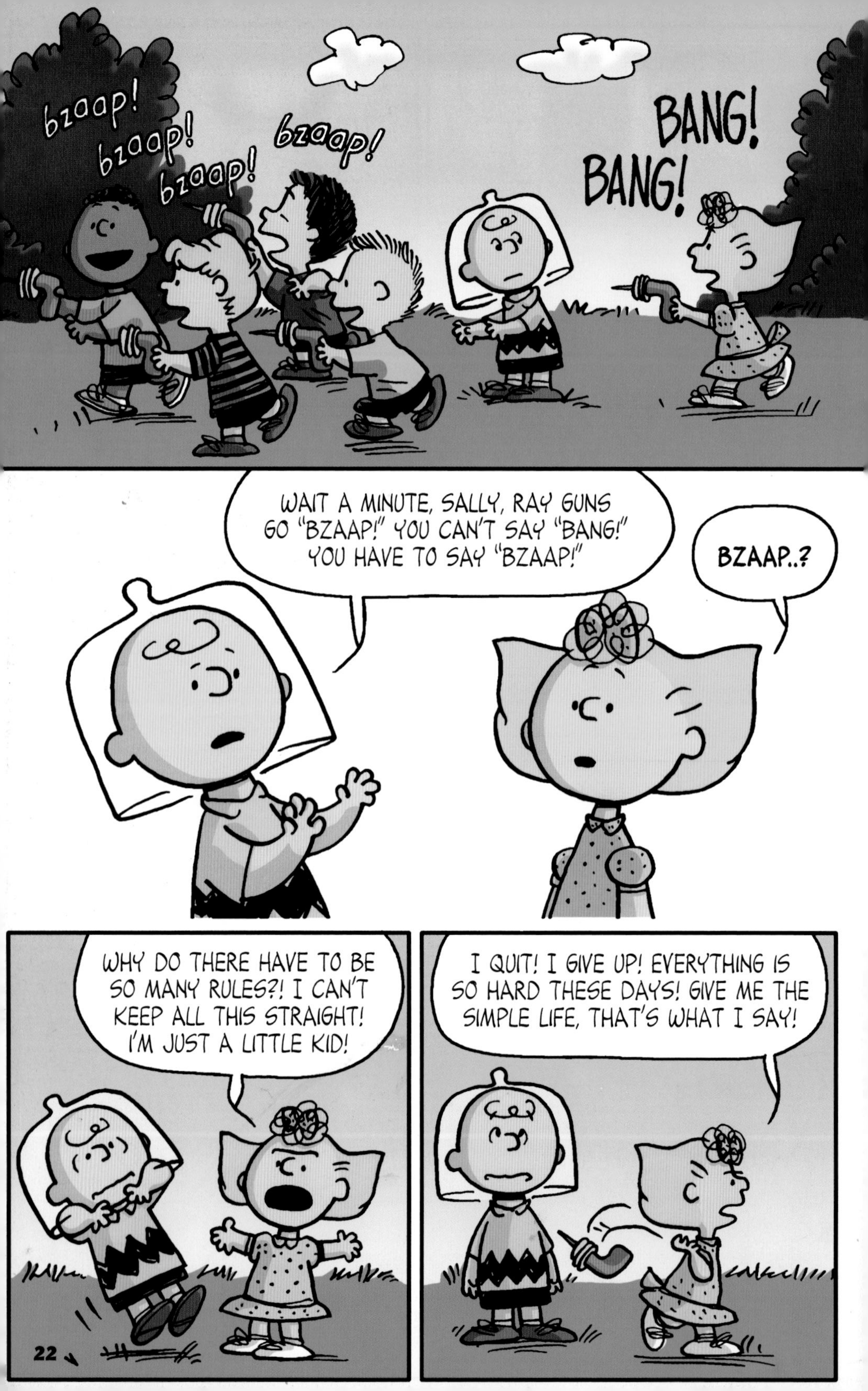
bzaap!
bzaap!
bzaap!
bzaap!
BANG!
BANG!
WAIT A MINUTE, SALLY, RAY GUNS GO "BZAAP!" YOU CAN'T SAY "BANG!" YOU HAVE TO SAY "BZAAP!"
BZAAP..?
WHY DO THERE HAVE TO BE SO MANY RULES?! I CAN'T KEEP ALL THIS STRAIGHT! I'M JUST A LITTLE KID!
I QUIT! I GIVE UP! EVERYTHING IS SO HARD THESE DAYS! GIVE ME THE SIMPLE LIFE, THAT'S WHAT I SAY!

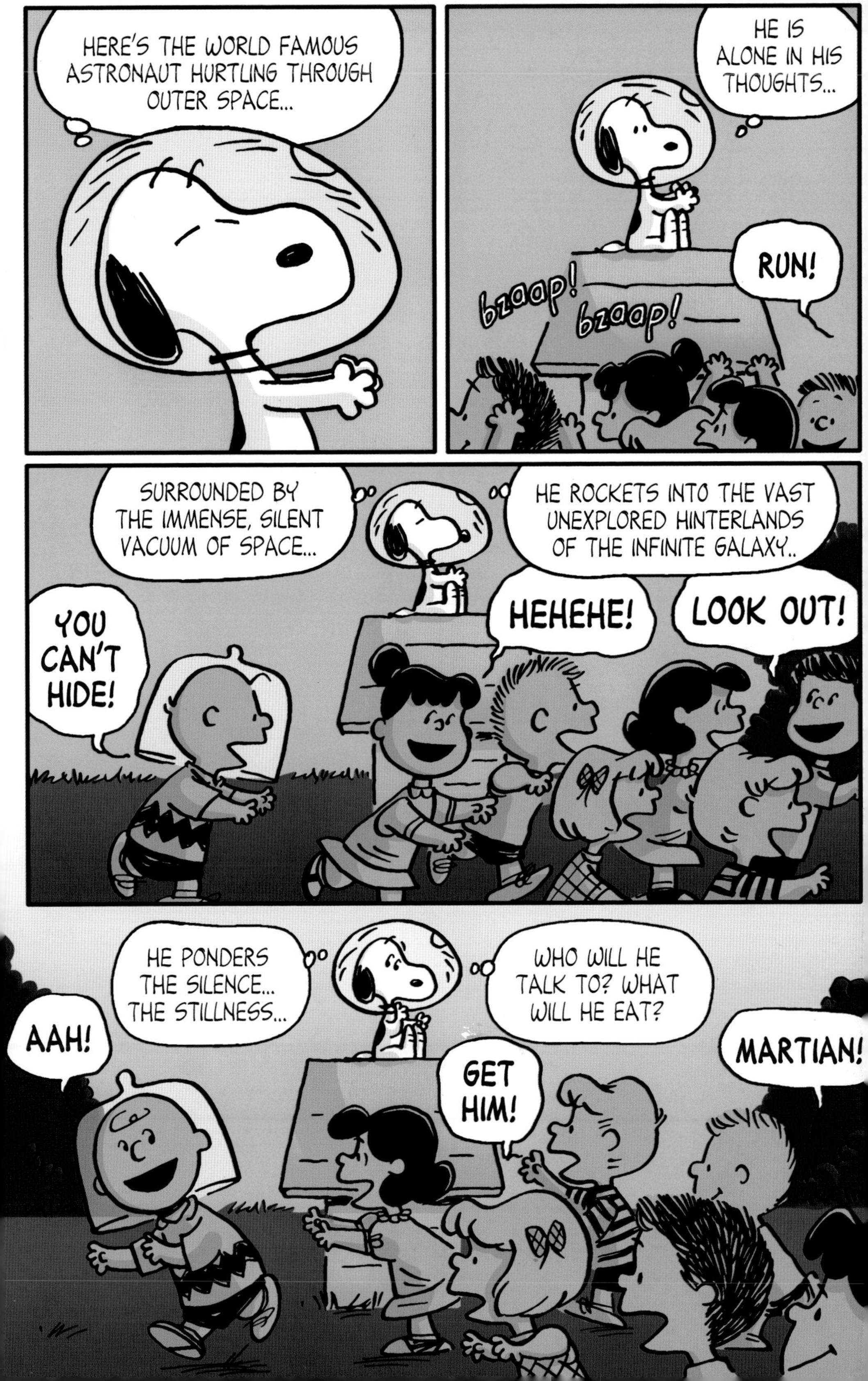
HERE'S THE WORLD FAMOUS ASTRONAUT HURTLING THROUGH OUTER SPACE...
HE IS ALONE IN HIS THOUGHTS...
bzaap! bzaap!
RUN!
SURROUNDED BY THE IMMENSE, SILENT VACUUM OF SPACE...
HE ROCKETS INTO THE VAST UNEXPLORED HINTERLANDS OF THE INFINITE GALAXY..
YOU CAN'T HIDE!
HEHEHE!
LOOK OUT!
HE PONDERS THE SILENCE... THE STILLNESS...
WHO WILL HE TALK TO? WHAT WILL HE EAT?
AAH!
GET HIM!
MARTIAN!

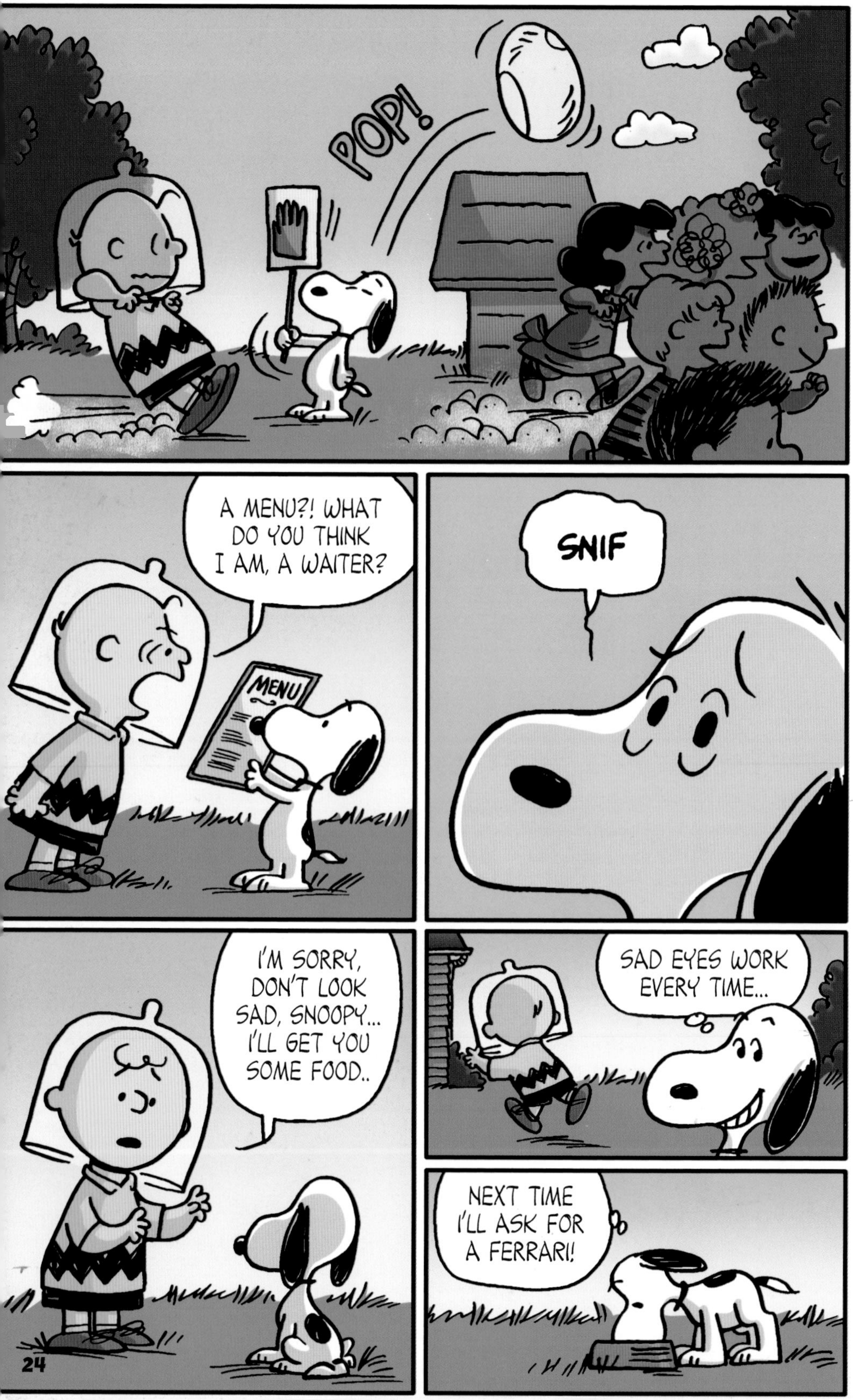
POP!
A MENU?! WHAT DO YOU THINK I AM, A WAITER?
MENU
SNIF
I'M SORRY, DON'T LOOK SAD, SNOOPY... I'LL GET YOU SOME FOOD..
SAD EYES WORK EVERY TIME...
NEXT TIME I'LL ASK FOR A FERRARI!

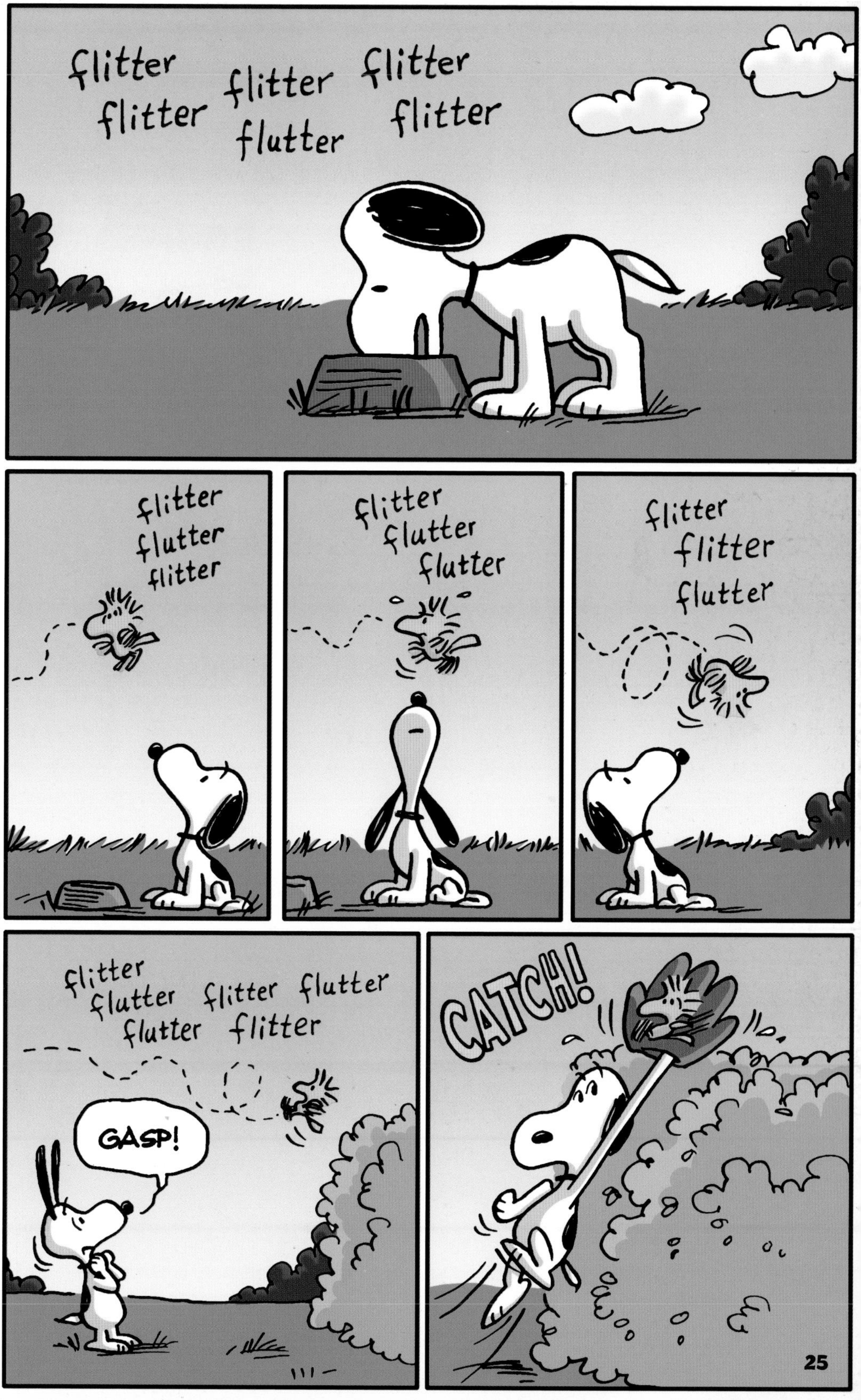
flitter
flitter flitter flitter
flutter flitter
flitter
flutter
flitter
flitter
flutter
flutter
flitter
flitter
flutter
flitter
flutter flitter flutter
flutter flitter
GASP!
CATCH!

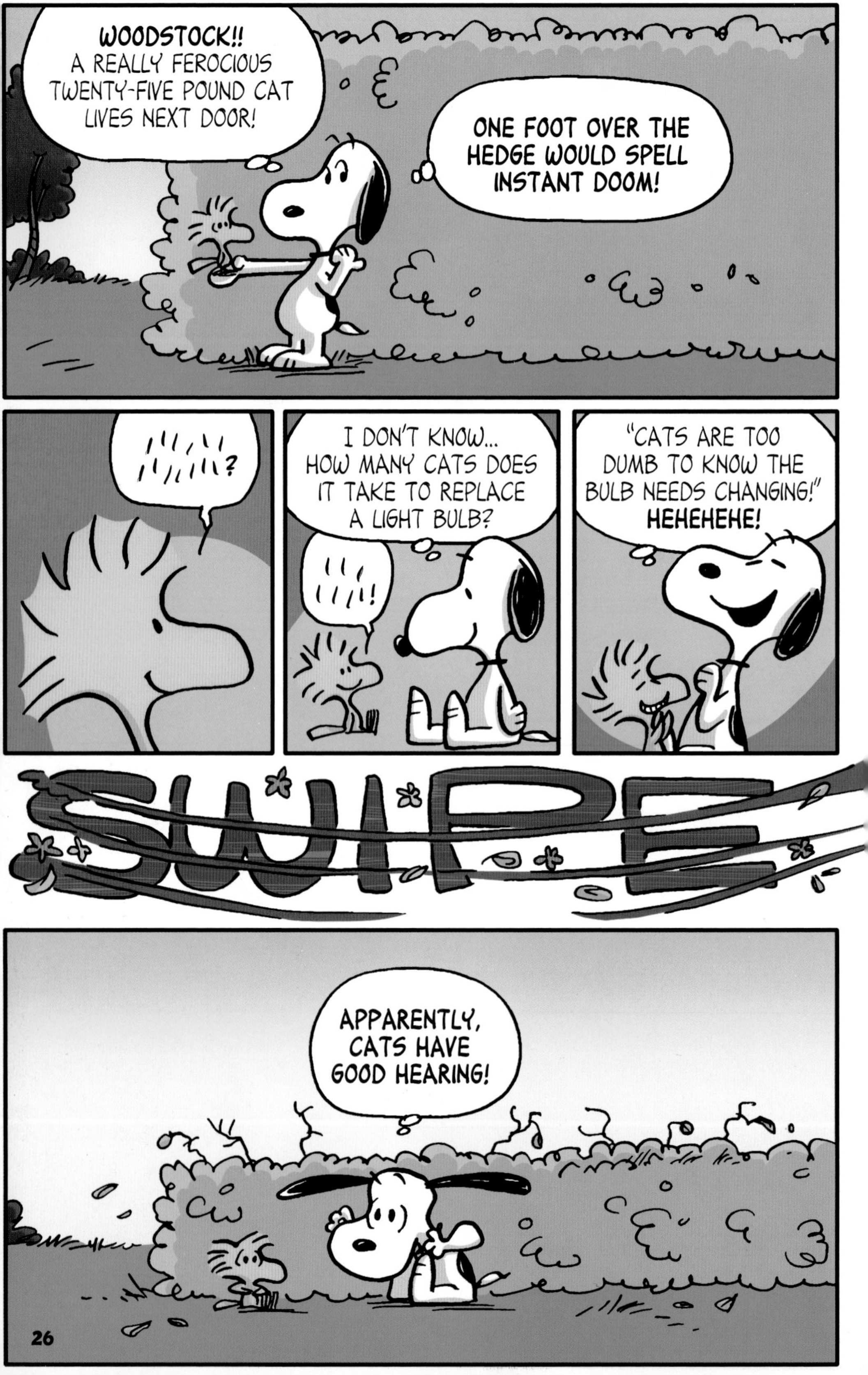
WOODSTOCK!! A REALLY FEROCIOUS TWENTY-FIVE POUND CAT LIVES NEXT DOOR!
ONE FOOT OVER THE HEDGE WOULD SPELL INSTANT DOOM!
?
I DON'T KNOW... HOW MANY CATS DOES IT TAKE TO REPLACE A LIGHT BULB?
!
"CATS ARE TOO DUMB TO KNOW THE BULB NEEDS CHANGING!" HEHEHEHE!
SWIPE
APPARENTLY, CATS HAVE GOOD HEARING!

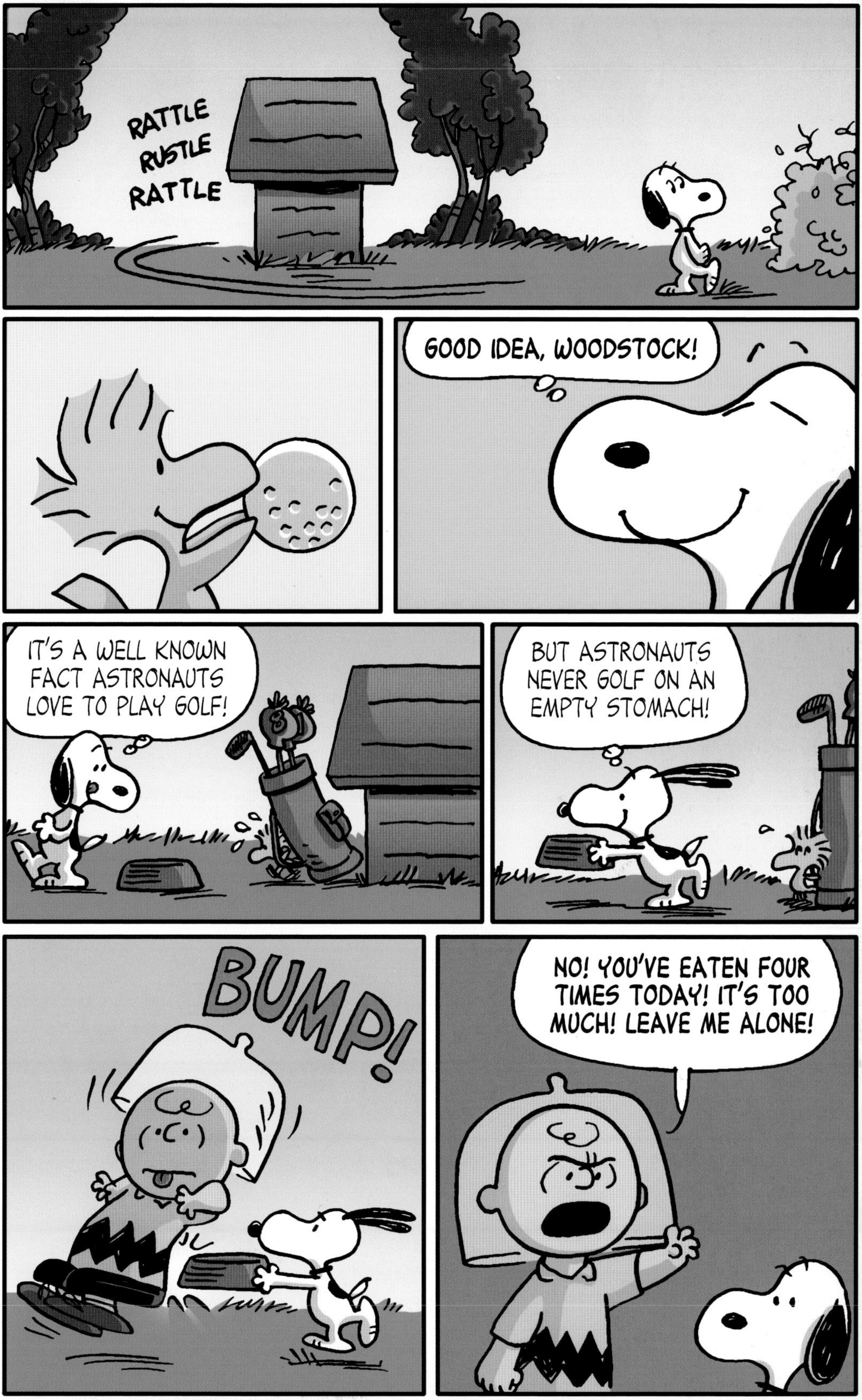
RATTLE
RUSTLE
RATTLE
GOOD IDEA, WOODSTOCK!
IT'S A WELL KNOWN FACT ASTRONAUTS LOVE TO PLAY GOLF!
BUT ASTRONAUTS NEVER GOLF ON AN EMPTY STOMACH!
BUMP!
NO! YOU'VE EATEN FOUR TIMES TODAY! IT'S TOO MUCH! LEAVE ME ALONE!

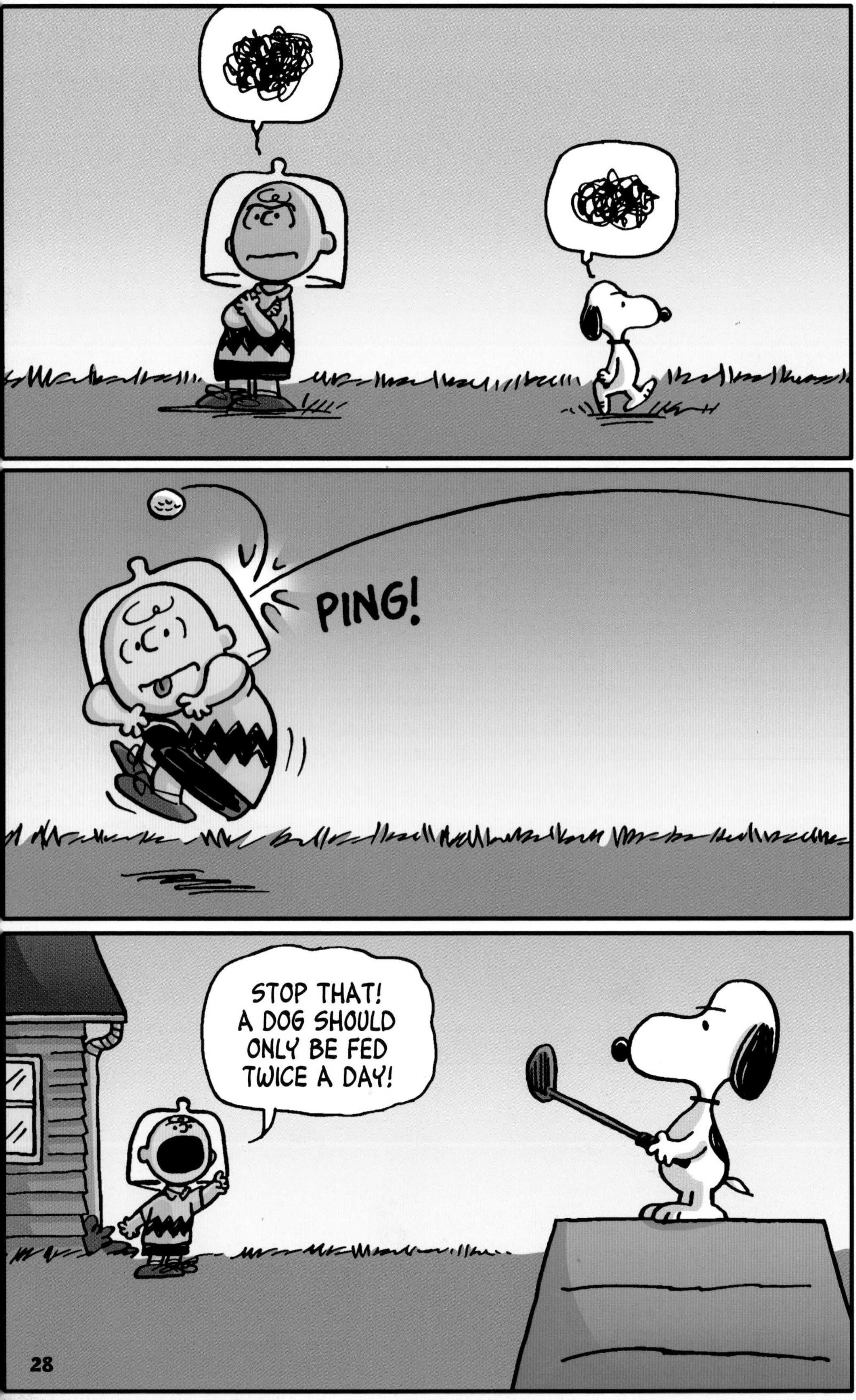
PING!
STOP THAT!
A DOG SHOULD
ONLY BE FED
TWICE A DAY!

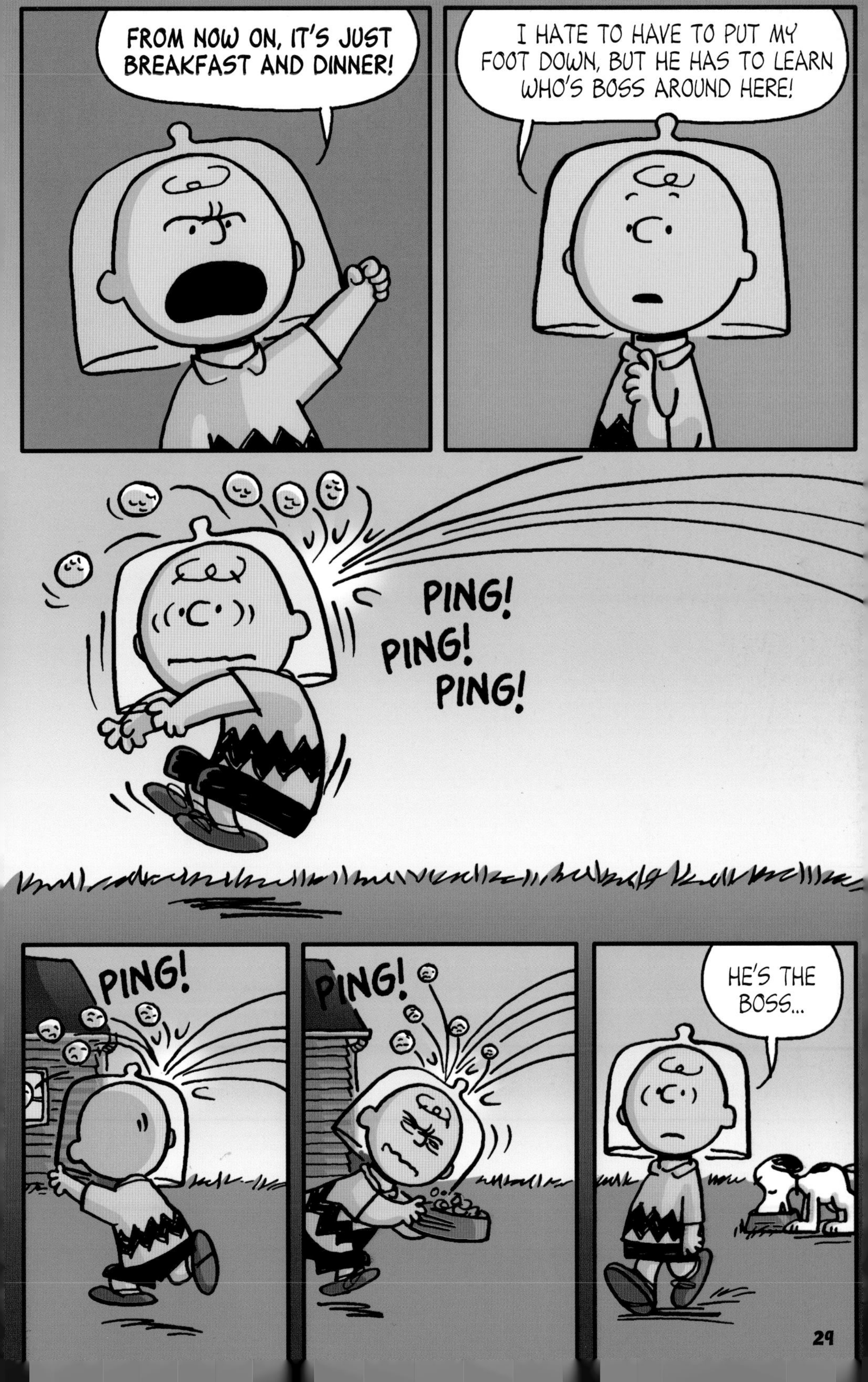
FROM NOW ON, IT'S JUST BREAKFAST AND DINNER!
I HATE TO HAVE TO PUT MY FOOT DOWN, BUT HE HAS TO LEARN WHO'S BOSS AROUND HERE!
PING!
PING!
PING!
PING!
PING!
HE'S THE BOSS...

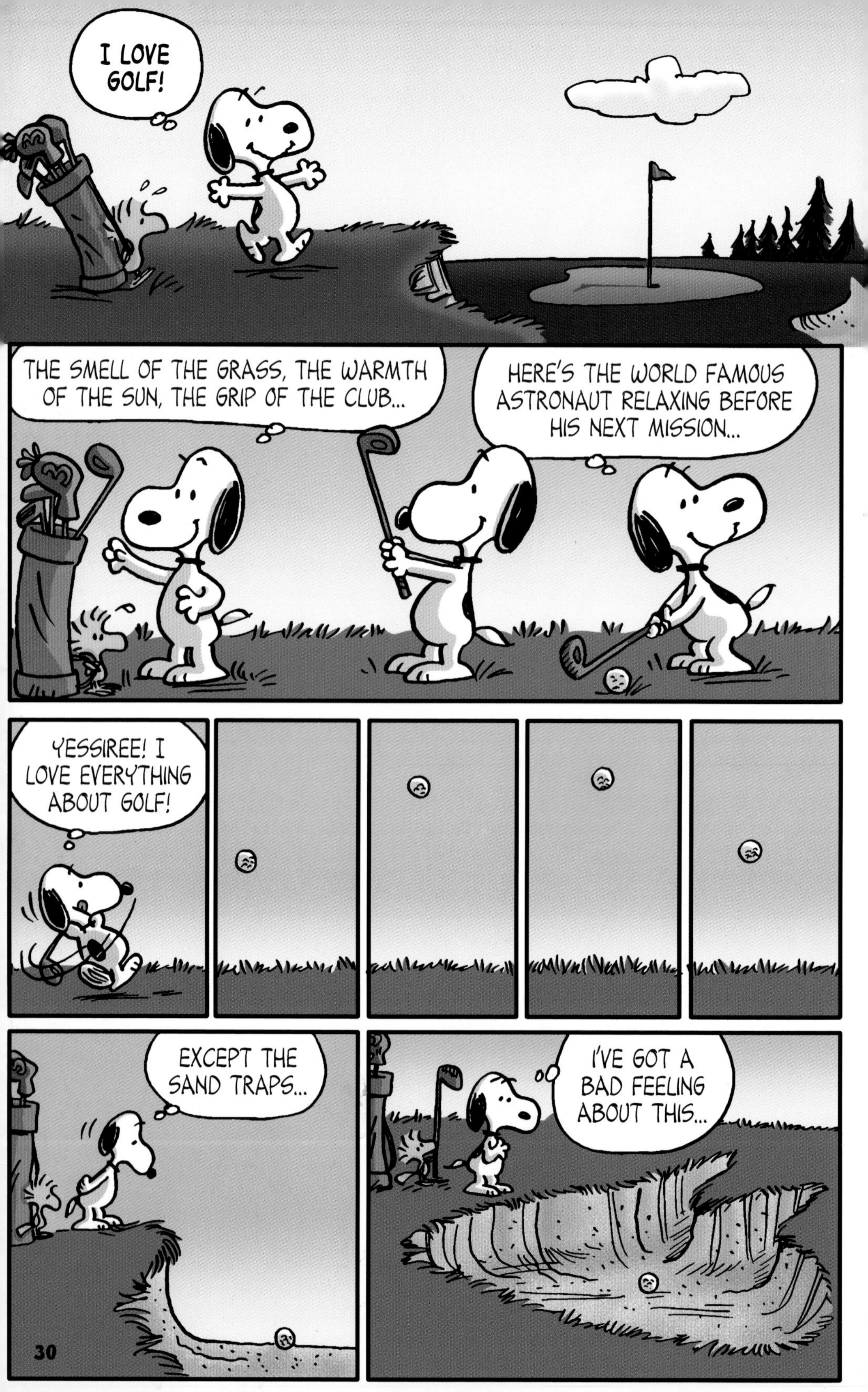
I LOVE GOLF!
THE SMELL OF THE GRASS, THE WARMTH OF THE SUN, THE GRIP OF THE CLUB...
HERE'S THE WORLD FAMOUS ASTRONAUT RELAXING BEFORE HIS NEXT MISSION...
YESSIREE! I LOVE EVERYTHING ABOUT GOLF!
EXCEPT THE SAND TRAPS...
I'VE GOT A BAD FEELING ABOUT THIS...

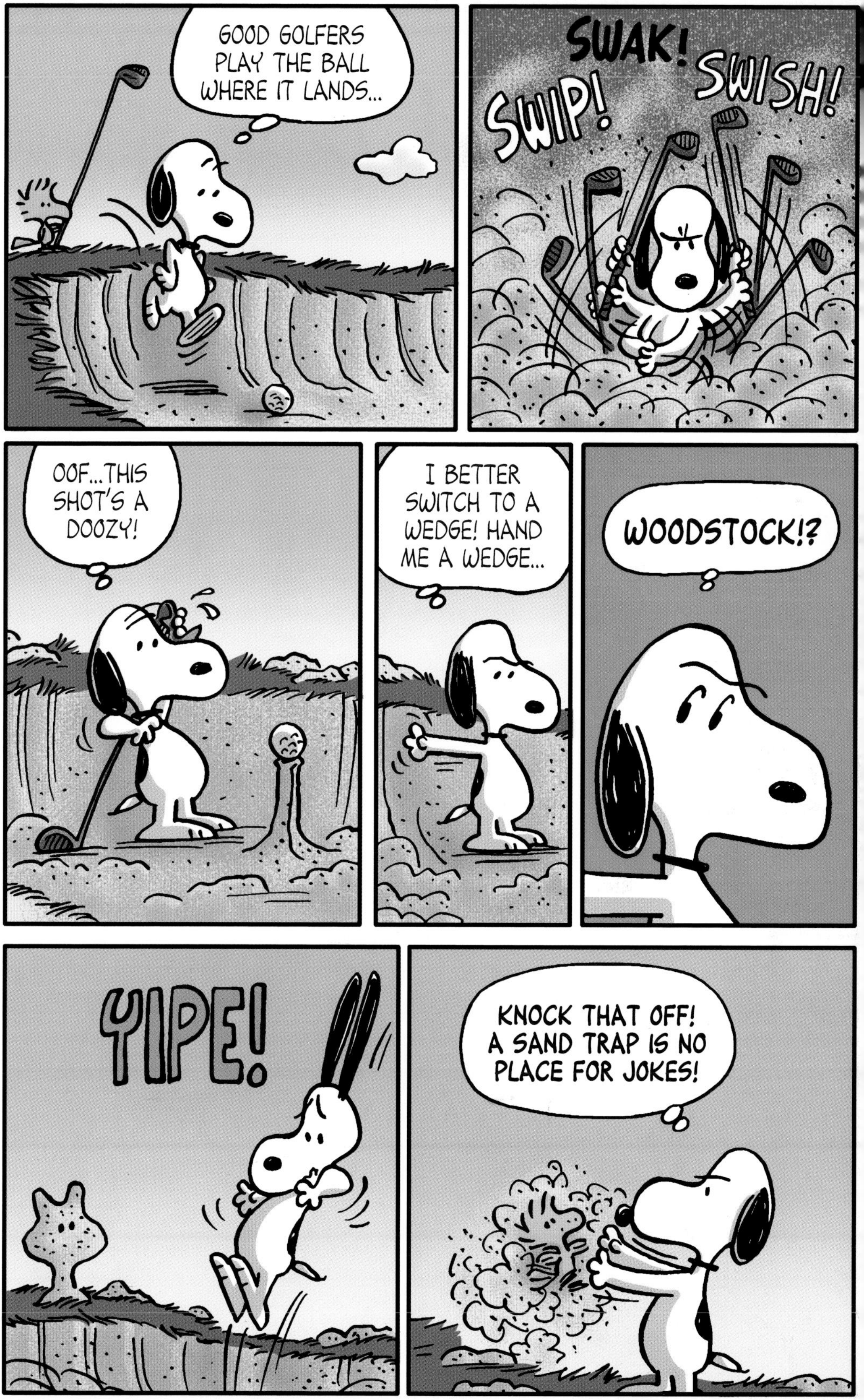
GOOD GOLFERS PLAY THE BALL WHERE IT LANDS...
SWAK!
SWIP!
SWISH!
OOF...THIS SHOT'S A DOOZY!
I BETTER SWITCH TO A WEDGE! HAND ME A WEDGE...
WOODSTOCK!?
YIPE!
KNOCK THAT OFF! A SAND TRAP IS NO PLACE FOR JOKES!

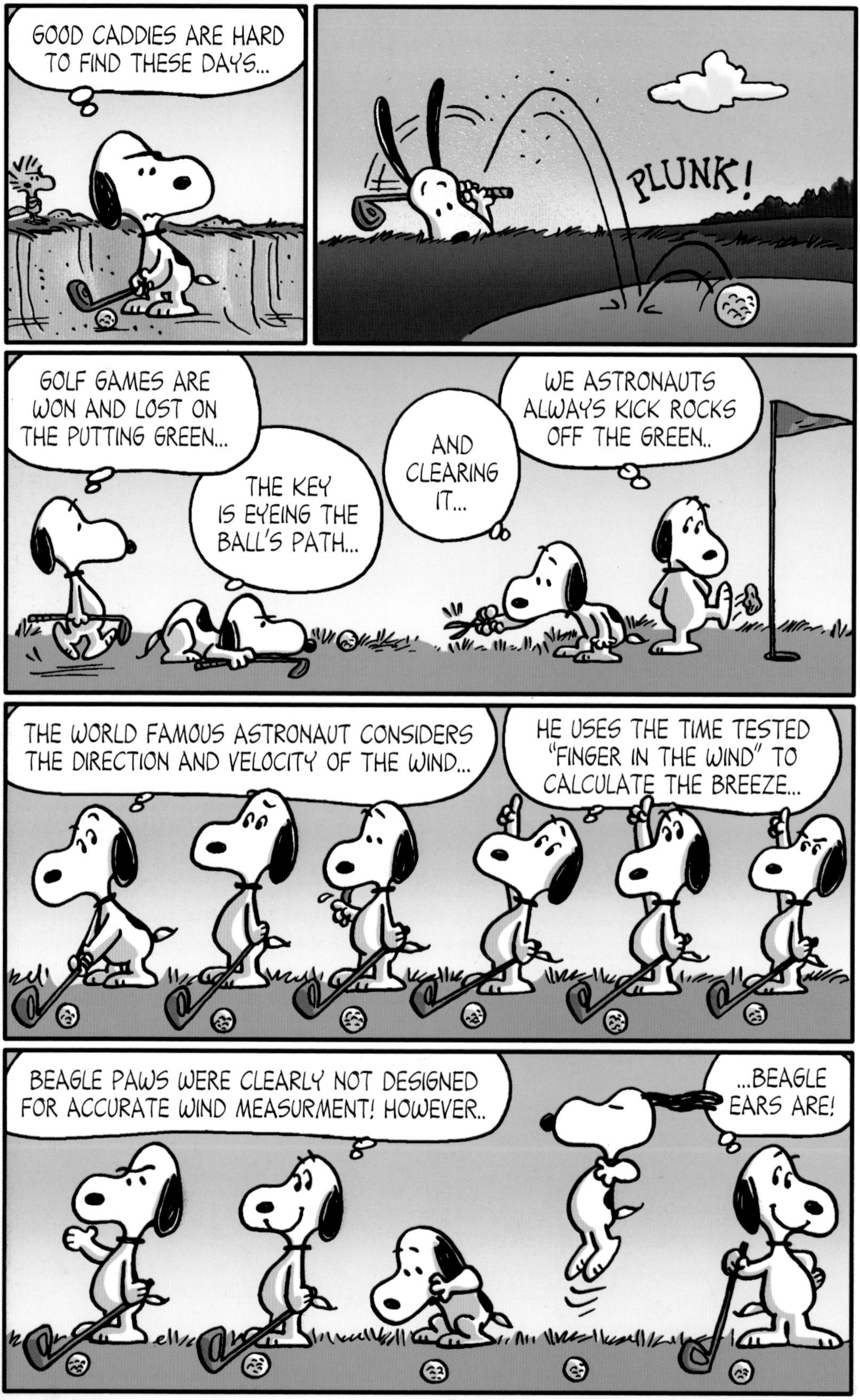
GOOD CADDIES ARE HARD TO FIND THESE DAYS...
PLUNK!
GOLF GAMES ARE WON AND LOST ON THE PUTTING GREEN...
THE KEY IS EYEING THE BALL'S PATH...
AND CLEARING IT...
WE ASTRONAUTS ALWAYS KICK ROCKS OFF THE GREEN..
THE WORLD FAMOUS ASTRONAUT CONSIDERS THE DIRECTION AND VELOCITY OF THE WIND...
HE USES THE TIME TESTED "FINGER IN THE WIND" TO CALCULATE THE BREEZE...
BEAGLE PAWS WERE CLEARLY NOT DESIGNED FOR ACCURATE WIND MEASURMENT! HOWEVER..
...BEAGLE EARS ARE!

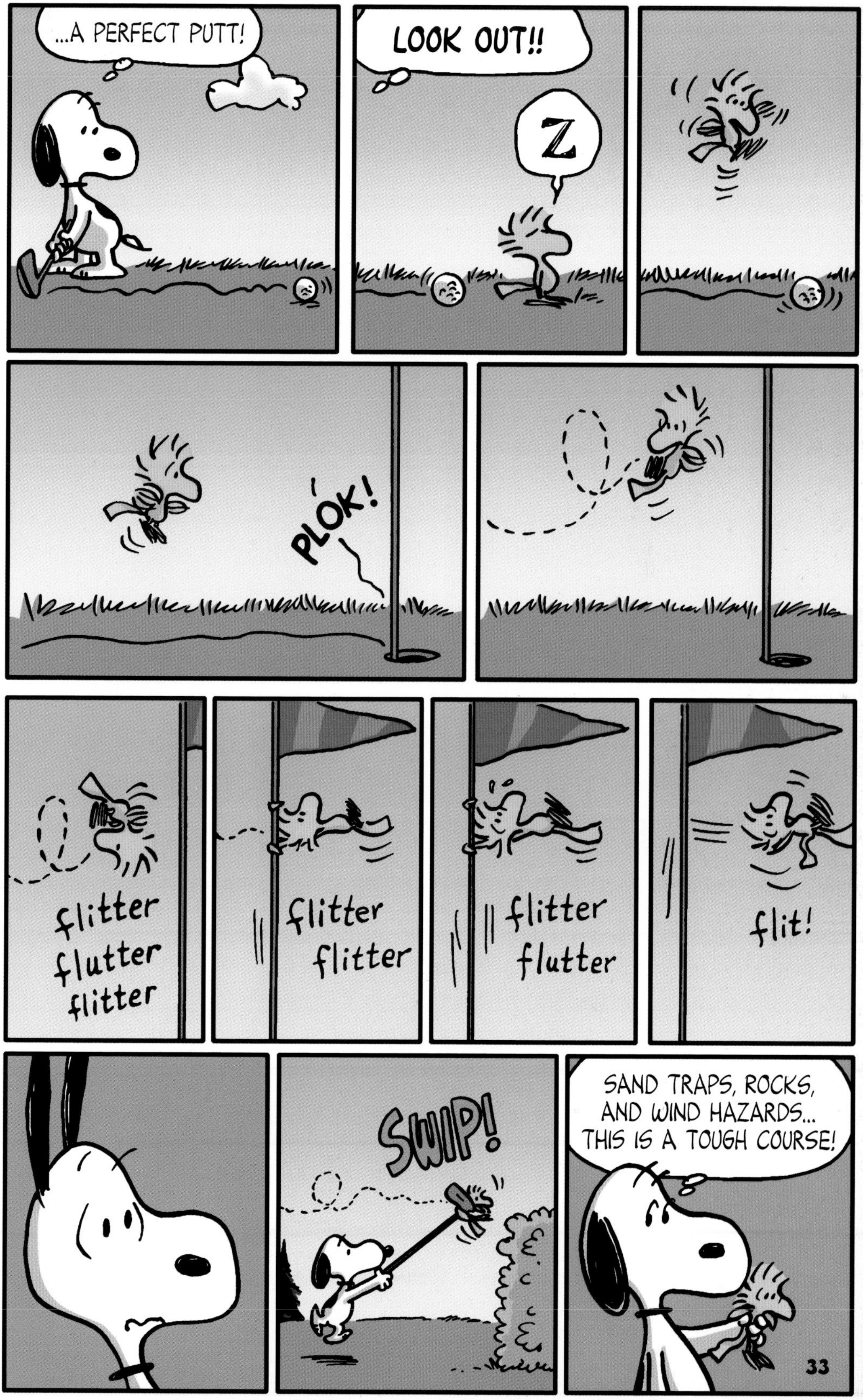
...A PERFECT PUTT!
LOOK OUT!!
Z
PLOK!
flitter
flutter
flitter
flitter
flitter
flitter
flutter
flit!
SWIP!
SAND TRAPS, ROCKS, AND WIND HAZARDS... THIS IS A TOUGH COURSE!

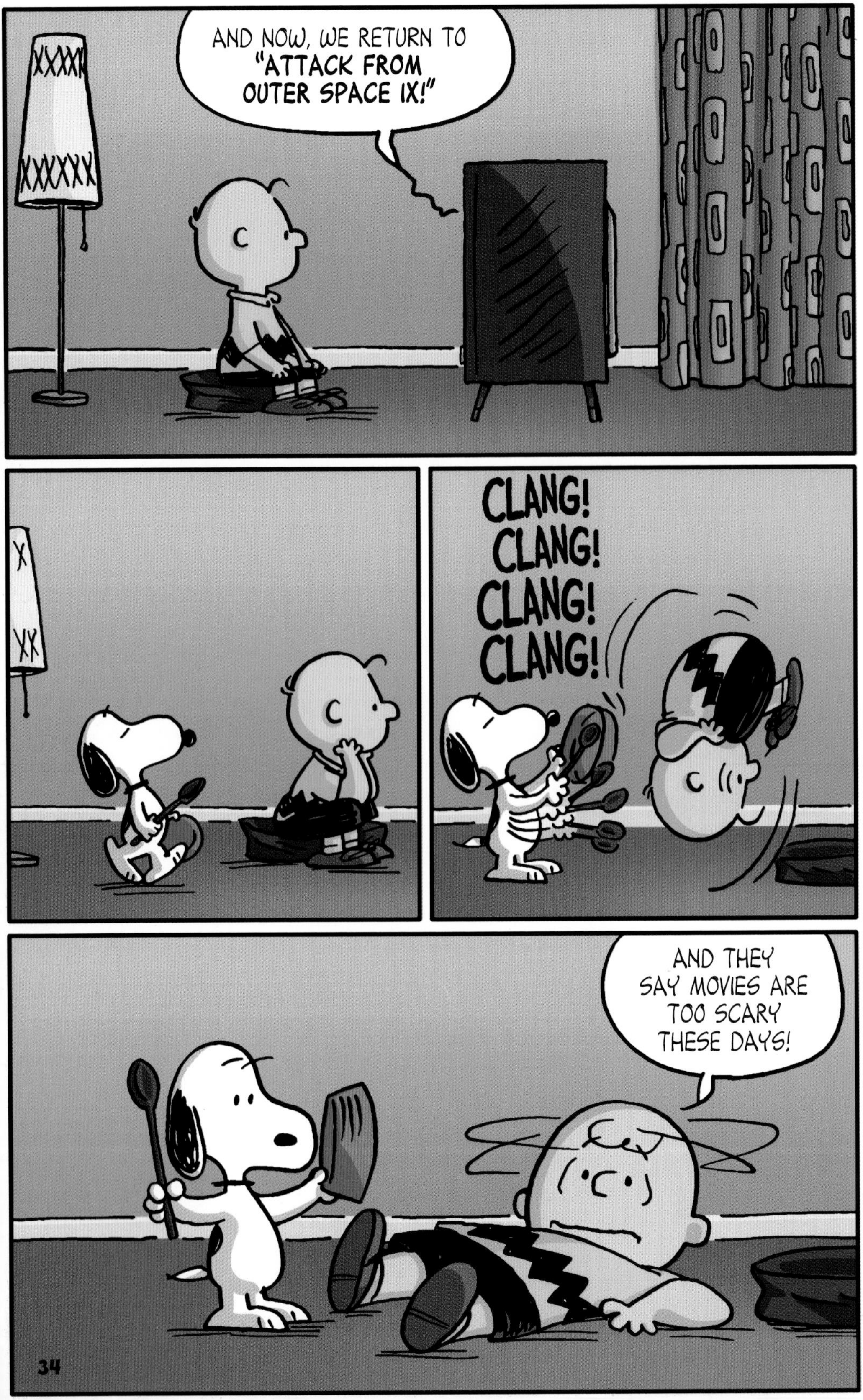
AND NOW, WE RETURN TO "ATTACK FROM OUTER SPACE IX!"
CLANG! CLANG! CLANG! CLANG!
AND THEY SAY MOVIES ARE TOO SCARY THESE DAYS!

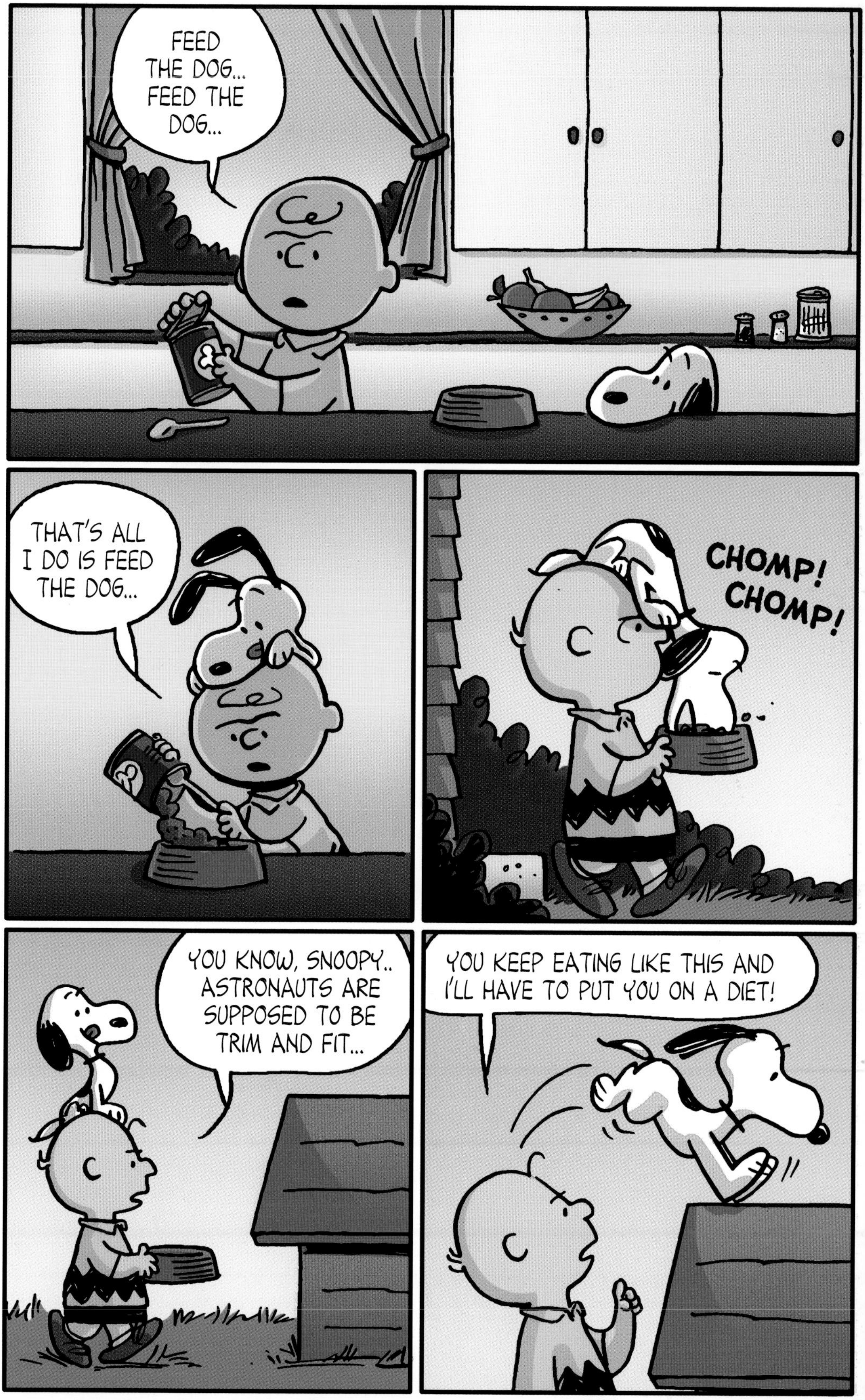
FEED THE DOG... FEED THE DOG...
THAT'S ALL I DO IS FEED THE DOG...
CHOMP! CHOMP!
YOU KNOW, SNOOPY.. ASTRONAUTS ARE SUPPOSED TO BE TRIM AND FIT...
YOU KEEP EATING LIKE THIS AND I'LL HAVE TO PUT YOU ON A DIET!

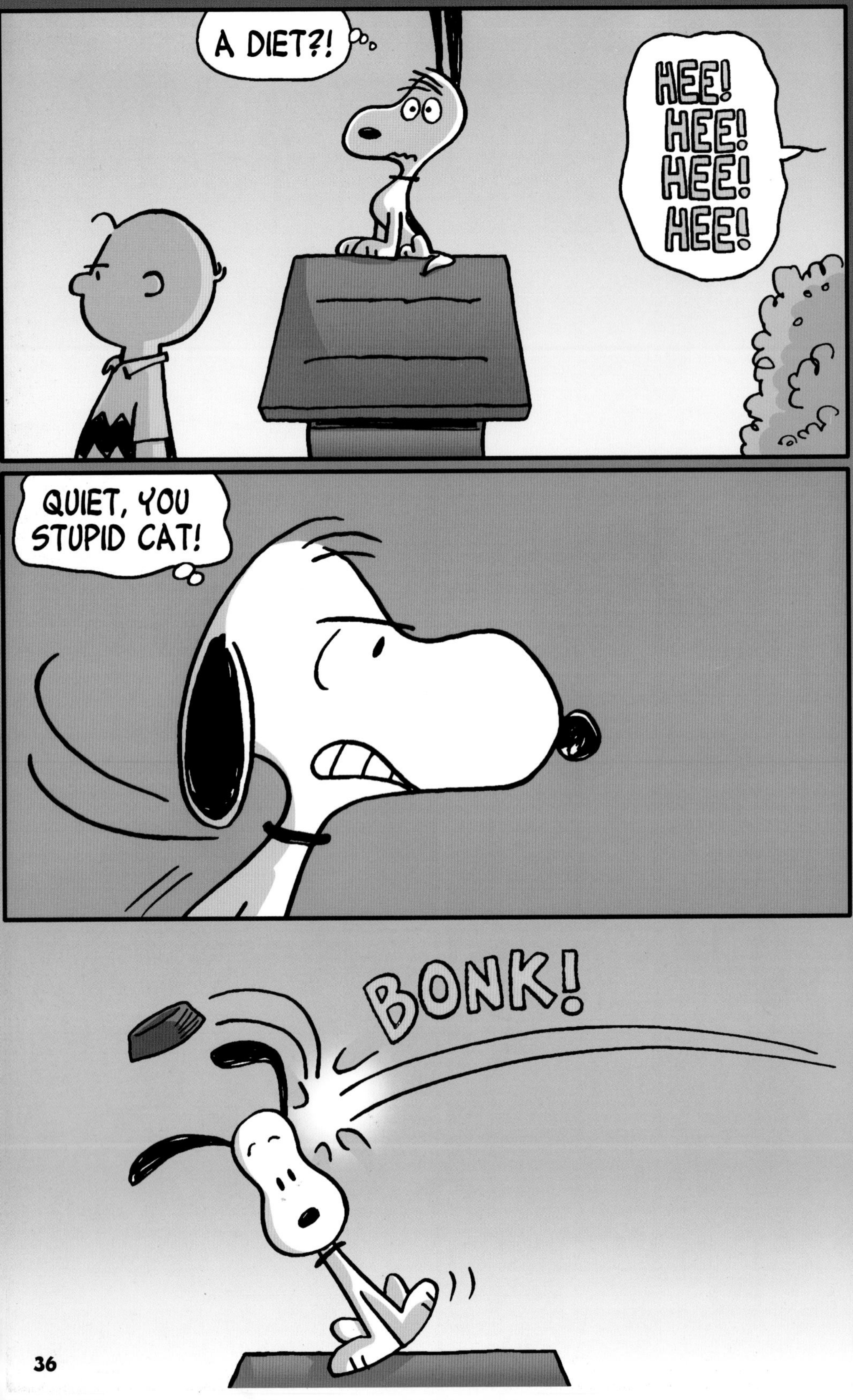
A DIET?!
HEE! HEE! HEE! HEE!
QUIET, YOU STUPID CAT!
BONK!

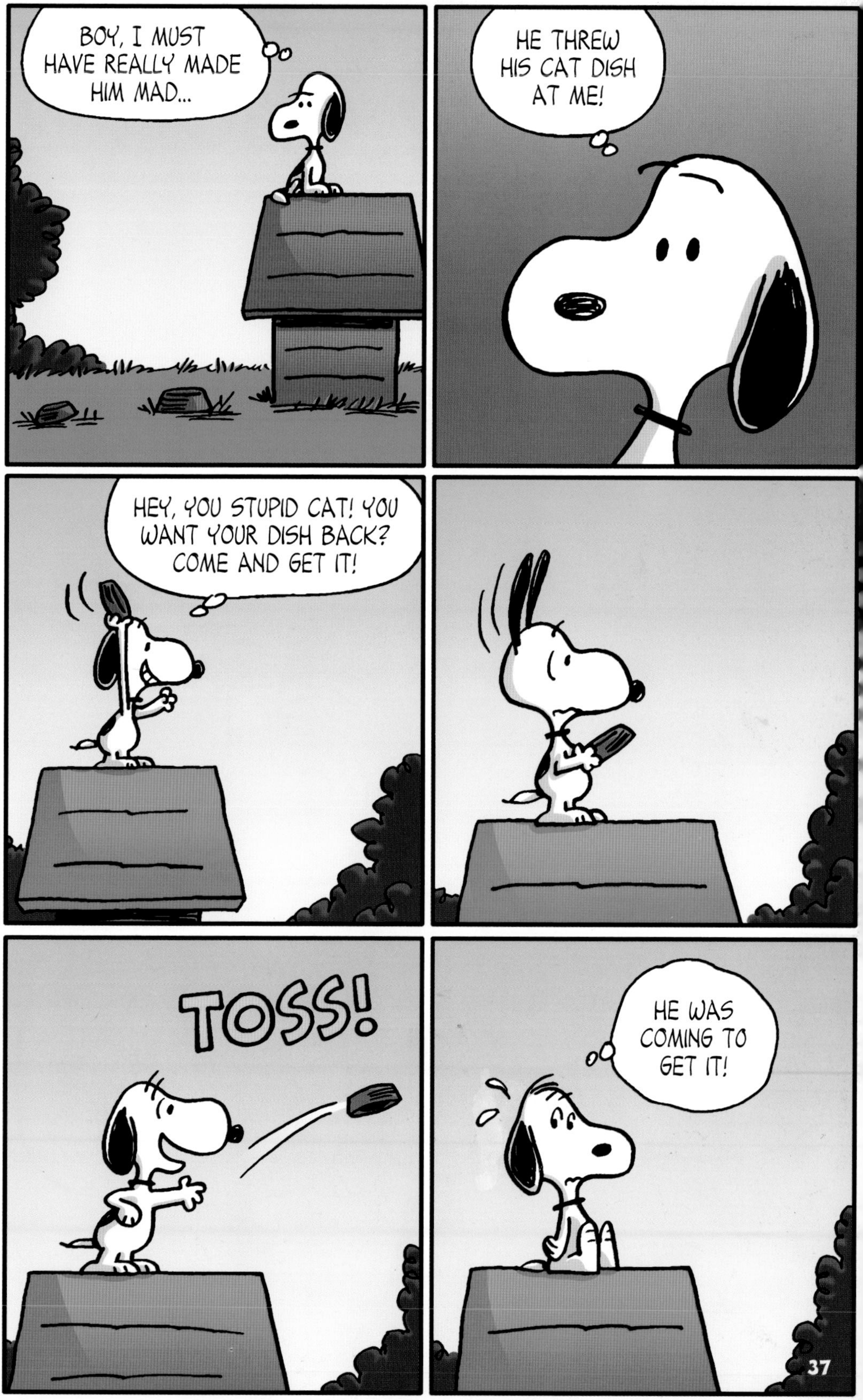
BOY, I MUST HAVE REALLY MADE HIM MAD...
HE THREW HIS CAT DISH AT ME!
HEY, YOU STUPID CAT! YOU WANT YOUR DISH BACK? COME AND GET IT!
TOSS!
HE WAS COMING TO GET IT!

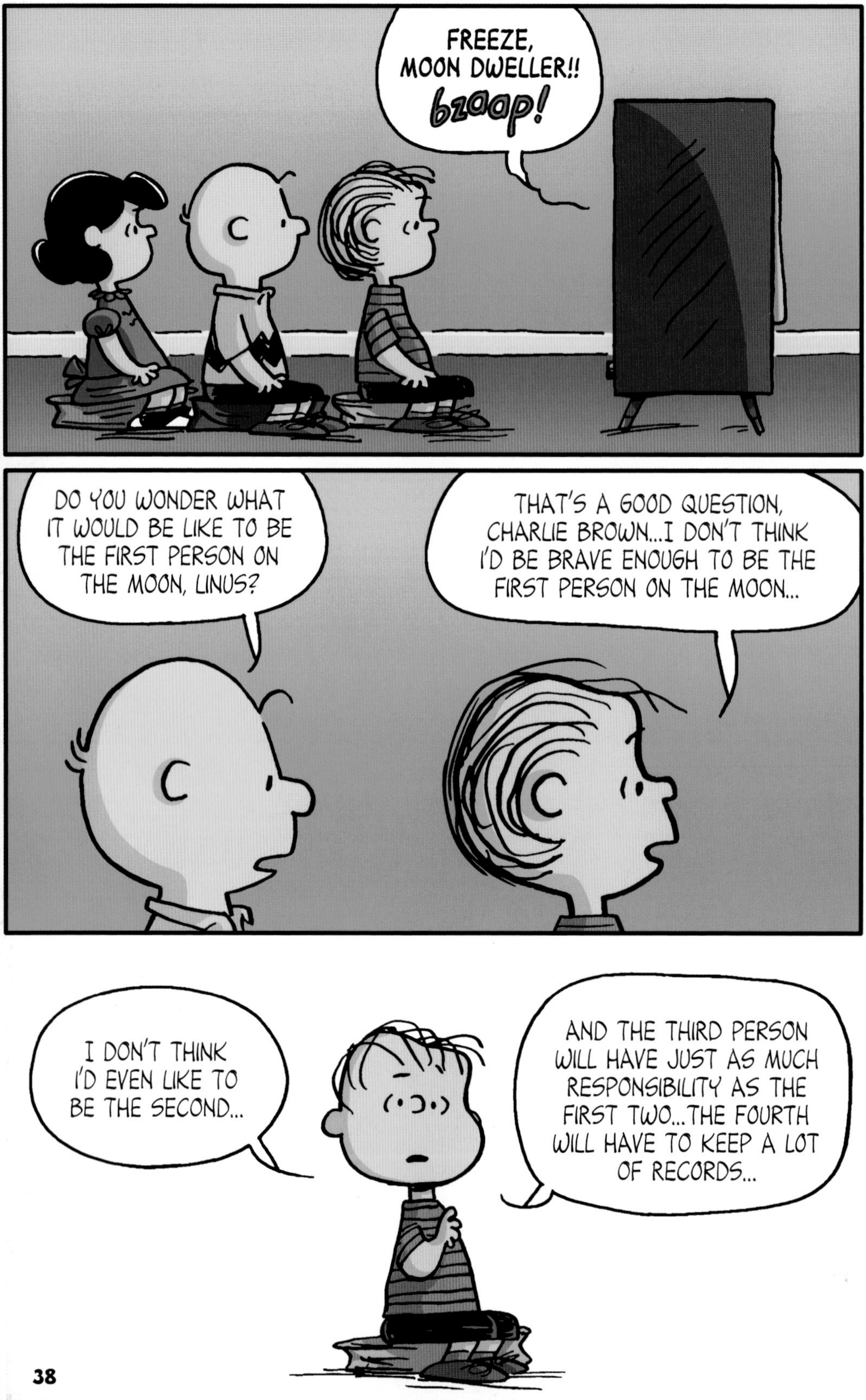
FREEZE, MOON DWELLER!! bzaap!
DO YOU WONDER WHAT IT WOULD BE LIKE TO BE THE FIRST PERSON ON THE MOON, LINUS?
THAT'S A GOOD QUESTION, CHARLIE BROWN...I DON'T THINK I'D BE BRAVE ENOUGH TO BE THE FIRST PERSON ON THE MOON...
I DON'T THINK I'D EVEN LIKE TO BE THE SECOND...
AND THE THIRD PERSON WILL HAVE JUST AS MUCH RESPONSIBILITY AS THE FIRST TWO...THE FOURTH WILL HAVE TO KEEP A LOT OF RECORDS...

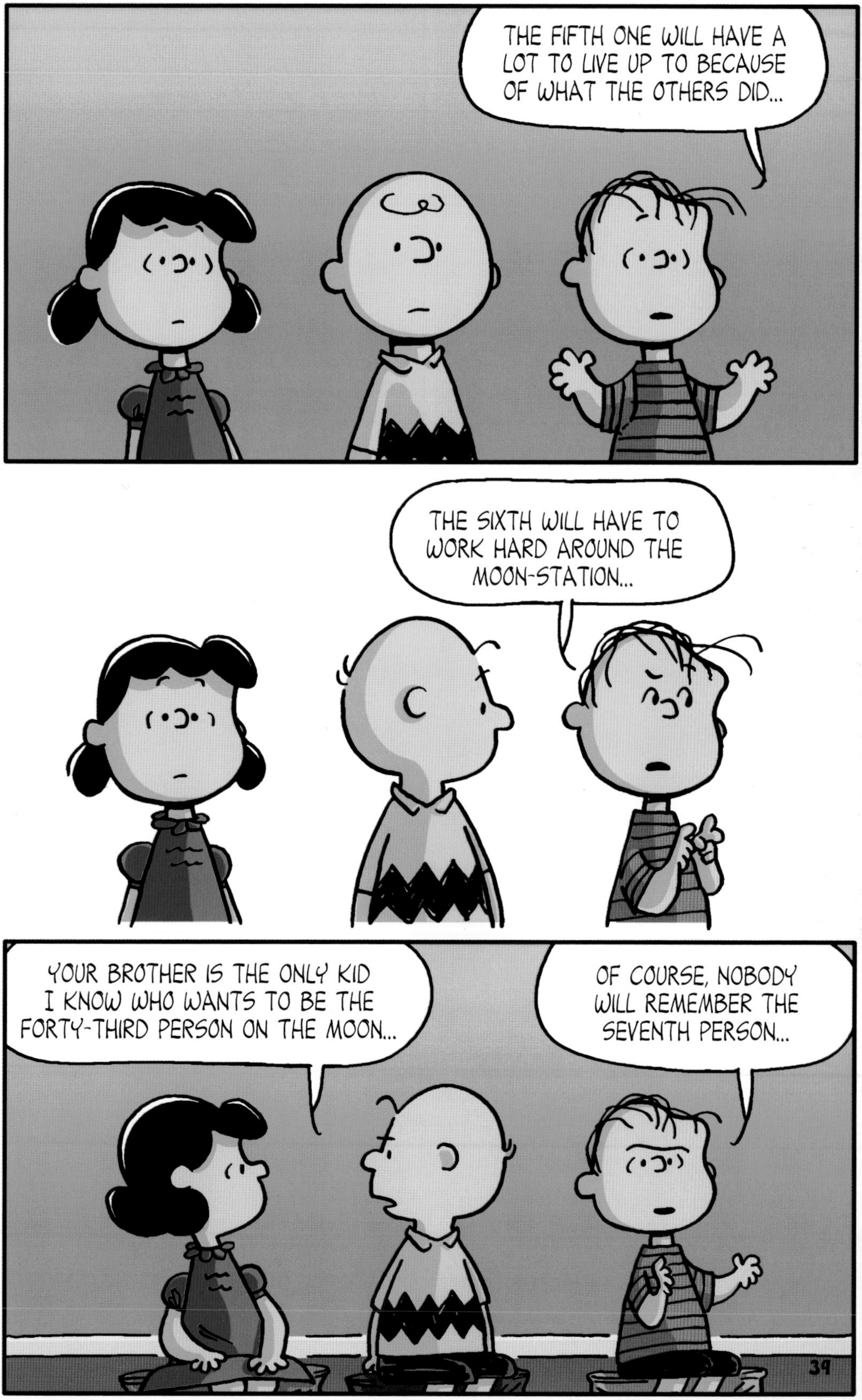
THE FIFTH ONE WILL HAVE A LOT TO LIVE UP TO BECAUSE OF WHAT THE OTHERS DID...
THE SIXTH WILL HAVE TO WORK HARD AROUND THE MOON-STATION...
YOUR BROTHER IS THE ONLY KID I KNOW WHO WANTS TO BE THE FORTY-THIRD PERSON ON THE MOON...
OF COURSE, NOBODY WILL REMEMBER THE SEVENTH PERSON...

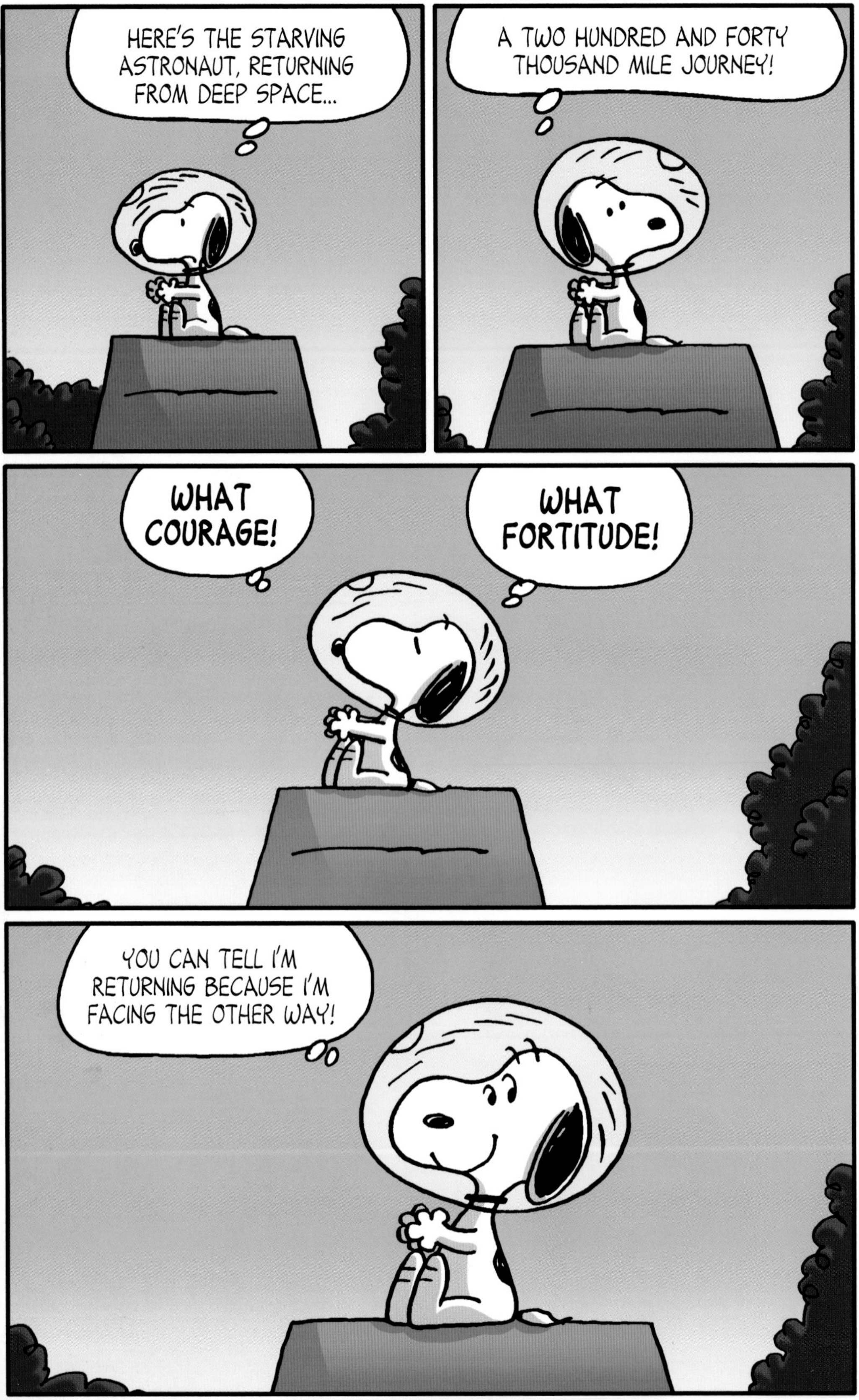
HERE'S THE STARVING ASTRONAUT, RETURNING FROM DEEP SPACE...
A TWO HUNDRED AND FORTY THOUSAND MILE JOURNEY!
WHAT COURAGE!
WHAT FORTITUDE!
YOU CAN TELL I'M RETURNING BECAUSE I'M FACING THE OTHER WAY!

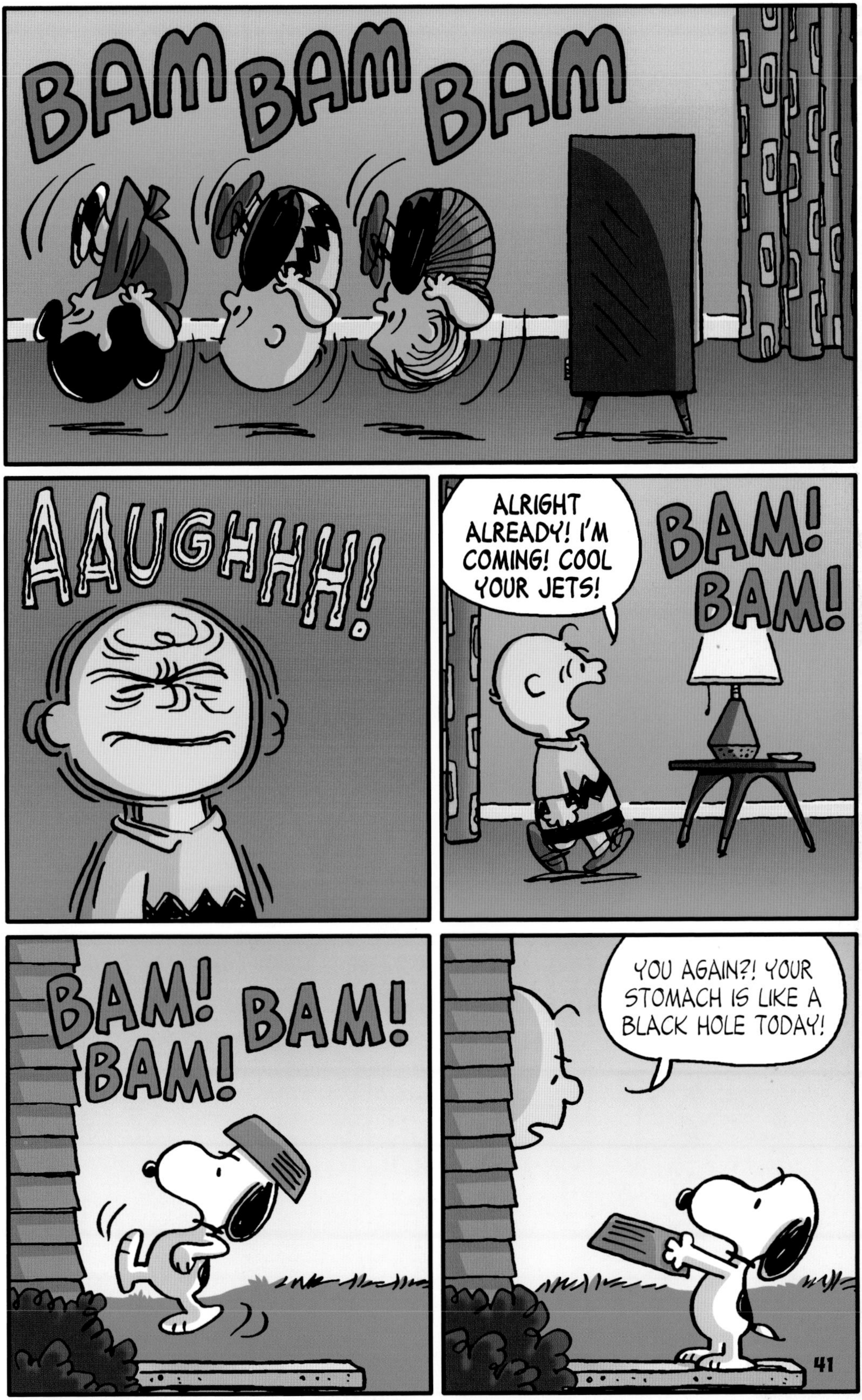
BAM BAM BAM
AAUGHHH!
ALRIGHT ALREADY! I'M COMING! COOL YOUR JETS!
BAM! BAM!
BAM! BAM! BAM!
YOU AGAIN?! YOUR STOMACH IS LIKE A BLACK HOLE TODAY!

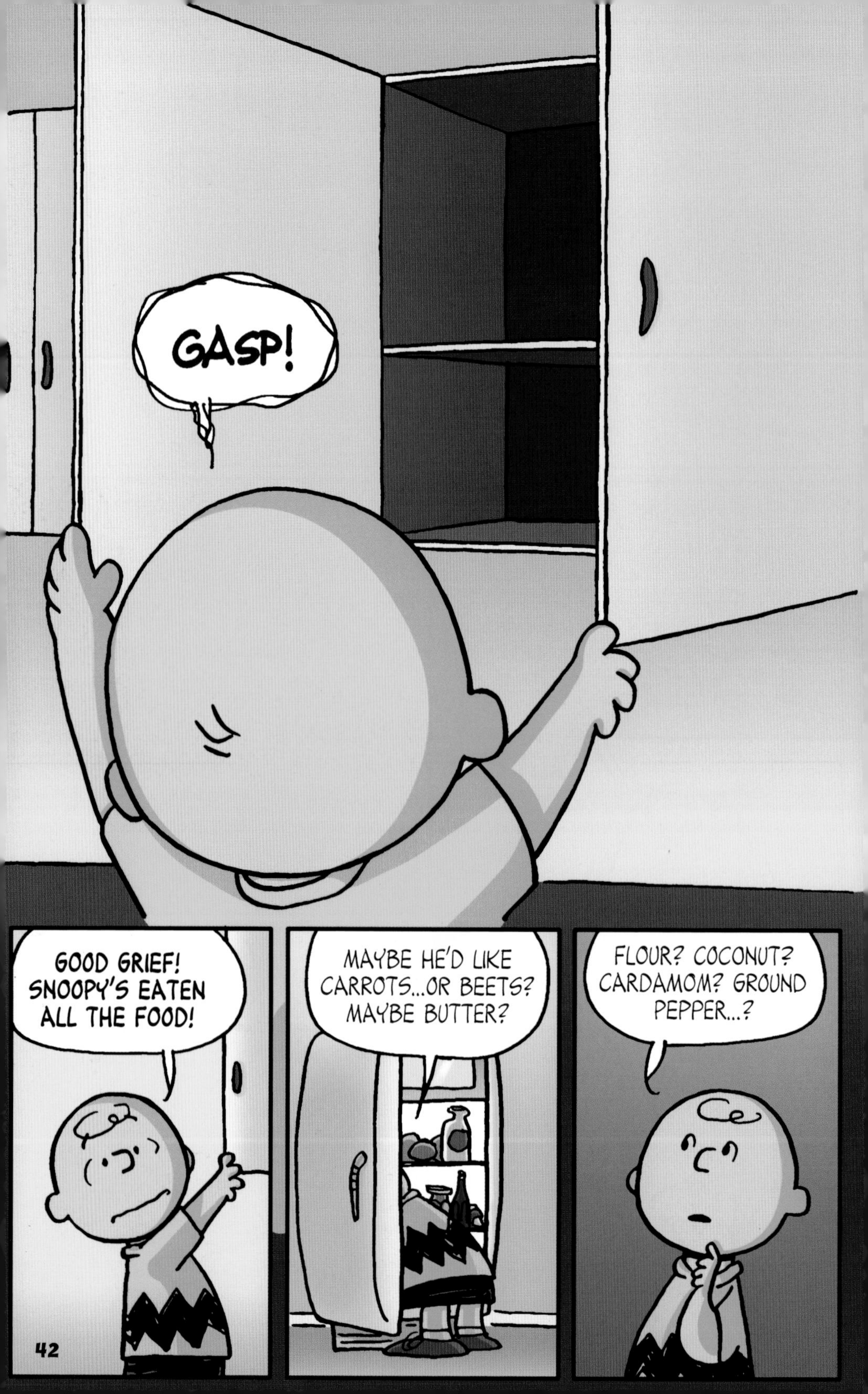
GASP!
GOOD GRIEF! SNOOPY'S EATEN ALL THE FOOD!
MAYBE HE'D LIKE CARROTS...OR BEETS? MAYBE BUTTER?
FLOUR? COCONUT? CARDAMOM? GROUND PEPPER...?

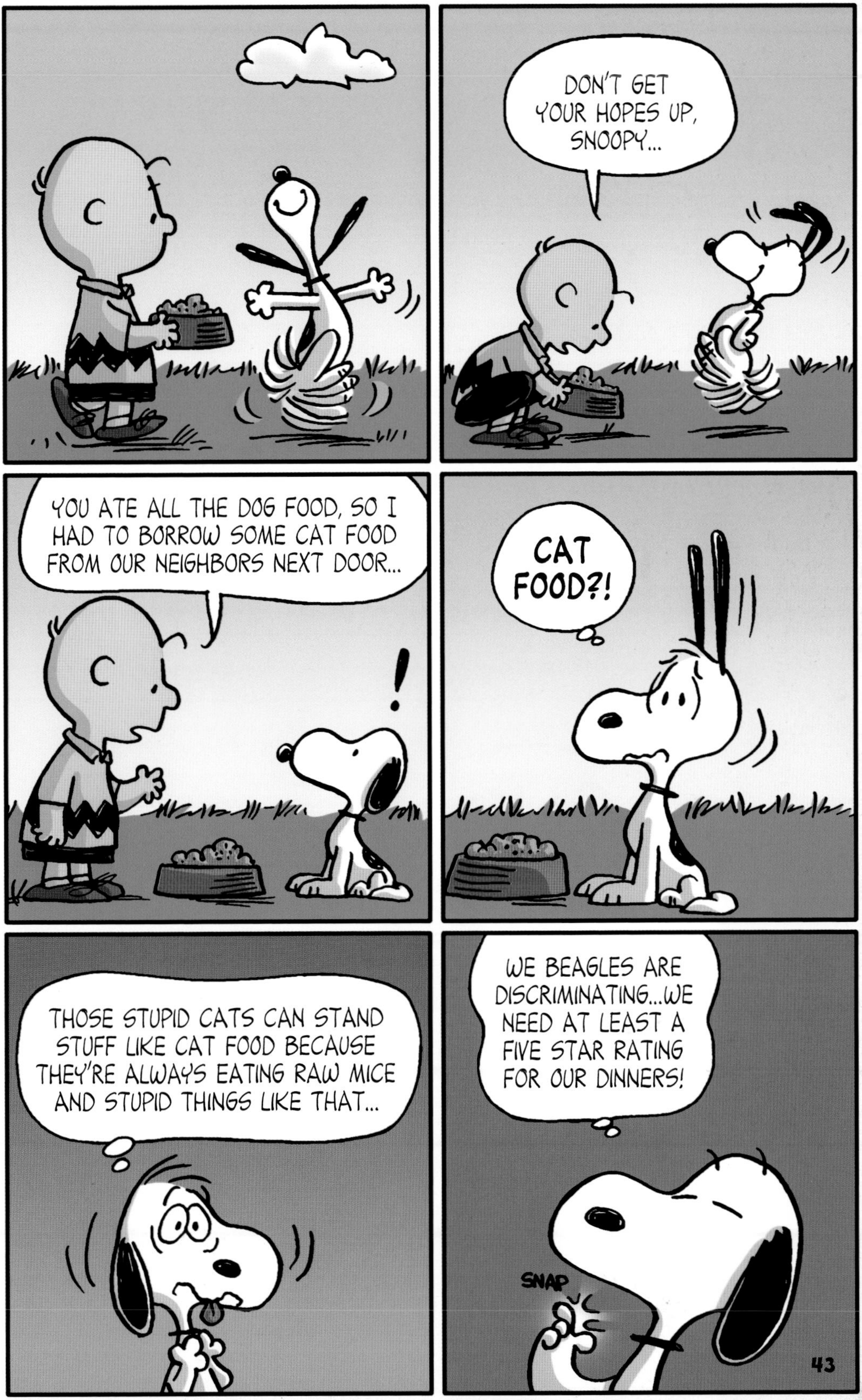
DON'T GET YOUR HOPES UP, SNOOPY...
YOU ATE ALL THE DOG FOOD, SO I HAD TO BORROW SOME CAT FOOD FROM OUR NEIGHBORS NEXT DOOR...
!
CAT FOOD?!
THOSE STUPID CATS CAN STAND STUFF LIKE CAT FOOD BECAUSE THEY'RE ALWAYS EATING RAW MICE AND STUPID THINGS LIKE THAT...
WE BEAGLES ARE DISCRIMINATING...WE NEED AT LEAST A FIVE STAR RATING FOR OUR DINNERS!
SNAP

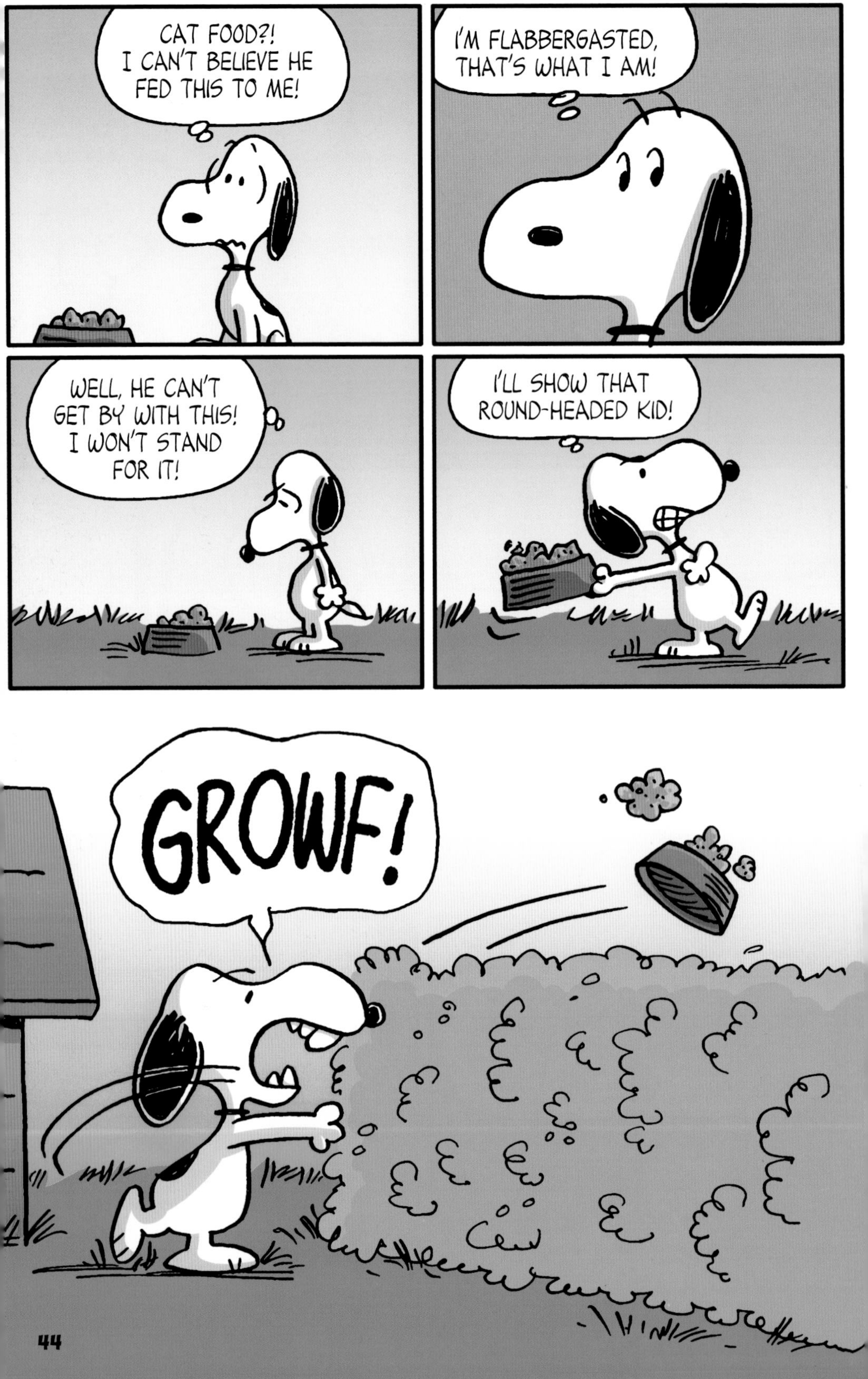
CAT FOOD?! I CAN'T BELIEVE HE FED THIS TO ME!
I'M FLABBERGASTED, THAT'S WHAT I AM!
WELL, HE CAN'T GET BY WITH THIS! I WON'T STAND FOR IT!
I'LL SHOW THAT ROUND-HEADED KID!
GROWF!

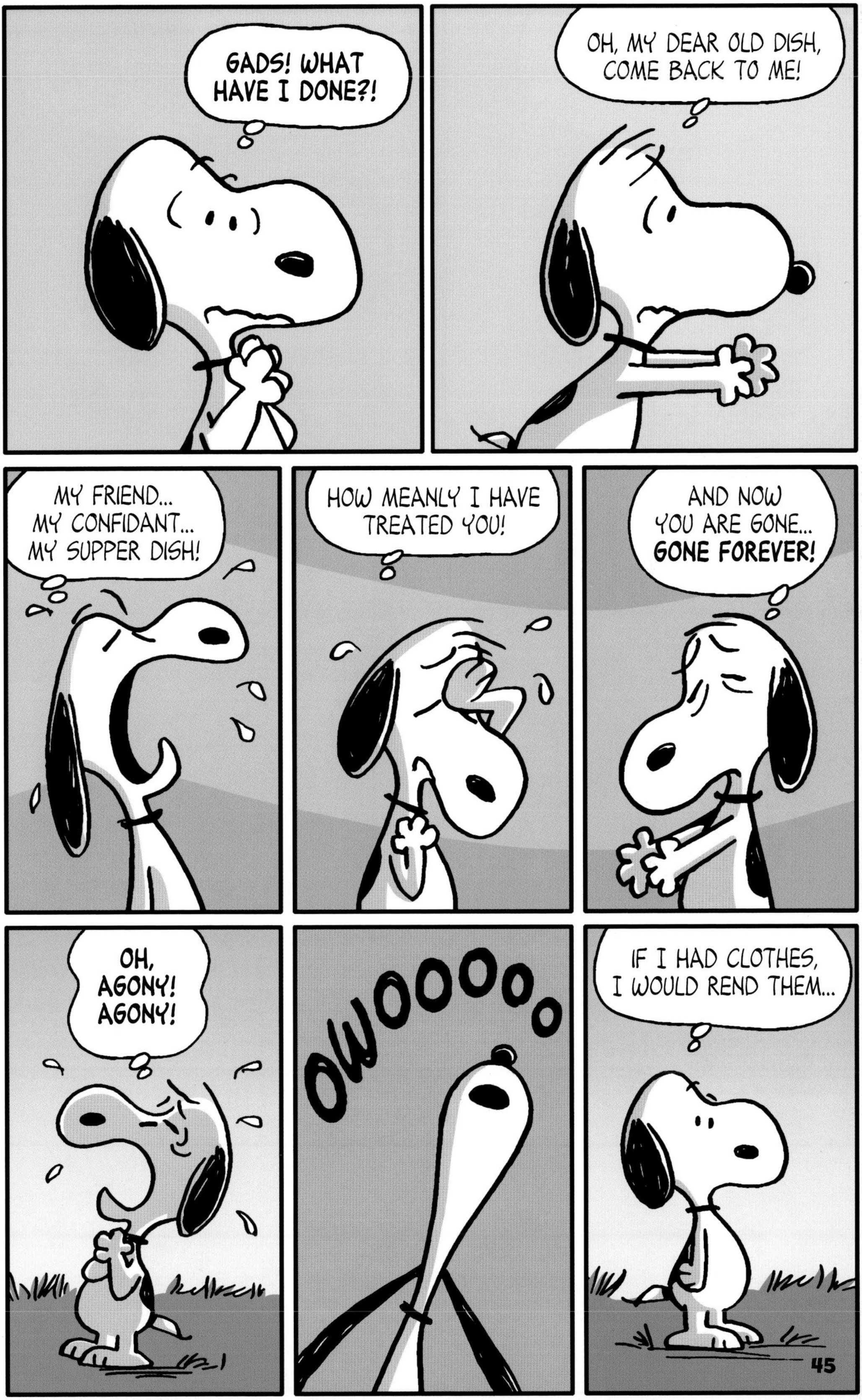
GADS! WHAT HAVE I DONE?!
OH, MY DEAR OLD DISH, COME BACK TO ME!
MY FRIEND... MY CONFIDANT... MY SUPPER DISH!
HOW MEANLY I HAVE TREATED YOU!
AND NOW YOU ARE GONE... GONE FOREVER!
OH, AGONY! AGONY!
OWOOOOO
IF I HAD CLOTHES, I WOULD REND THEM...

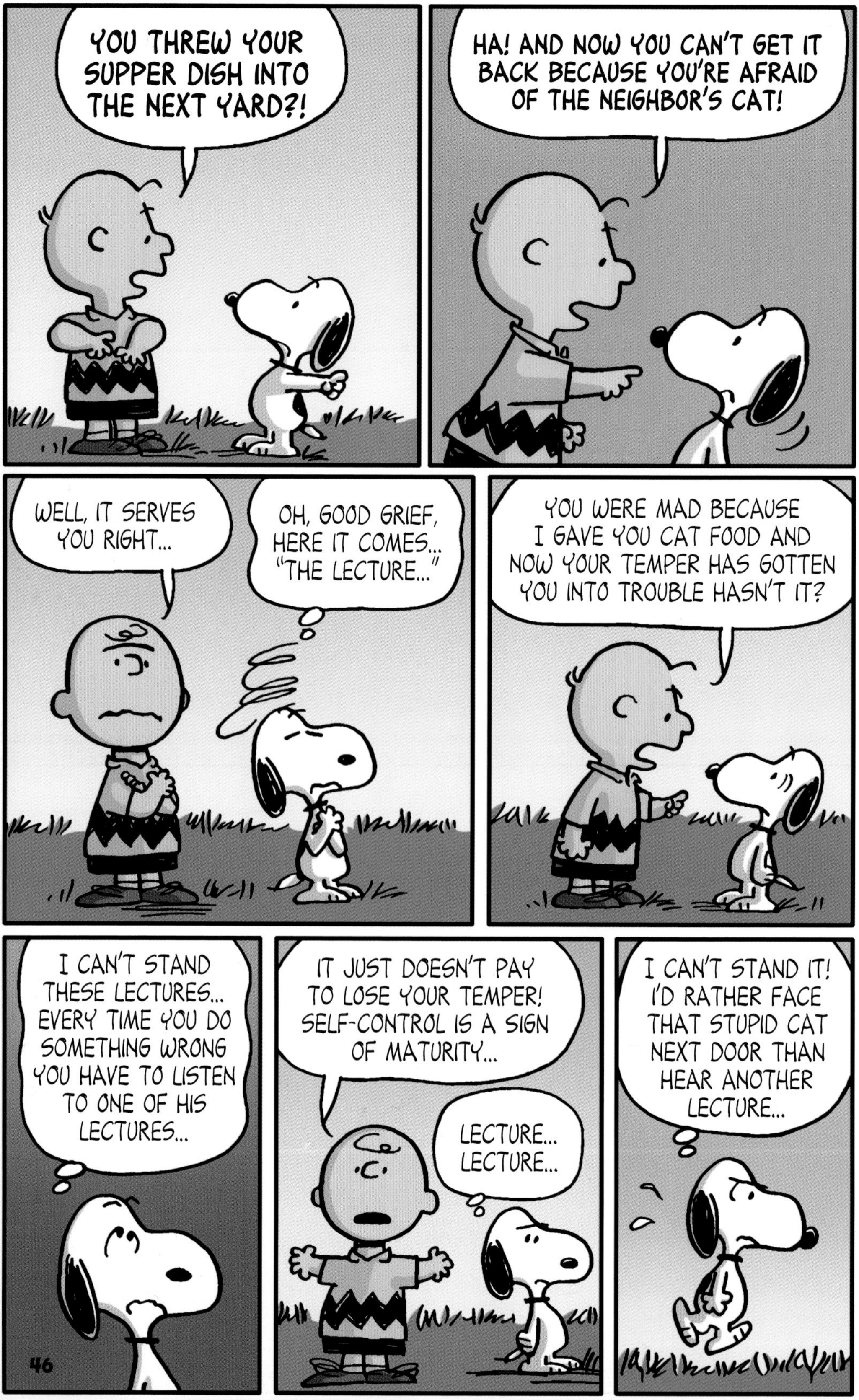
YOU THREW YOUR SUPPER DISH INTO THE NEXT YARD?!
HA! AND NOW YOU CAN'T GET IT BACK BECAUSE YOU'RE AFRAID OF THE NEIGHBOR'S CAT!
WELL, IT SERVES YOU RIGHT...
OH, GOOD GRIEF, HERE IT COMES... "THE LECTURE..."
YOU WERE MAD BECAUSE I GAVE YOU CAT FOOD AND NOW YOUR TEMPER HAS GOTTEN YOU INTO TROUBLE HASN'T IT?
I CAN'T STAND THESE LECTURES... EVERY TIME YOU DO SOMETHING WRONG YOU HAVE TO LISTEN TO ONE OF HIS LECTURES...
IT JUST DOESN'T PAY TO LOSE YOUR TEMPER! SELF-CONTROL IS A SIGN OF MATURITY...
LECTURE... LECTURE...
I CAN'T STAND IT! I'D RATHER FACE THAT STUPID CAT NEXT DOOR THAN HEAR ANOTHER LECTURE...

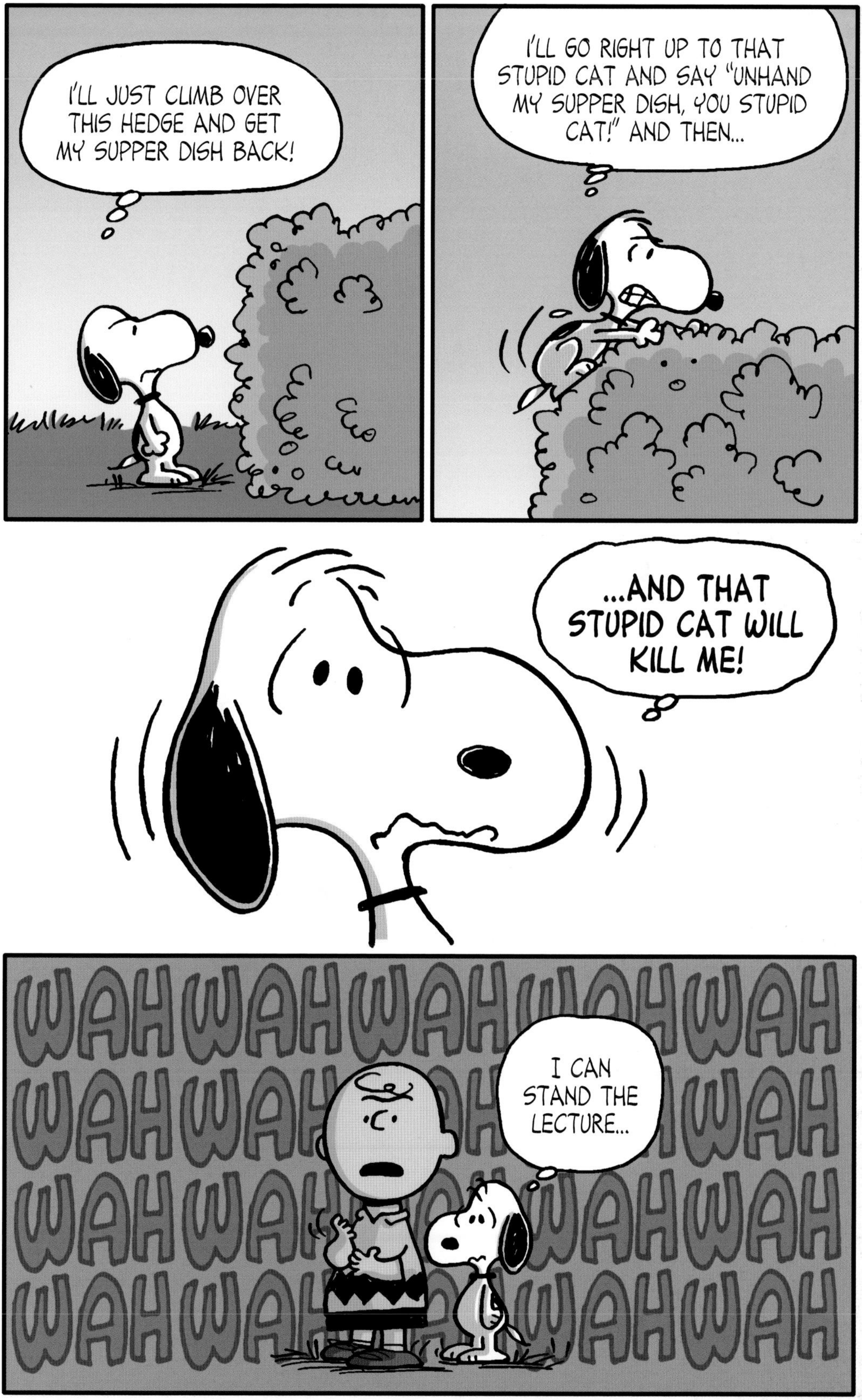

I'LL JUST CLIMB OVER THIS HEDGE AND GET MY SUPPER DISH BACK!
I'LL GO RIGHT UP TO THAT STUPID CAT AND SAY "UNHAND MY SUPPER DISH, YOU STUPID CAT!" AND THEN...
...AND THAT STUPID CAT WILL KILL ME!
WAHWAHWAHWAHWAH
I CAN STAND THE LECTURE...

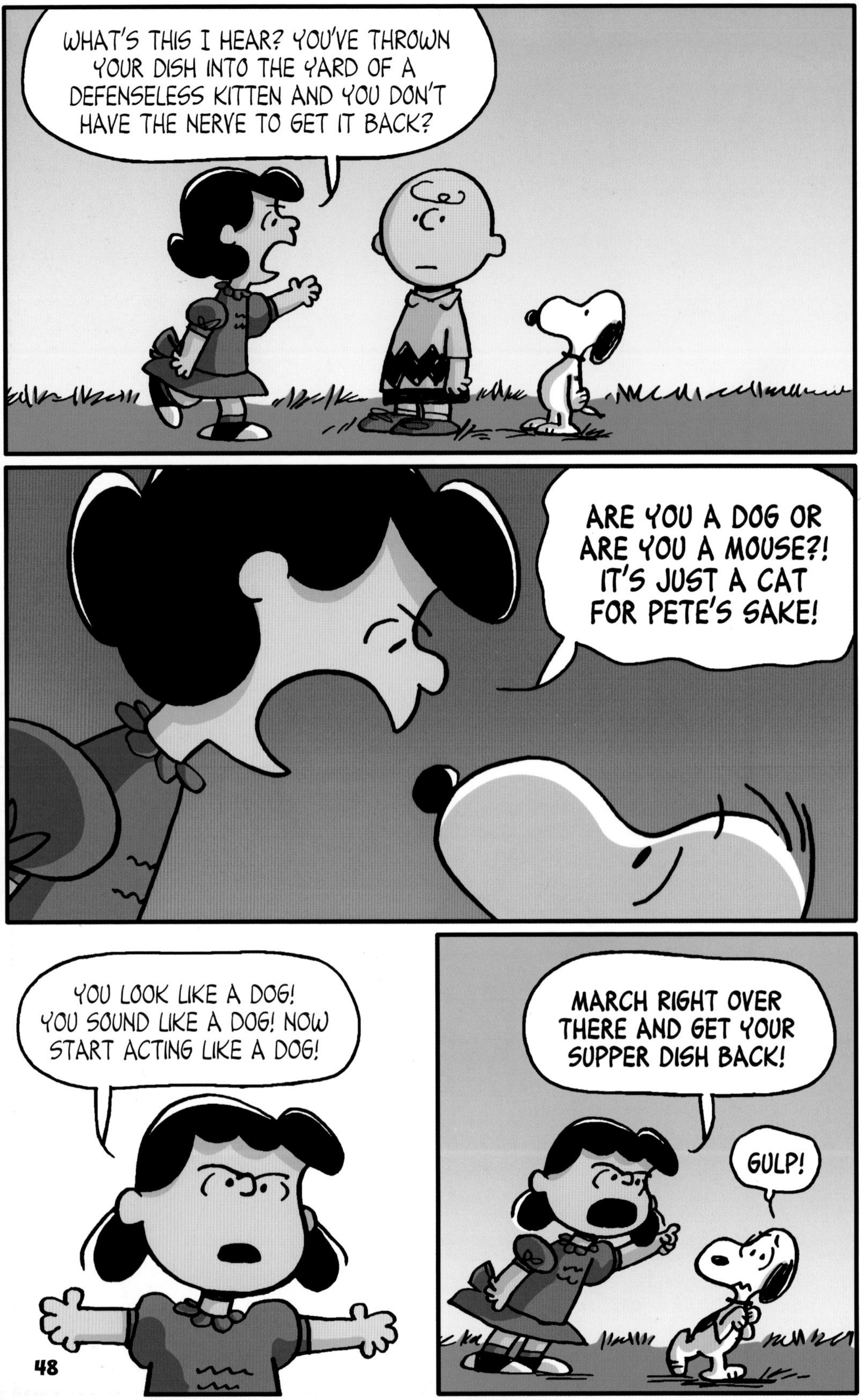
WHAT'S THIS I HEAR? YOU'VE THROWN YOUR DISH INTO THE YARD OF A DEFENSELESS KITTEN AND YOU DON'T HAVE THE NERVE TO GET IT BACK?
ARE YOU A DOG OR ARE YOU A MOUSE?! IT'S JUST A CAT FOR PETE'S SAKE!
YOU LOOK LIKE A DOG! YOU SOUND LIKE A DOG! NOW START ACTING LIKE A DOG!
MARCH RIGHT OVER THERE AND GET YOUR SUPPER DISH BACK!
GULP!

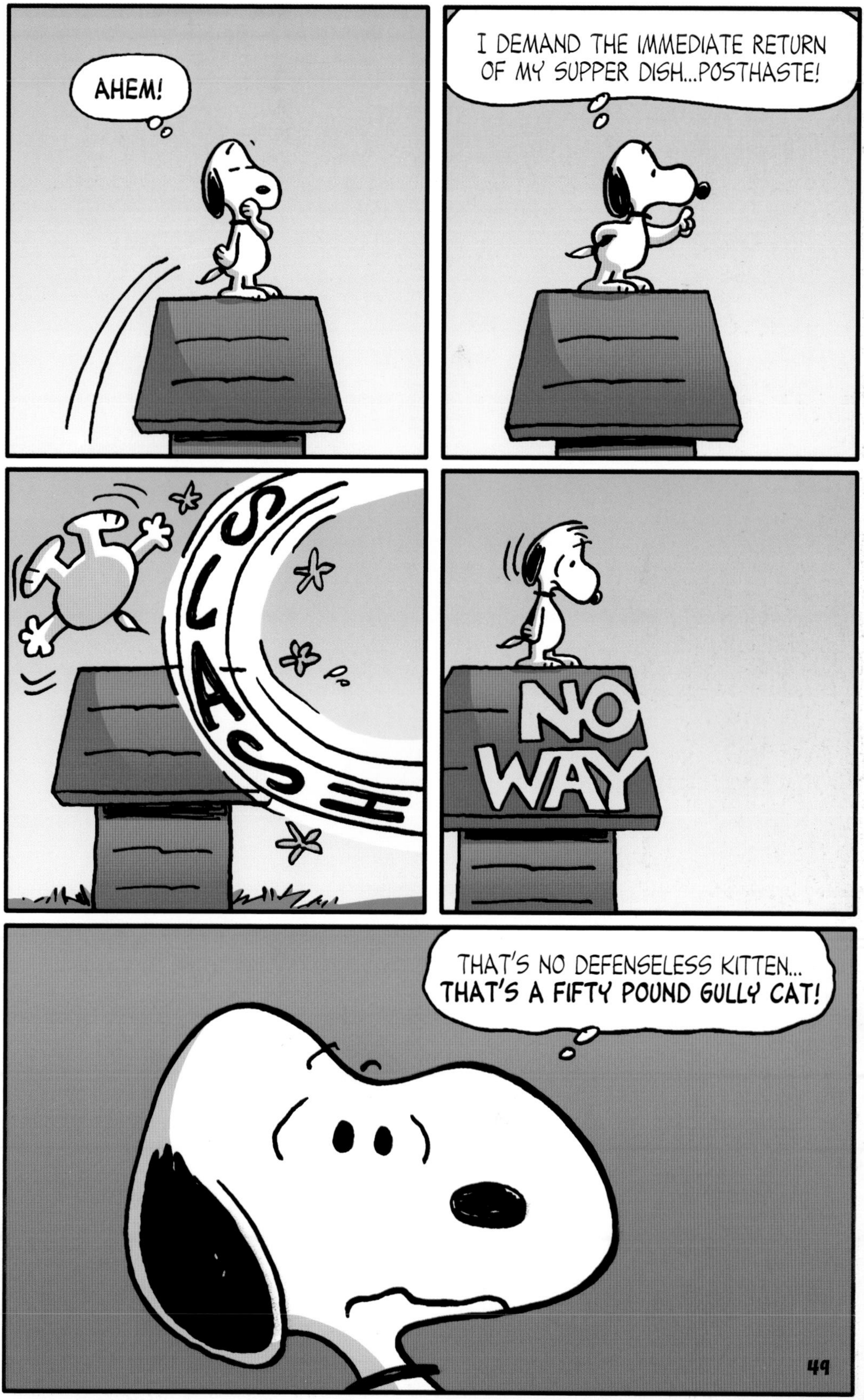
AHEM!
I DEMAND THE IMMEDIATE RETURN OF MY SUPPER DISH...POSTHASTE!
SLASH
NO WAY
THAT'S NO DEFENSELESS KITTEN... THAT'S A FIFTY POUND GULLY CAT!

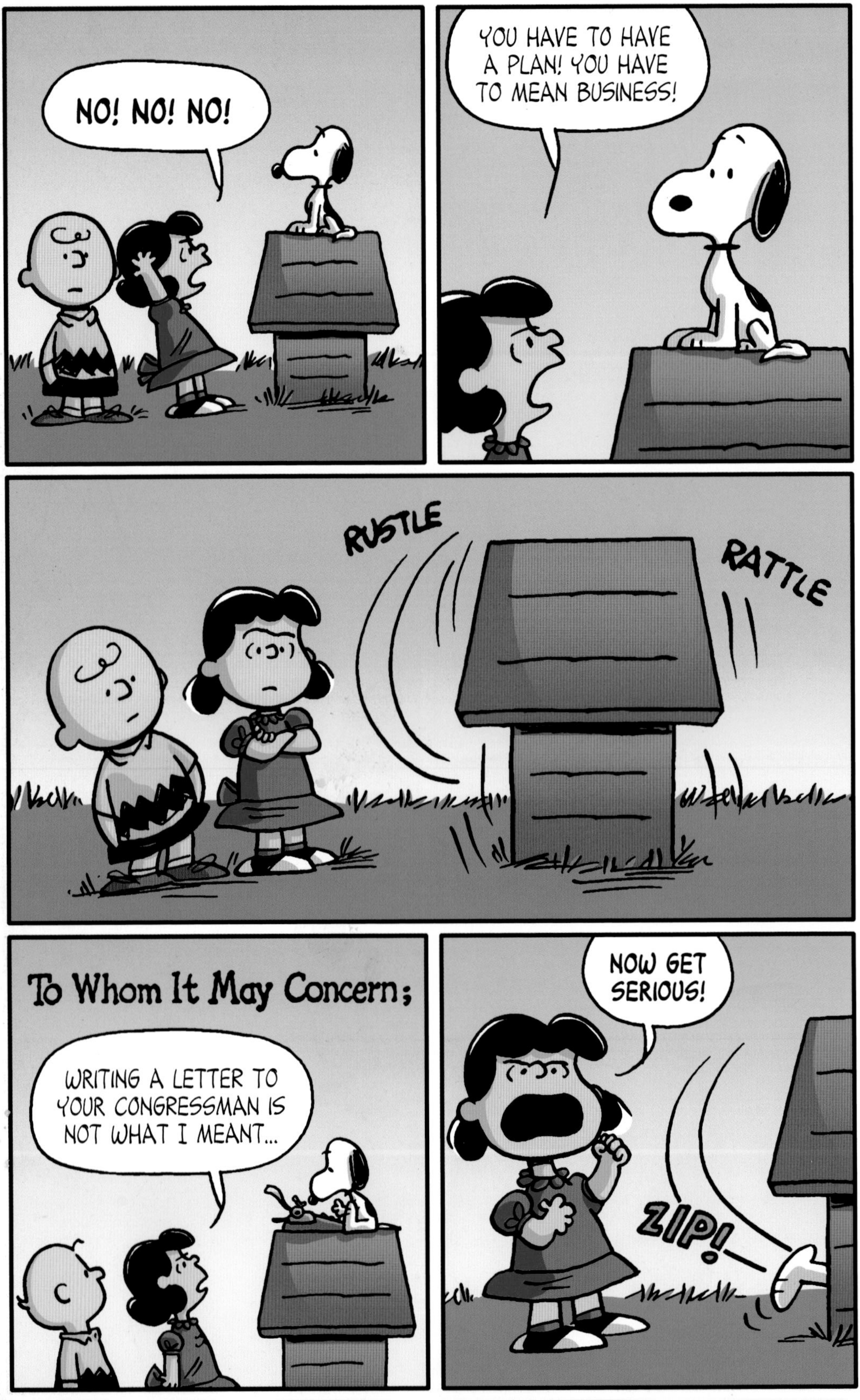
NO! NO! NO!
YOU HAVE TO HAVE A PLAN! YOU HAVE TO MEAN BUSINESS!
RUSTLE
RATTLE
To Whom It May Concern;
WRITING A LETTER TO YOUR CONGRESSMAN IS NOT WHAT I MEANT...
NOW GET SERIOUS!
ZIP!

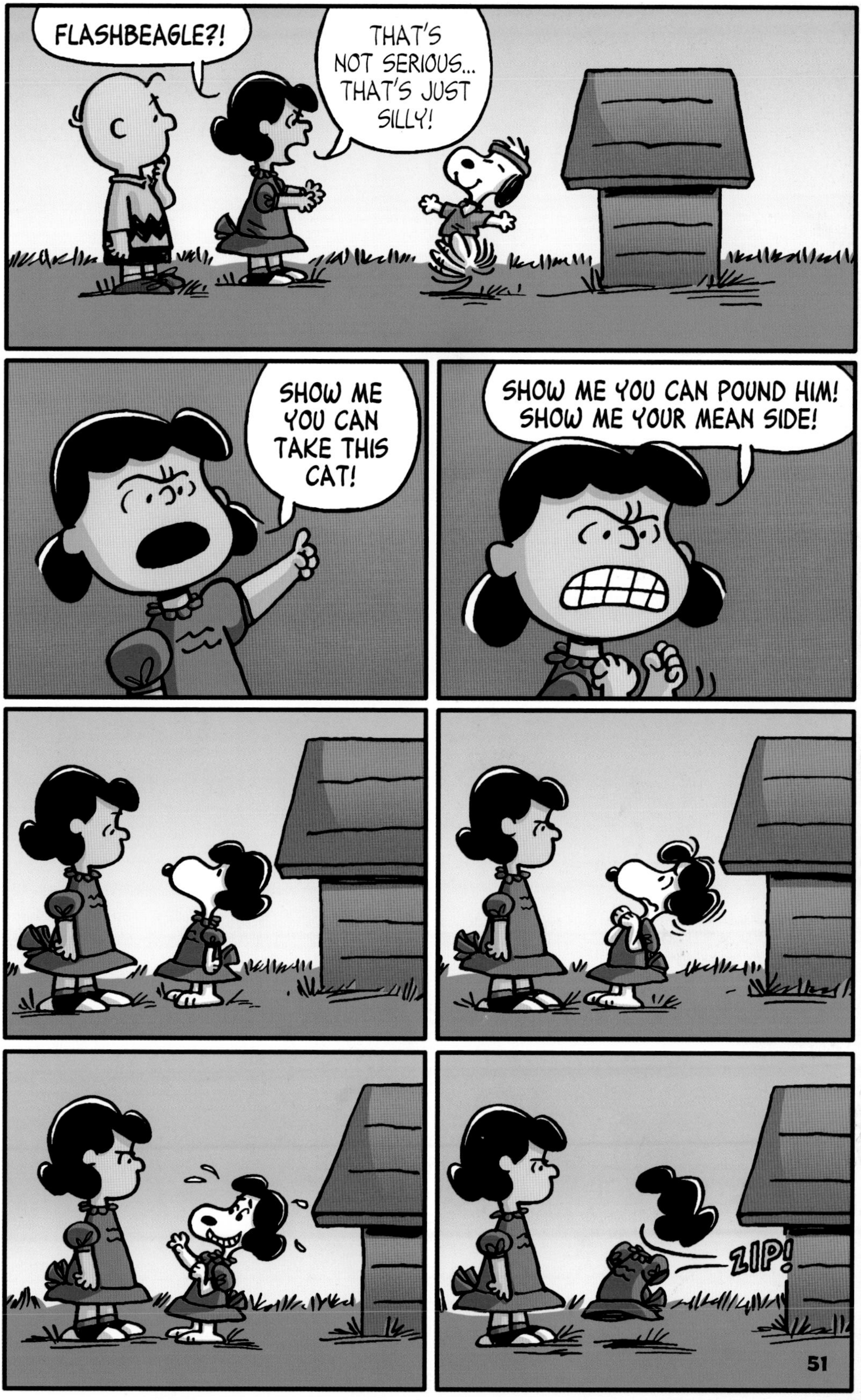
FLASHBEAGLE?!
THAT'S NOT SERIOUS... THAT'S JUST SILLY!
SHOW ME YOU CAN TAKE THIS CAT!
SHOW ME YOU CAN POUND HIM! SHOW ME YOUR MEAN SIDE!
ZIP!

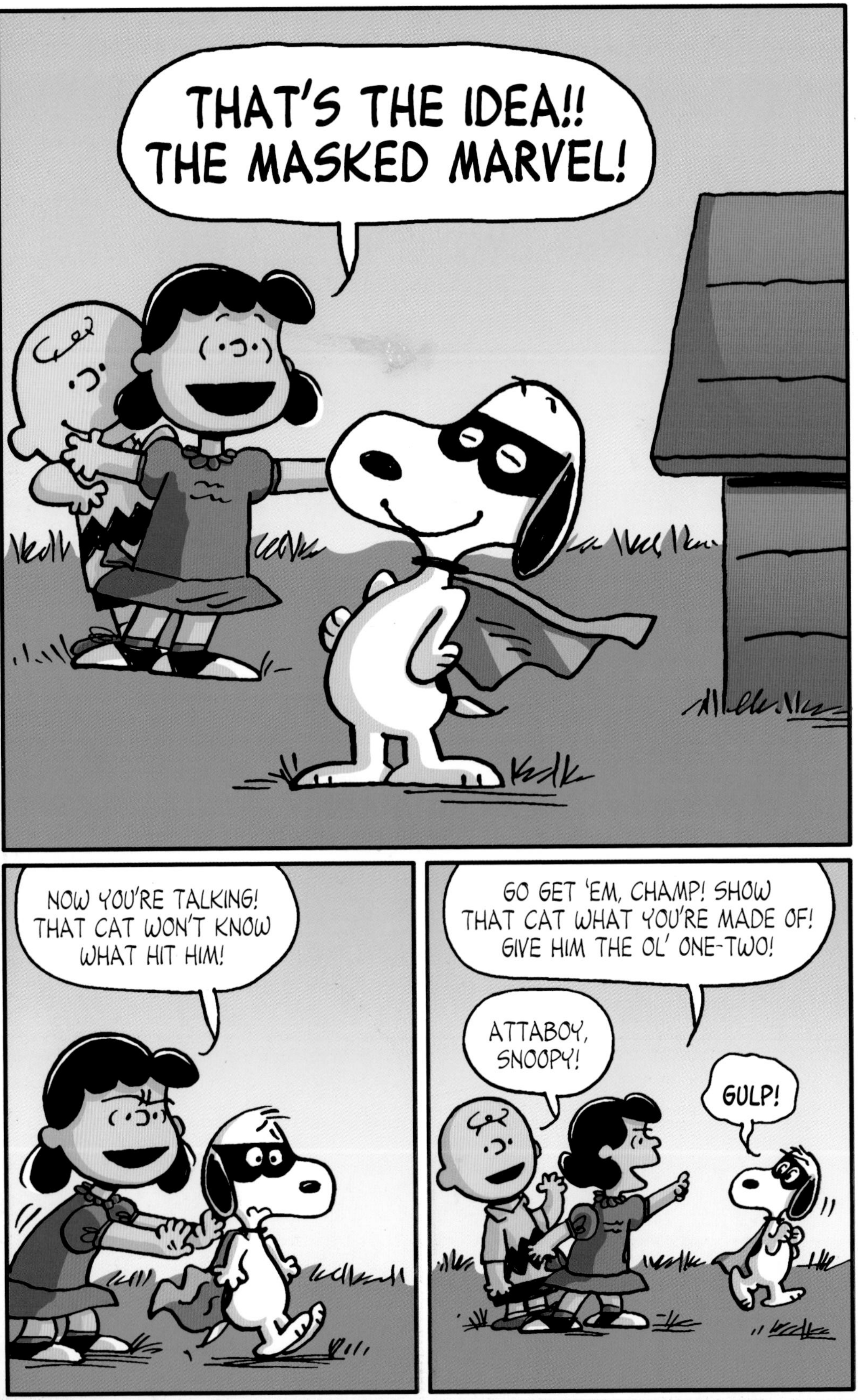
THAT'S THE IDEA!! THE MASKED MARVEL!
NOW YOU'RE TALKING! THAT CAT WON'T KNOW WHAT HIT HIM!
GO GET 'EM, CHAMP! SHOW THAT CAT WHAT YOU'RE MADE OF! GIVE HIM THE OL' ONE-TWO!
ATTABOY, SNOOPY!
GULP!

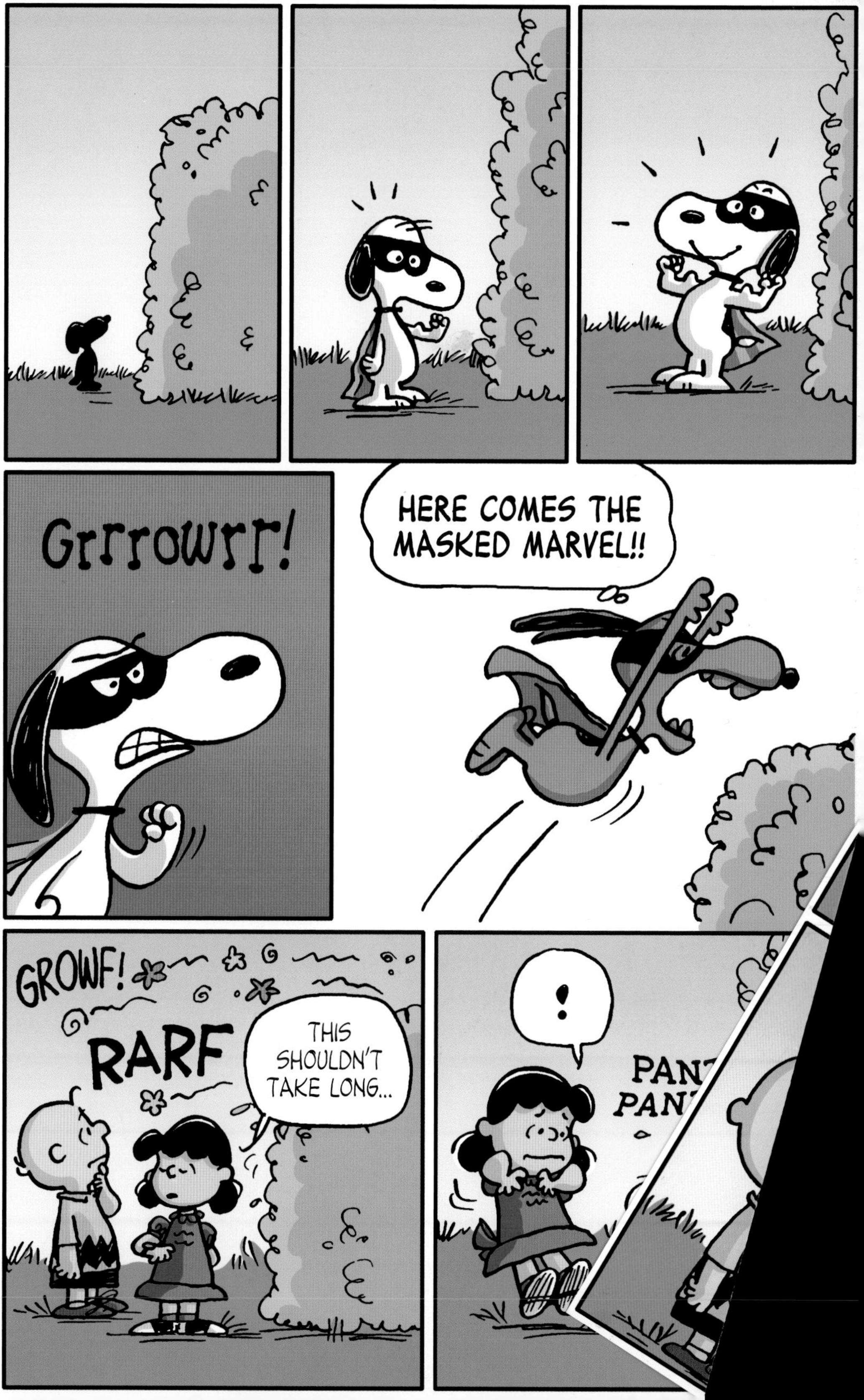
Grrrowrr!
HERE COMES THE MASKED MARVEL!!
GROWF!
RARF
THIS SHOULDN'T TAKE LONG...
!
PAN
PAN

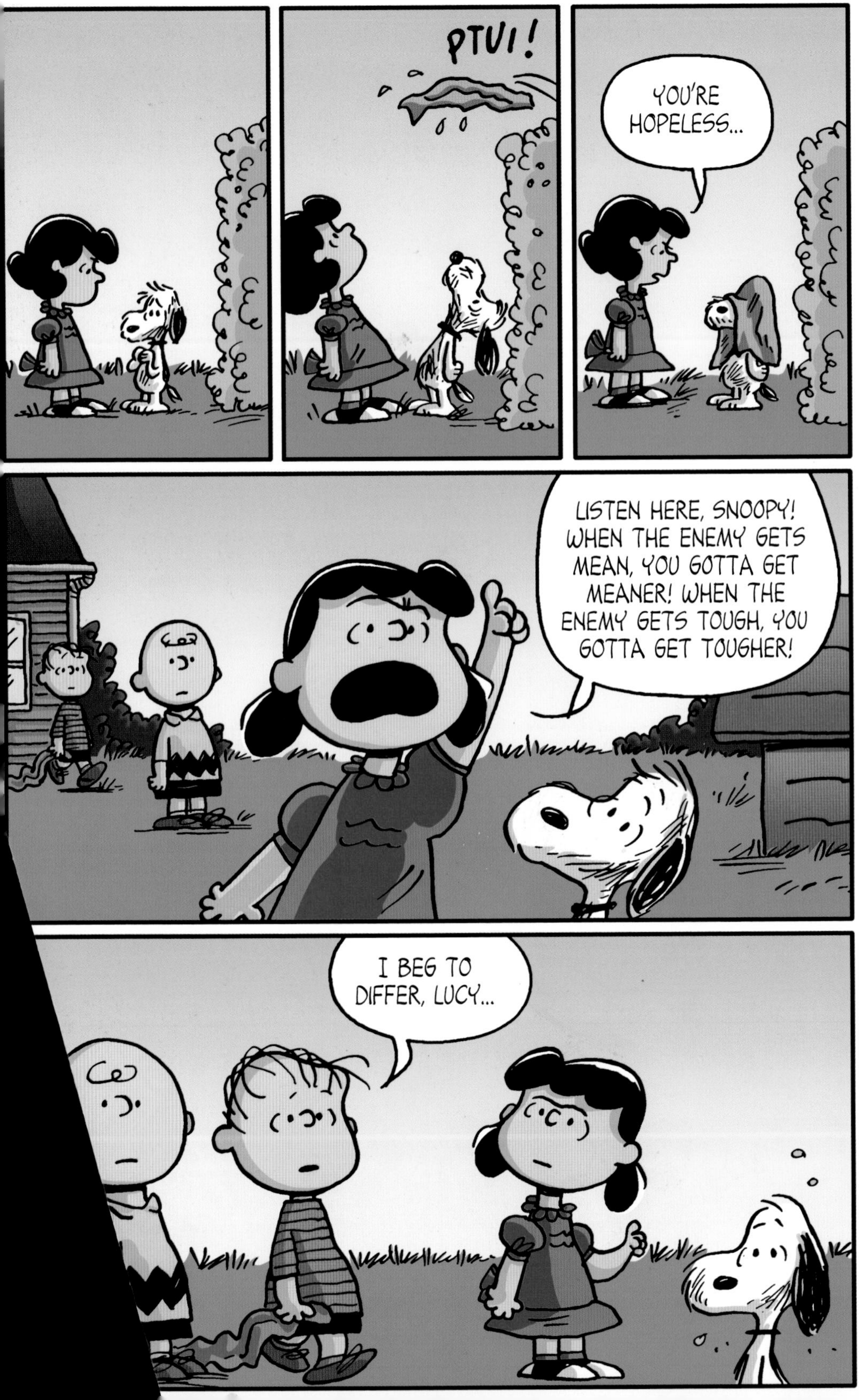
PTUI!
YOU'RE HOPELESS...
LISTEN HERE, SNOOPY! WHEN THE ENEMY GETS MEAN, YOU GOTTA GET MEANER! WHEN THE ENEMY GETS TOUGH, YOU GOTTA GET TOUGHER!
I BEG TO DIFFER, LUCY...

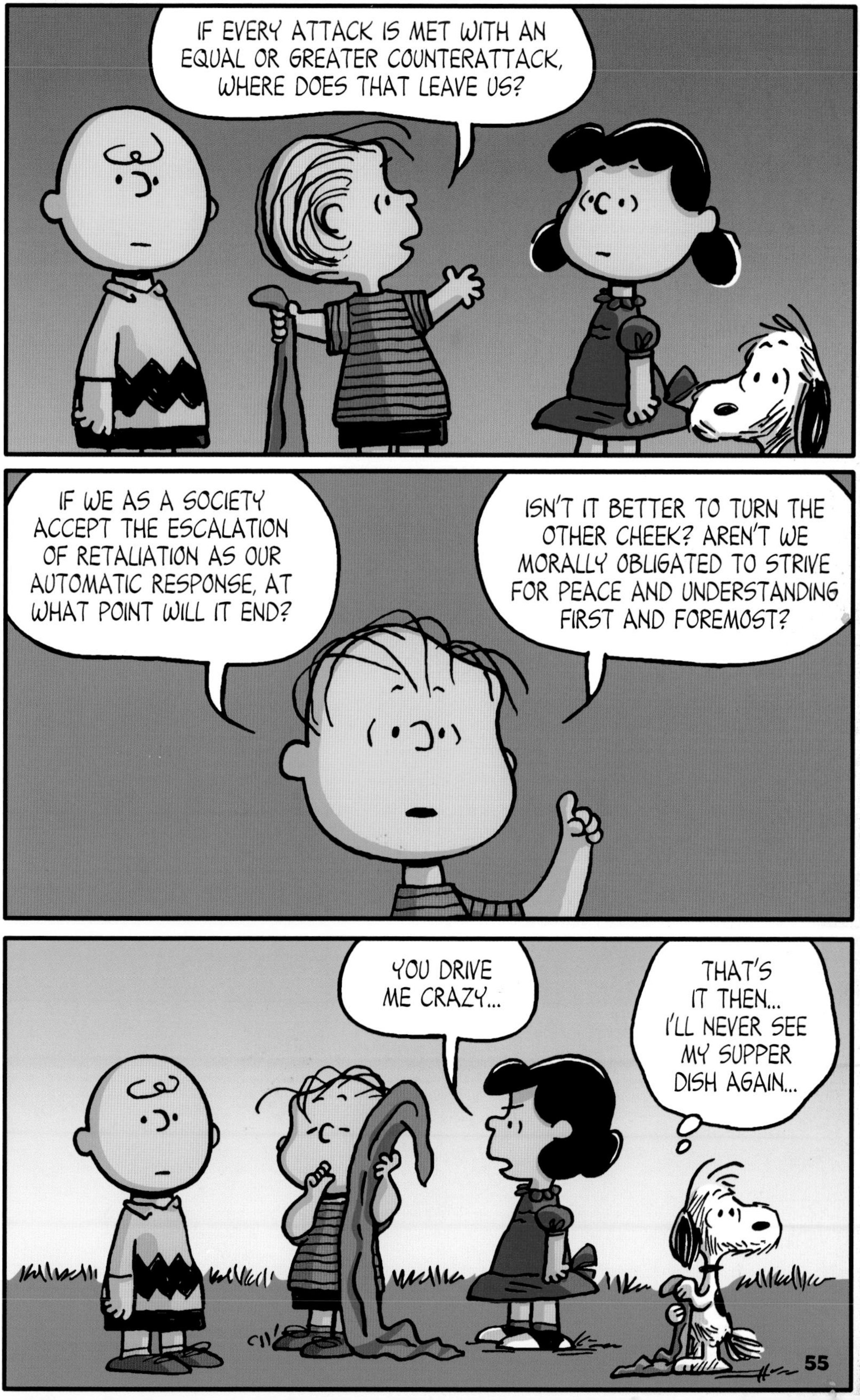
IF EVERY ATTACK IS MET WITH AN EQUAL OR GREATER COUNTERATTACK, WHERE DOES THAT LEAVE US?
IF WE AS A SOCIETY ACCEPT THE ESCALATION OF RETALIATION AS OUR AUTOMATIC RESPONSE, AT WHAT POINT WILL IT END?
ISN'T IT BETTER TO TURN THE OTHER CHEEK? AREN'T WE MORALLY OBLIGATED TO STRIVE FOR PEACE AND UNDERSTANDING FIRST AND FOREMOST?
YOU DRIVE ME CRAZY...
THAT'S IT THEN... I'LL NEVER SEE MY SUPPER DISH AGAIN...

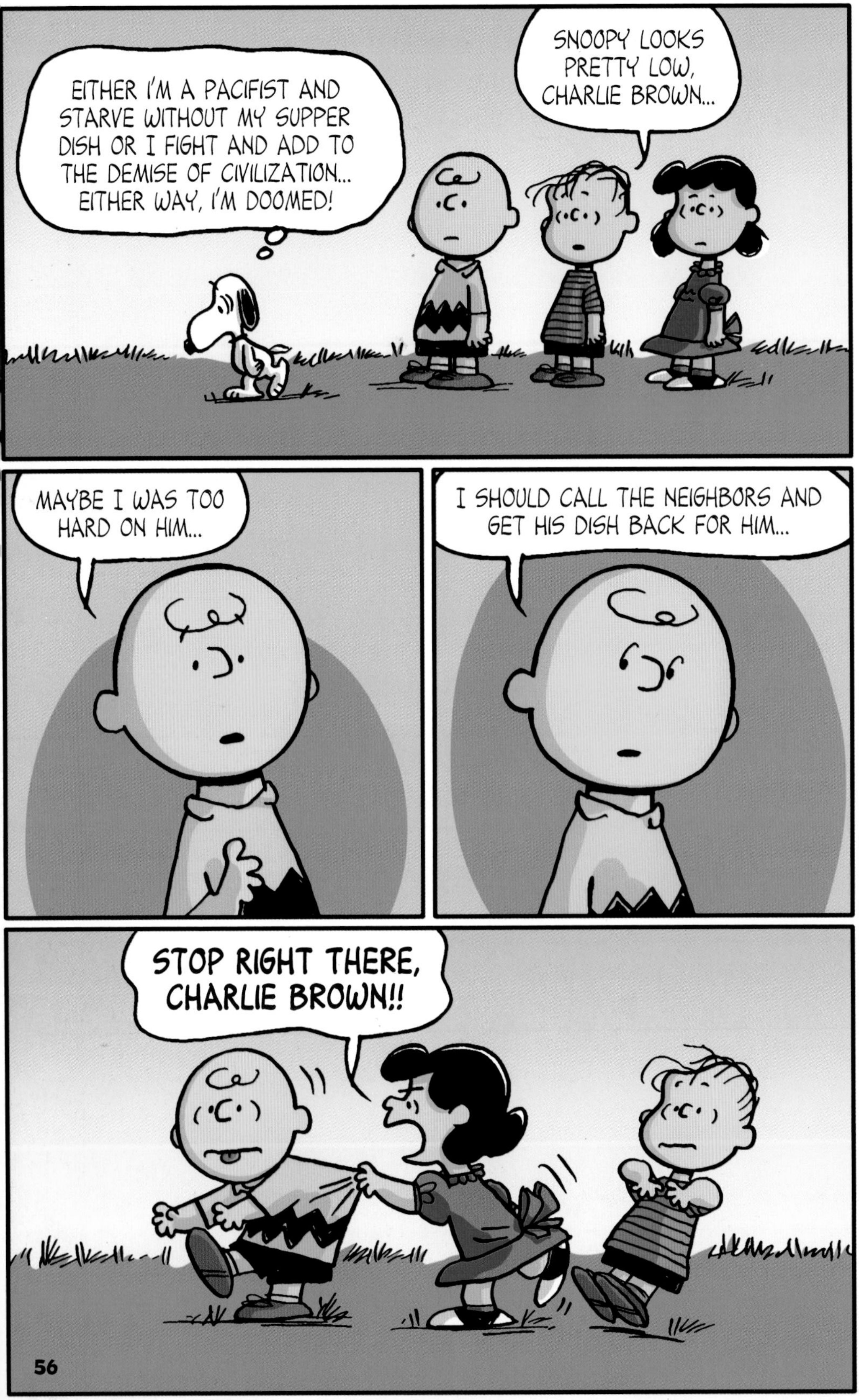
EITHER I'M A PACIFIST AND STARVE WITHOUT MY SUPPER DISH OR I FIGHT AND ADD TO THE DEMISE OF CIVILIZATION... EITHER WAY, I'M DOOMED!
SNOOPY LOOKS PRETTY LOW, CHARLIE BROWN...
MAYBE I WAS TOO HARD ON HIM...
I SHOULD CALL THE NEIGHBORS AND GET HIS DISH BACK FOR HIM...
STOP RIGHT THERE, CHARLIE BROWN!!

HE'LL NEVER AMOUNT TO ANYTHING IF YOU CODDLE HIM!

I SAY MAKE HIM GET HIS OWN BOWL! HE THREW IT OVER THERE, DIDN'T HE?

HE MADE HIS OWN BED, MAKE HIM LIE IN IT!

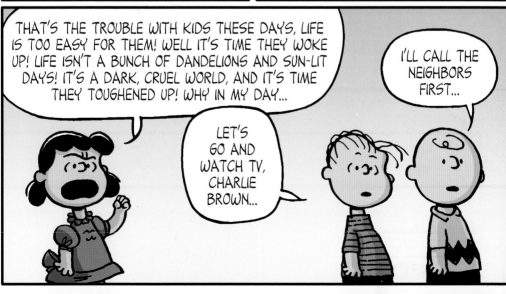

THAT'S THE TROUBLE WITH KIDS THESE DAYS, LIFE IS TOO EASY FOR THEM! WELL IT'S TIME THEY WOKE UP! LIFE ISN'T A BUNCH OF DANDELIONS AND SUN-LIT DAYS! IT'S A DARK, CRUEL WORLD, AND IT'S TIME THEY TOUGHENED UP! WHY IN MY DAY...

LET'S GO AND WATCH TV, CHARLIE BROWN...

I'LL CALL THE NEIGHBORS FIRST...

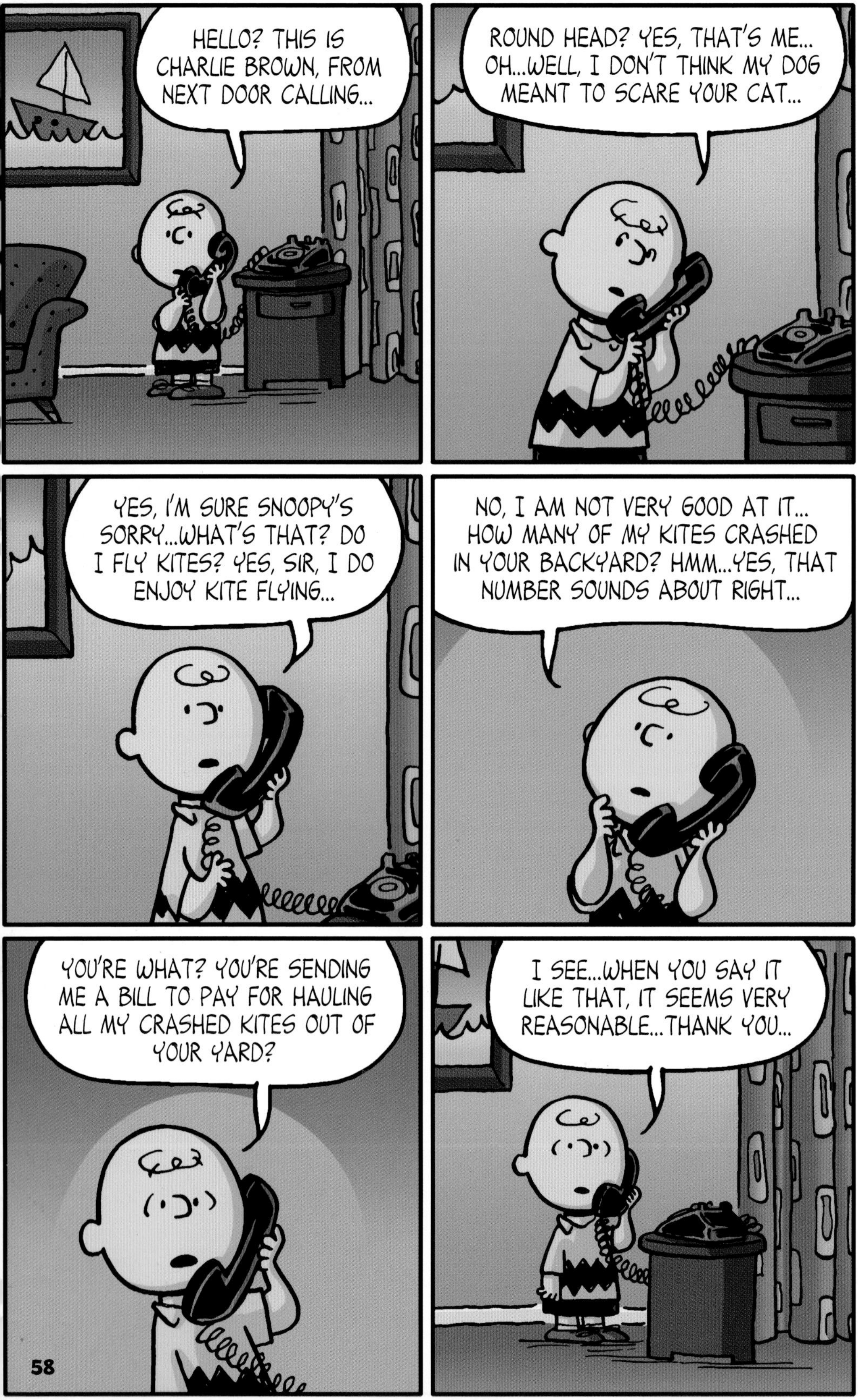
HELLO? THIS IS CHARLIE BROWN, FROM NEXT DOOR CALLING...
ROUND HEAD? YES, THAT'S ME... OH...WELL, I DON'T THINK MY DOG MEANT TO SCARE YOUR CAT...
YES, I'M SURE SNOOPY'S SORRY...WHAT'S THAT? DO I FLY KITES? YES, SIR, I DO ENJOY KITE FLYING...
NO, I AM NOT VERY GOOD AT IT... HOW MANY OF MY KITES CRASHED IN YOUR BACKYARD? HMM...YES, THAT NUMBER SOUNDS ABOUT RIGHT...
YOU'RE WHAT? YOU'RE SENDING ME A BILL TO PAY FOR HAULING ALL MY CRASHED KITES OUT OF YOUR YARD?
I SEE...WHEN YOU SAY IT LIKE THAT, IT SEEMS VERY REASONABLE...THANK YOU...

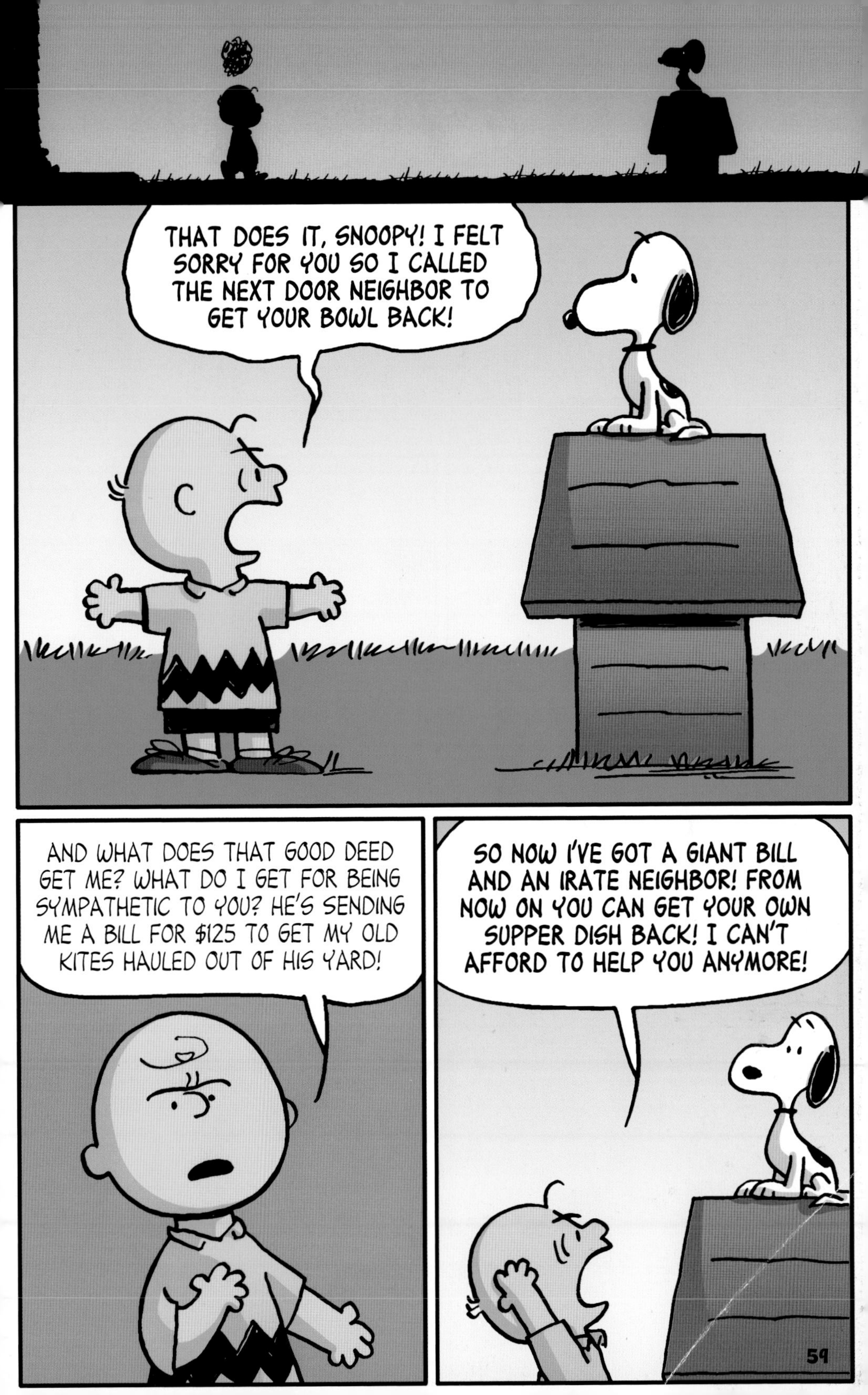
THAT DOES IT, SNOOPY! I FELT SORRY FOR YOU SO I CALLED THE NEXT DOOR NEIGHBOR TO GET YOUR BOWL BACK!
AND WHAT DOES THAT GOOD DEED GET ME? WHAT DO I GET FOR BEING SYMPATHETIC TO YOU? HE'S SENDING ME A BILL FOR $125 TO GET MY OLD KITES HAULED OUT OF HIS YARD!
SO NOW I'VE GOT A GIANT BILL AND AN IRATE NEIGHBOR! FROM NOW ON YOU CAN GET YOUR OWN SUPPER DISH BACK! I CAN'T AFFORD TO HELP YOU ANYMORE!

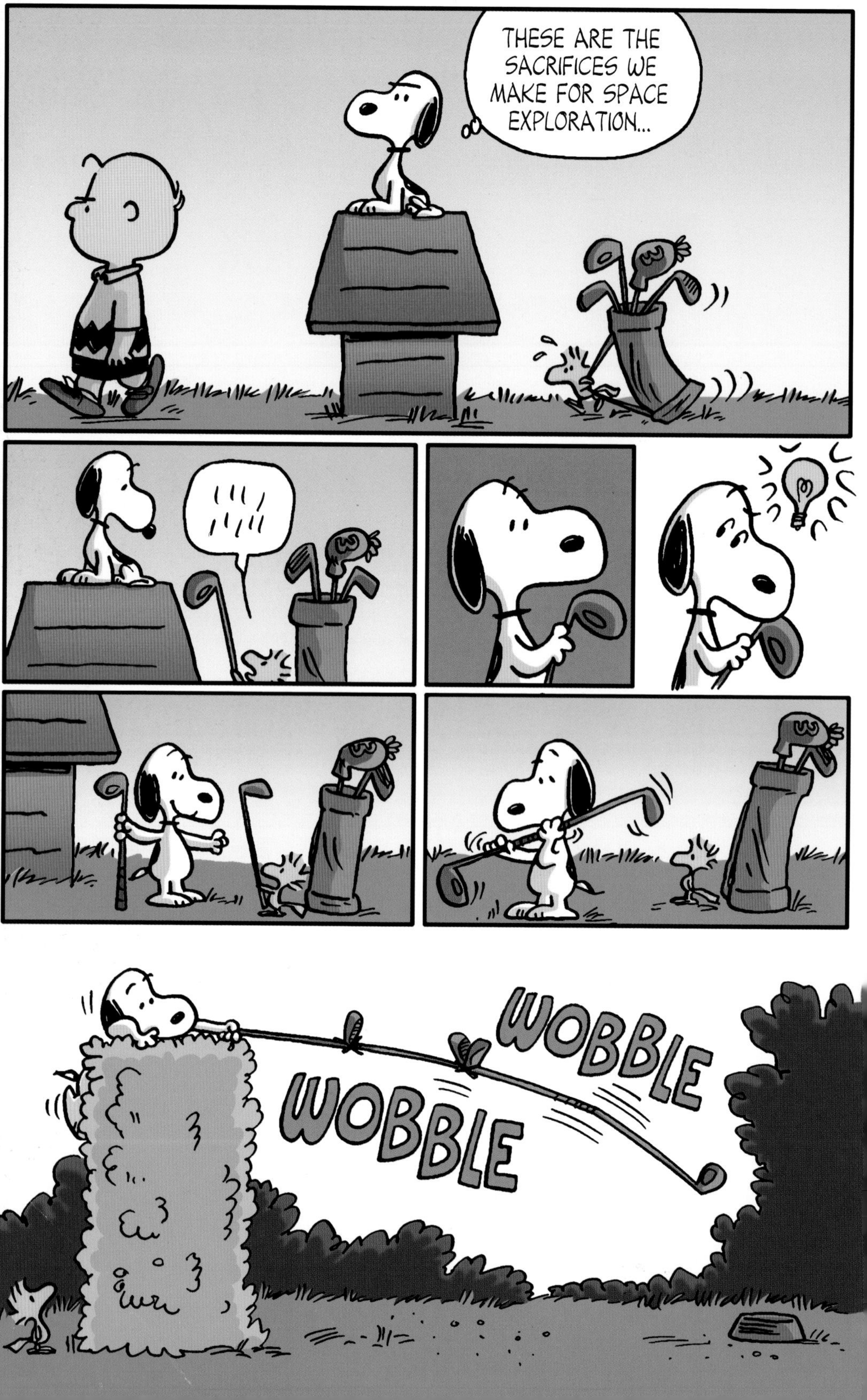
THESE ARE THE SACRIFICES WE MAKE FOR SPACE EXPLORATION...
WOBBLE
WOBBLE

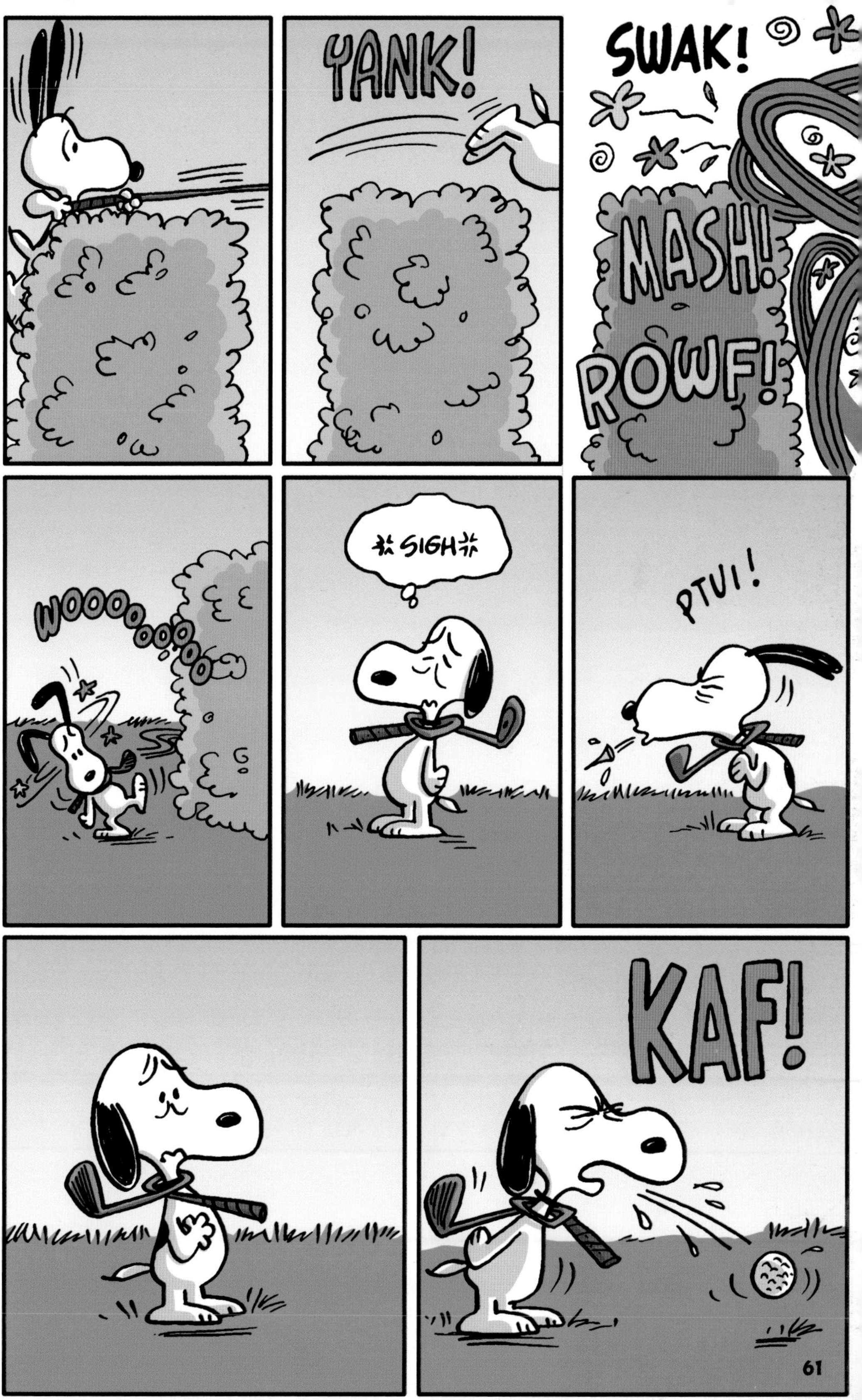
YANK!
SWAK!
MASH!
ROWF!
WOOOOOOOOOO
SIGH
PTUI!
KAF!

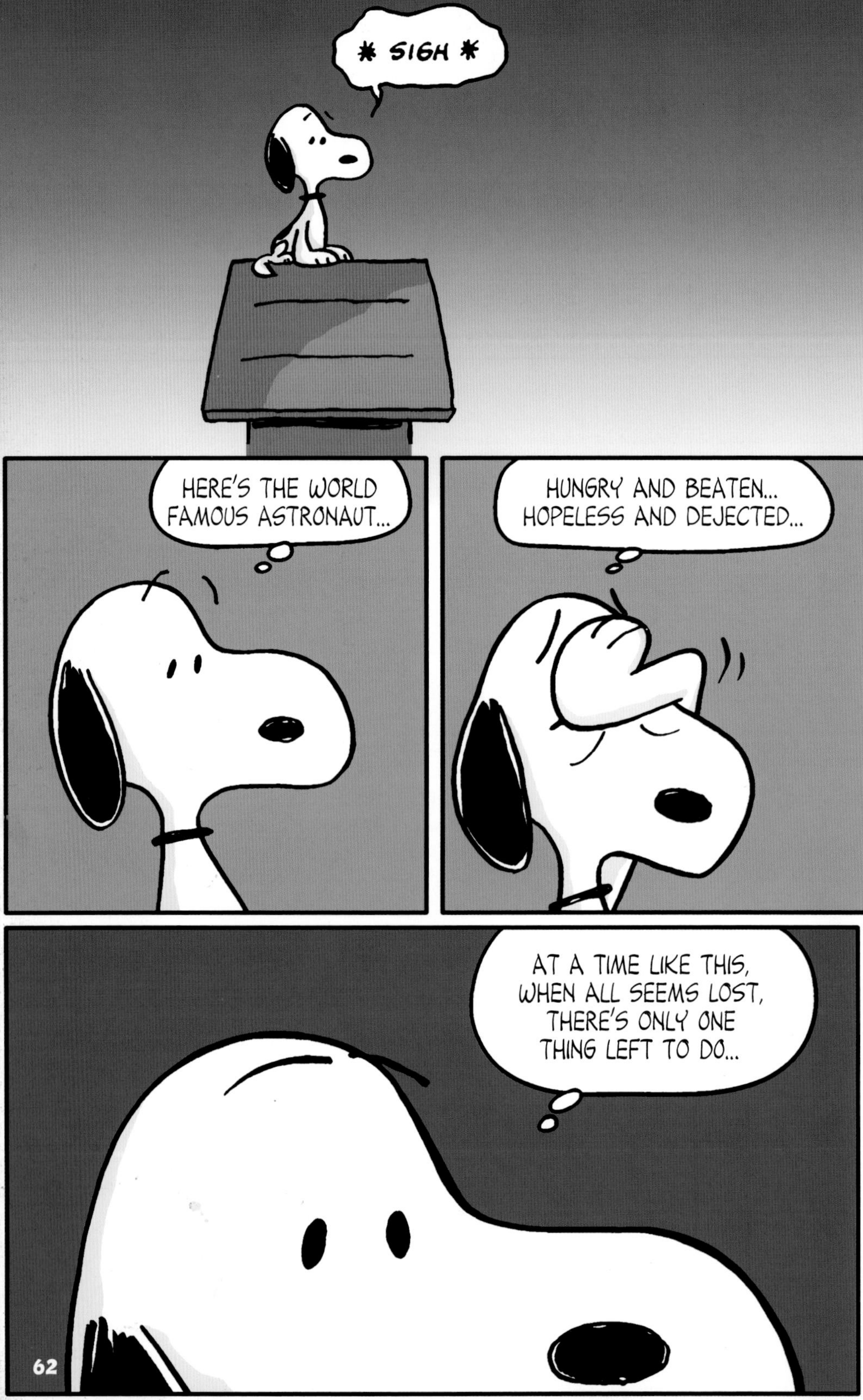
* SIGH *
HERE'S THE WORLD FAMOUS ASTRONAUT...
HUNGRY AND BEATEN... HOPELESS AND DEJECTED...
AT A TIME LIKE THIS, WHEN ALL SEEMS LOST, THERE'S ONLY ONE THING LEFT TO DO...

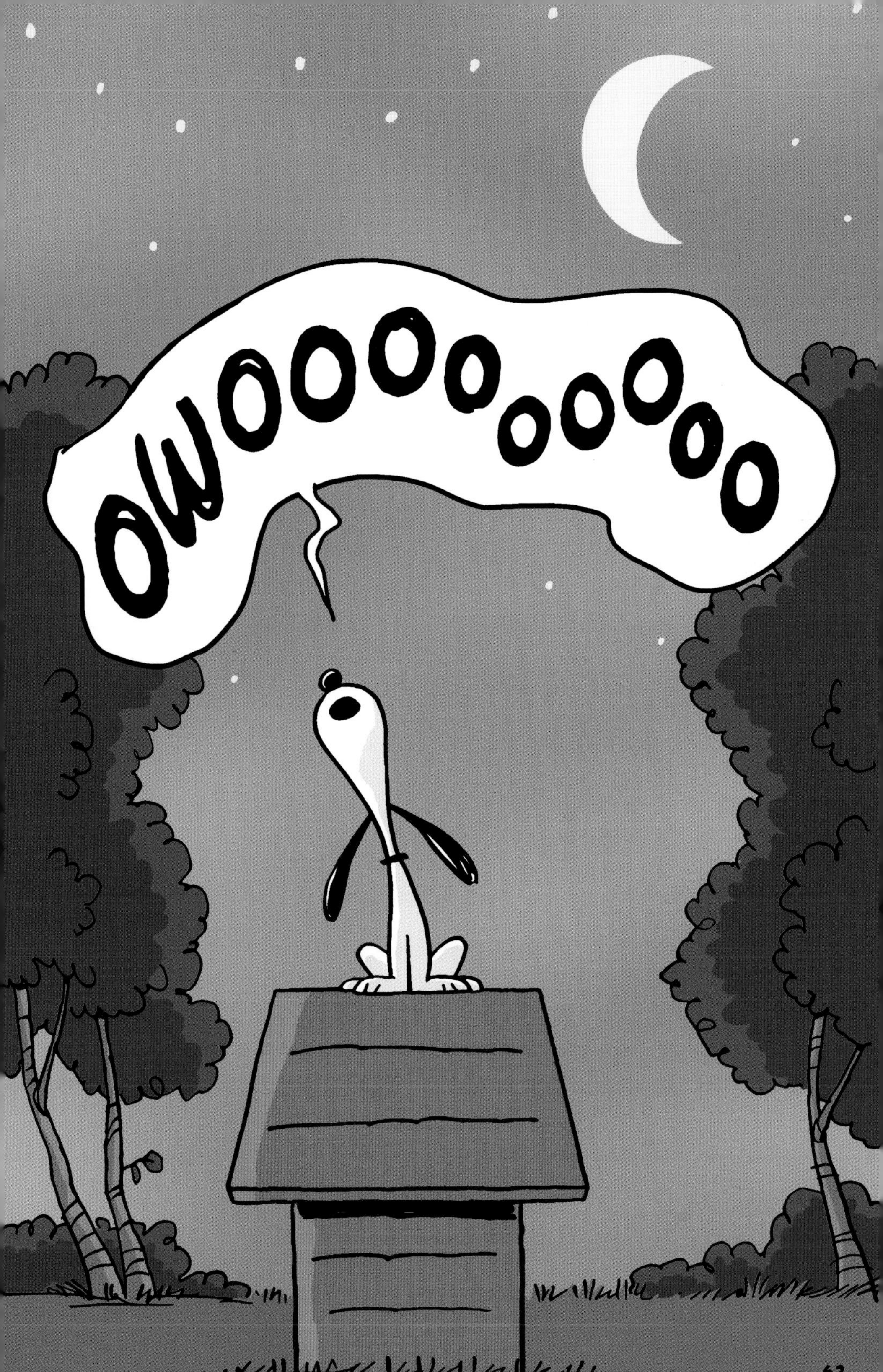
OWOOOOOOOOO

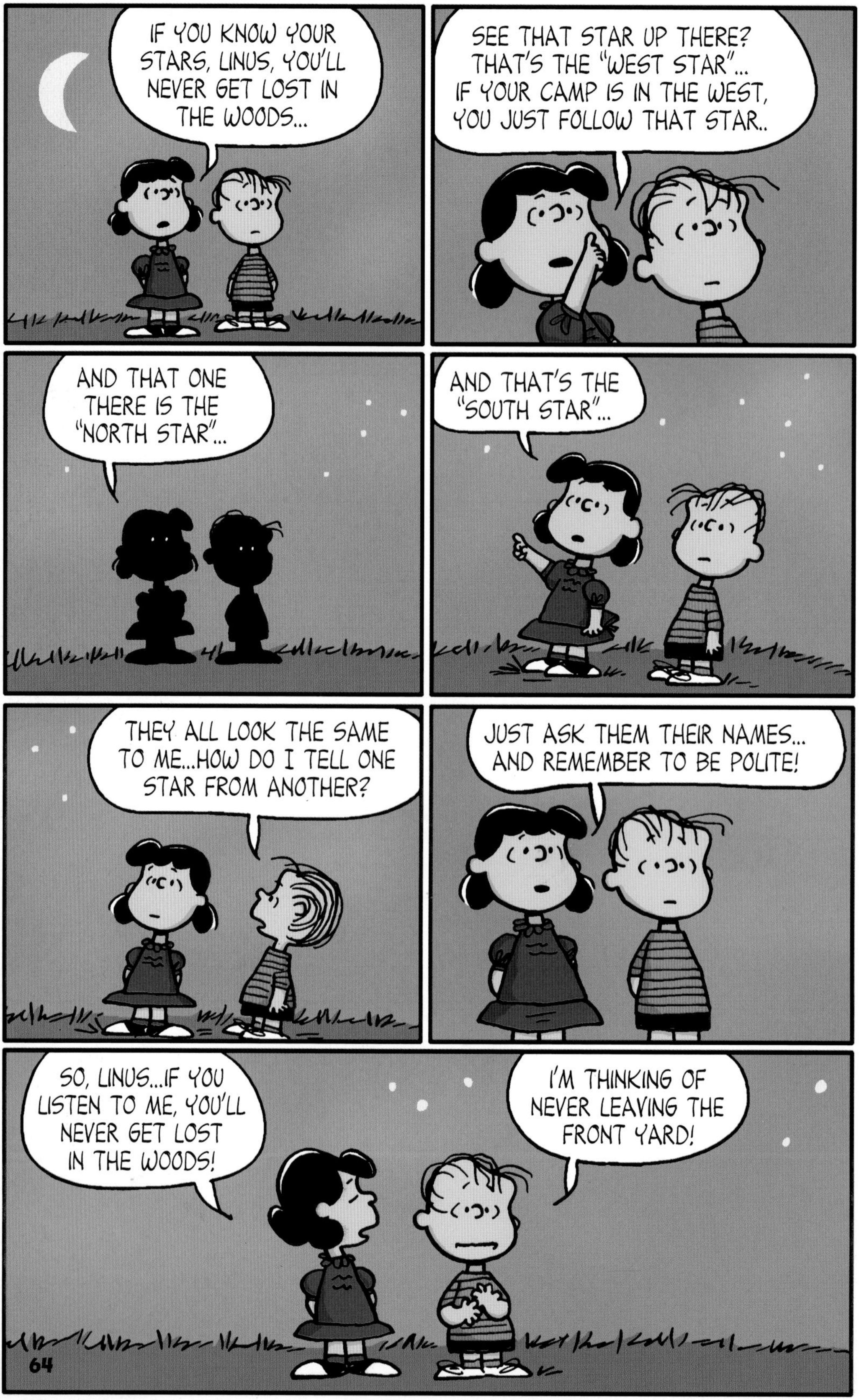
IF YOU KNOW YOUR STARS, LINUS, YOU'LL NEVER GET LOST IN THE WOODS...
SEE THAT STAR UP THERE? THAT'S THE "WEST STAR"... IF YOUR CAMP IS IN THE WEST, YOU JUST FOLLOW THAT STAR..
AND THAT ONE THERE IS THE "NORTH STAR"...
AND THAT'S THE "SOUTH STAR"...
THEY ALL LOOK THE SAME TO ME...HOW DO I TELL ONE STAR FROM ANOTHER?
JUST ASK THEM THEIR NAMES... AND REMEMBER TO BE POLITE!
SO, LINUS...IF YOU LISTEN TO ME, YOU'LL NEVER GET LOST IN THE WOODS!
I'M THINKING OF NEVER LEAVING THE FRONT YARD!

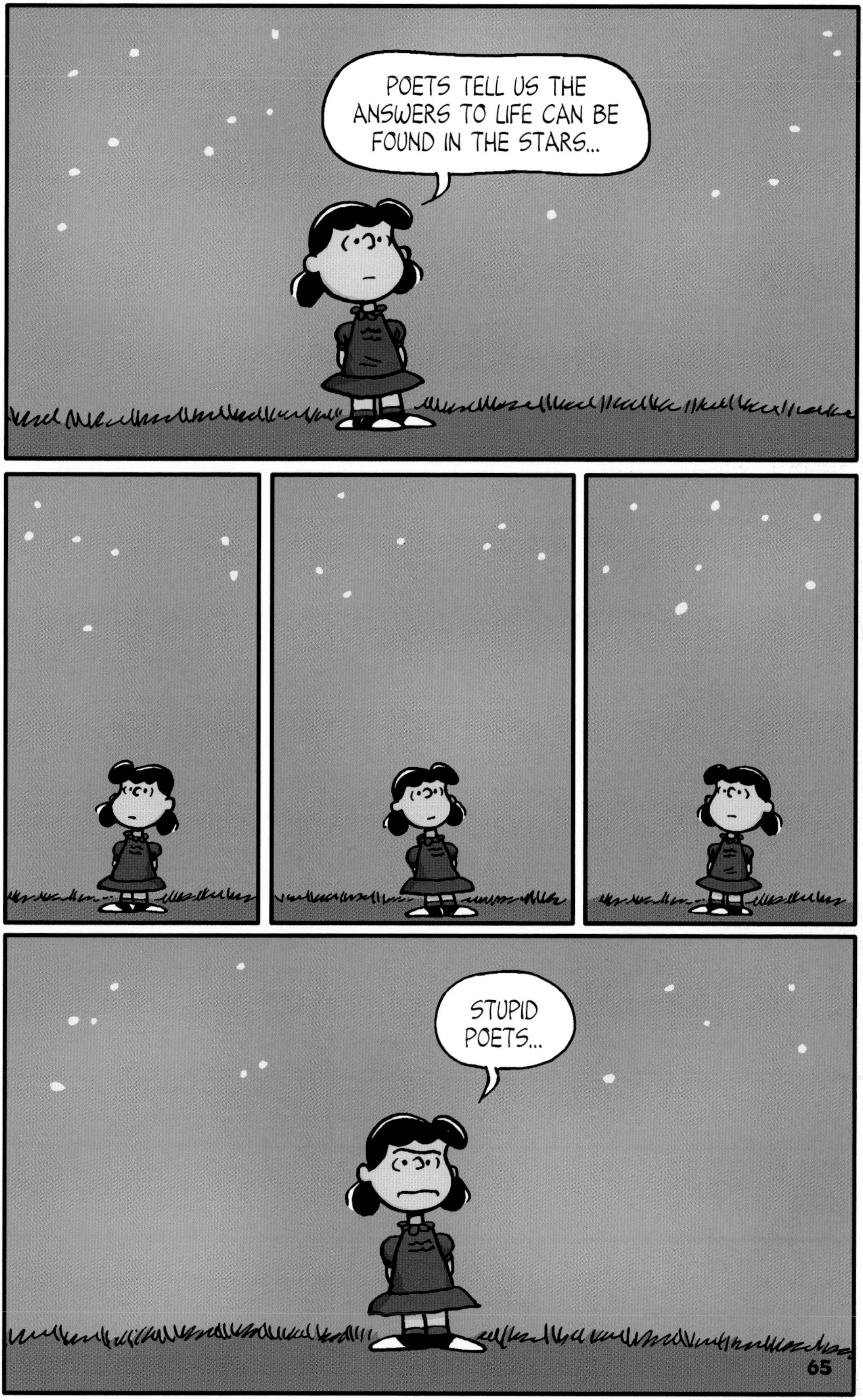
POETS TELL US THE ANSWERS TO LIFE CAN BE FOUND IN THE STARS...
STUPID POETS...

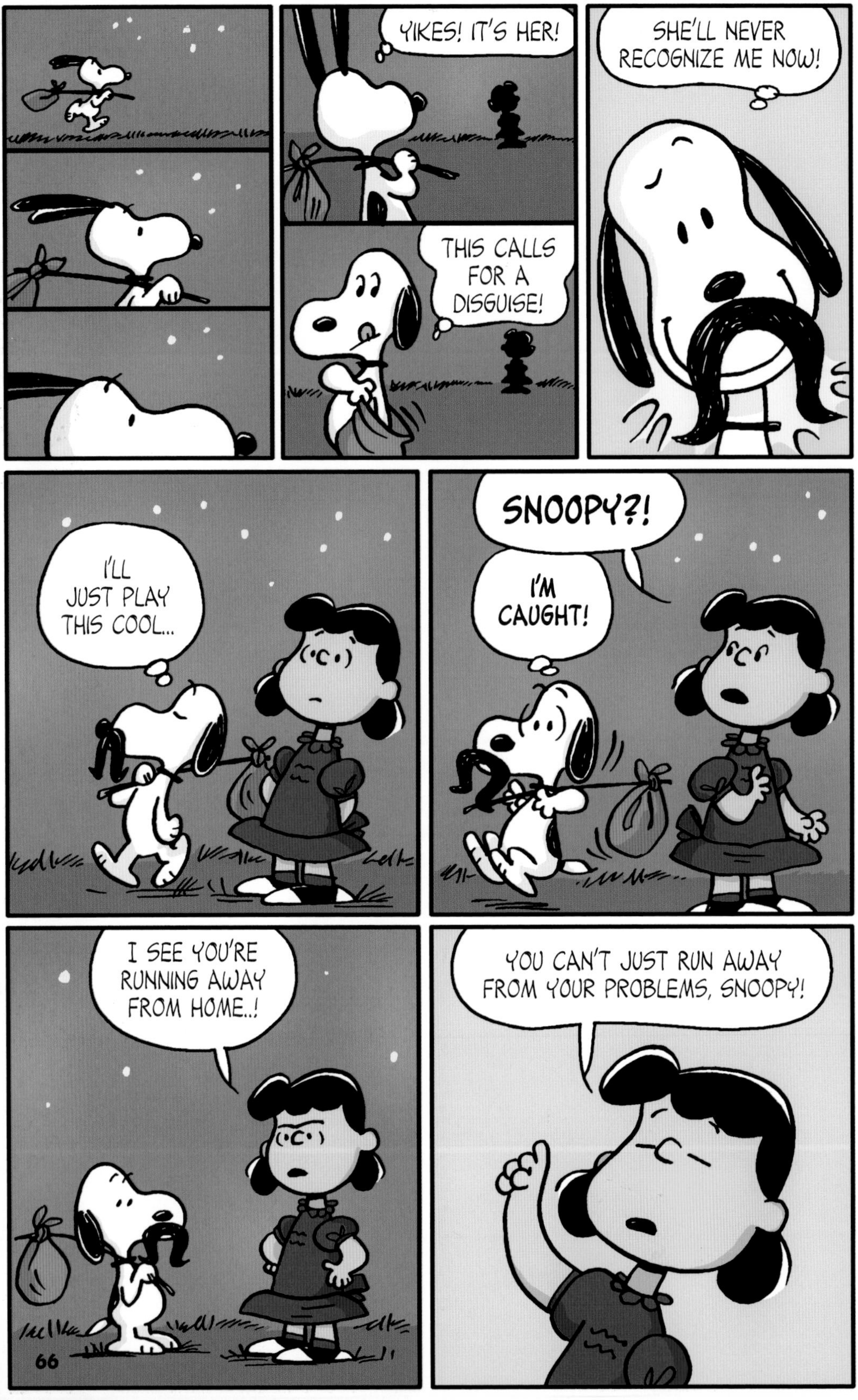
YIKES! IT'S HER!
SHE'LL NEVER RECOGNIZE ME NOW!
THIS CALLS FOR A DISGUISE!
I'LL JUST PLAY THIS COOL...
SNOOPY?!
I'M CAUGHT!
I SEE YOU'RE RUNNING AWAY FROM HOME..!
YOU CAN'T JUST RUN AWAY FROM YOUR PROBLEMS, SNOOPY!

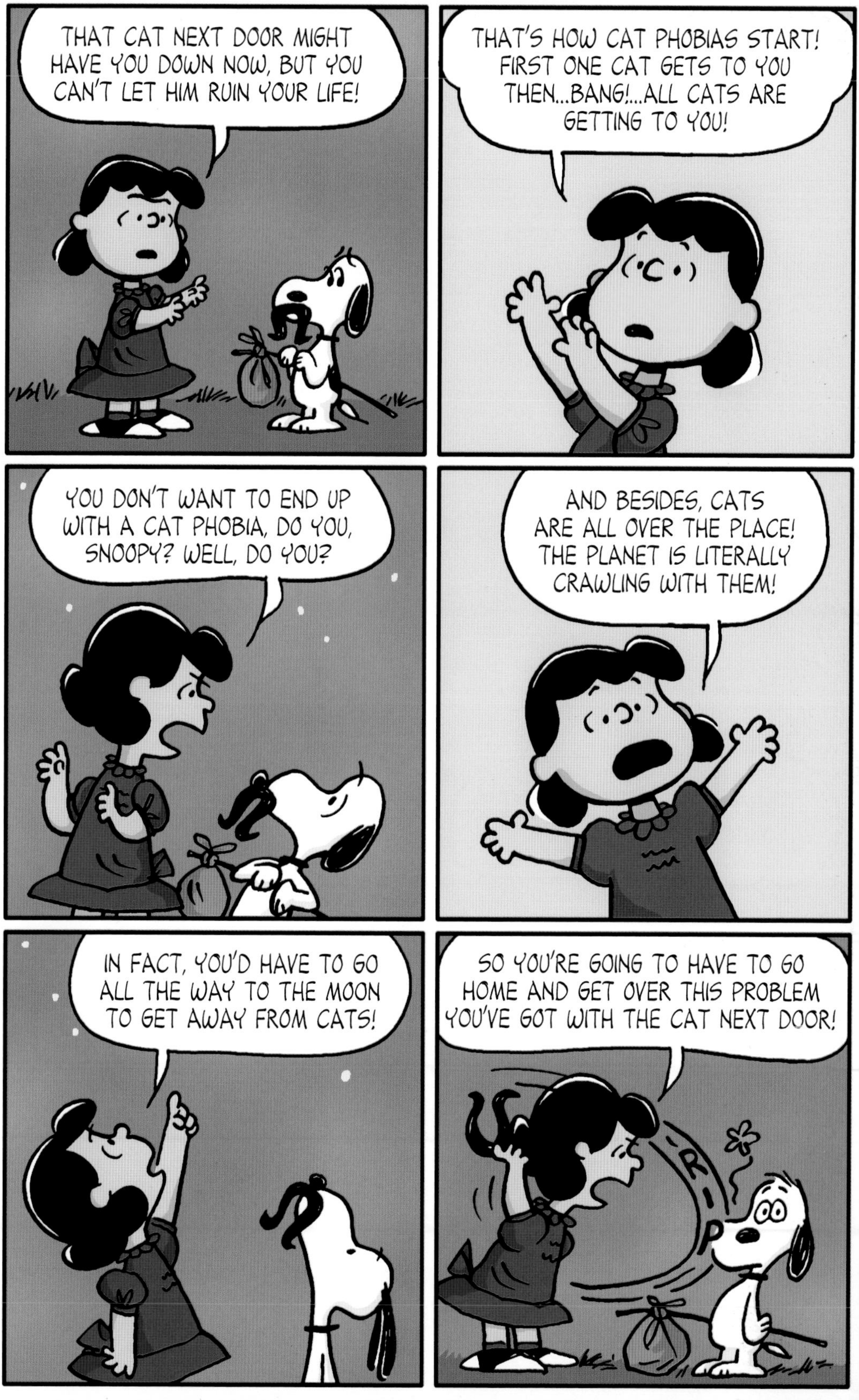
THAT CAT NEXT DOOR MIGHT HAVE YOU DOWN NOW, BUT YOU CAN'T LET HIM RUIN YOUR LIFE!
THAT'S HOW CAT PHOBIAS START! FIRST ONE CAT GETS TO YOU THEN...BANG!...ALL CATS ARE GETTING TO YOU!
YOU DON'T WANT TO END UP WITH A CAT PHOBIA, DO YOU, SNOOPY? WELL, DO YOU?
AND BESIDES, CATS ARE ALL OVER THE PLACE! THE PLANET IS LITERALLY CRAWLING WITH THEM!
IN FACT, YOU'D HAVE TO GO ALL THE WAY TO THE MOON TO GET AWAY FROM CATS!
SO YOU'RE GOING TO HAVE TO GO HOME AND GET OVER THIS PROBLEM YOU'VE GOT WITH THE CAT NEXT DOOR!
R
P

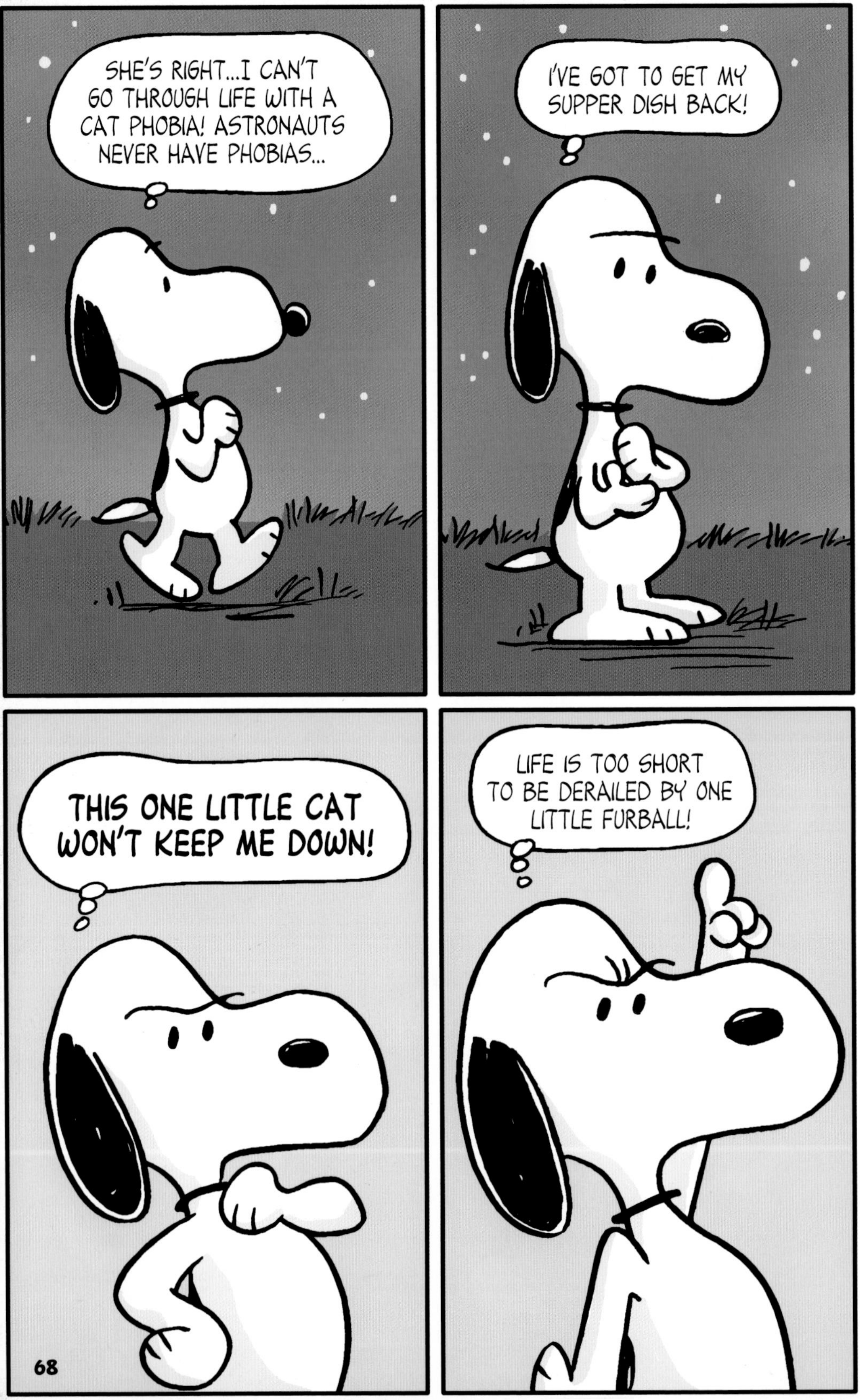
SHE'S RIGHT...I CAN'T GO THROUGH LIFE WITH A CAT PHOBIA! ASTRONAUTS NEVER HAVE PHOBIAS...
I'VE GOT TO GET MY SUPPER DISH BACK!
THIS ONE LITTLE CAT WON'T KEEP ME DOWN!
LIFE IS TOO SHORT TO BE DERAILED BY ONE LITTLE FURBALL!

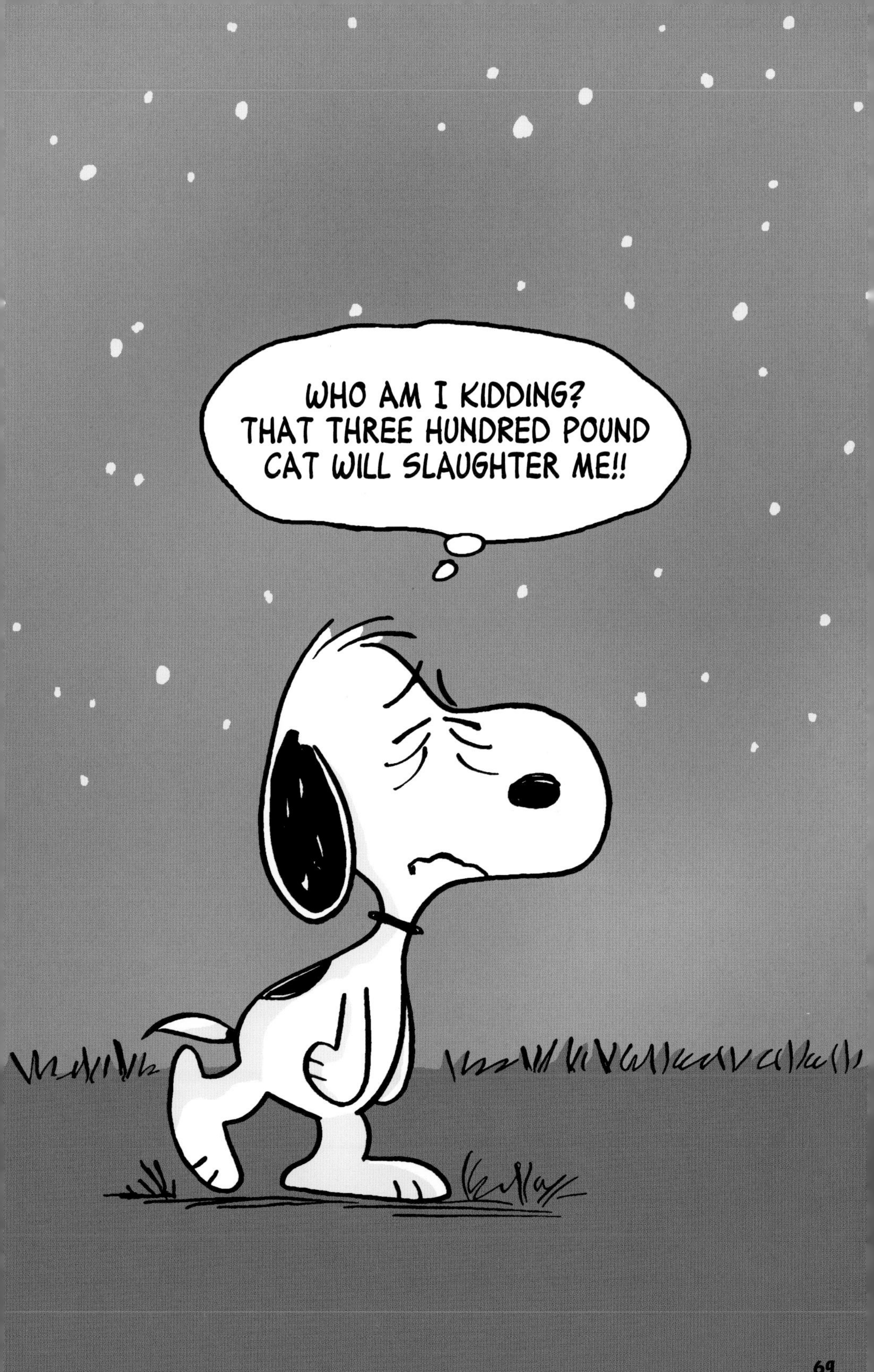
WHO AM I KIDDING? THAT THREE HUNDRED POUND CAT WILL SLAUGHTER ME!!

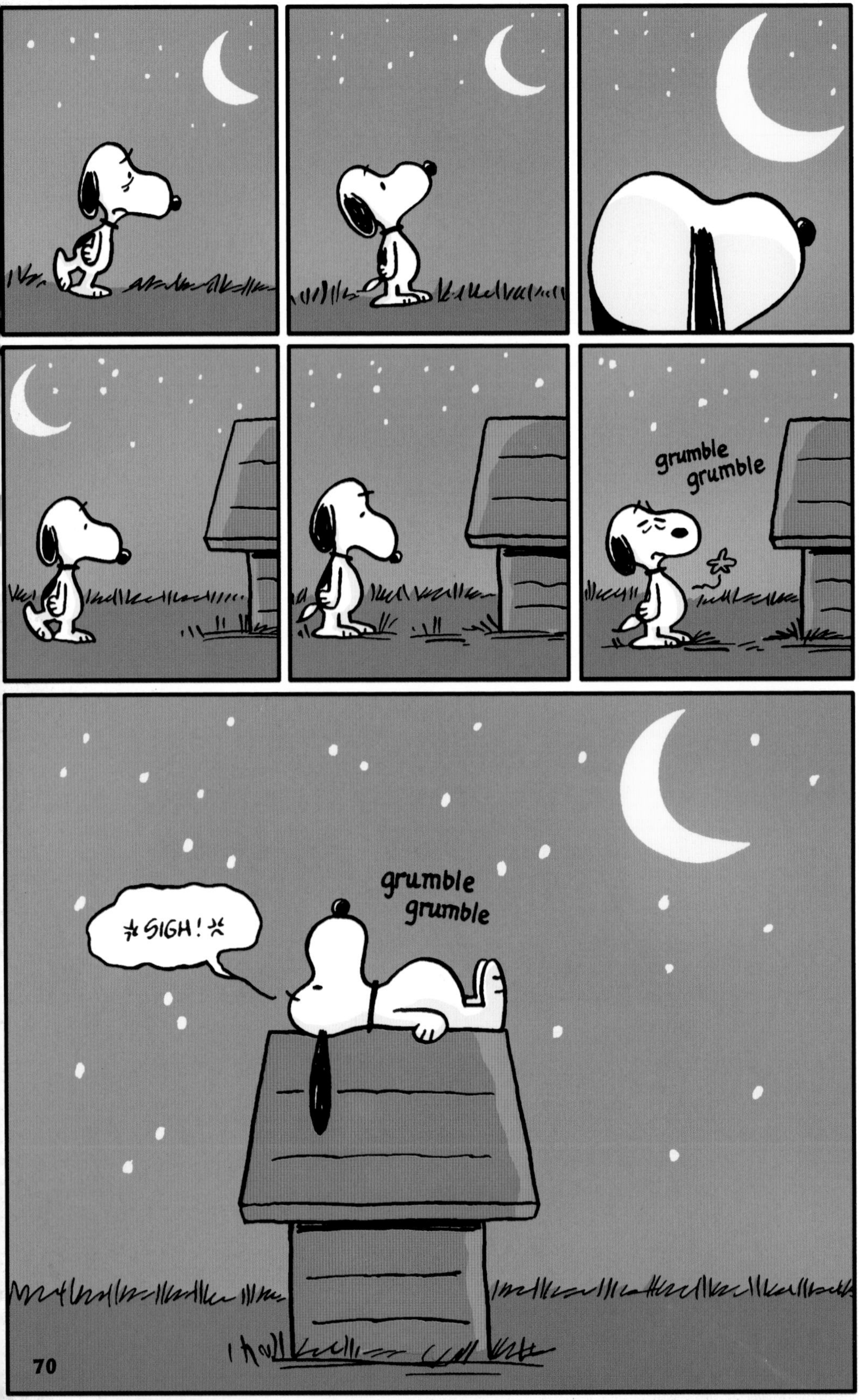
grumble
grumble
grumble
grumble
*SIGH!*

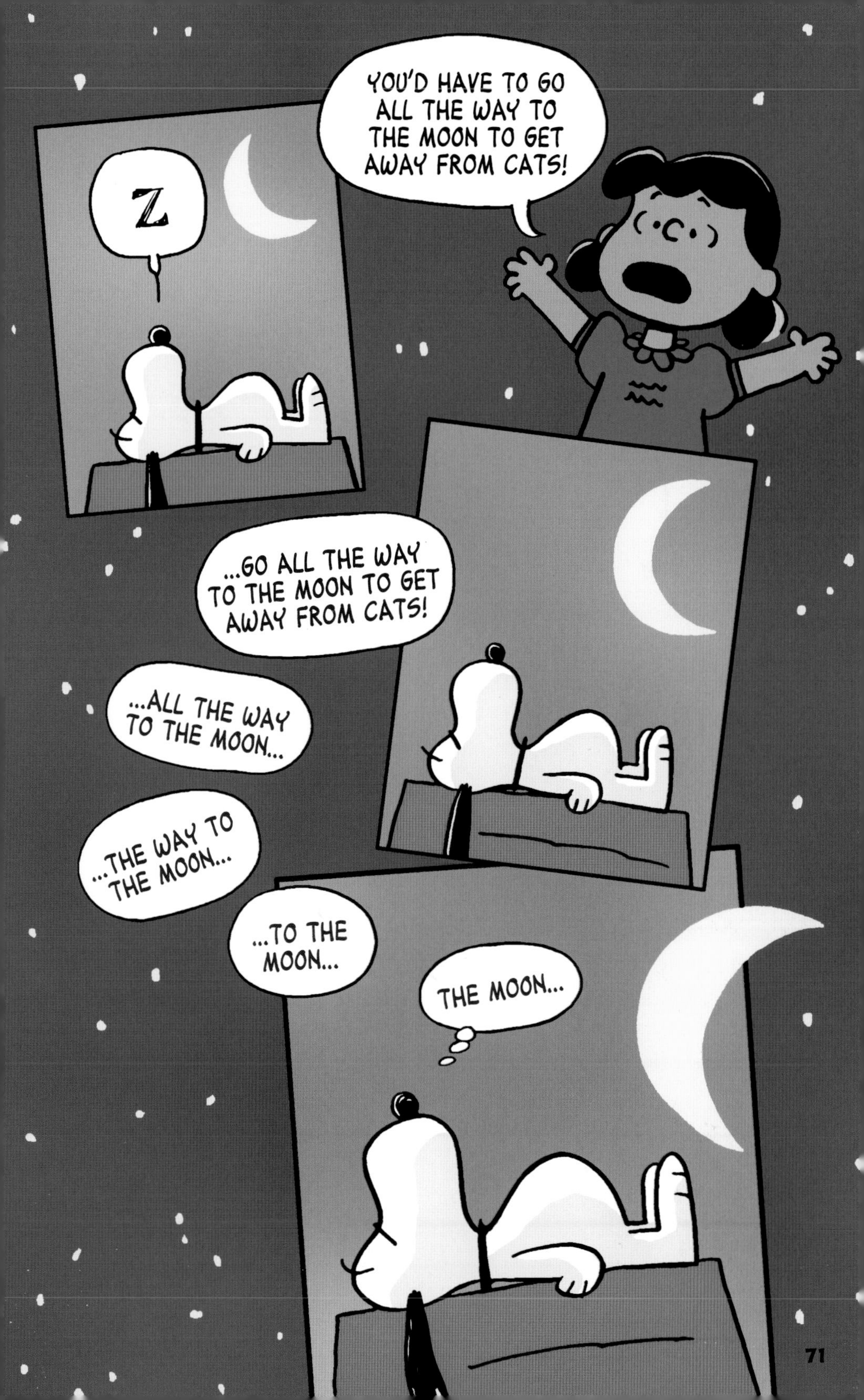
Z
YOU'D HAVE TO GO ALL THE WAY TO THE MOON TO GET AWAY FROM CATS!
...GO ALL THE WAY TO THE MOON TO GET AWAY FROM CATS!
...ALL THE WAY TO THE MOON...
...THE WAY TO THE MOON...
...TO THE MOON...
THE MOON...

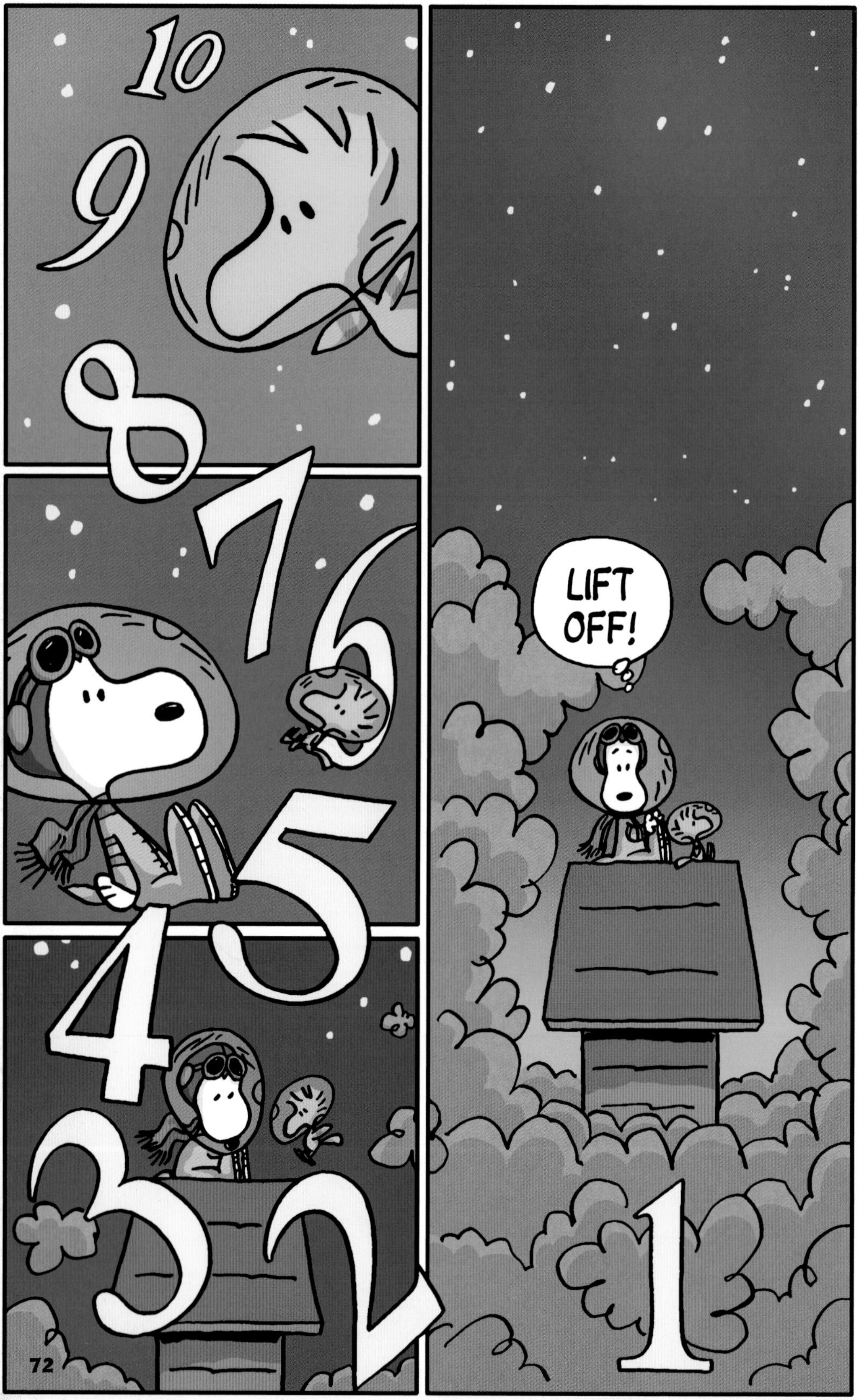
10
9
8
7
6
5
4
3
2
1
LIFT OFF!

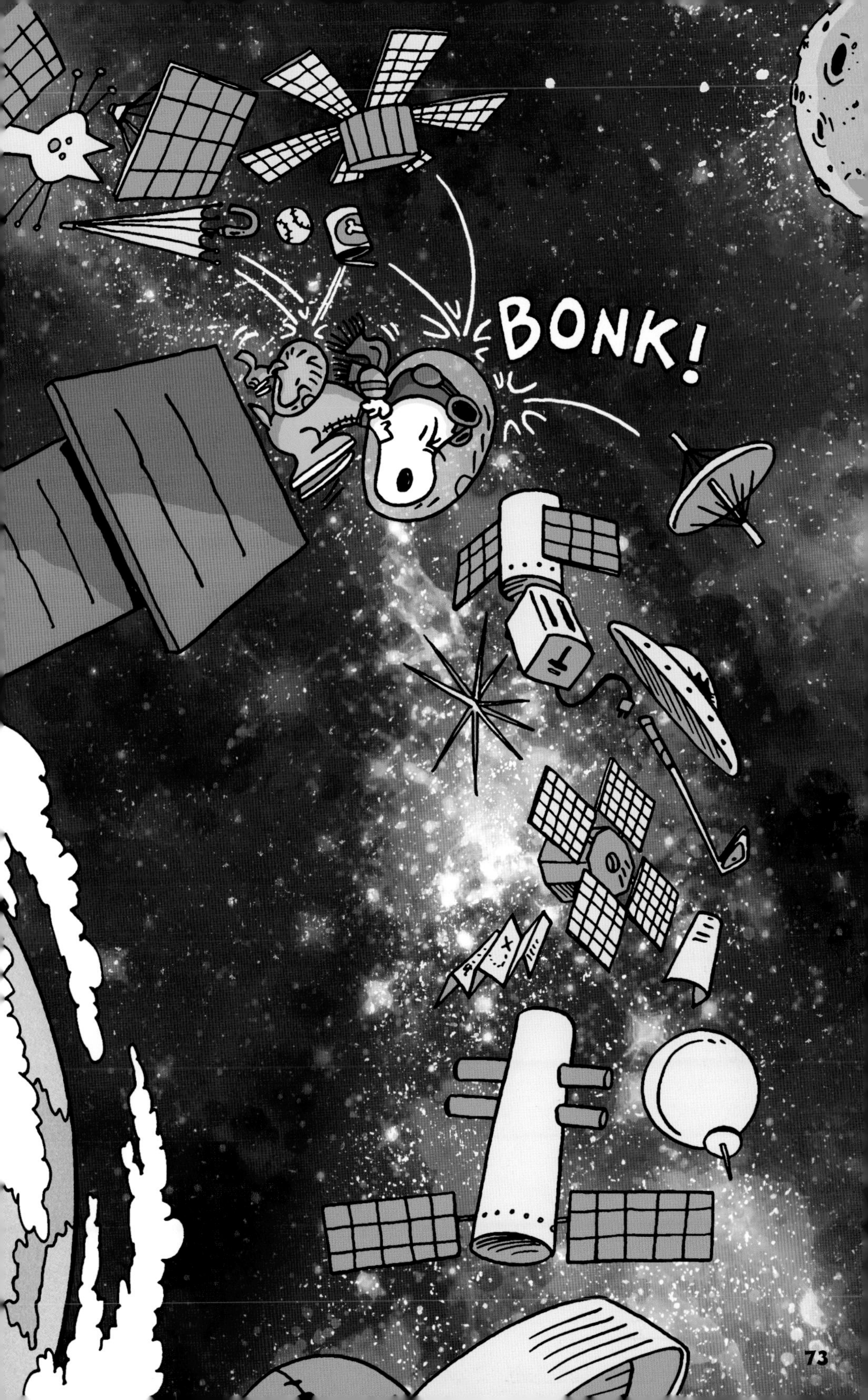
BONK!

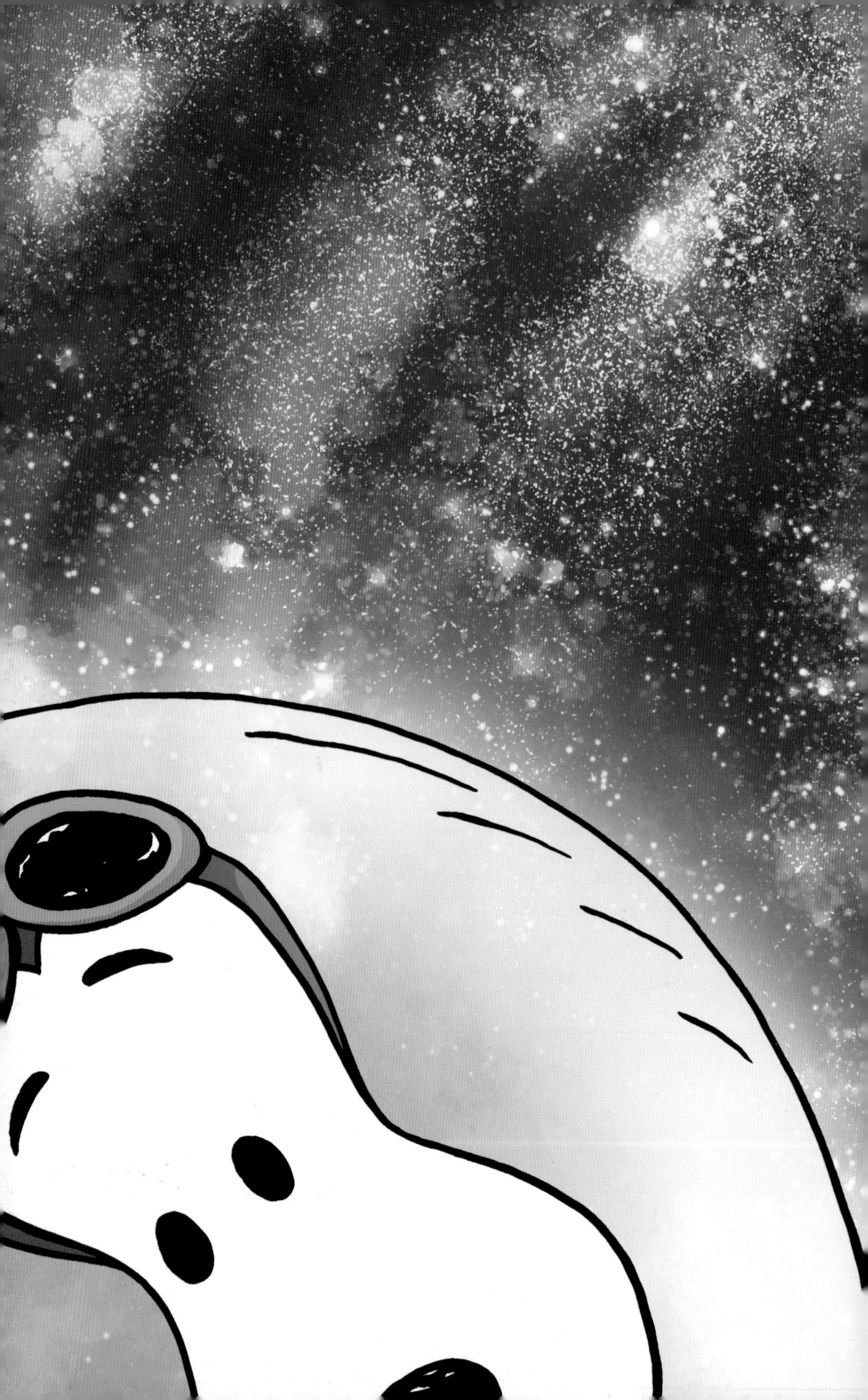

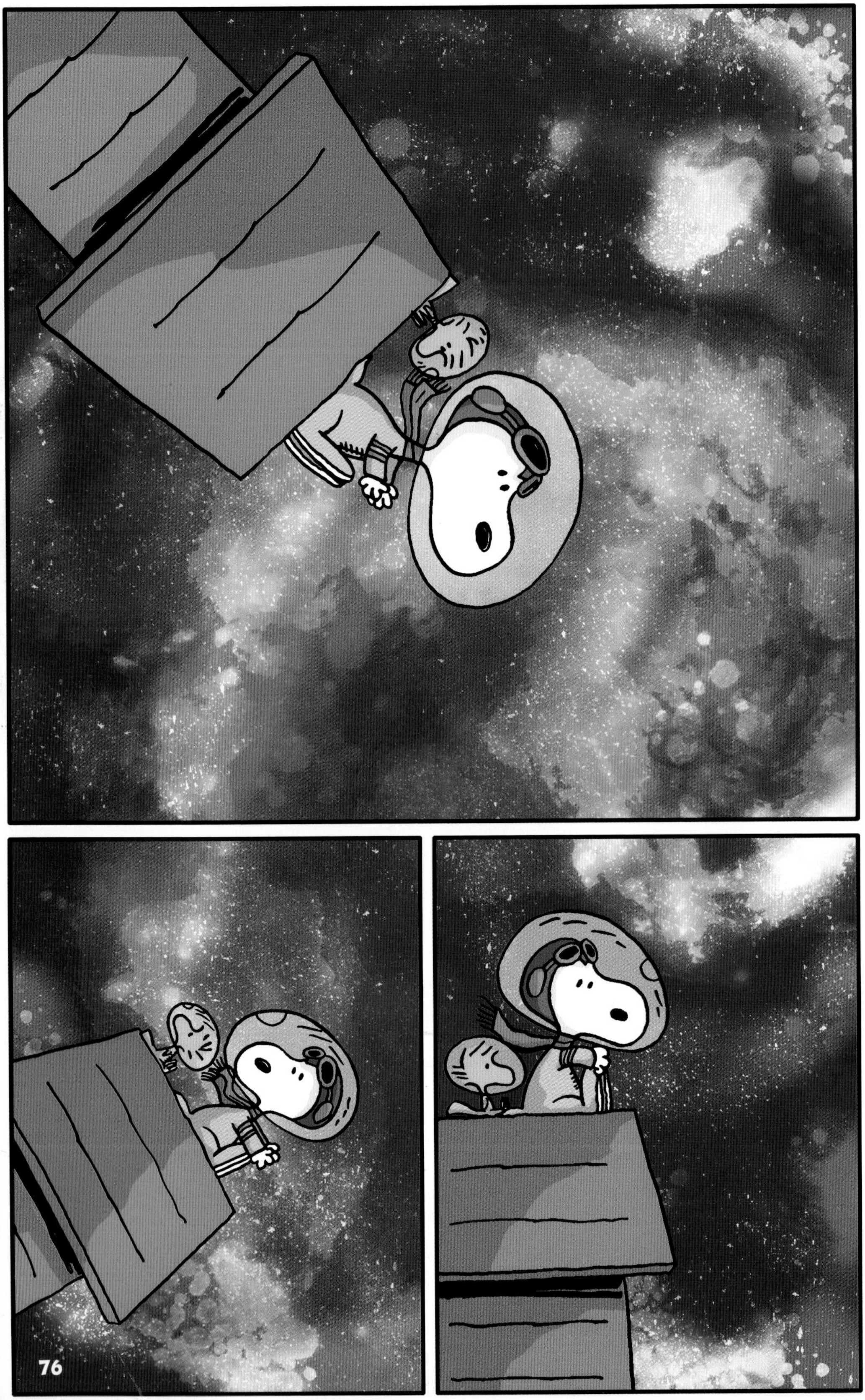

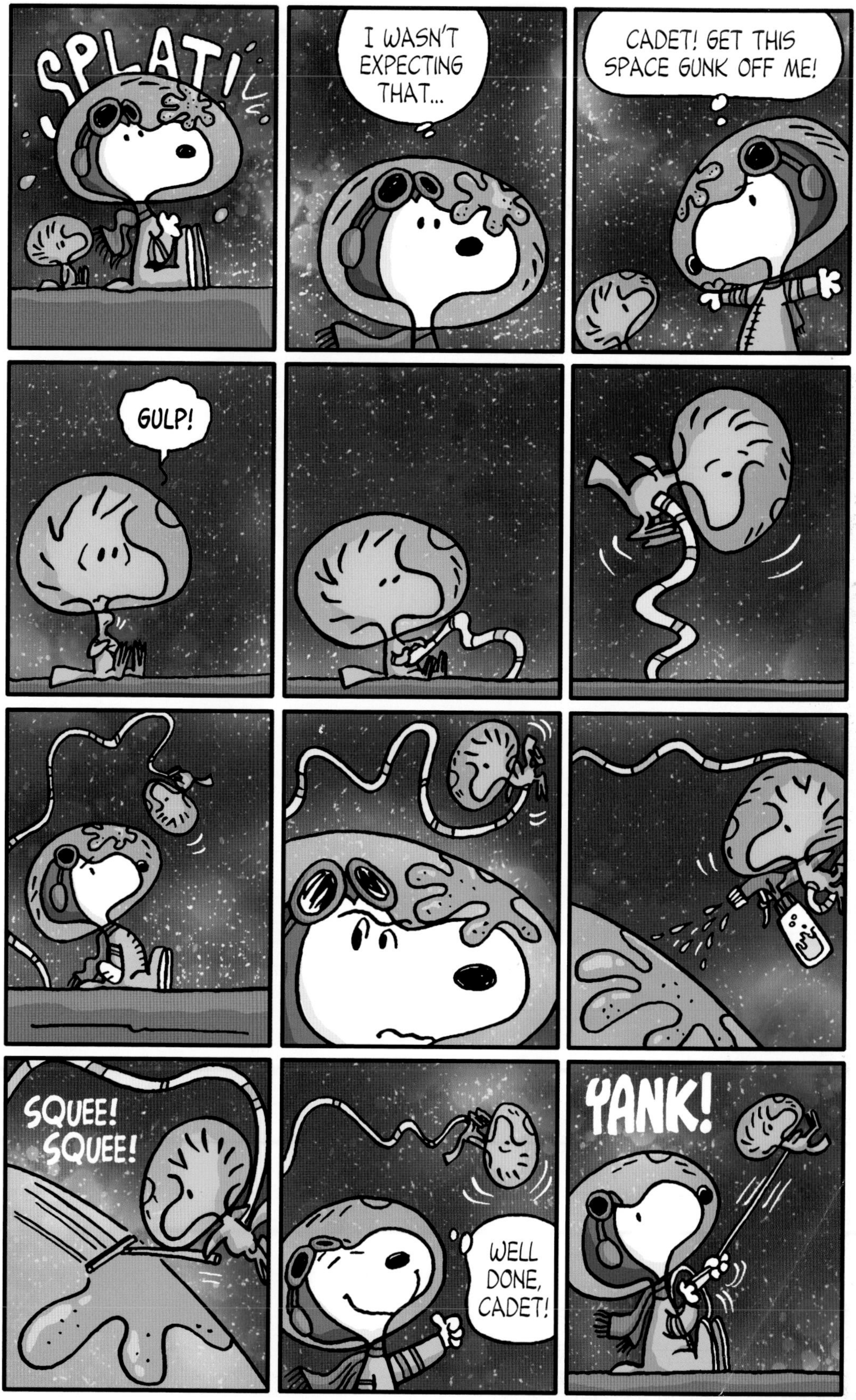
SPLAT!
I WASN'T EXPECTING THAT...
CADET! GET THIS SPACE GUNK OFF ME!
GULP!
SQUEE! SQUEE!
WELL DONE, CADET!
YANK!

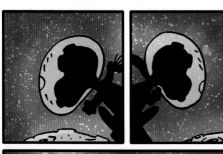

HOUSTON, THIS IS SNOOPY...

WHAM!

THE BEAGLE HAS LANDED!

WAIT HERE, CADET! I'LL SEE IF IT'S SAFE!

POOF!

*GASP!*
I CAN'T BELIEVE MY EYES!

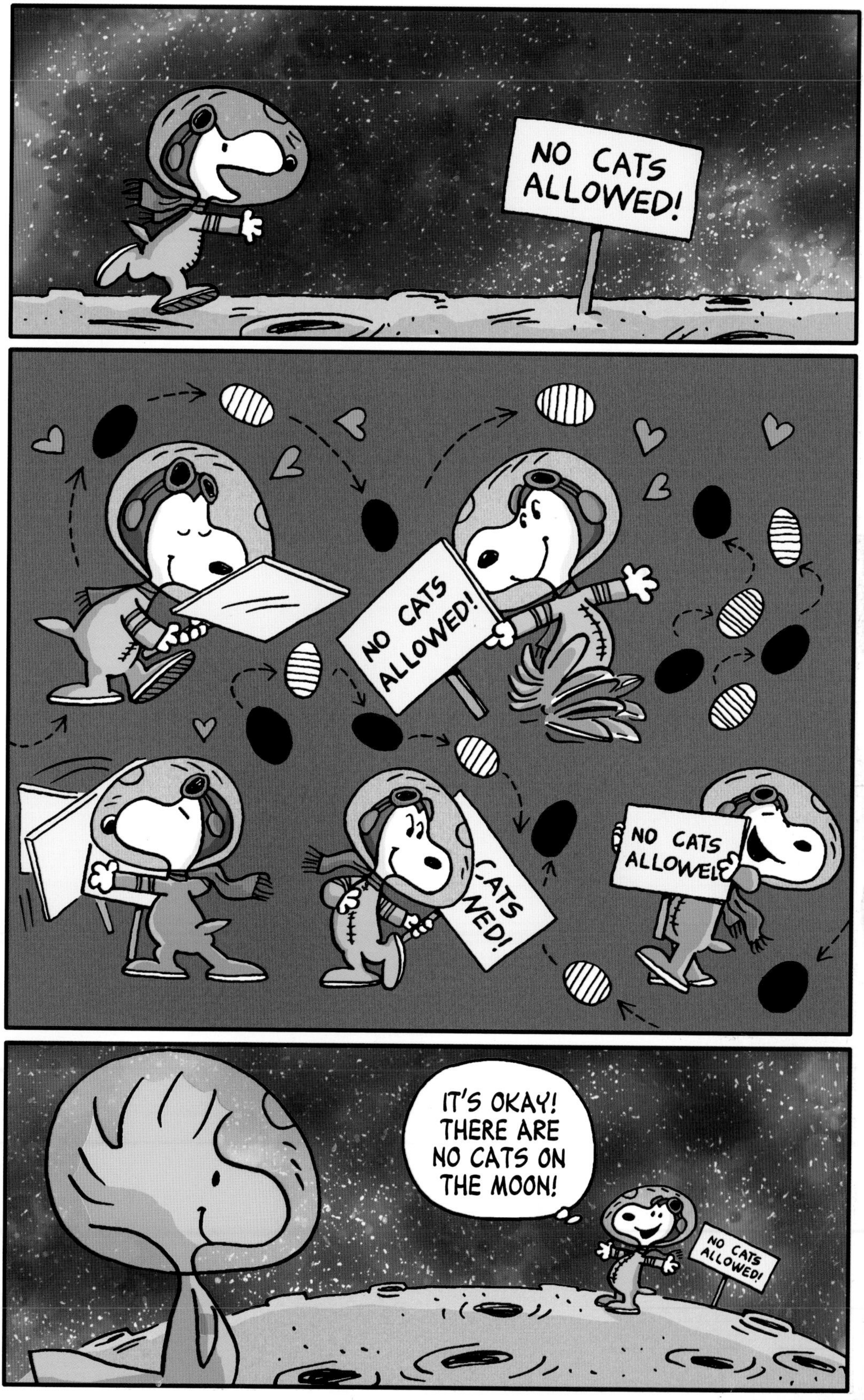
NO CATS ALLOWED!
NO CATS ALLOWED!
CATS WED!
NO CATS
IT'S OKAY! THERE ARE NO CATS ON THE MOON!
NO CATS ALLOWED!

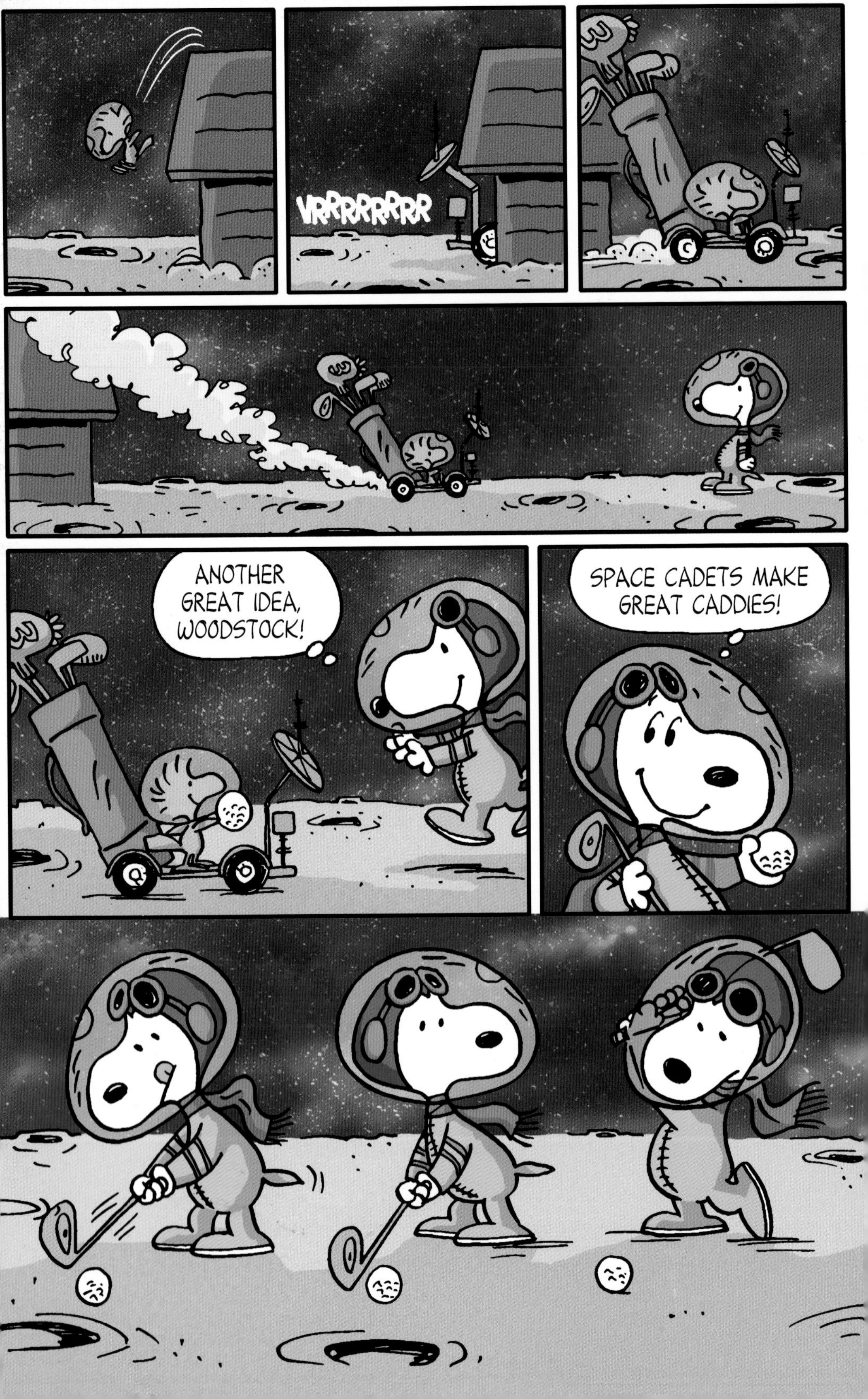
VRRRRRRRR
ANOTHER GREAT IDEA, WOODSTOCK!
SPACE CADETS MAKE GREAT CADDIES!

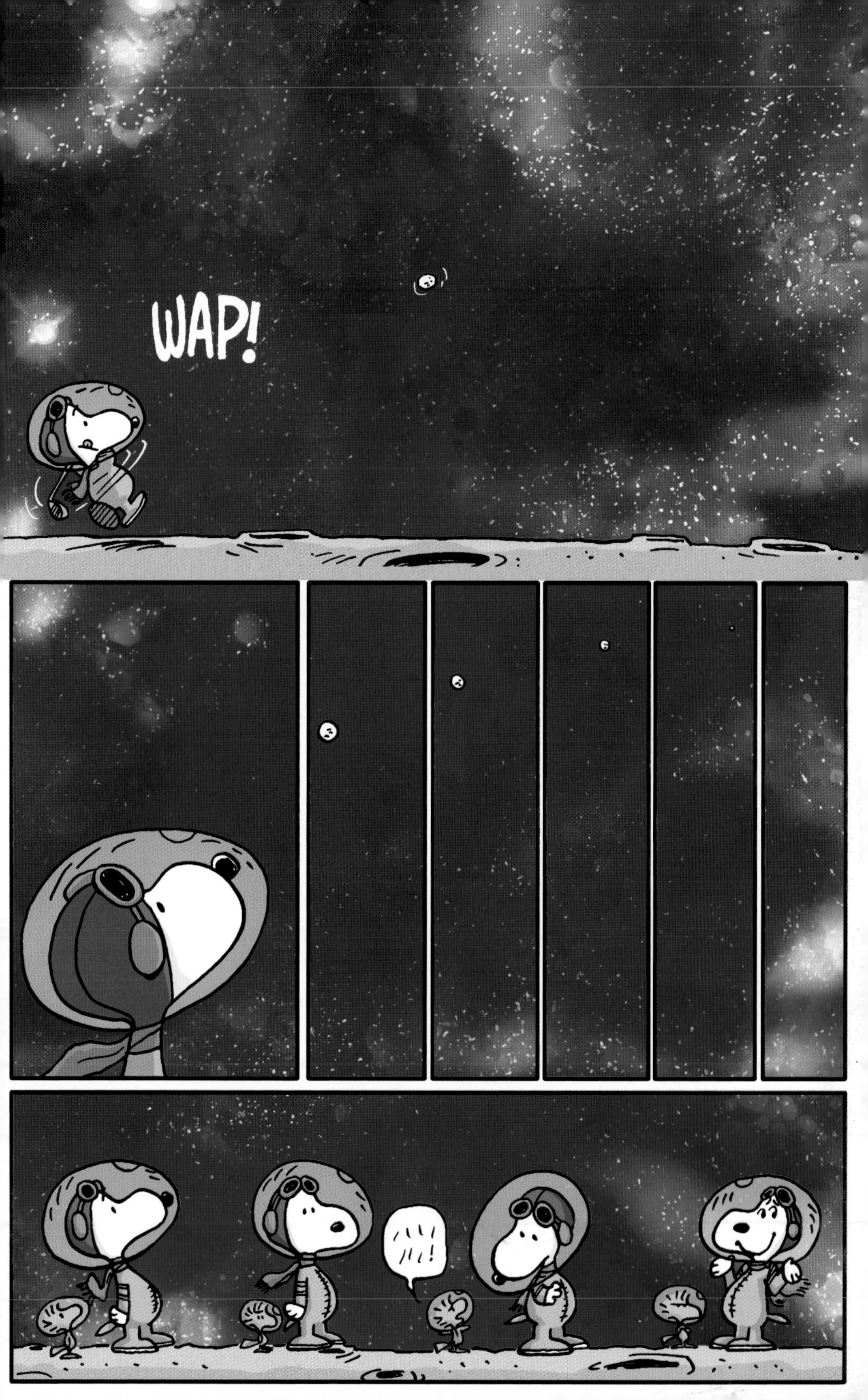
WAP!

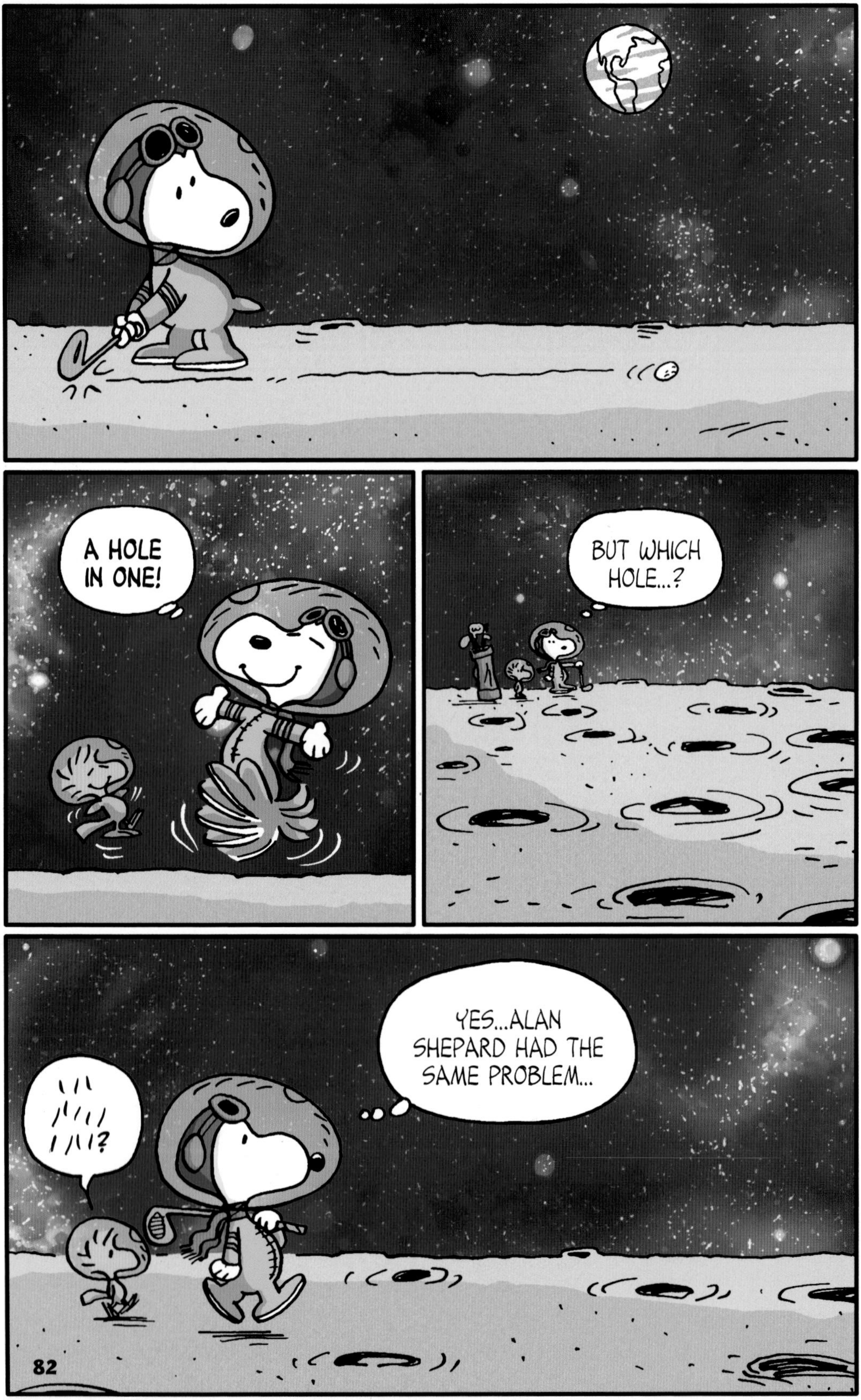
A HOLE IN ONE!
BUT WHICH HOLE...?
YES...ALAN SHEPARD HAD THE SAME PROBLEM...

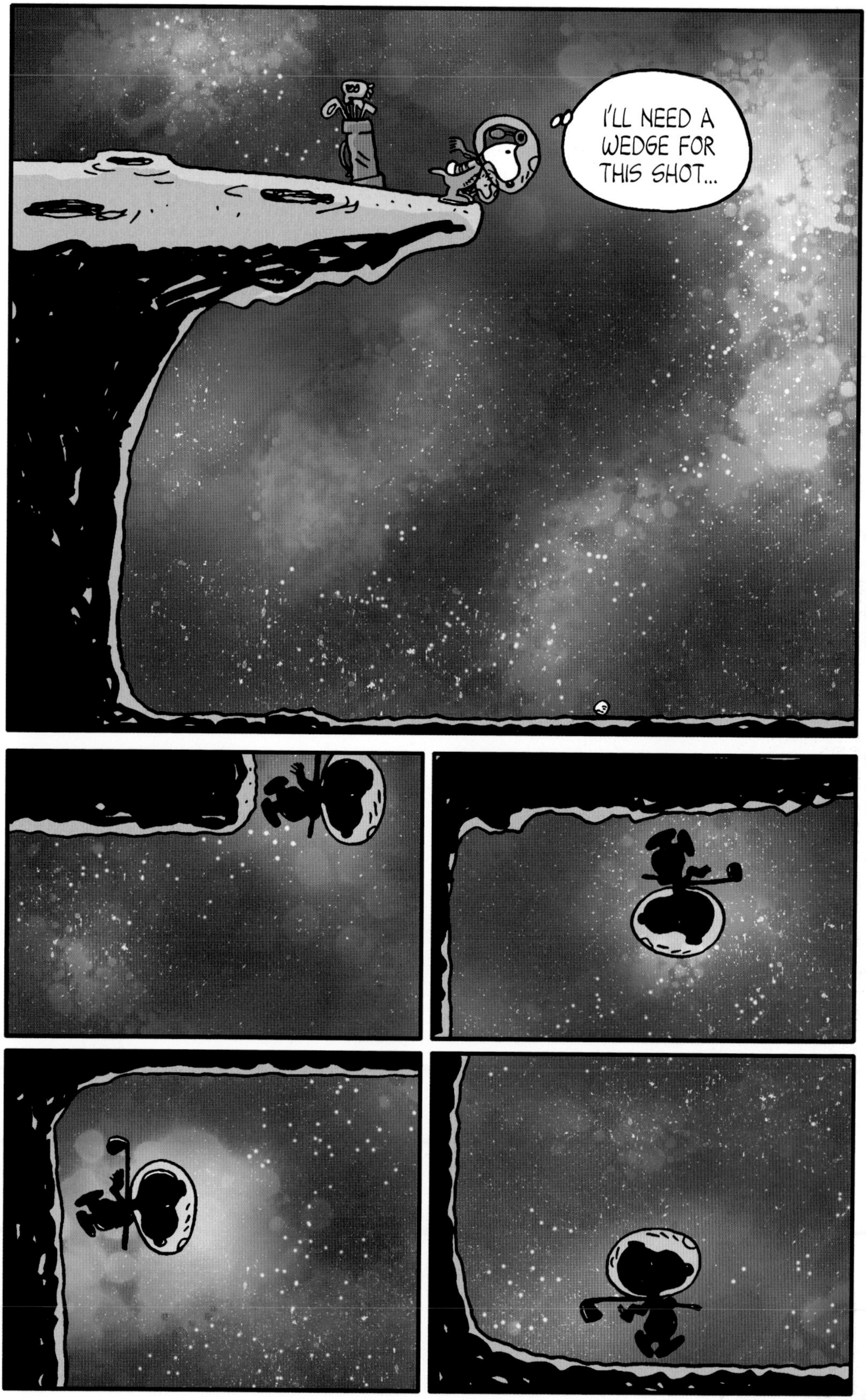
I'LL NEED A WEDGE FOR THIS SHOT...

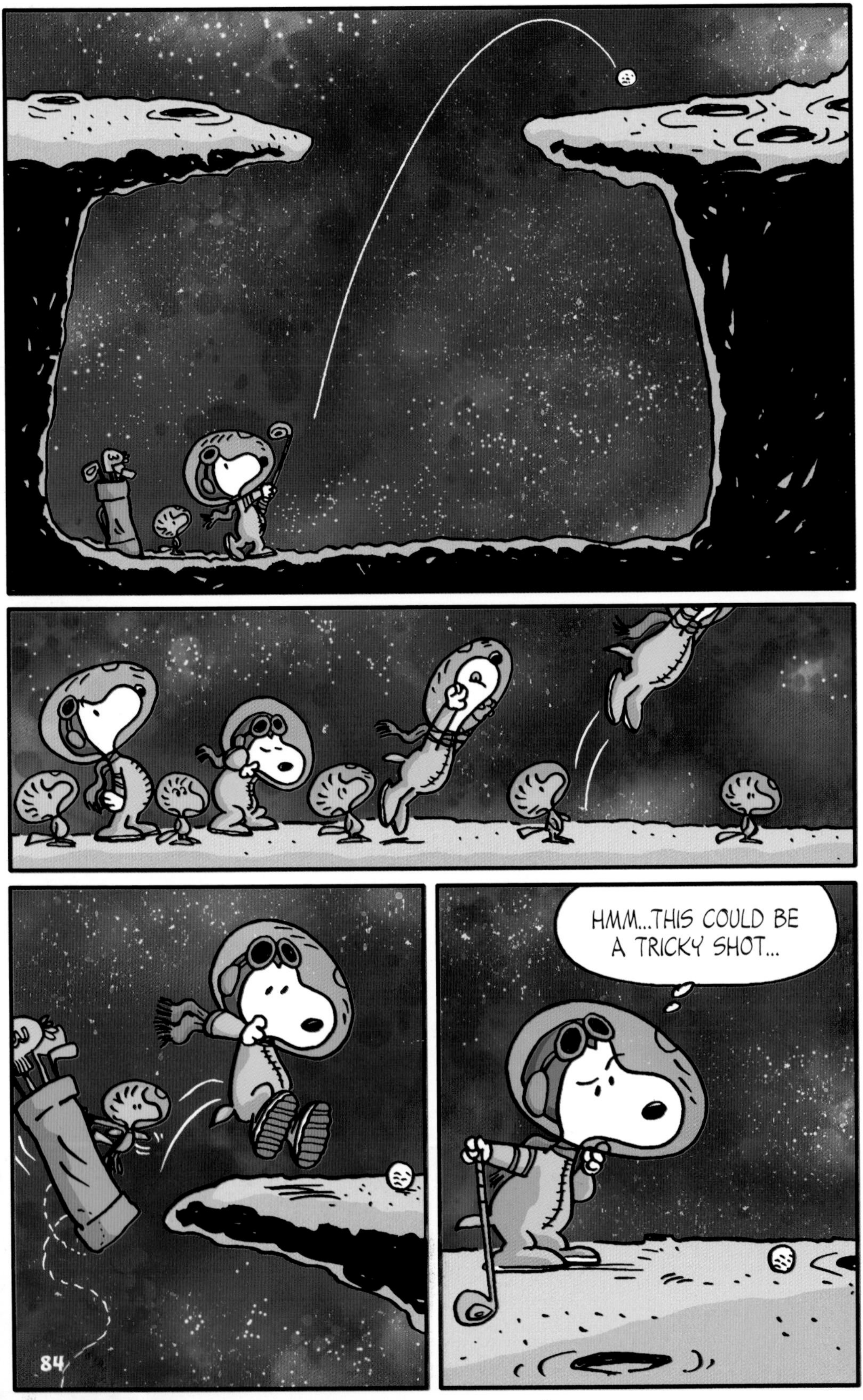
HMM...THIS COULD BE A TRICKY SHOT...

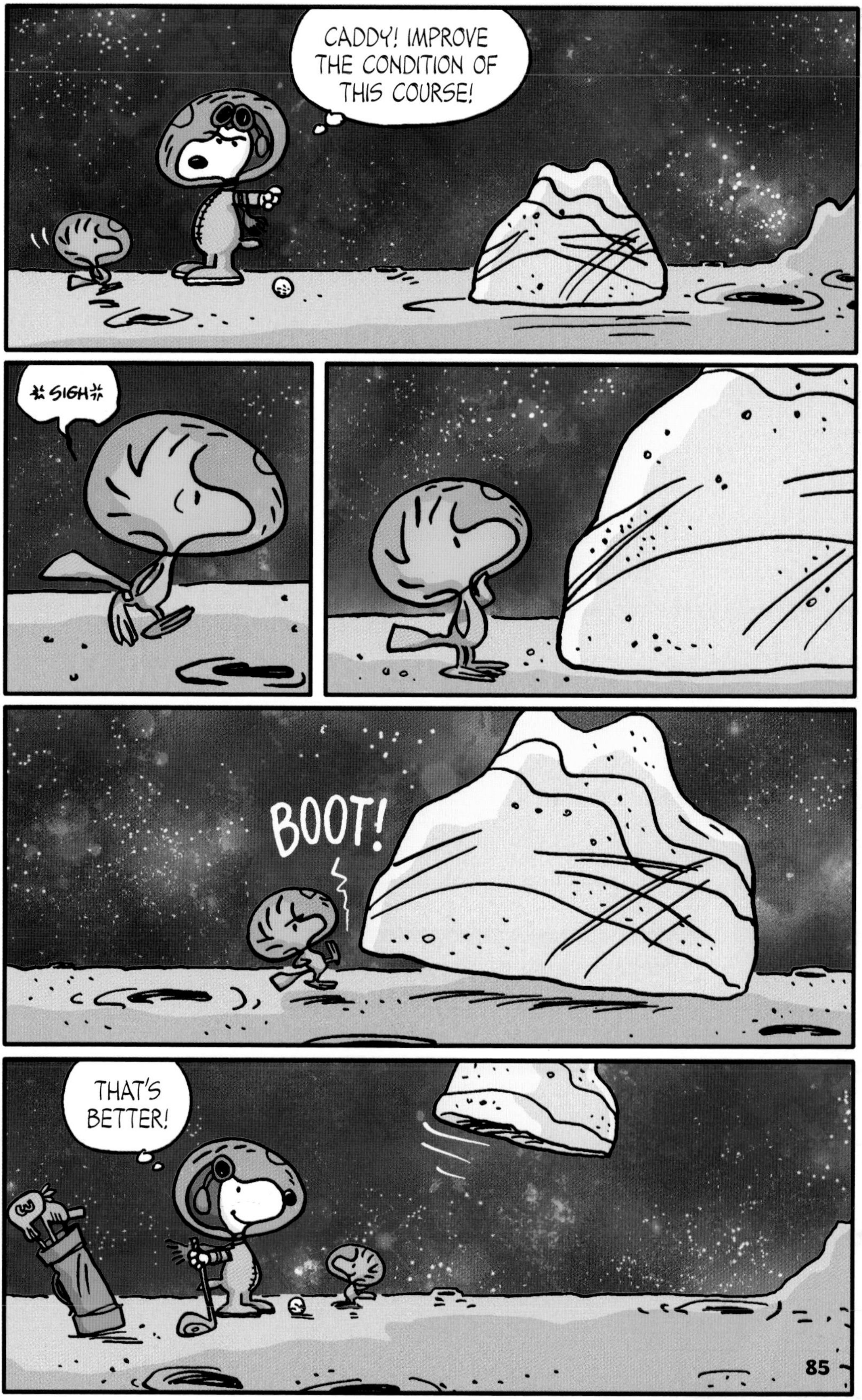
CADDY! IMPROVE THE CONDITION OF THIS COURSE!
SIGH
BOOT!
THAT'S BETTER!

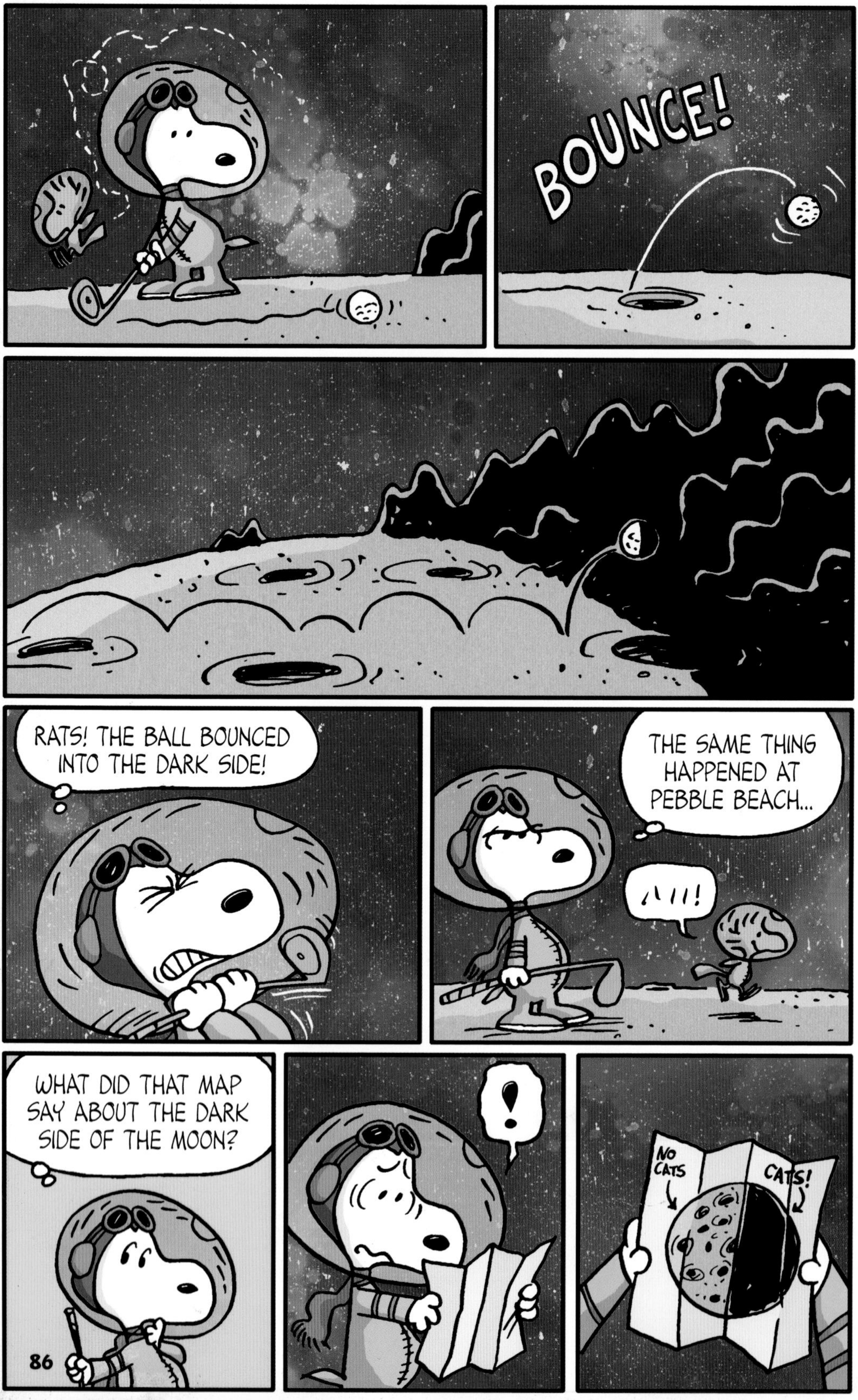
BOUNCE!
RATS! THE BALL BOUNCED INTO THE DARK SIDE!
THE SAME THING HAPPENED AT PEBBLE BEACH...
HA!!
WHAT DID THAT MAP SAY ABOUT THE DARK SIDE OF THE MOON?
!
NO CATS
CATS!

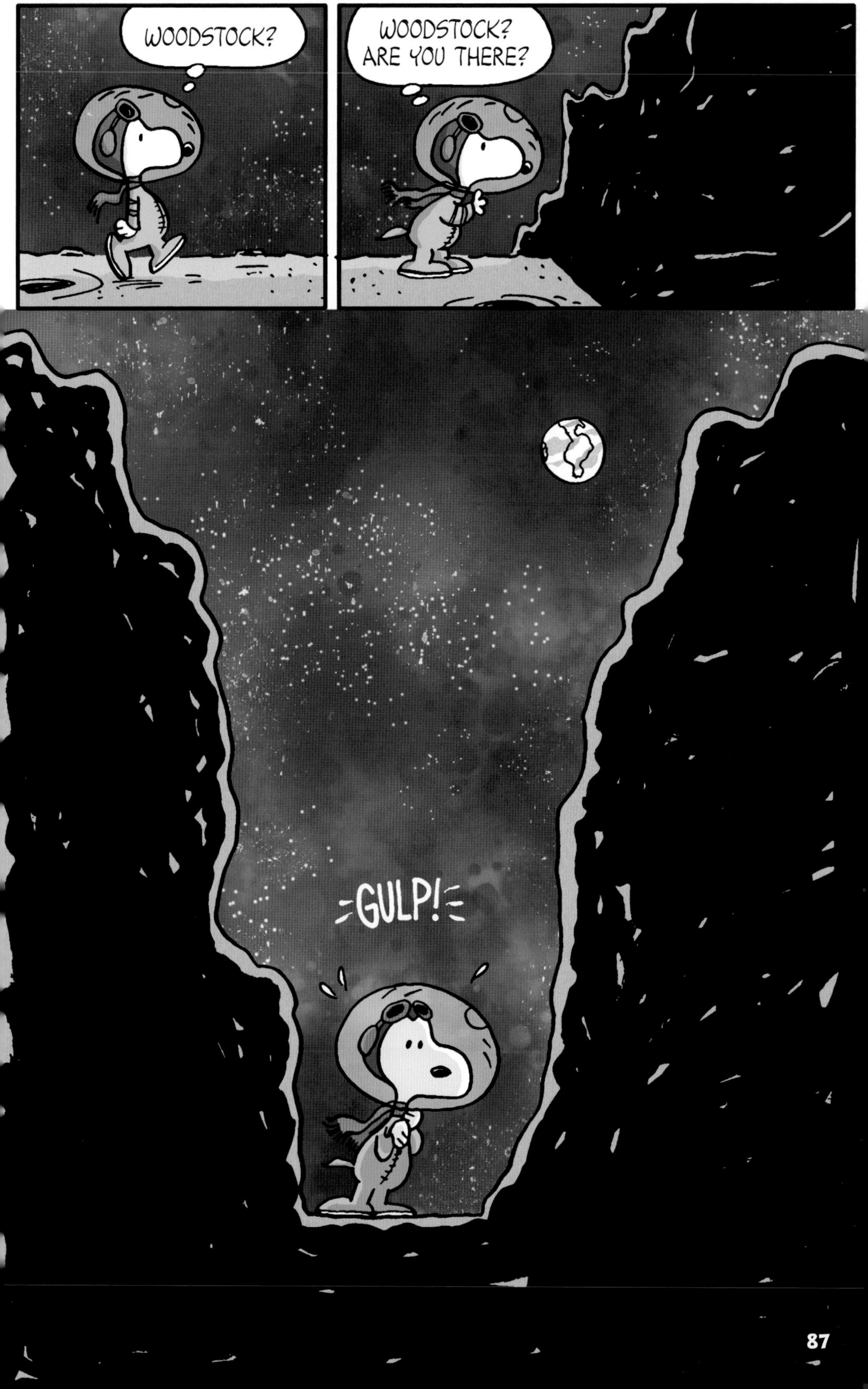
WOODSTOCK?
WOODSTOCK? ARE YOU THERE?
GULP!

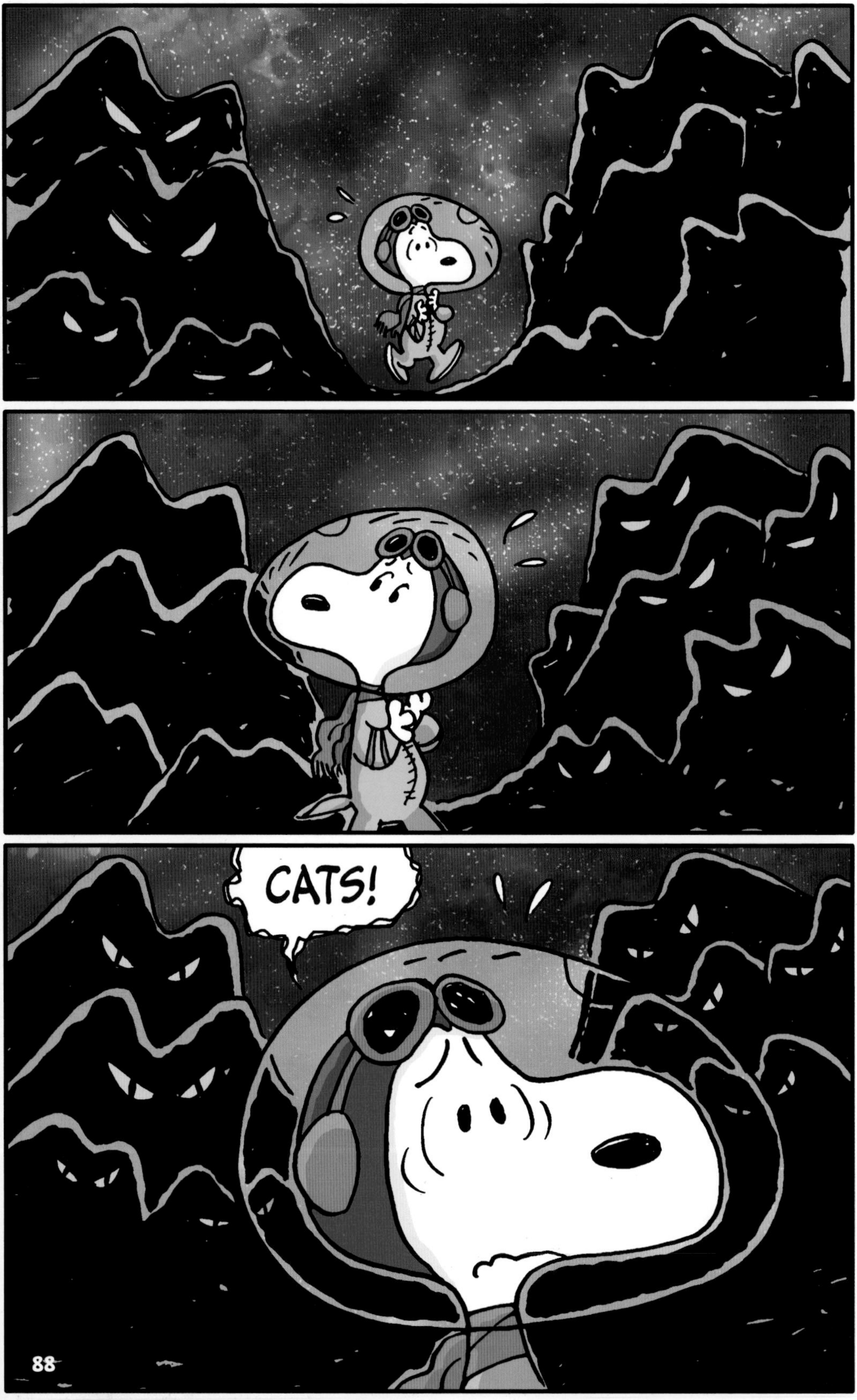
CATS!

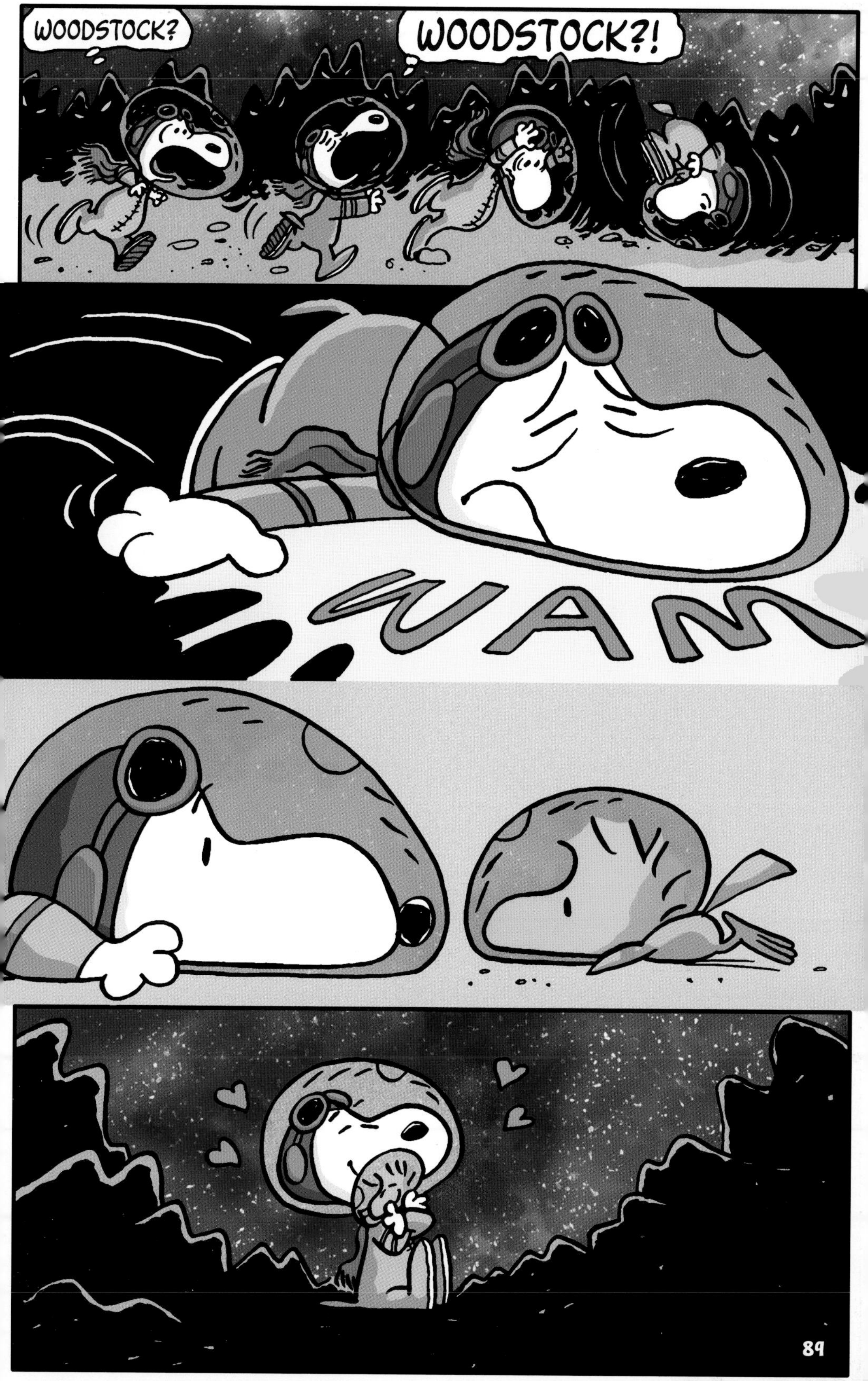
WOODSTOCK?
WOODSTOCK?!
WAM

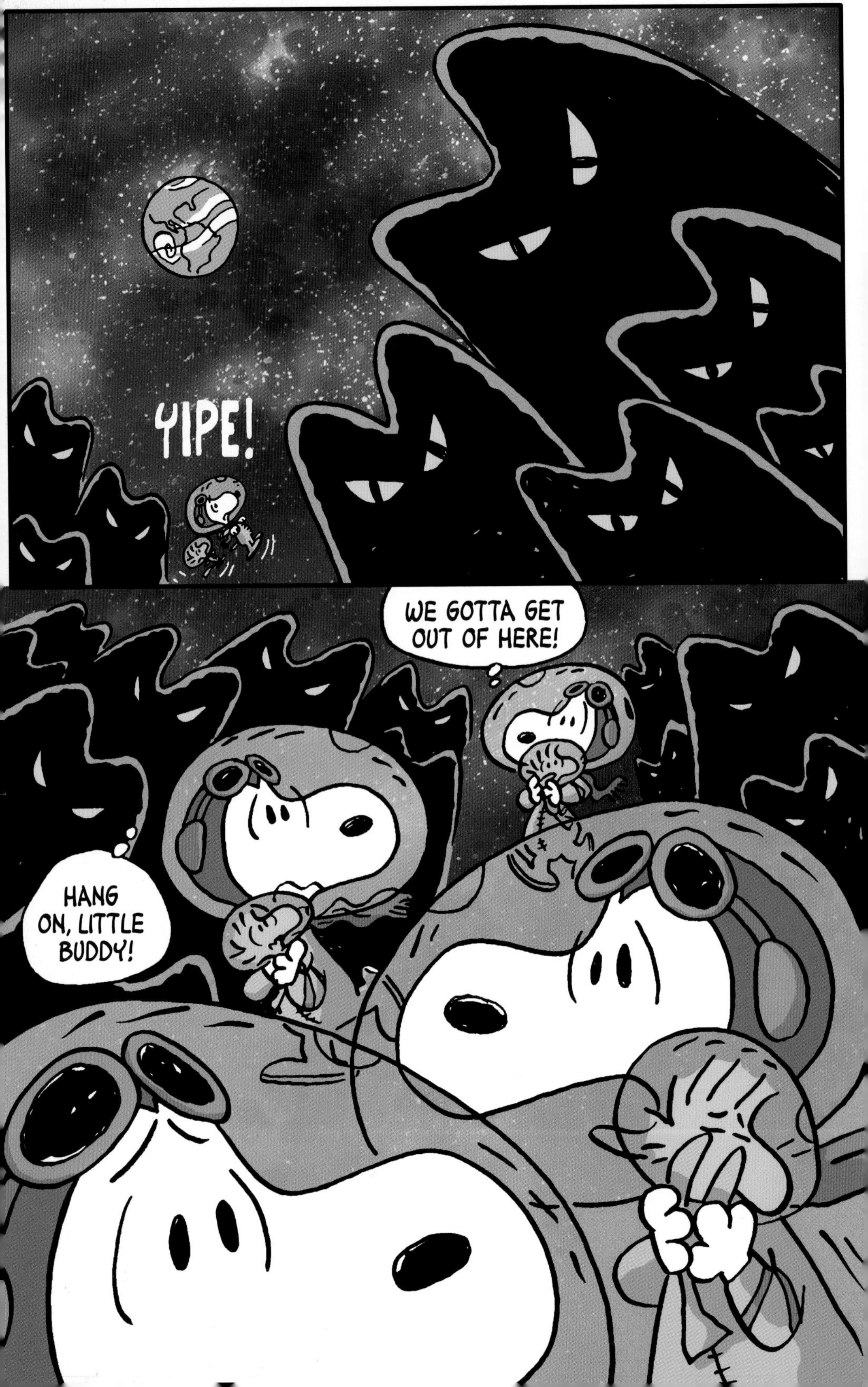
YIPE!
WE GOTTA GET OUT OF HERE!
HANG ON, LITTLE BUDDY!

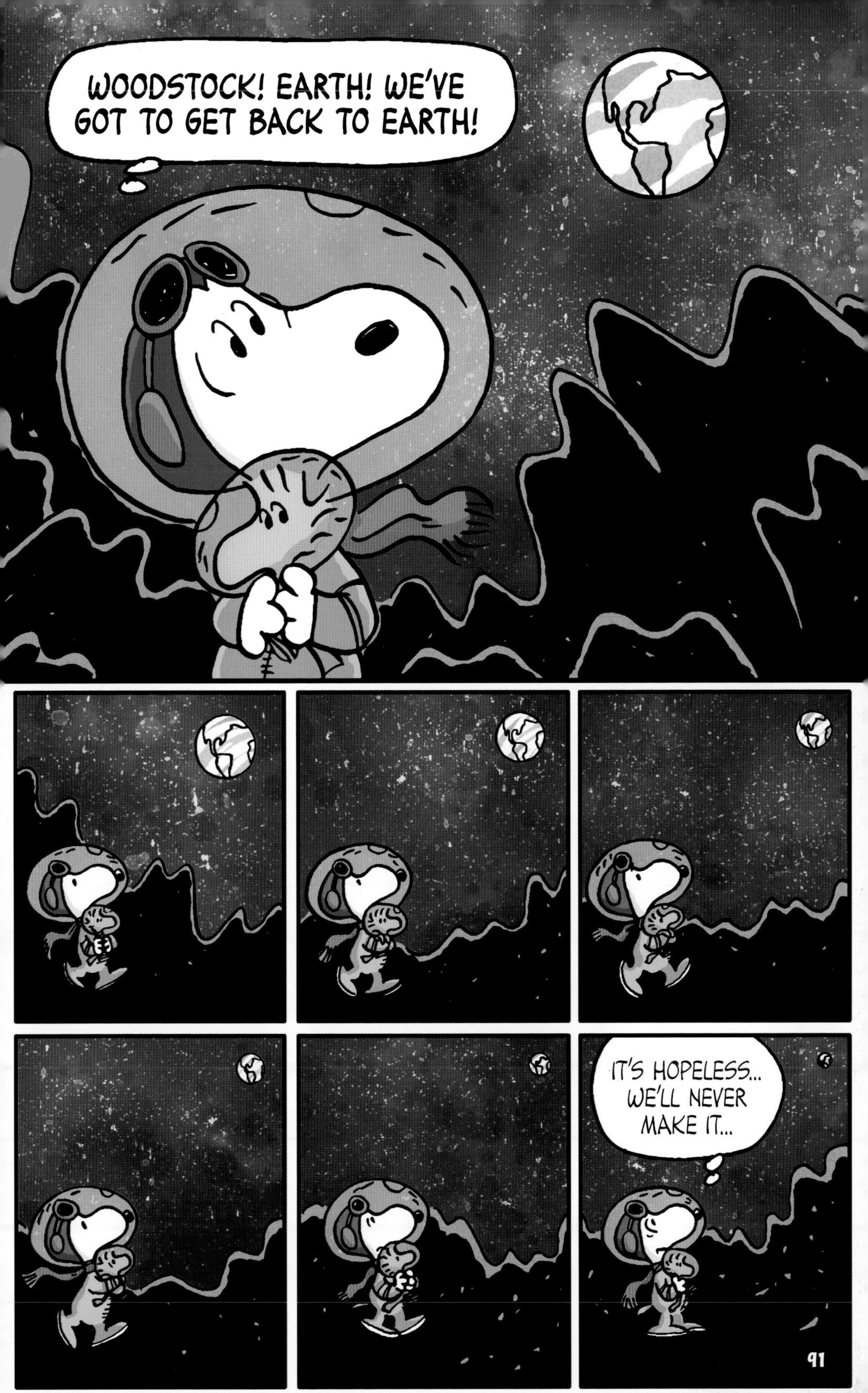
WOODSTOCK! EARTH! WE'VE GOT TO GET BACK TO EARTH!
IT'S HOPELESS... WE'LL NEVER MAKE IT...

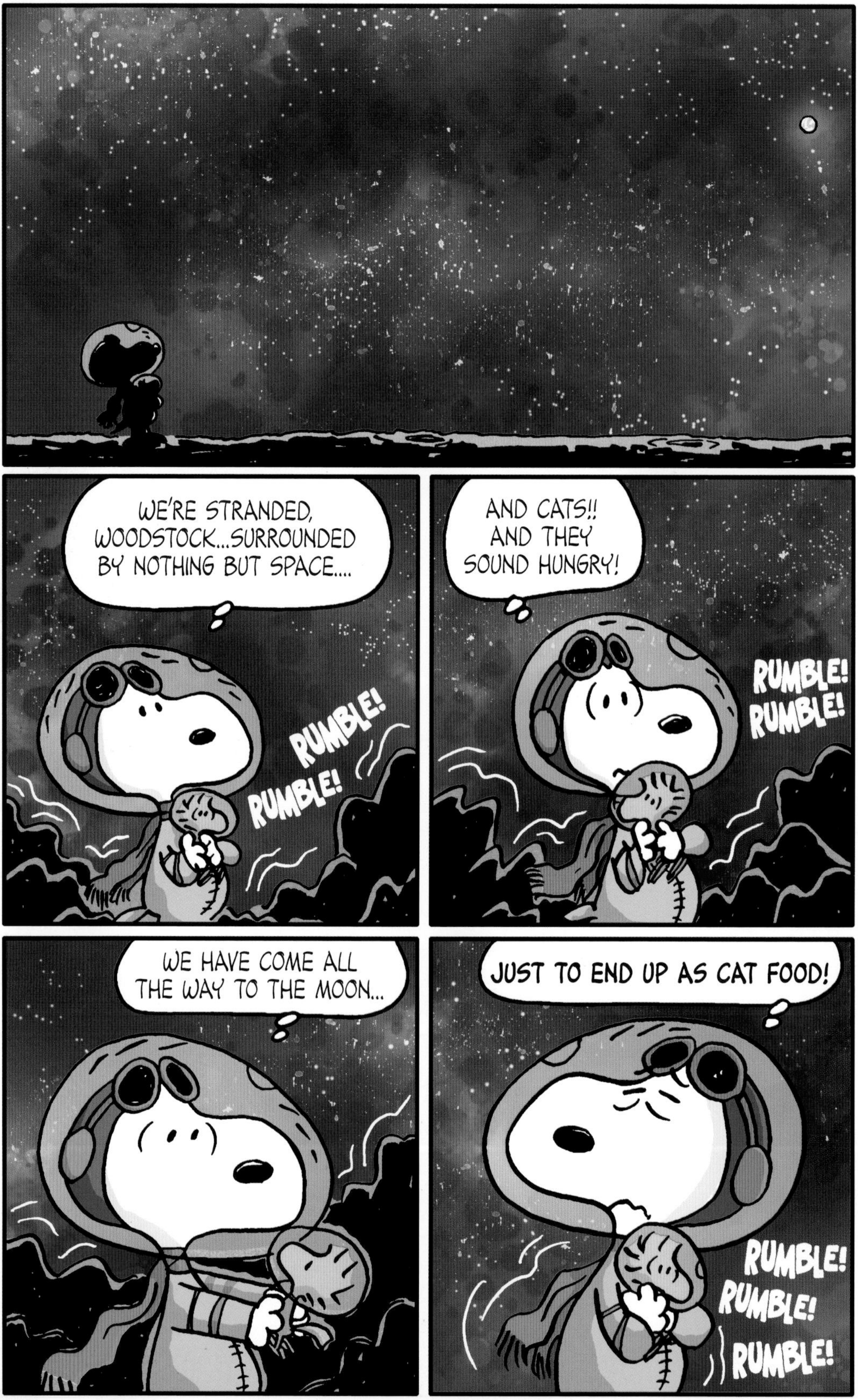

WE'RE STRANDED, WOODSTOCK...SURROUNDED BY NOTHING BUT SPACE....
RUMBLE!
RUMBLE!
AND CATS!! AND THEY SOUND HUNGRY!
RUMBLE!
RUMBLE!
WE HAVE COME ALL THE WAY TO THE MOON...
JUST TO END UP AS CAT FOOD!
RUMBLE!
RUMBLE!
RUMBLE!

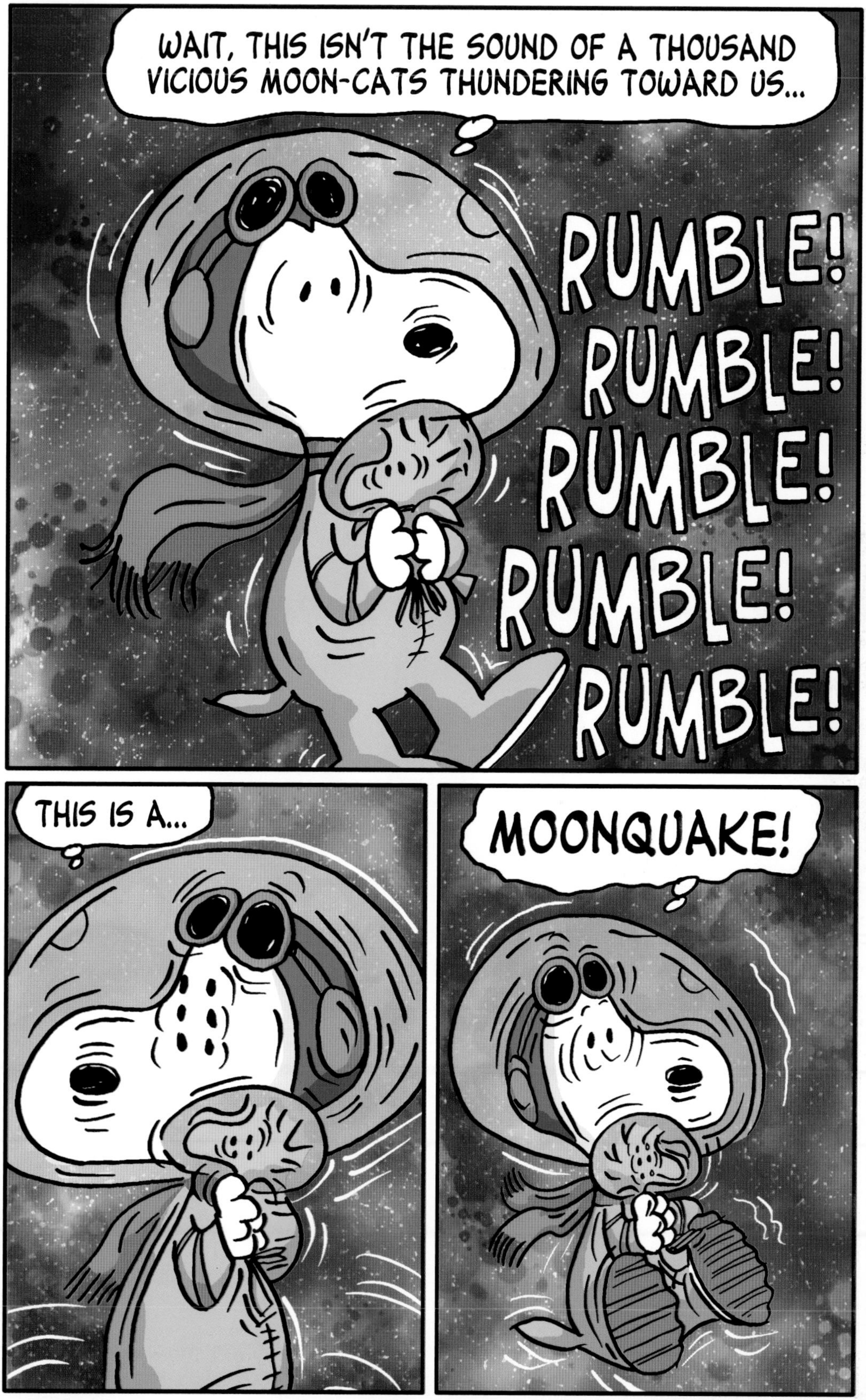
WAIT, THIS ISN'T THE SOUND OF A THOUSAND VICIOUS MOON-CATS THUNDERING TOWARD US...
RUMBLE! RUMBLE! RUMBLE! RUMBLE! RUMBLE!
THIS IS A...
MOONQUAKE!

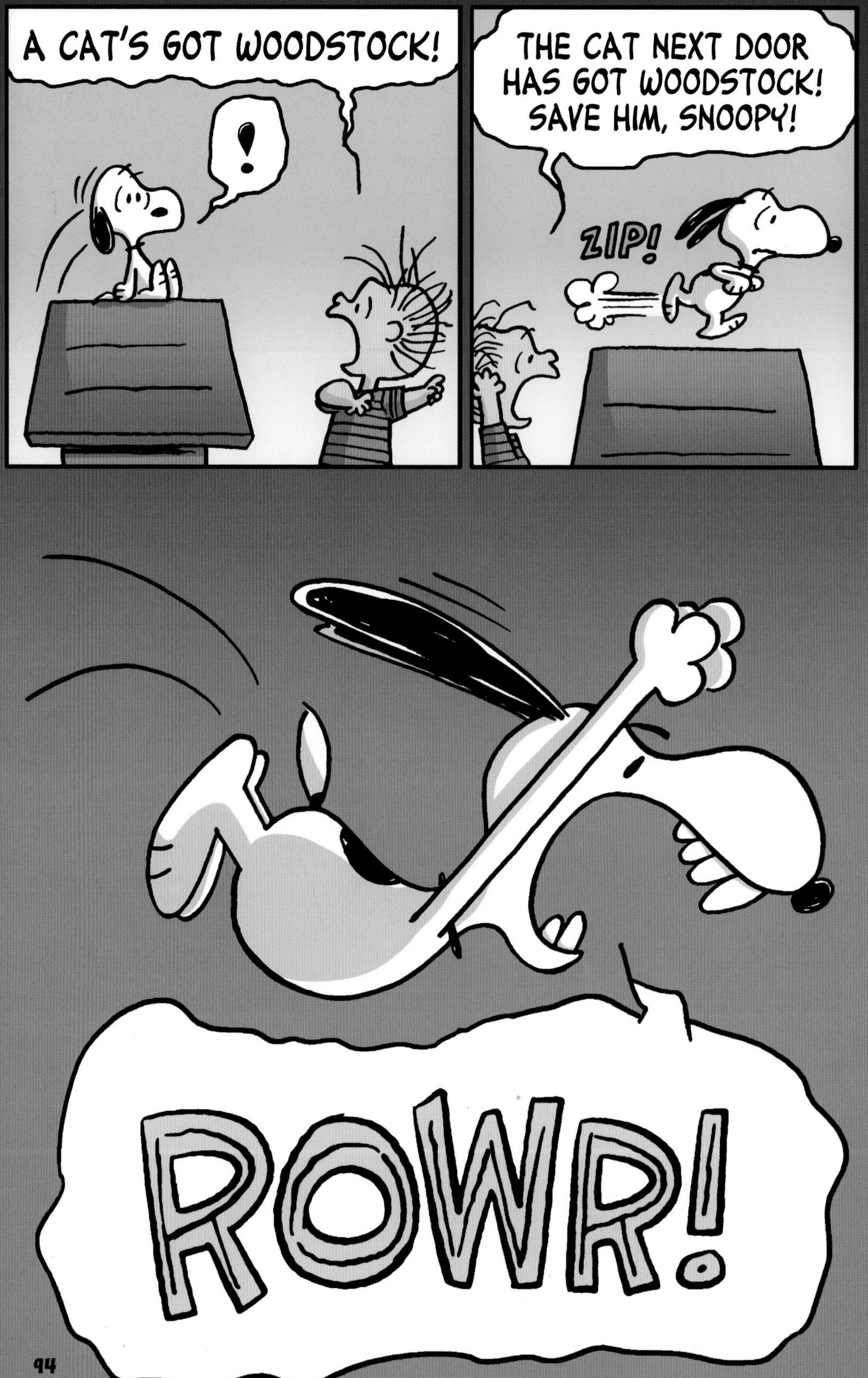
A CAT'S GOT WOODSTOCK!
!
THE CAT NEXT DOOR HAS GOT WOODSTOCK! SAVE HIM, SNOOPY!
ZIP!
ROWR!

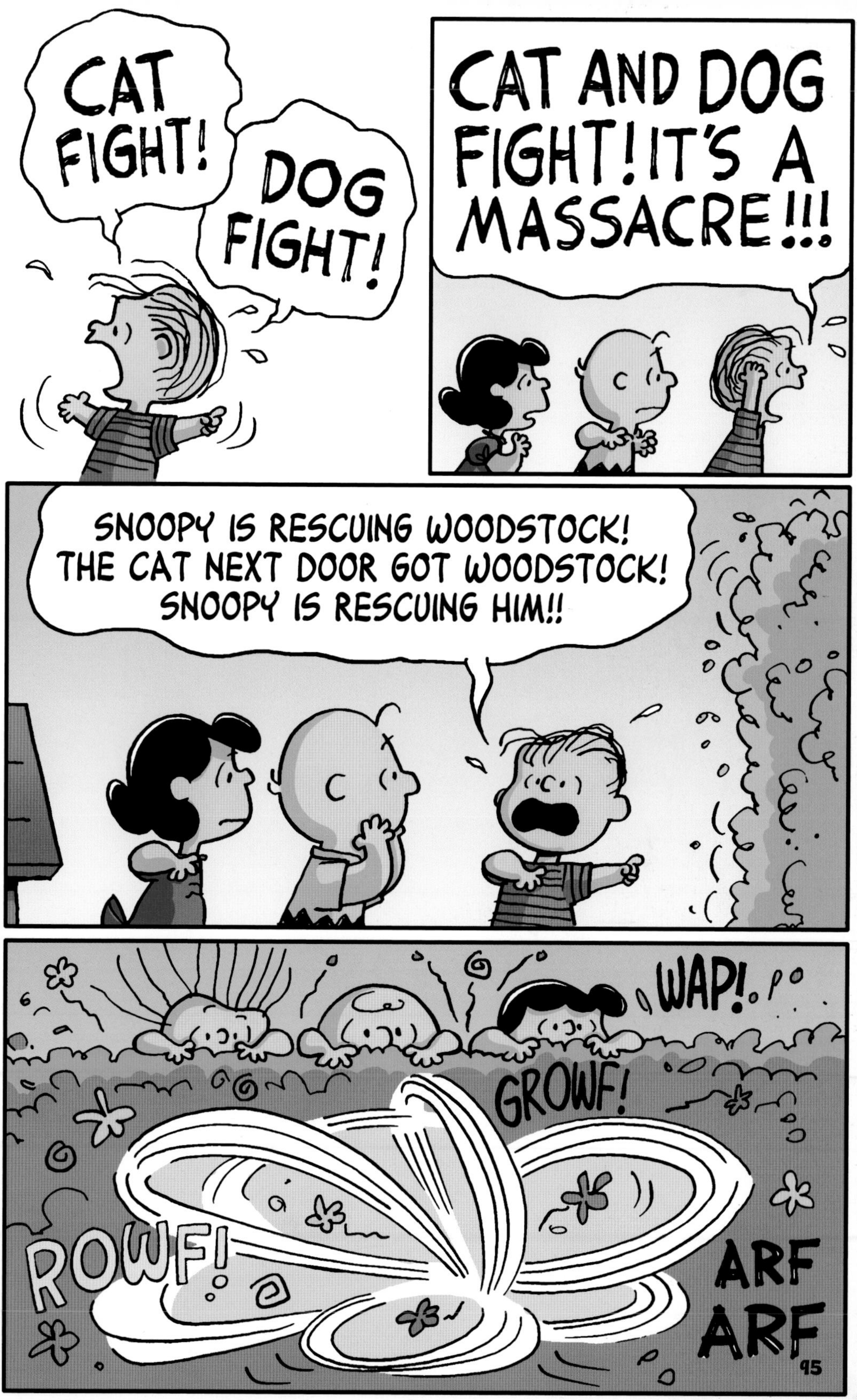
CAT FIGHT!
DOG FIGHT!
CAT AND DOG FIGHT! IT'S A MASSACRE!!!
SNOOPY IS RESCUING WOODSTOCK! THE CAT NEXT DOOR GOT WOODSTOCK! SNOOPY IS RESCUING HIM!!
WAP!
GROWF!
ROWF!
ARF ARF

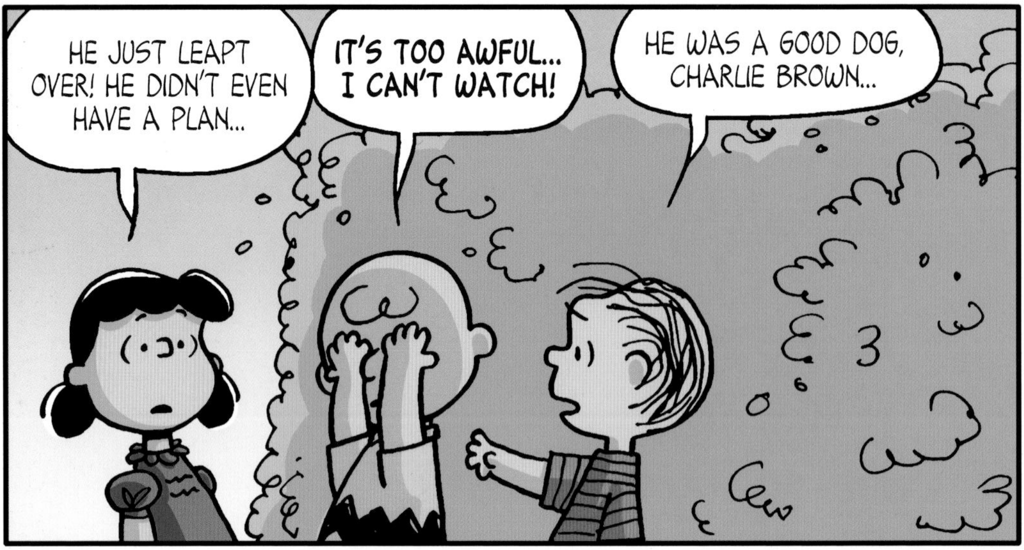
HE JUST LEAPT OVER! HE DIDN'T EVEN HAVE A PLAN...
IT'S TOO AWFUL... I CAN'T WATCH!
HE WAS A GOOD DOG, CHARLIE BROWN...

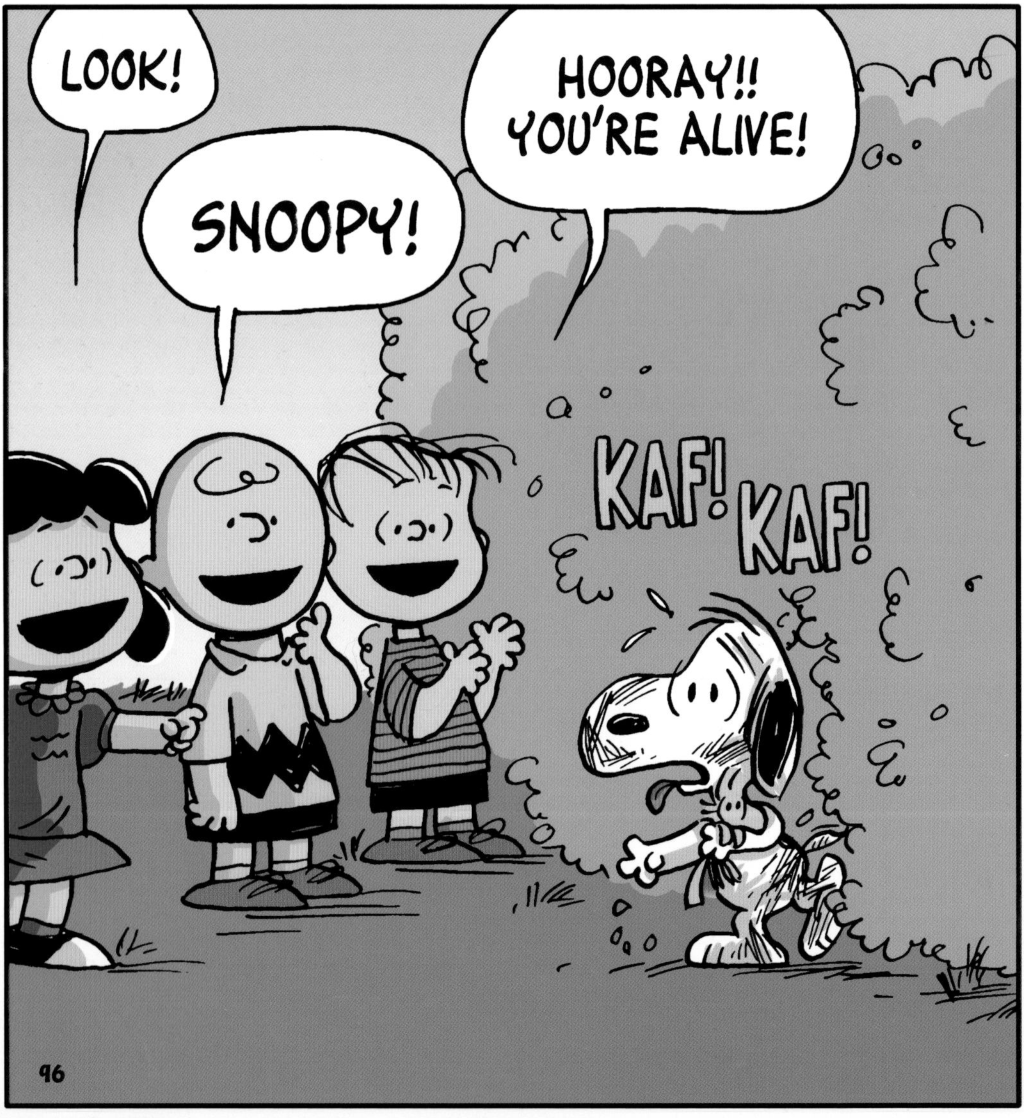
LOOK!
SNOOPY!
HOORAY!! YOU'RE ALIVE!
KAF! KAF!

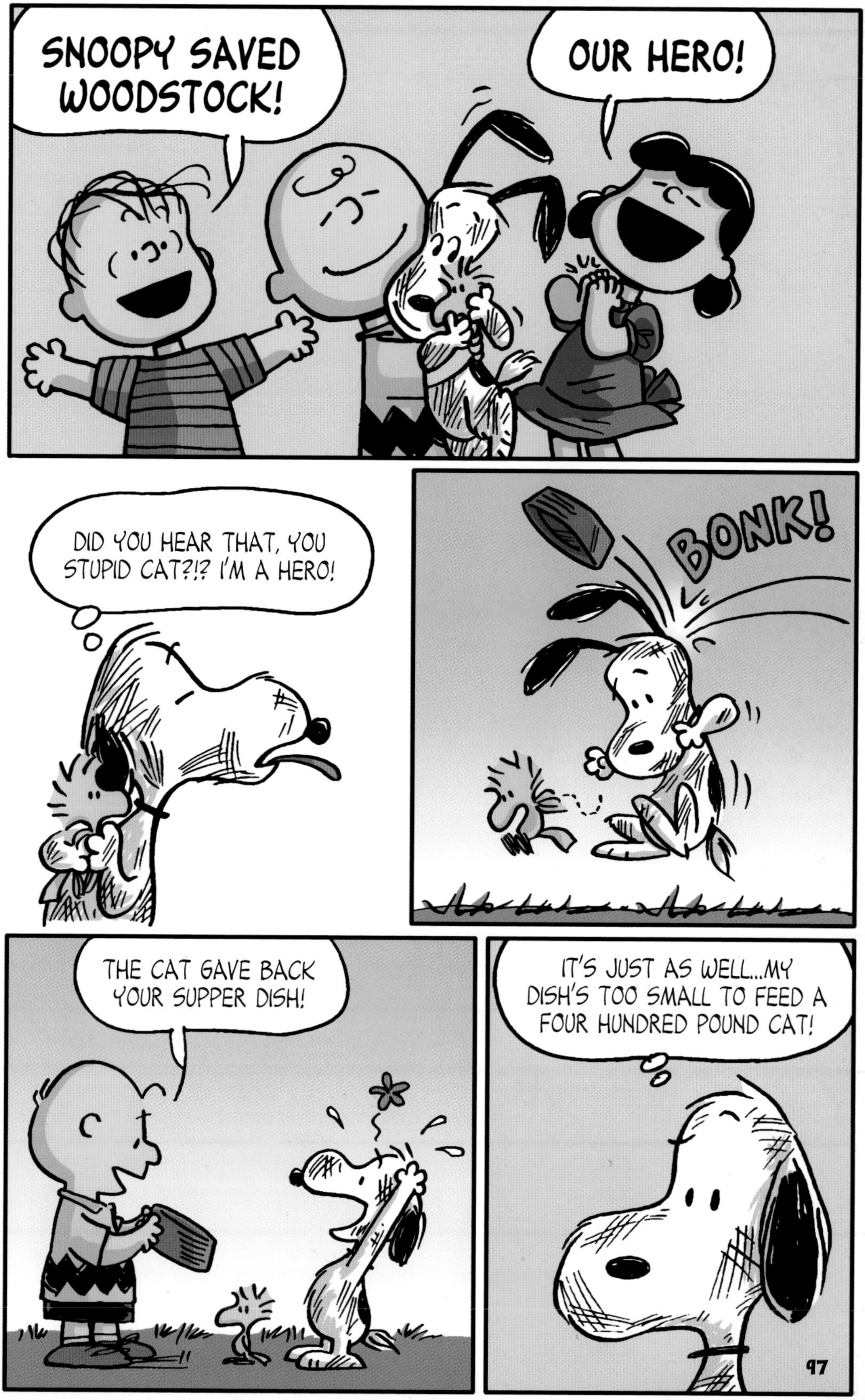
SNOOPY SAVED WOODSTOCK!
OUR HERO!
DID YOU HEAR THAT, YOU STUPID CAT?!? I'M A HERO!
BONK!
THE CAT GAVE BACK YOUR SUPPER DISH!
IT'S JUST AS WELL...MY DISH'S TOO SMALL TO FEED A FOUR HUNDRED POUND CAT!

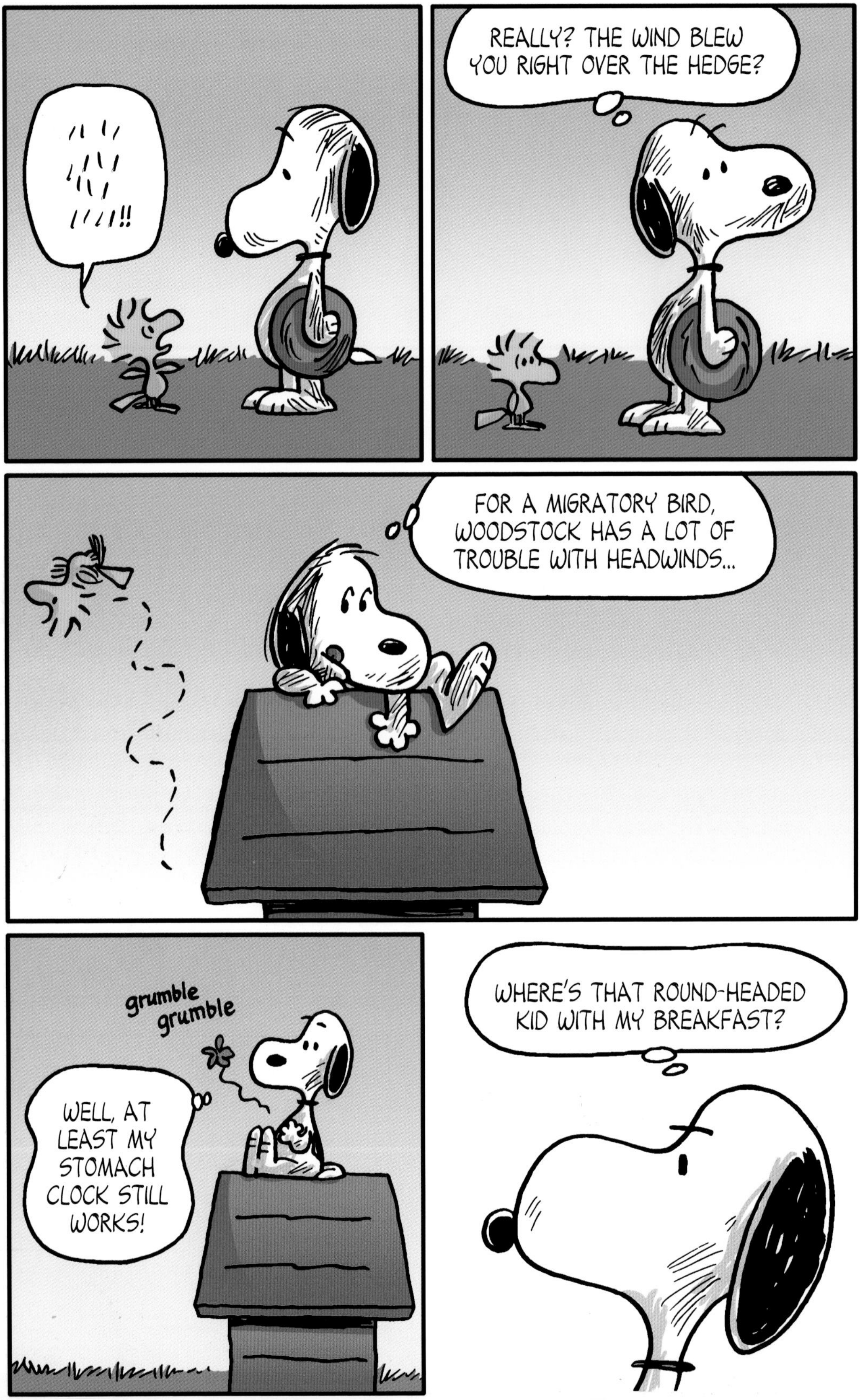

REALLY? THE WIND BLEW YOU RIGHT OVER THE HEDGE?
FOR A MIGRATORY BIRD, WOODSTOCK HAS A LOT OF TROUBLE WITH HEADWINDS...
grumble grumble
WELL, AT LEAST MY STOMACH CLOCK STILL WORKS!
WHERE'S THAT ROUND-HEADED KID WITH MY BREAKFAST?

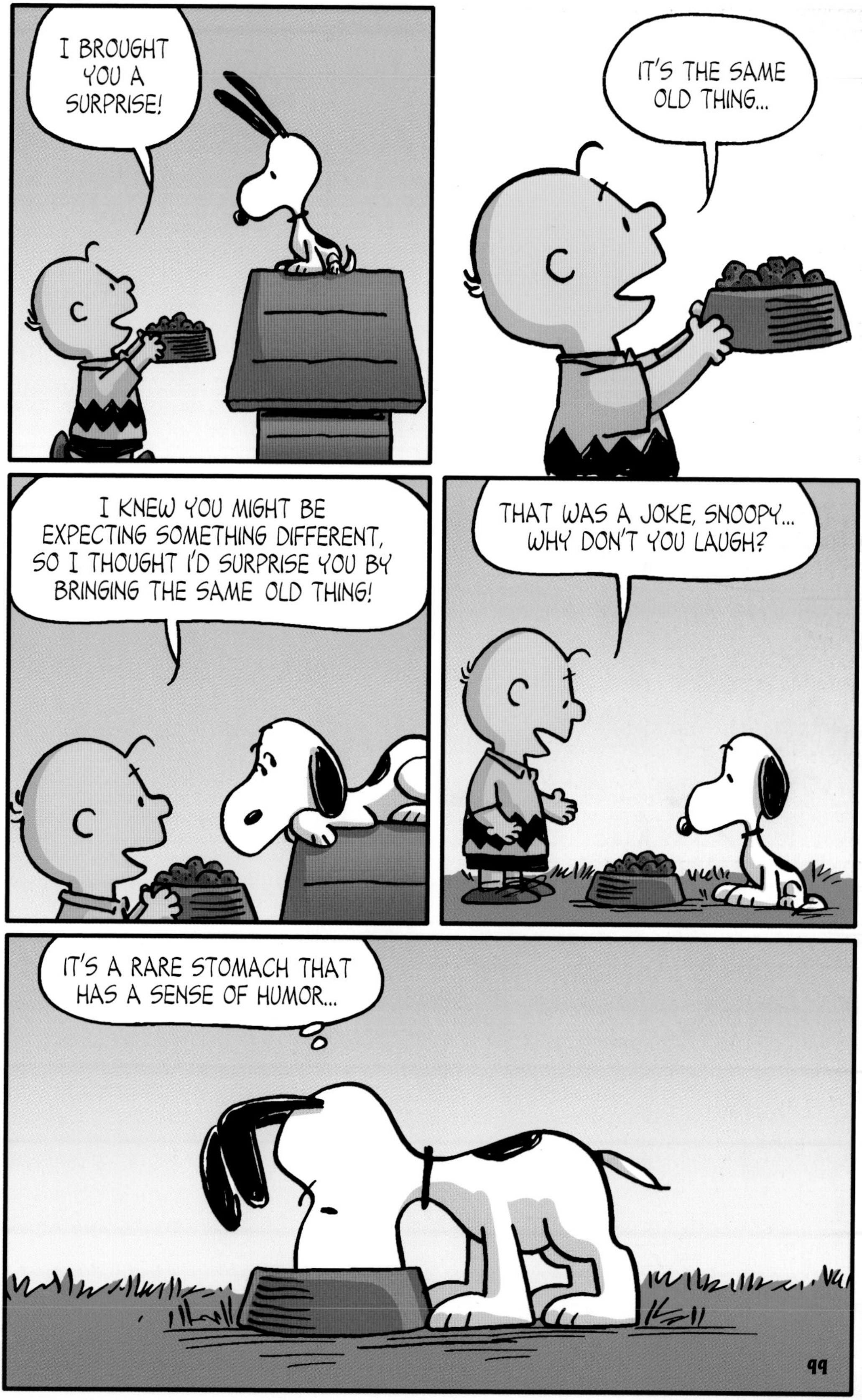
I BROUGHT YOU A SURPRISE!
IT'S THE SAME OLD THING...
I KNEW YOU MIGHT BE EXPECTING SOMETHING DIFFERENT, SO I THOUGHT I'D SURPRISE YOU BY BRINGING THE SAME OLD THING!
THAT WAS A JOKE, SNOOPY... WHY DON'T YOU LAUGH?
IT'S A RARE STOMACH THAT HAS A SENSE OF HUMOR...

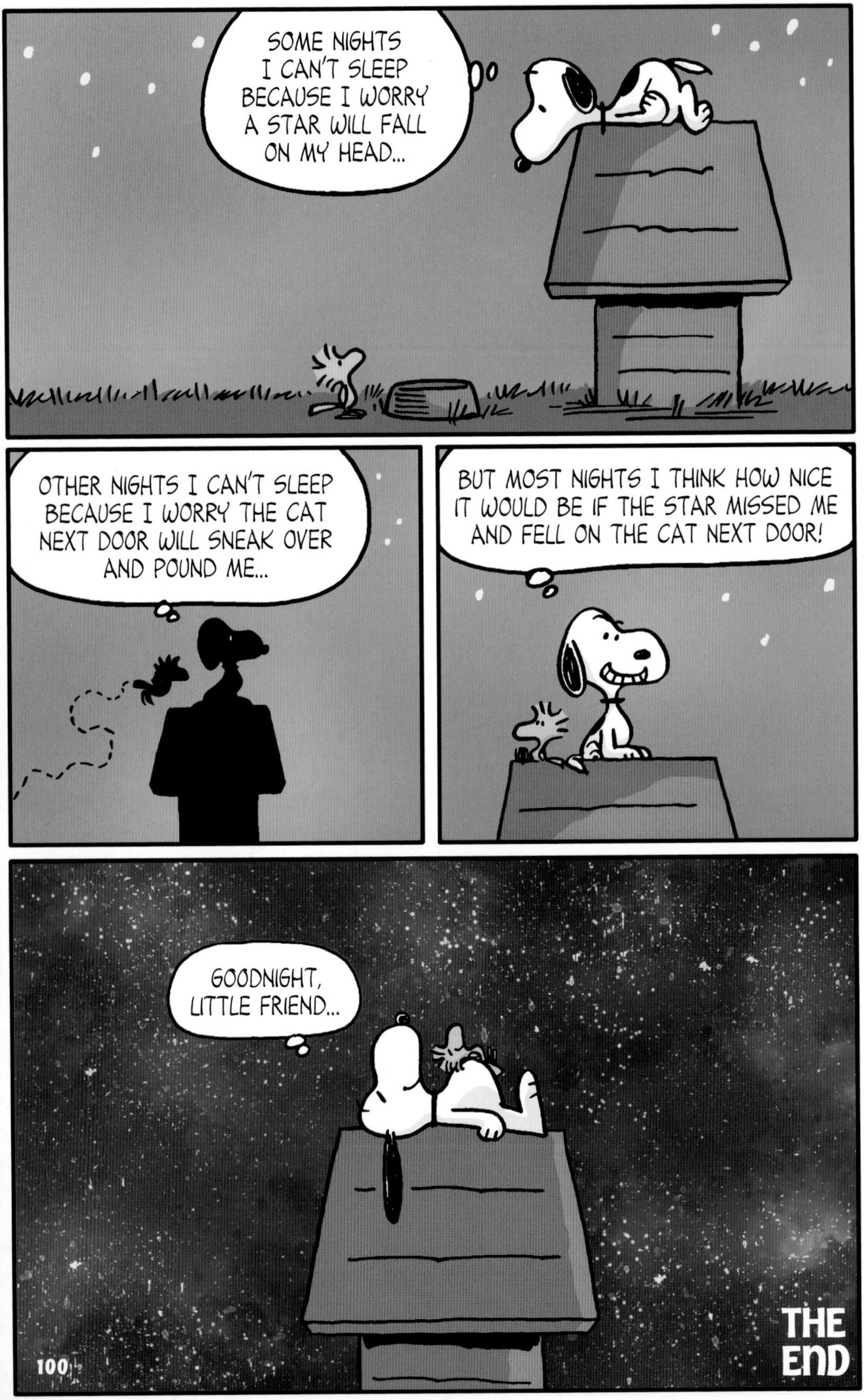
SOME NIGHTS I CAN'T SLEEP BECAUSE I WORRY A STAR WILL FALL ON MY HEAD...
OTHER NIGHTS I CAN'T SLEEP BECAUSE I WORRY THE CAT NEXT DOOR WILL SNEAK OVER AND POUND ME...
BUT MOST NIGHTS I THINK HOW NICE IT WOULD BE IF THE STAR MISSED ME AND FELL ON THE CAT NEXT DOOR!
GOODNIGHT, LITTLE FRIEND...
THE END

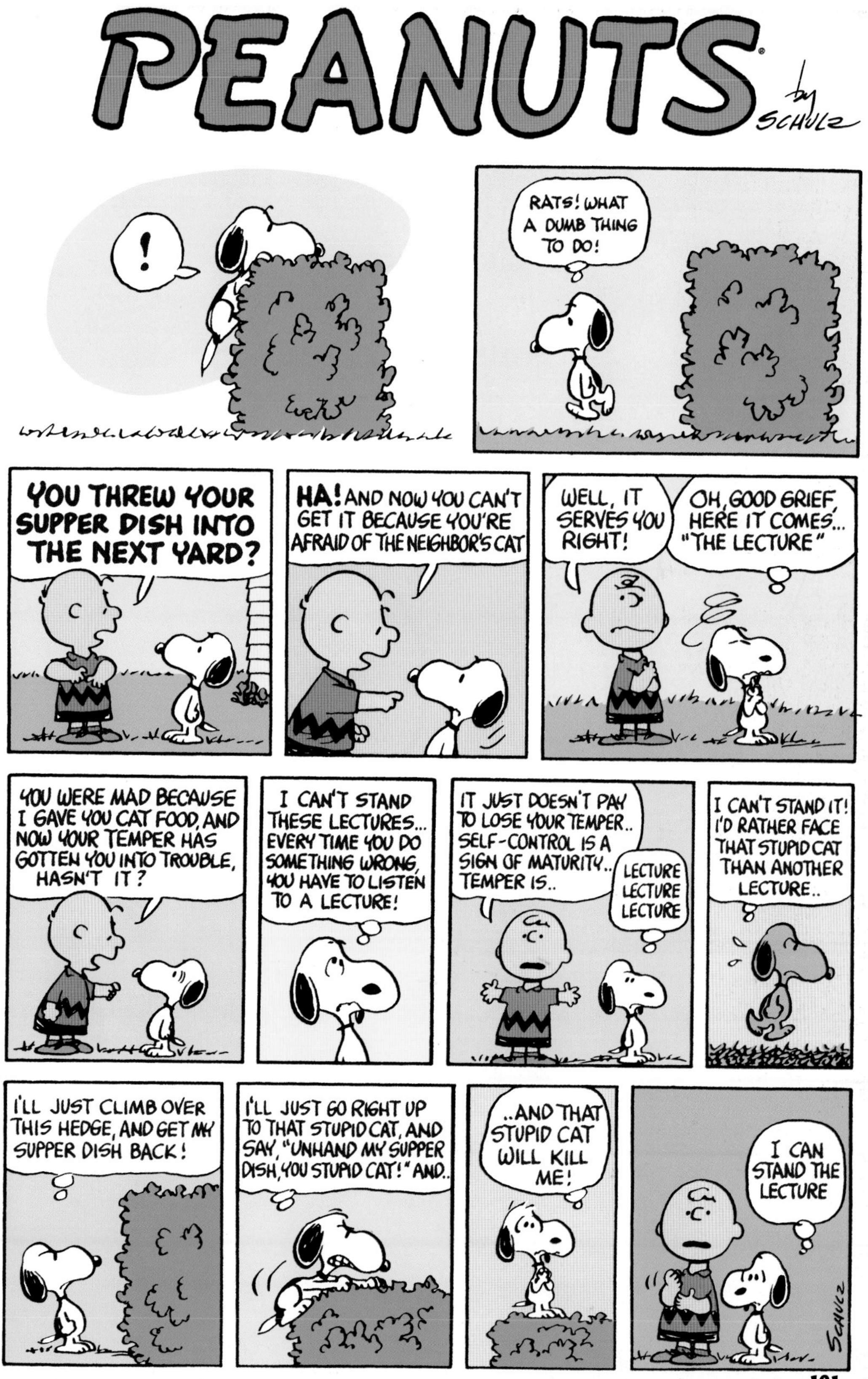
PEANUTS
by SCHULZ
!
RATS! WHAT A DUMB THING TO DO!
YOU THREW YOUR SUPPER DISH INTO THE NEXT YARD?
HA! AND NOW YOU CAN'T GET IT BECAUSE YOU'RE AFRAID OF THE NEIGHBOR'S CAT
WELL, IT SERVES YOU RIGHT!
OH, GOOD GRIEF, HERE IT COMES... "THE LECTURE"
YOU WERE MAD BECAUSE I GAVE YOU CAT FOOD, AND NOW YOUR TEMPER HAS GOTTEN YOU INTO TROUBLE, HASN'T IT?
I CAN'T STAND THESE LECTURES... EVERY TIME YOU DO SOMETHING WRONG, YOU HAVE TO LISTEN TO A LECTURE!
IT JUST DOESN'T PAY TO LOSE YOUR TEMPER.. SELF-CONTROL IS A SIGN OF MATURITY.. TEMPER IS..
LECTURE LECTURE LECTURE
I CAN'T STAND IT! I'D RATHER FACE THAT STUPID CAT THAN ANOTHER LECTURE..
I'LL JUST CLIMB OVER THIS HEDGE, AND GET MY SUPPER DISH BACK!
I'LL JUST GO RIGHT UP TO THAT STUPID CAT, AND SAY, "UNHAND MY SUPPER DISH, YOU STUPID CAT!" AND..
..AND THAT STUPID CAT WILL KILL ME!
I CAN STAND THE LECTURE
SCHULZ

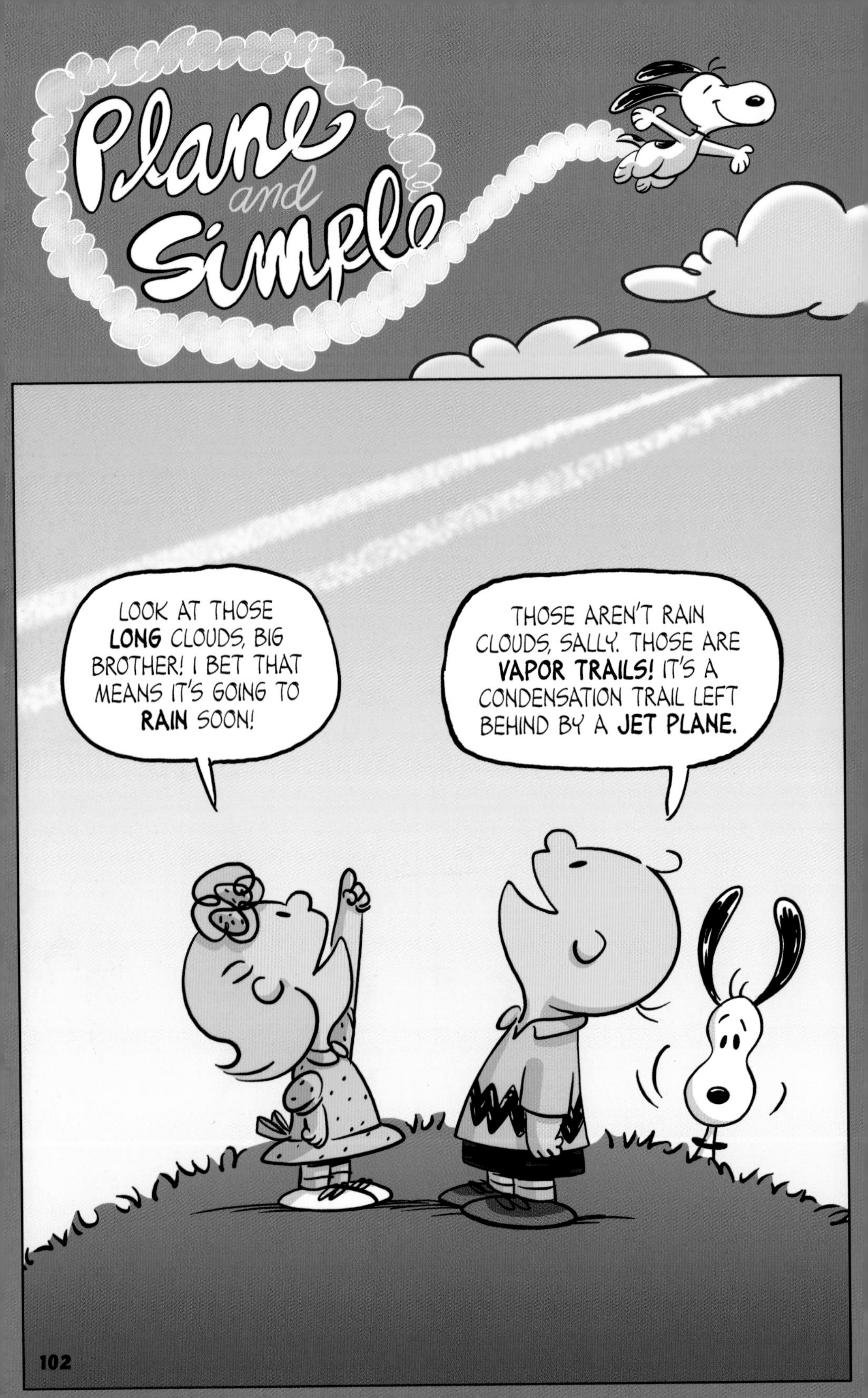
Plane and Simple
LOOK AT THOSE LONG CLOUDS, BIG BROTHER! I BET THAT MEANS IT'S GOING TO RAIN SOON!
THOSE AREN'T RAIN CLOUDS, SALLY. THOSE ARE VAPOR TRAILS! IT'S A CONDENSATION TRAIL LEFT BEHIND BY A JET PLANE.

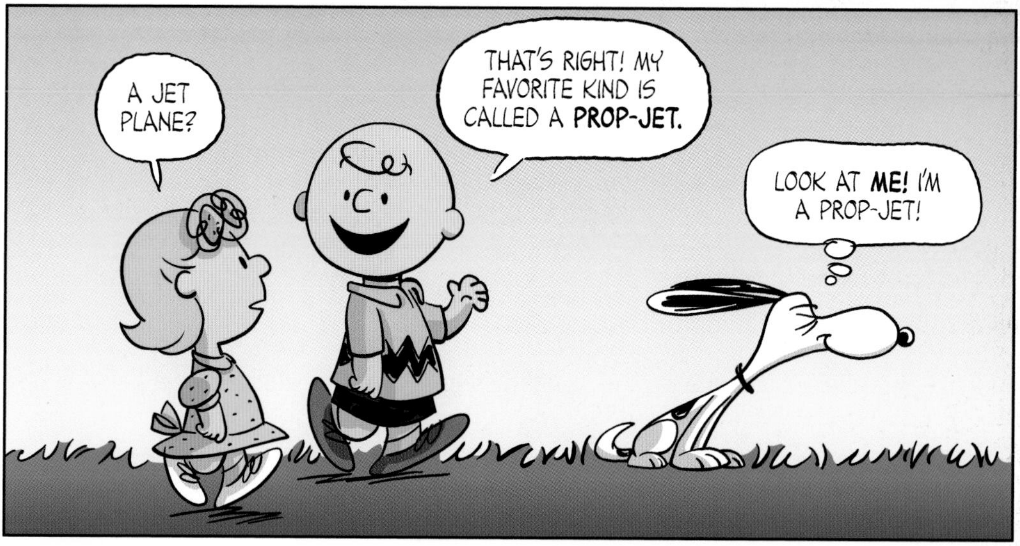
A JET PLANE?
THAT'S RIGHT! MY FAVORITE KIND IS CALLED A **PROP-JET.**
LOOK AT **ME!** I'M A PROP-JET!

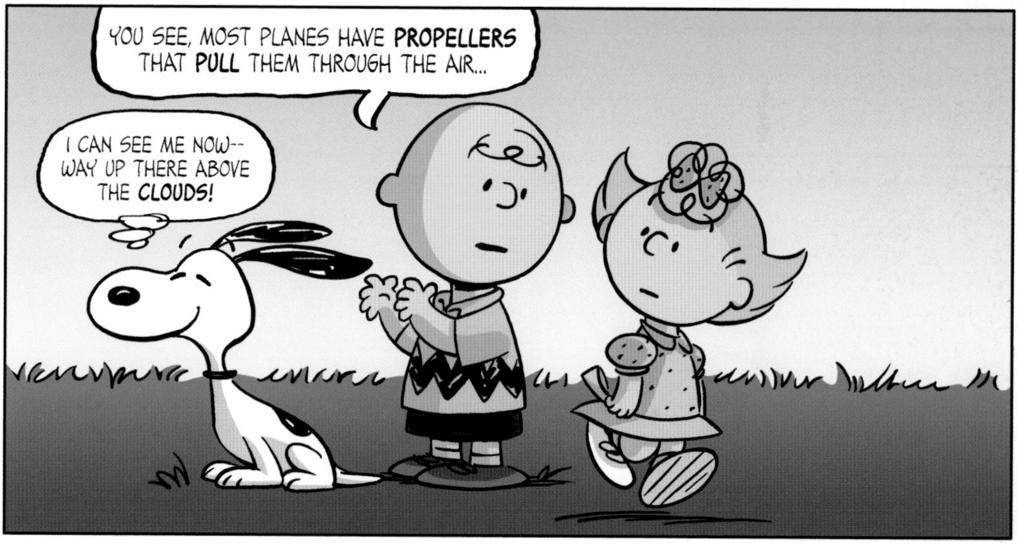
YOU SEE, MOST PLANES HAVE **PROPELLERS** THAT **PULL** THEM THROUGH THE AIR...
I CAN SEE ME NOW-- WAY UP THERE ABOVE THE **CLOUDS!**

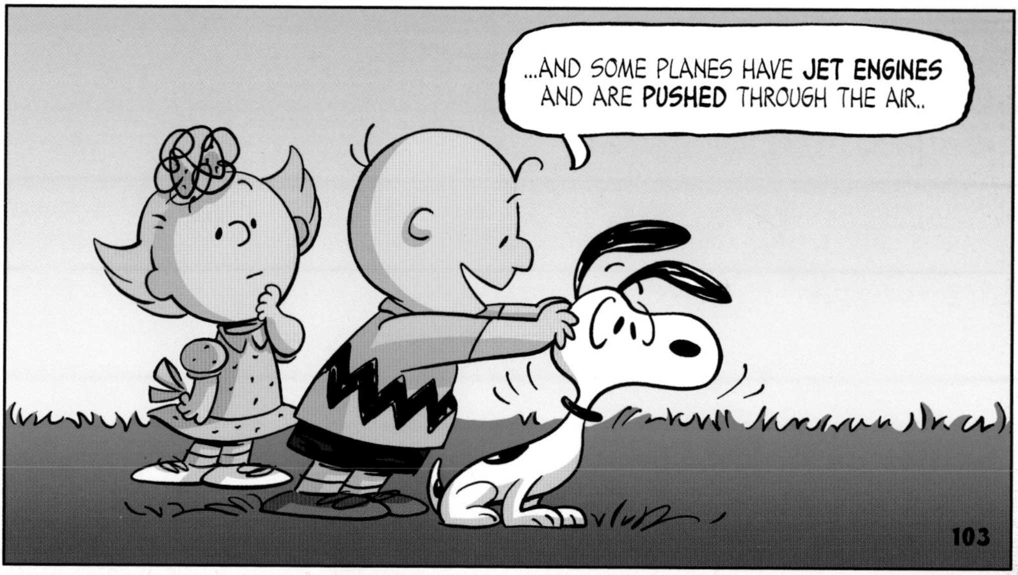
...AND SOME PLANES HAVE **JET ENGINES** AND ARE **PUSHED** THROUGH THE AIR..

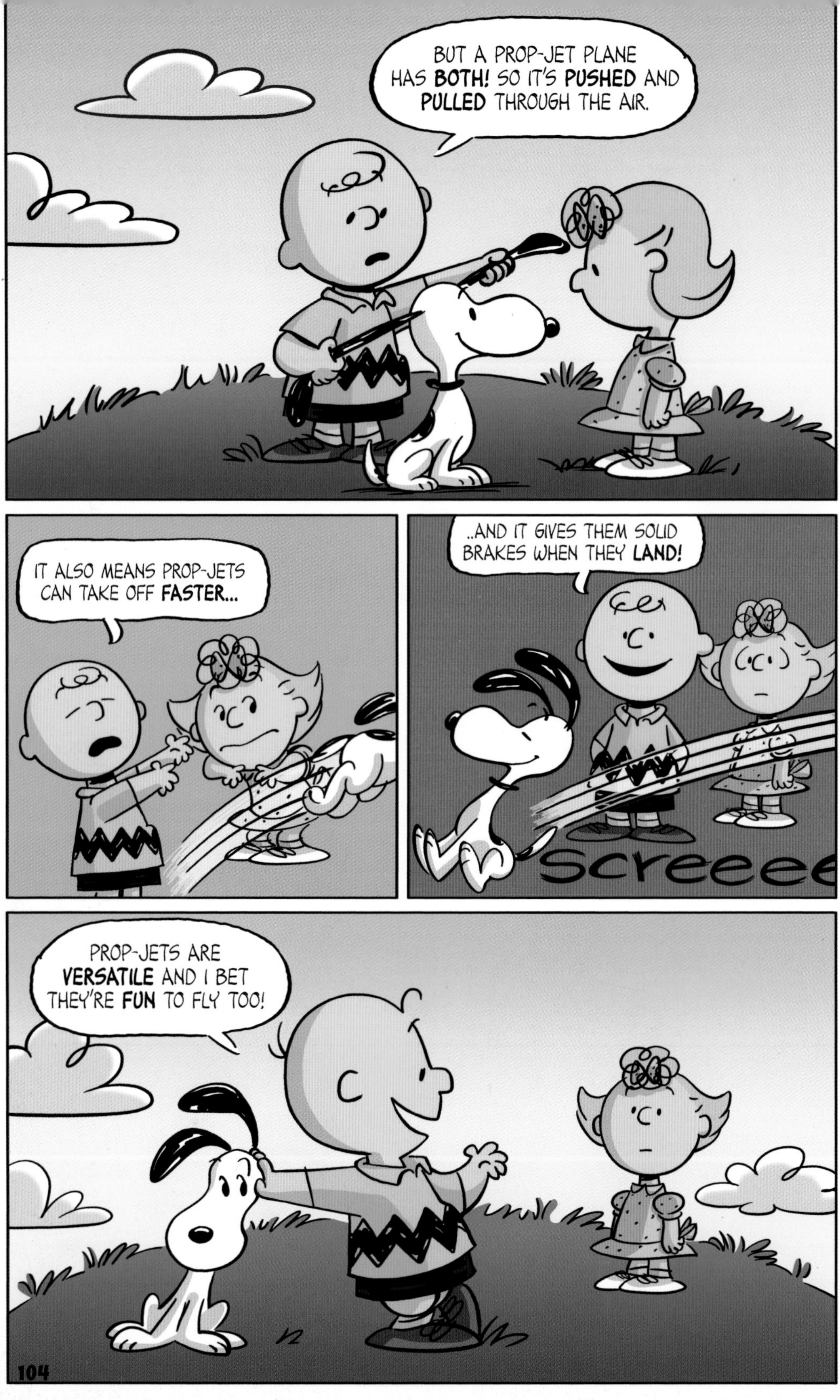
BUT A PROP-JET PLANE HAS BOTH! SO IT'S PUSHED AND PULLED THROUGH THE AIR.
IT ALSO MEANS PROP-JETS CAN TAKE OFF FASTER...
..AND IT GIVES THEM SOLID BRAKES WHEN THEY LAND!
SCREEEE
PROP-JETS ARE VERSATILE AND I BET THEY'RE FUN TO FLY TOO!

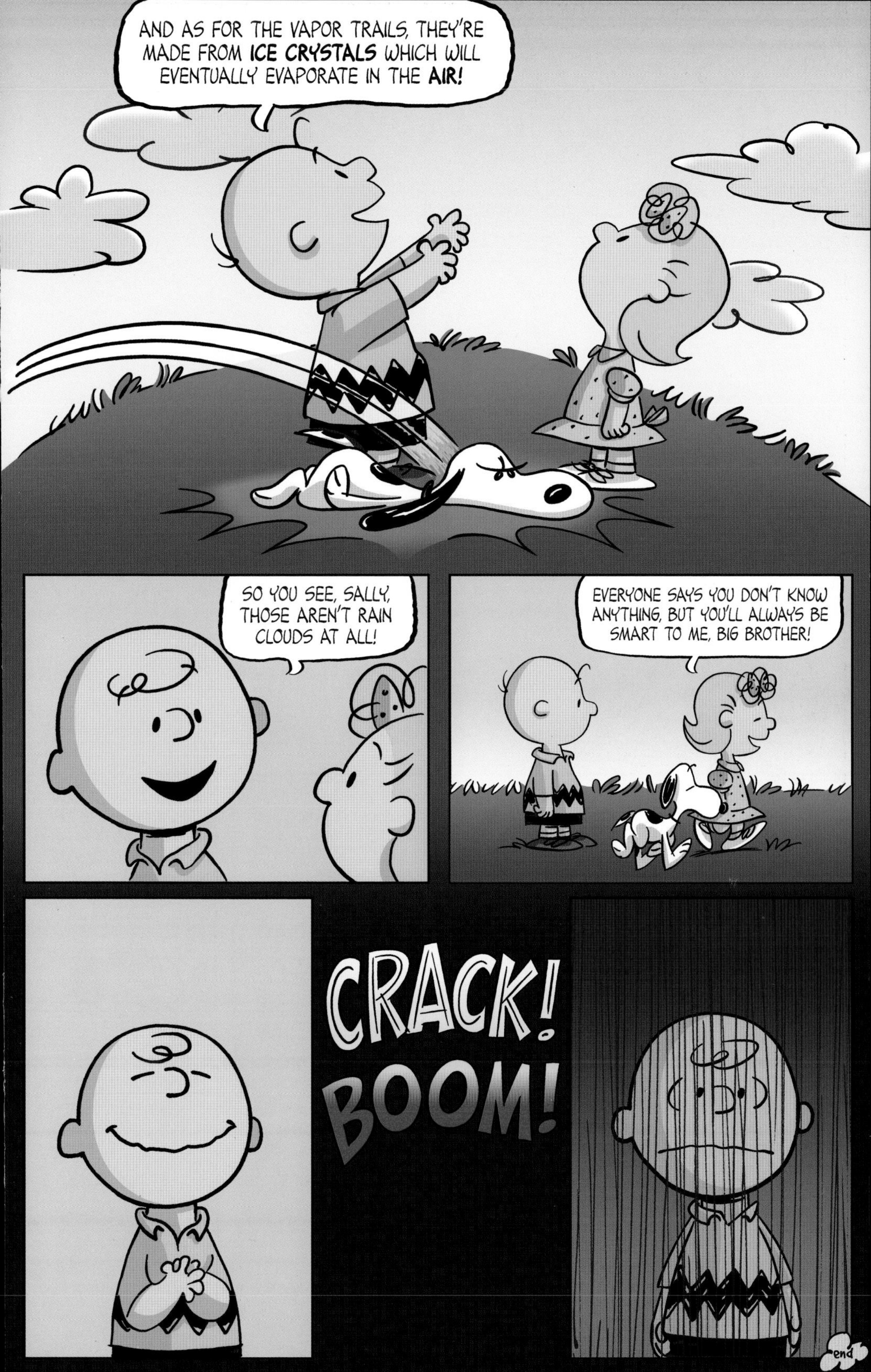
AND AS FOR THE VAPOR TRAILS, THEY'RE MADE FROM **ICE CRYSTALS** WHICH WILL EVENTUALLY EVAPORATE IN THE **AIR!**
SO YOU SEE, SALLY, THOSE AREN'T RAIN CLOUDS AT ALL!
EVERYONE SAYS YOU DON'T KNOW ANYTHING, BUT YOU'LL ALWAYS BE SMART TO ME, BIG BROTHER!
CRACK!
BOOM!
end

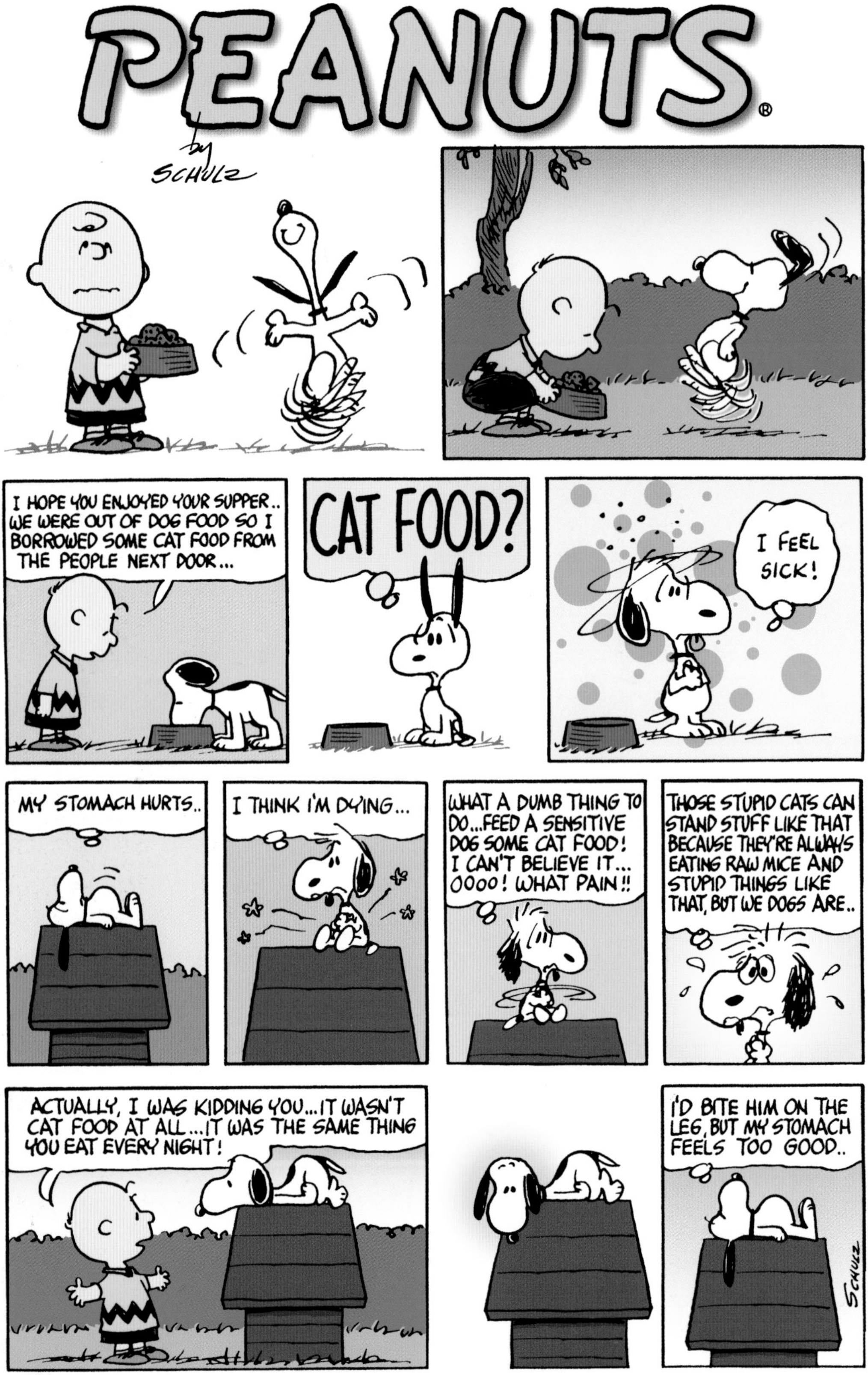
PEANUTS®
by SCHULZ
I HOPE YOU ENJOYED YOUR SUPPER.. WE WERE OUT OF DOG FOOD SO I BORROWED SOME CAT FOOD FROM THE PEOPLE NEXT DOOR...
CAT FOOD?
I FEEL SICK!
MY STOMACH HURTS..
I THINK I'M DYING...
WHAT A DUMB THING TO DO...FEED A SENSITIVE DOG SOME CAT FOOD! I CAN'T BELIEVE IT... OOOO! WHAT PAIN!!
THOSE STUPID CATS CAN STAND STUFF LIKE THAT BECAUSE THEY'RE ALWAYS EATING RAW MICE AND STUPID THINGS LIKE THAT, BUT WE DOGS ARE..
ACTUALLY, I WAS KIDDING YOU...IT WASN'T CAT FOOD AT ALL...IT WAS THE SAME THING YOU EAT EVERY NIGHT!
I'D BITE HIM ON THE LEG, BUT MY STOMACH FEELS TOO GOOD..
SCHULZ

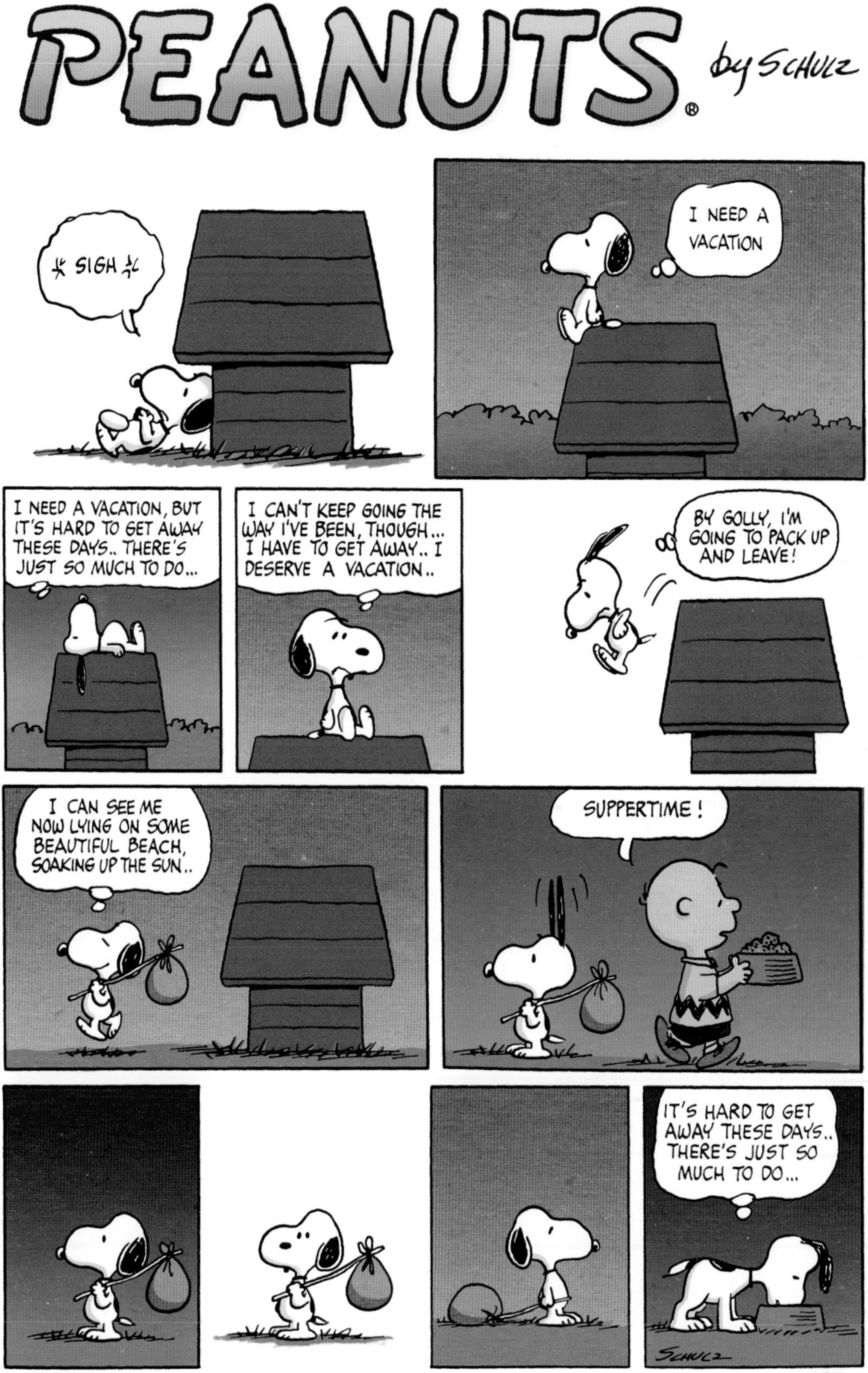
PEANUTS
by SCHULZ
SIGH
I NEED A VACATION
I NEED A VACATION, BUT IT'S HARD TO GET AWAY THESE DAYS.. THERE'S JUST SO MUCH TO DO...
I CAN'T KEEP GOING THE WAY I'VE BEEN, THOUGH... I HAVE TO GET AWAY.. I DESERVE A VACATION..
BY GOLLY, I'M GOING TO PACK UP AND LEAVE!
I CAN SEE ME NOW LYING ON SOME BEAUTIFUL BEACH, SOAKING UP THE SUN..
SUPPERTIME!
IT'S HARD TO GET AWAY THESE DAYS.. THERE'S JUST SO MUCH TO DO...
SCHULZ

# FOOD FOR FRAUGHT

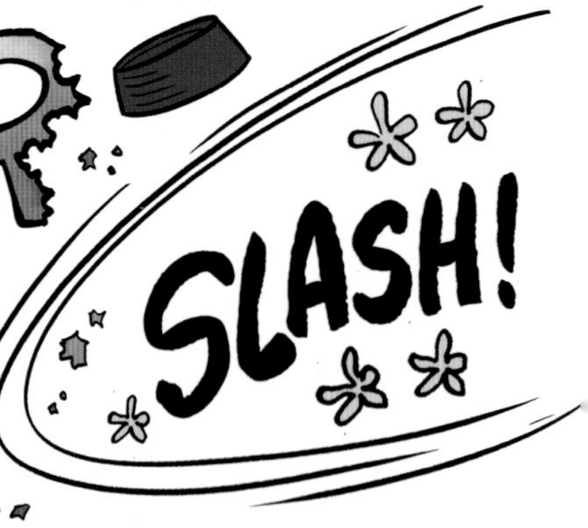
SLASH!

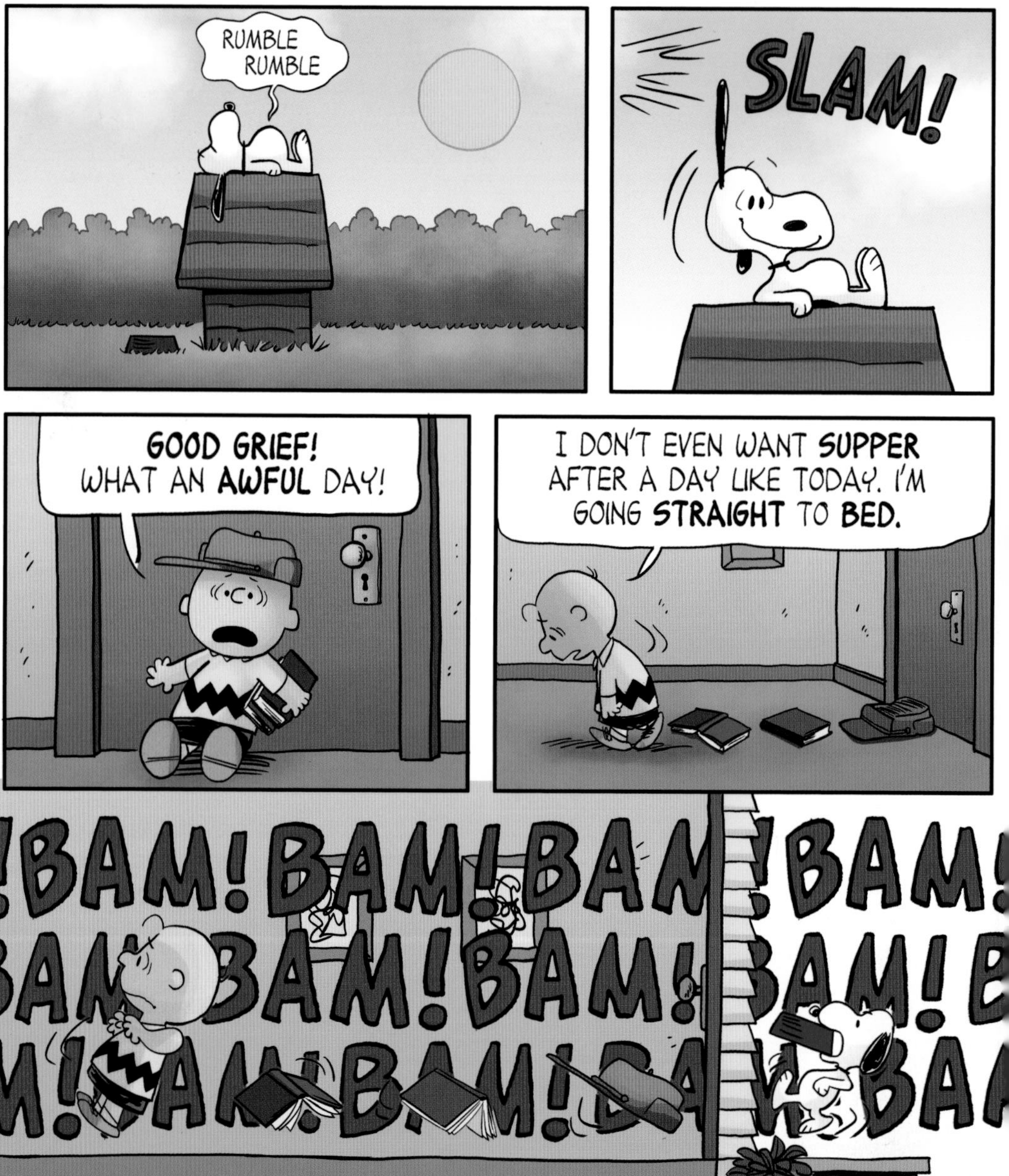
RUMBLE RUMBLE
SLAM!
GOOD GRIEF! WHAT AN AWFUL DAY!
I DON'T EVEN WANT SUPPER AFTER A DAY LIKE TODAY. I'M GOING STRAIGHT TO BED.
BAM! BAM! BAM! BAM!
BAM! BAM! BAM! BAM!
BAM! BAM! BAM!

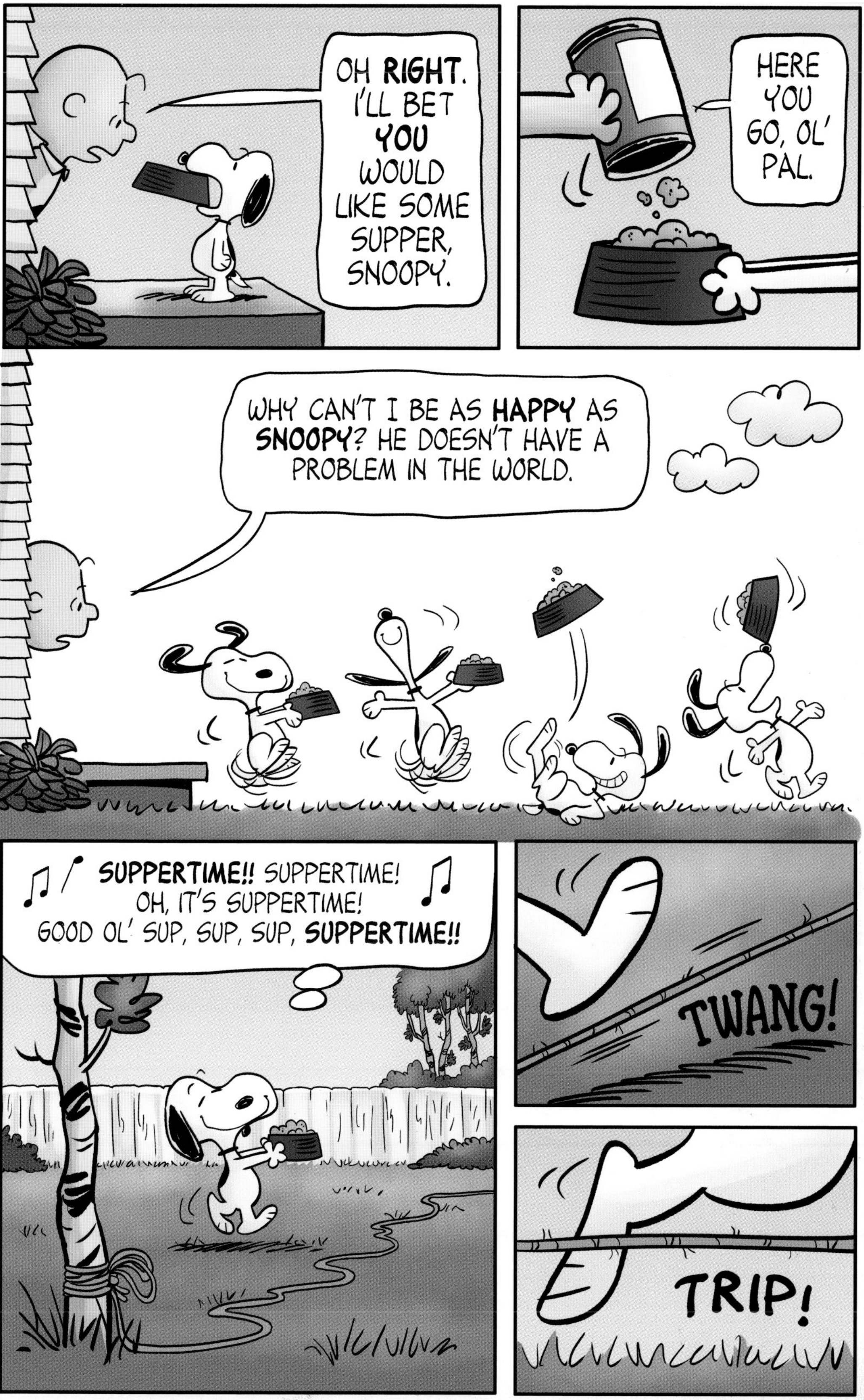
OH RIGHT. I'LL BET YOU WOULD LIKE SOME SUPPER, SNOOPY.
HERE YOU GO, OL' PAL.
WHY CAN'T I BE AS HAPPY AS SNOOPY? HE DOESN'T HAVE A PROBLEM IN THE WORLD.
♫♪ SUPPERTIME!! SUPPERTIME! OH, IT'S SUPPERTIME! GOOD OL' SUP, SUP, SUP, SUPPERTIME!! ♫
TWANG!
TRIP!

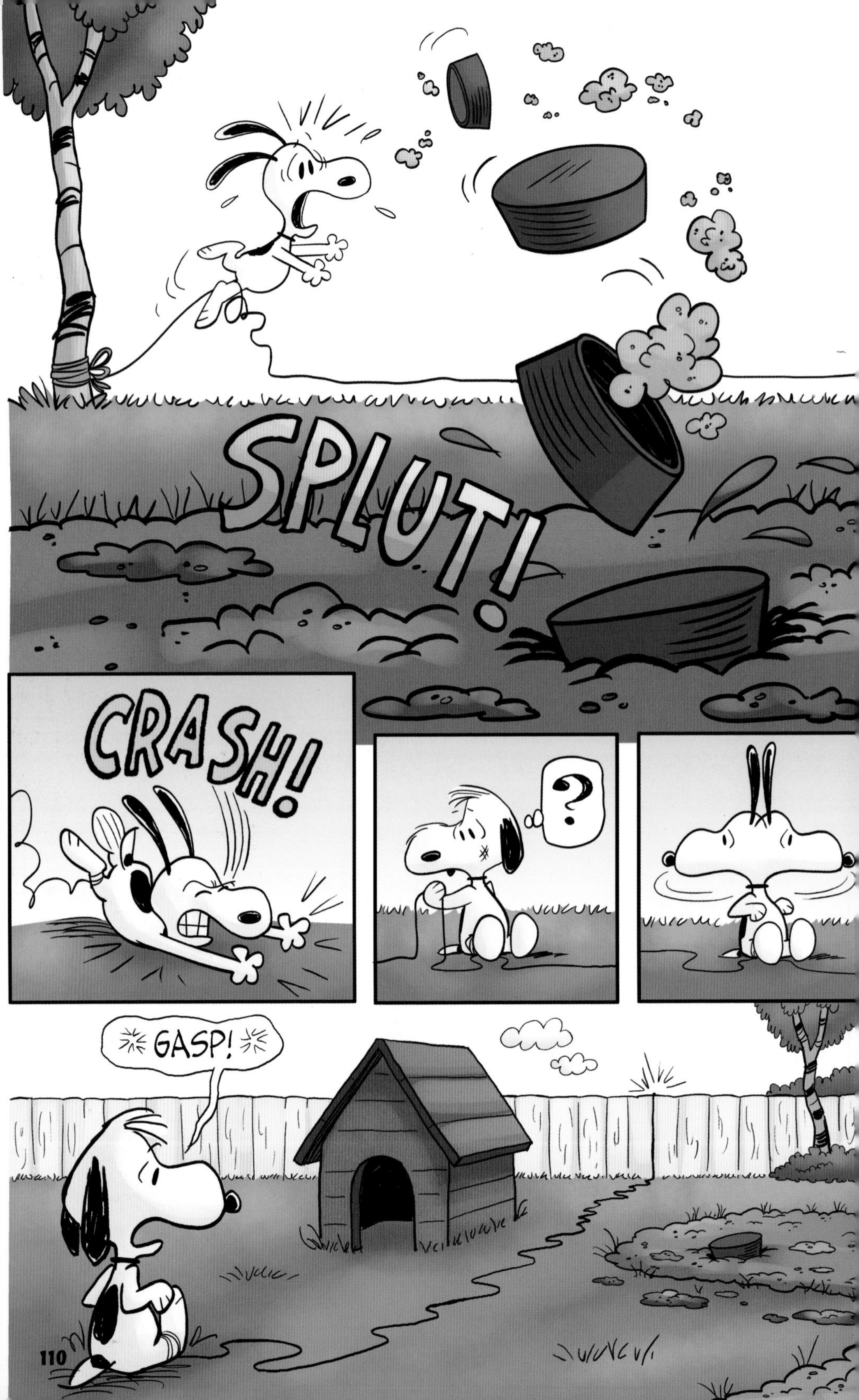
SPLUT!
CRASH!
?
GASP!

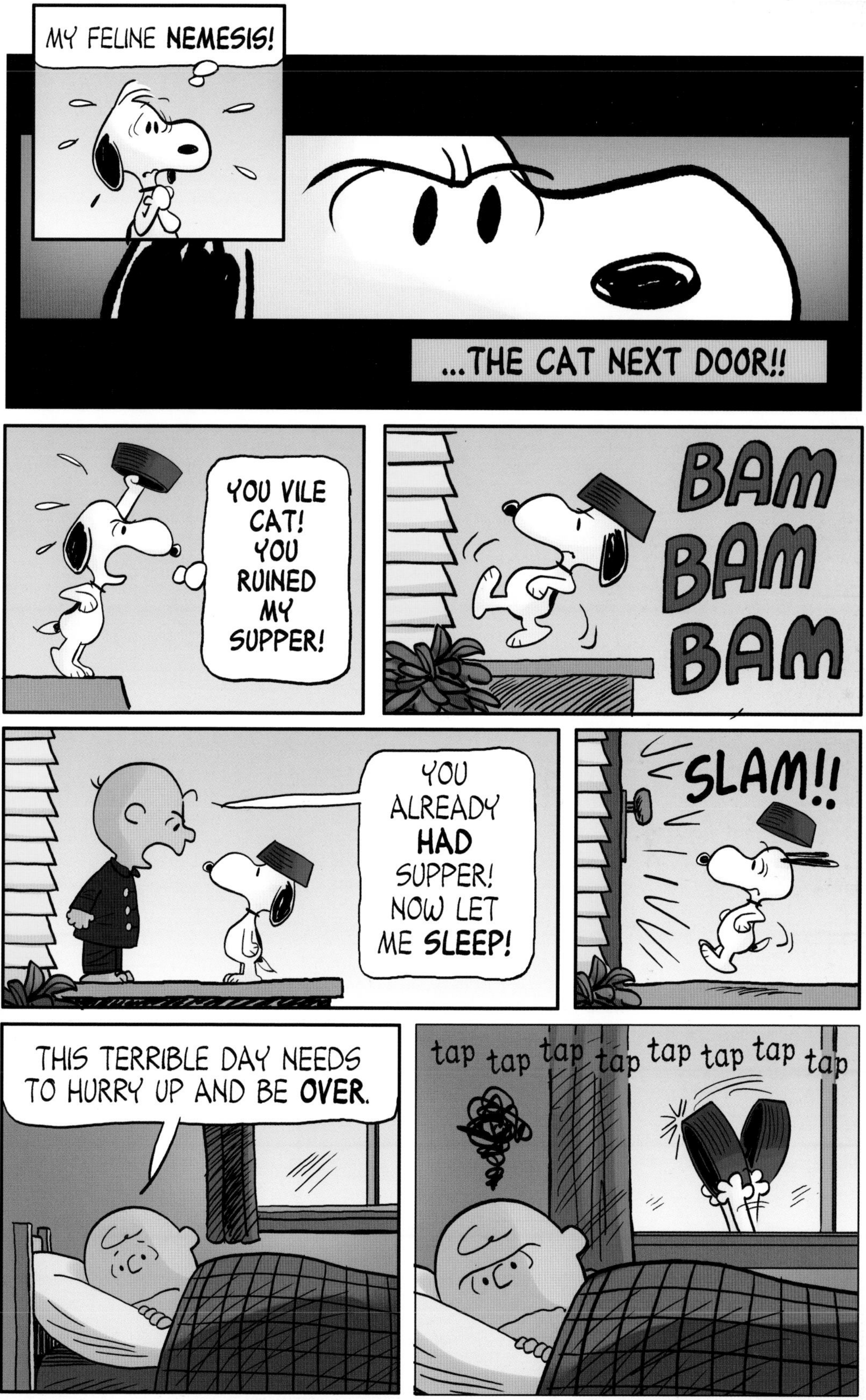

MY FELINE NEMESIS!
...THE CAT NEXT DOOR!!
YOU VILE CAT! YOU RUINED MY SUPPER!
BAM BAM BAM
YOU ALREADY HAD SUPPER! NOW LET ME SLEEP!
SLAM!!
THIS TERRIBLE DAY NEEDS TO HURRY UP AND BE OVER.
tap tap tap tap tap tap tap tap

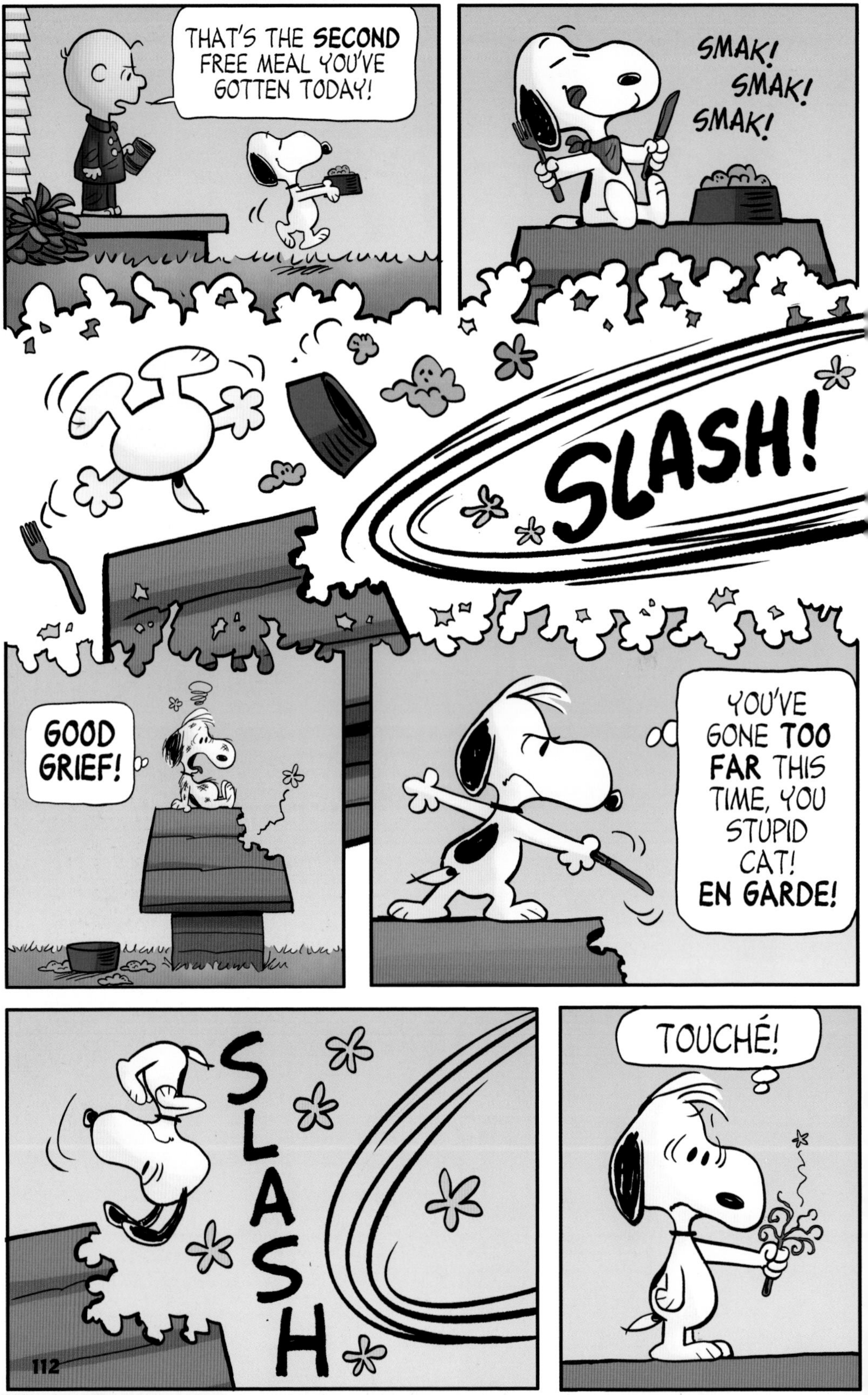
THAT'S THE SECOND FREE MEAL YOU'VE GOTTEN TODAY!
SMAK! SMAK! SMAK!
SLASH!
GOOD GRIEF!
YOU'VE GONE TOO FAR THIS TIME, YOU STUPID CAT! EN GARDE!
SLASH
TOUCHÉ!

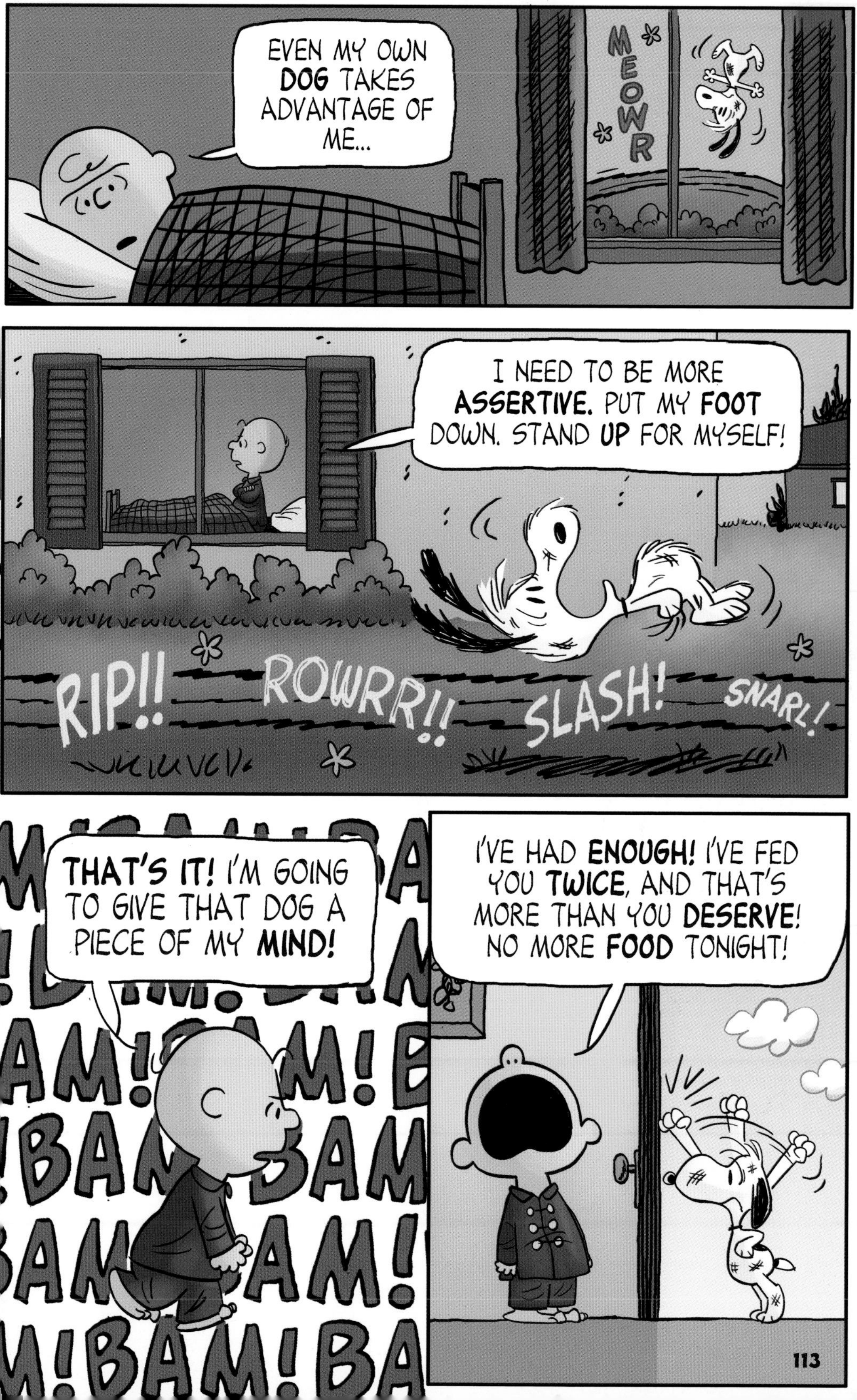
EVEN MY OWN DOG TAKES ADVANTAGE OF ME...
MEOWR
I NEED TO BE MORE ASSERTIVE. PUT MY FOOT DOWN. STAND UP FOR MYSELF!
RIP!!
ROWRR!!
SLASH!
SNARL!
THAT'S IT! I'M GOING TO GIVE THAT DOG A PIECE OF MY MIND!
BAM! BAM!
I'VE HAD ENOUGH! I'VE FED YOU TWICE, AND THAT'S MORE THAN YOU DESERVE! NO MORE FOOD TONIGHT!

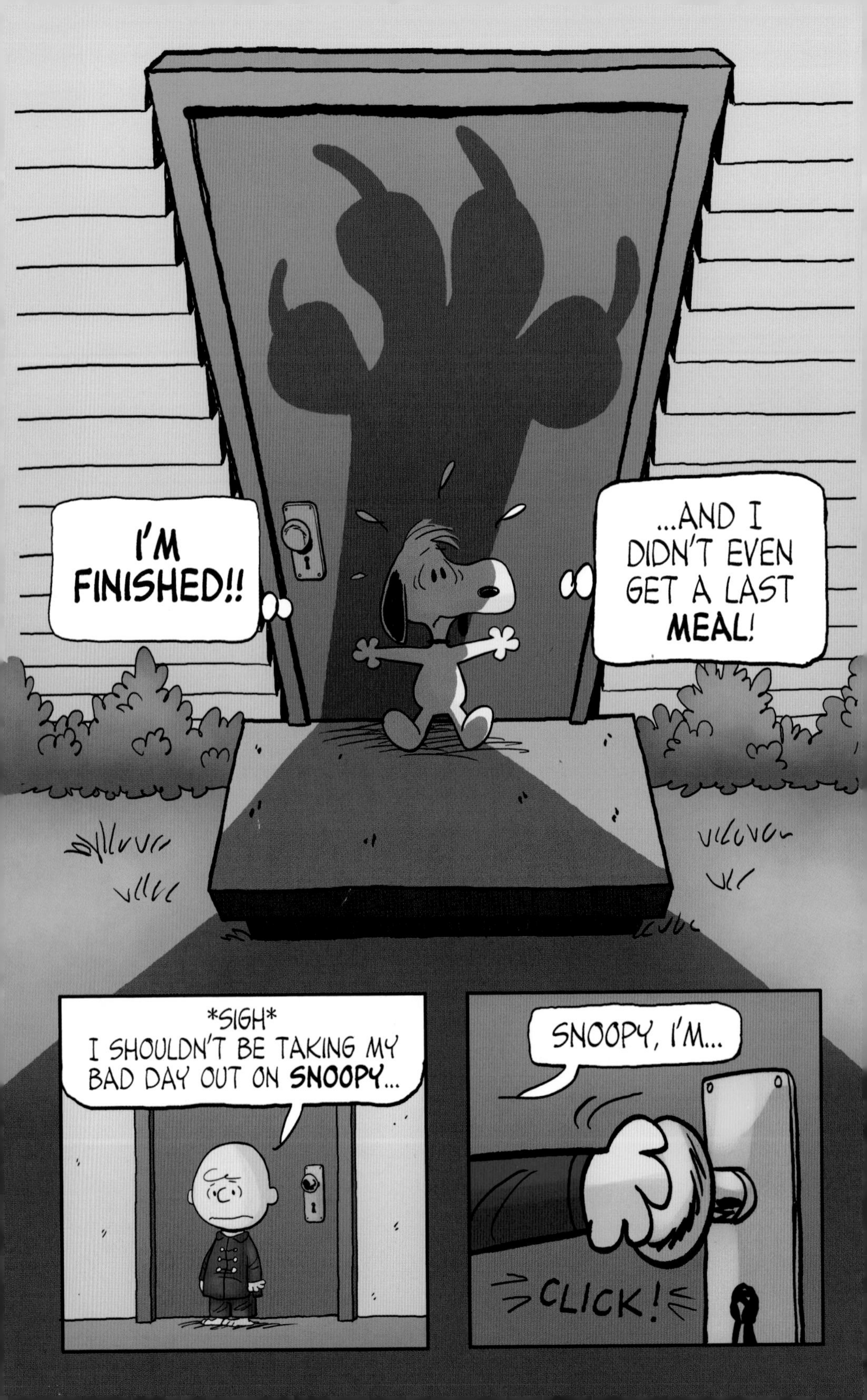
I'M FINISHED!!
...AND I DIDN'T EVEN GET A LAST MEAL!
*SIGH* I SHOULDN'T BE TAKING MY BAD DAY OUT ON SNOOPY...
SNOOPY, I'M...
CLICK!

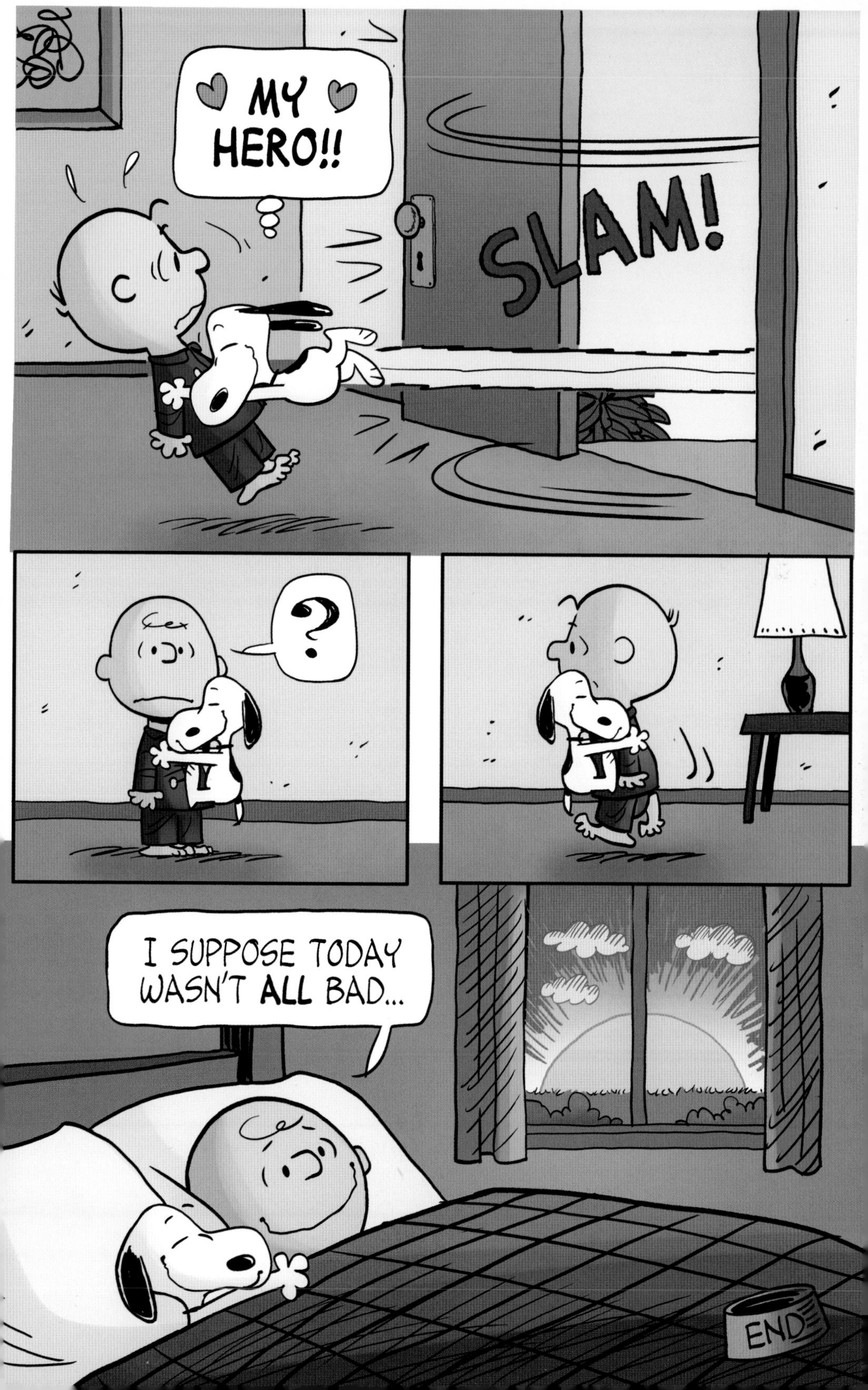
MY HERO!!
SLAM!
?
I SUPPOSE TODAY WASN'T ALL BAD...
END

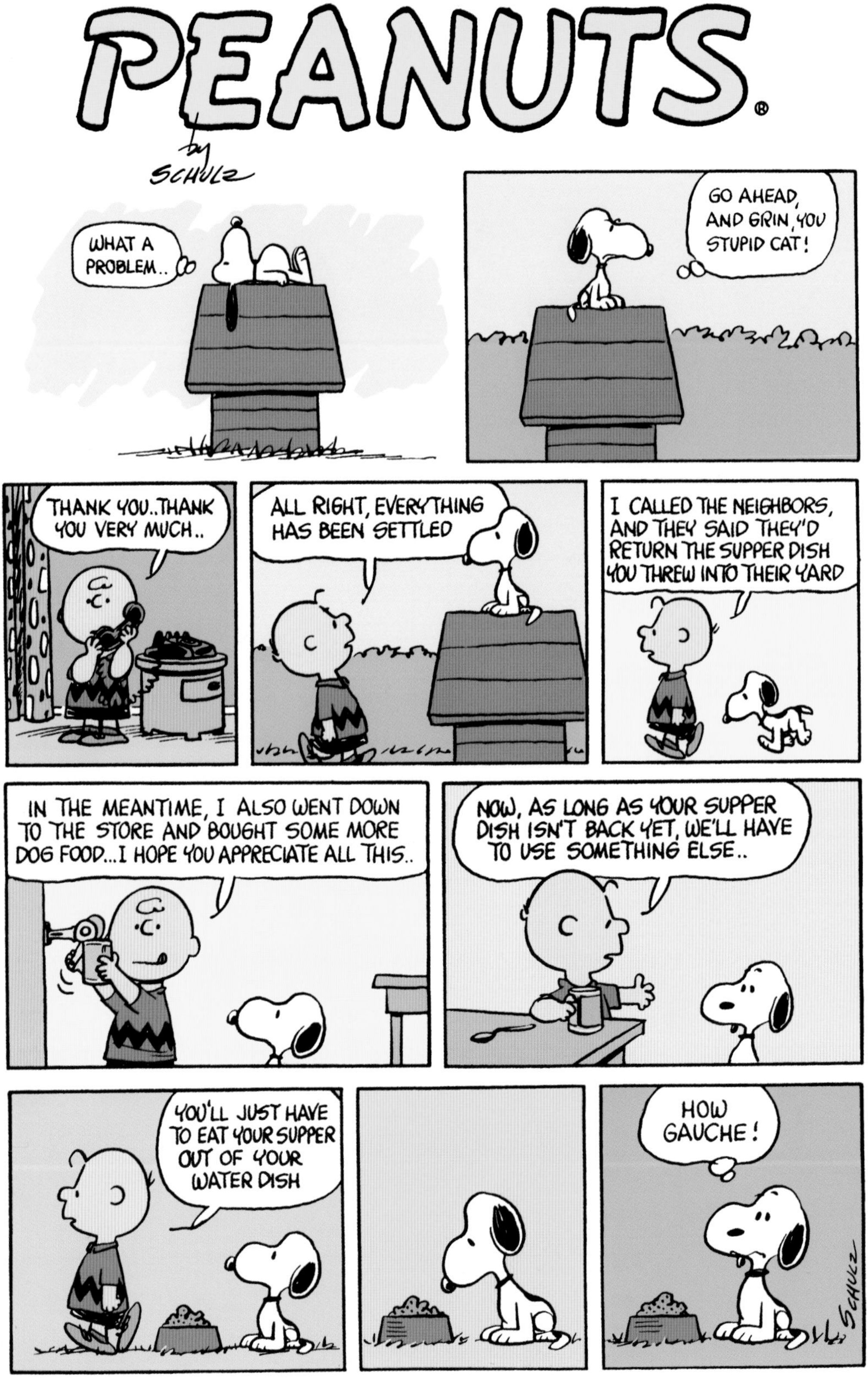
PEANUTS®
by SCHULZ
WHAT A PROBLEM..
GO AHEAD, AND GRIN, YOU STUPID CAT!
THANK YOU..THANK YOU VERY MUCH..
ALL RIGHT, EVERYTHING HAS BEEN SETTLED
I CALLED THE NEIGHBORS, AND THEY SAID THEY'D RETURN THE SUPPER DISH YOU THREW INTO THEIR YARD
IN THE MEANTIME, I ALSO WENT DOWN TO THE STORE AND BOUGHT SOME MORE DOG FOOD...I HOPE YOU APPRECIATE ALL THIS..
NOW, AS LONG AS YOUR SUPPER DISH ISN'T BACK YET, WE'LL HAVE TO USE SOMETHING ELSE..
YOU'LL JUST HAVE TO EAT YOUR SUPPER OUT OF YOUR WATER DISH
HOW GAUCHE!
SCHULZ

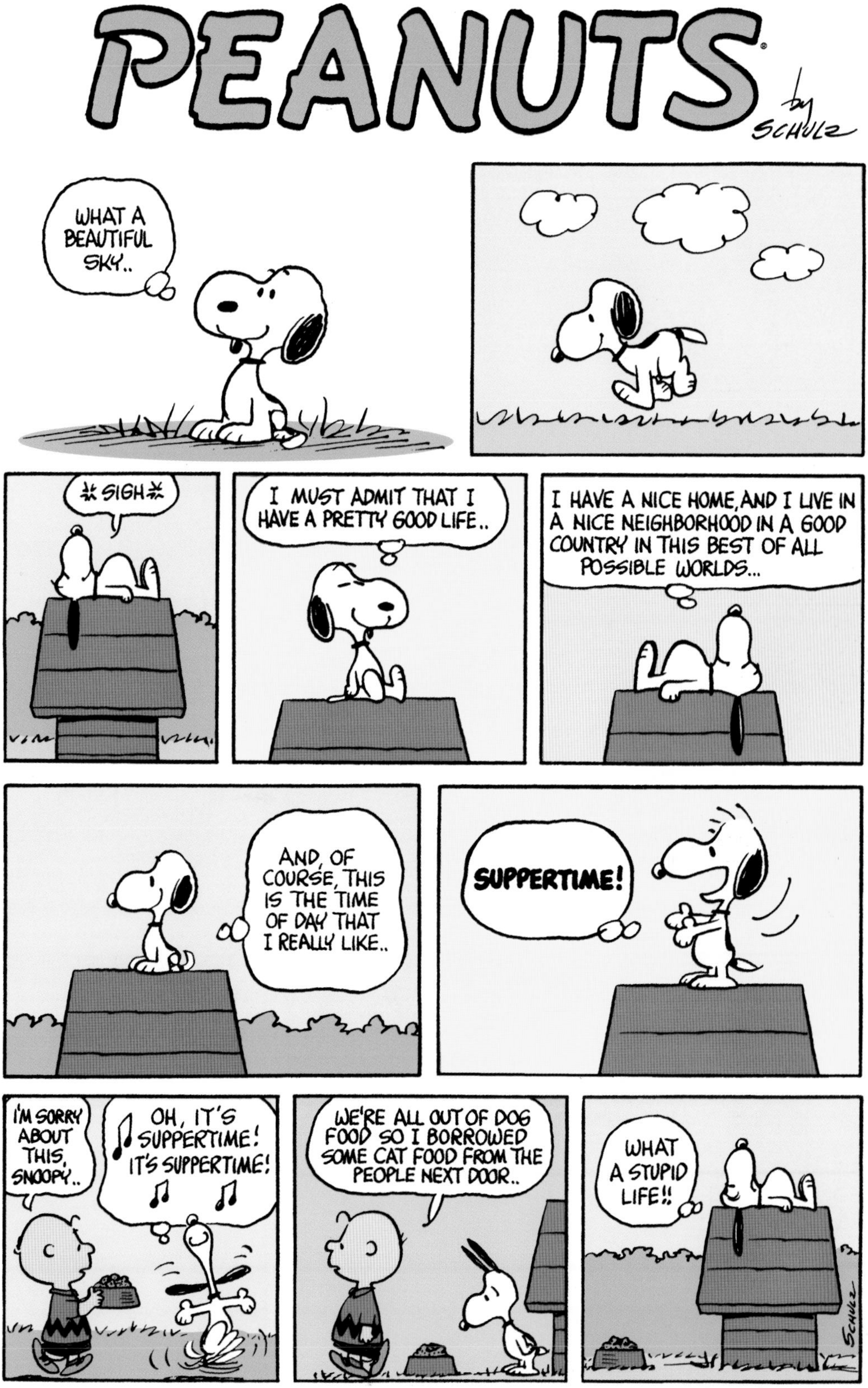
PEANUTS
by SCHULZ
WHAT A BEAUTIFUL SKY..
*SIGH*
I MUST ADMIT THAT I HAVE A PRETTY GOOD LIFE..
I HAVE A NICE HOME, AND I LIVE IN A NICE NEIGHBORHOOD IN A GOOD COUNTRY IN THIS BEST OF ALL POSSIBLE WORLDS...
AND, OF COURSE, THIS IS THE TIME OF DAY THAT I REALLY LIKE..
SUPPERTIME!
I'M SORRY ABOUT THIS, SNOOPY..
OH, IT'S SUPPERTIME! IT'S SUPPERTIME!
WE'RE ALL OUT OF DOG FOOD SO I BORROWED SOME CAT FOOD FROM THE PEOPLE NEXT DOOR..
WHAT A STUPID LIFE!!
SCHULZ

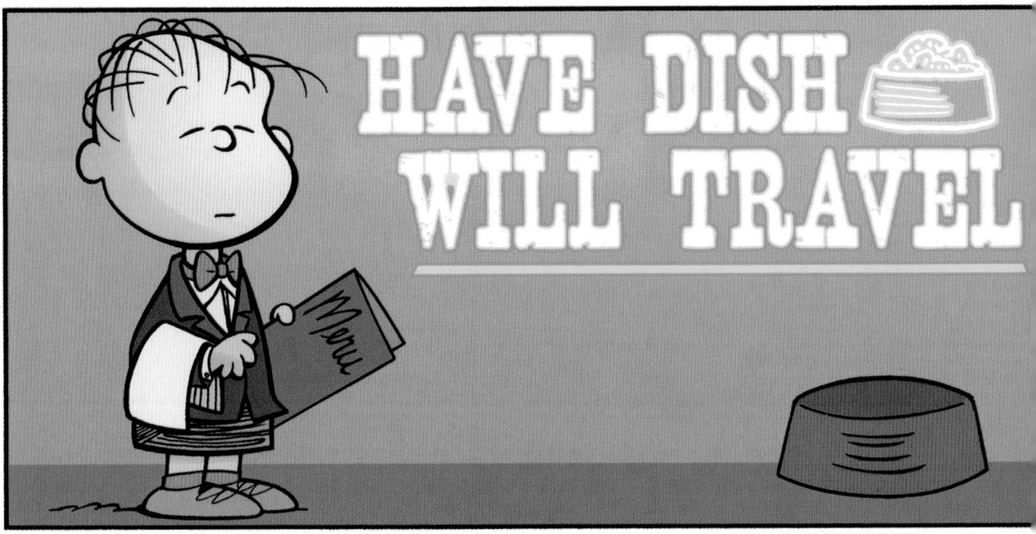
HAVE DISH
WILL TRAVEL
Menu

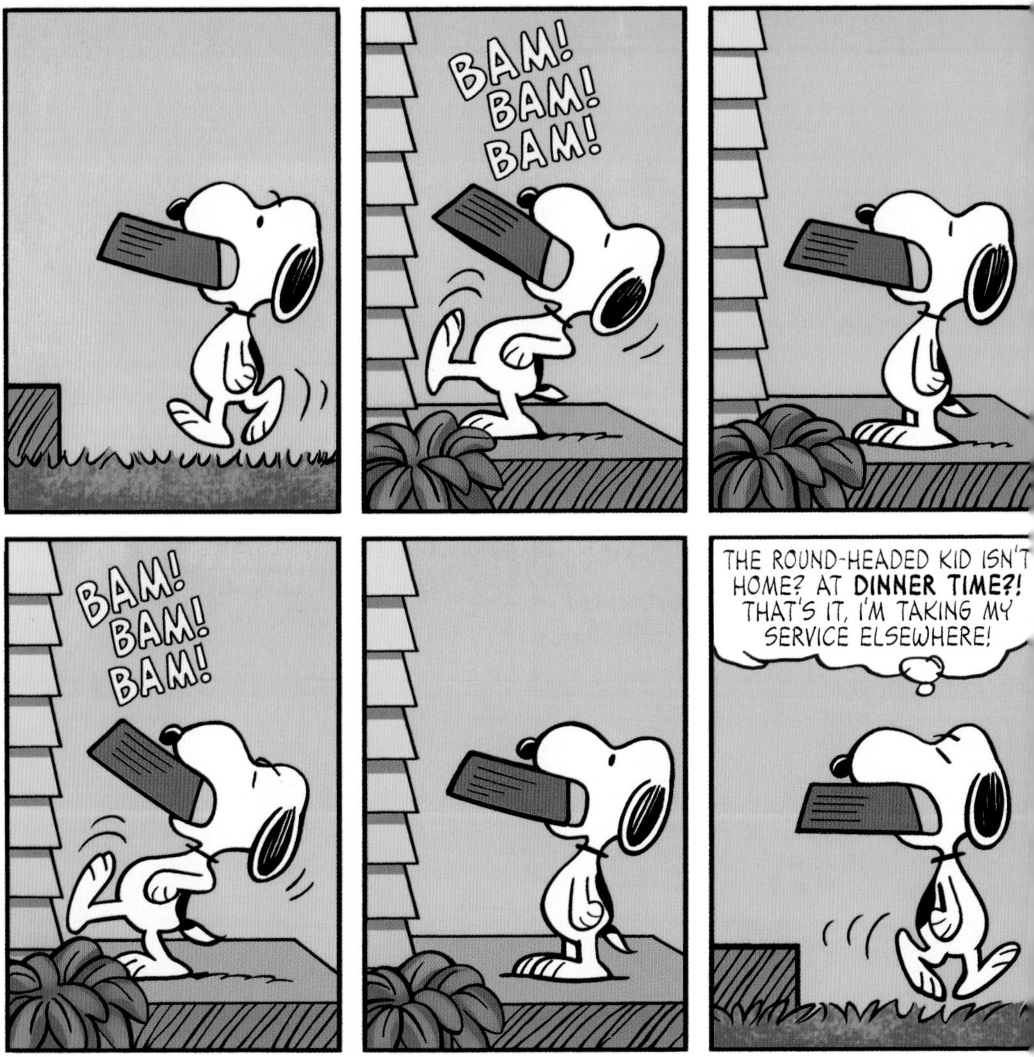
BAM! BAM! BAM!
BAM! BAM! BAM!
THE ROUND-HEADED KID ISN'T HOME? AT **DINNER TIME?!** THAT'S IT, I'M TAKING MY SERVICE ELSEWHERE!

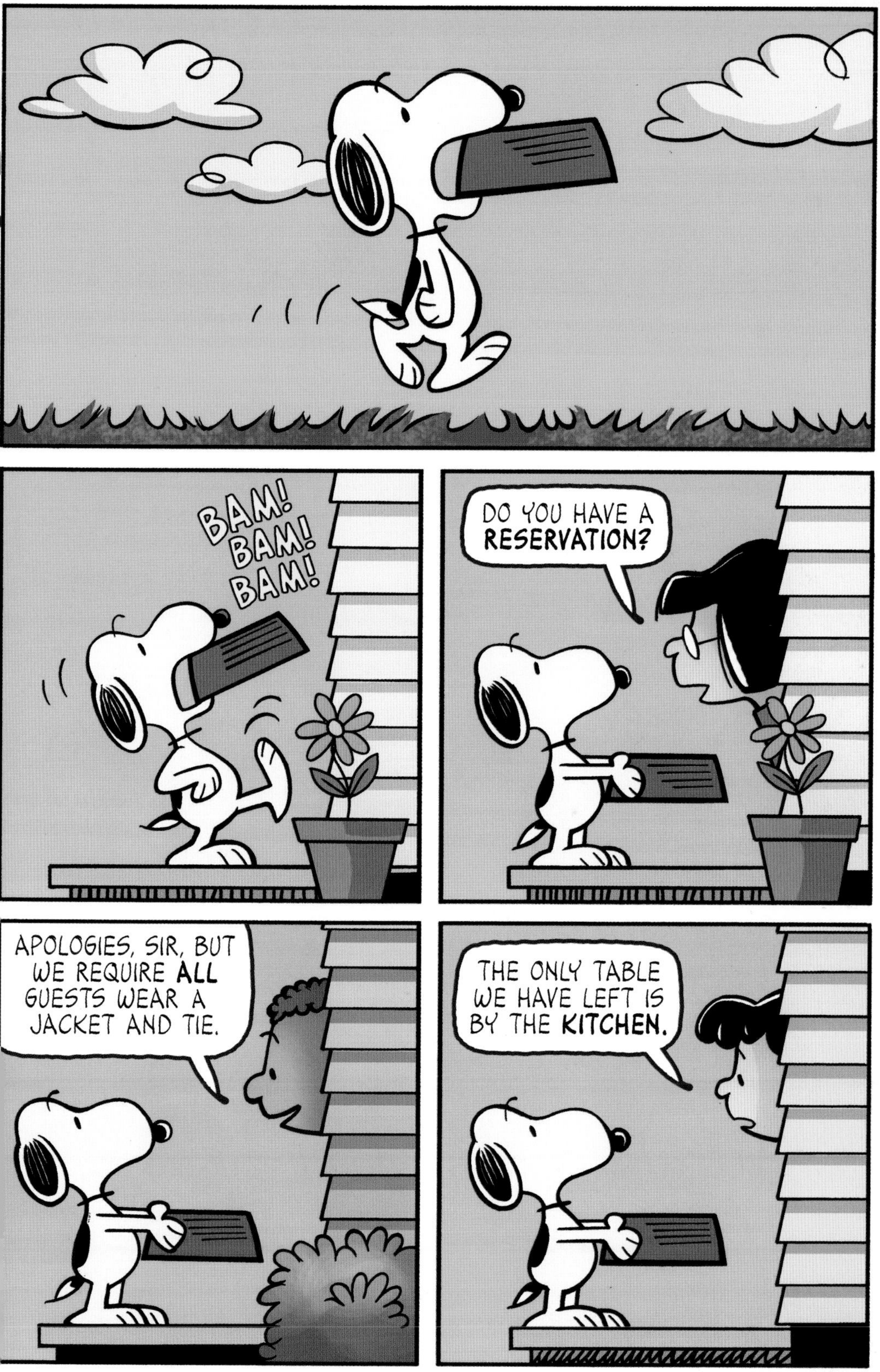
BAM!
BAM!
BAM!
DO YOU HAVE A RESERVATION?
APOLOGIES, SIR, BUT WE REQUIRE ALL GUESTS WEAR A JACKET AND TIE.
THE ONLY TABLE WE HAVE LEFT IS BY THE KITCHEN.

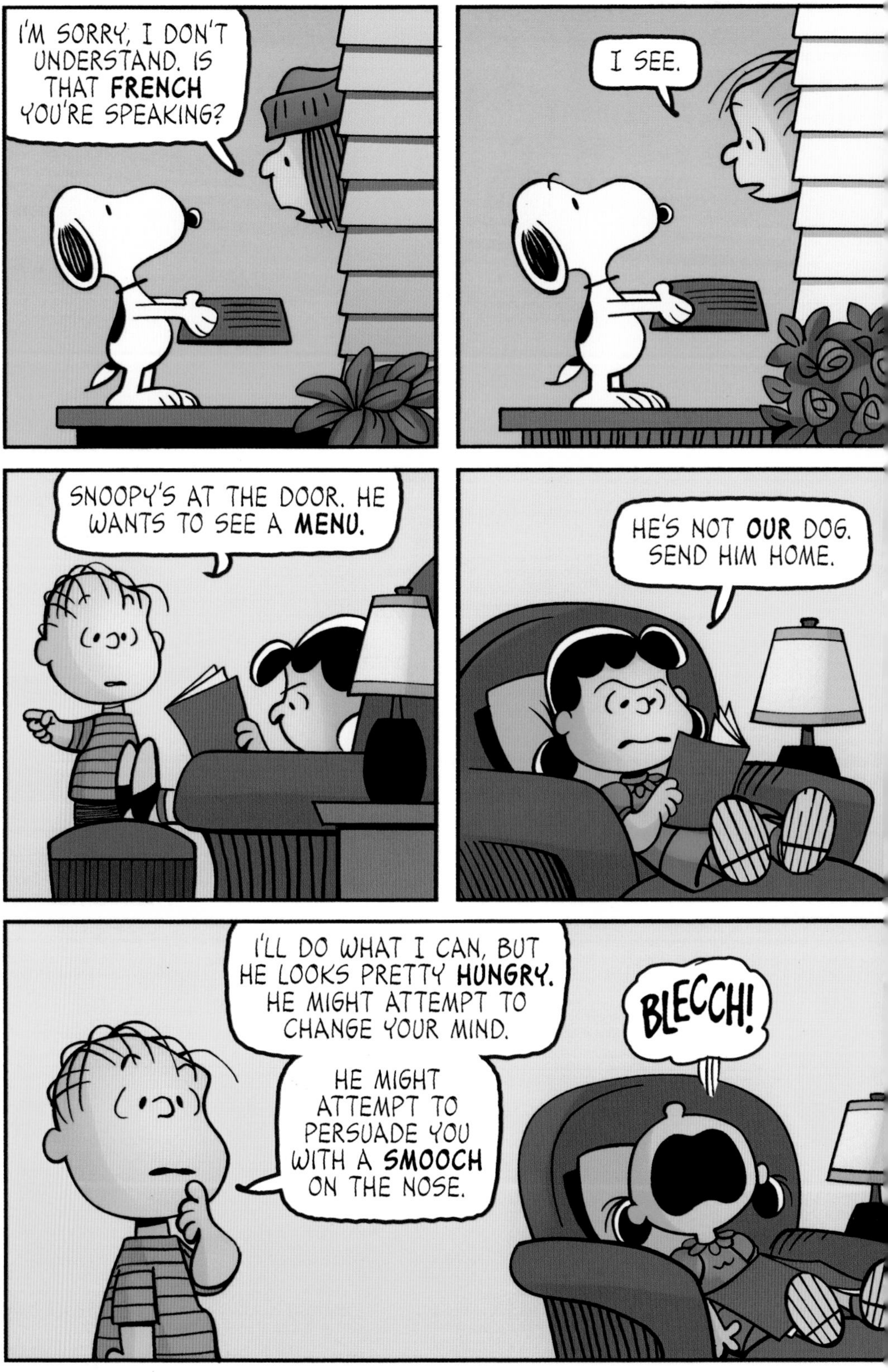
I'M SORRY, I DON'T UNDERSTAND. IS THAT **FRENCH** YOU'RE SPEAKING?
I SEE.
SNOOPY'S AT THE DOOR. HE WANTS TO SEE A **MENU.**
HE'S NOT **OUR** DOG. SEND HIM HOME.
I'LL DO WHAT I CAN, BUT HE LOOKS PRETTY **HUNGRY.** HE MIGHT ATTEMPT TO CHANGE YOUR MIND.
HE MIGHT ATTEMPT TO PERSUADE YOU WITH A **SMOOCH** ON THE NOSE.
BLECCH!

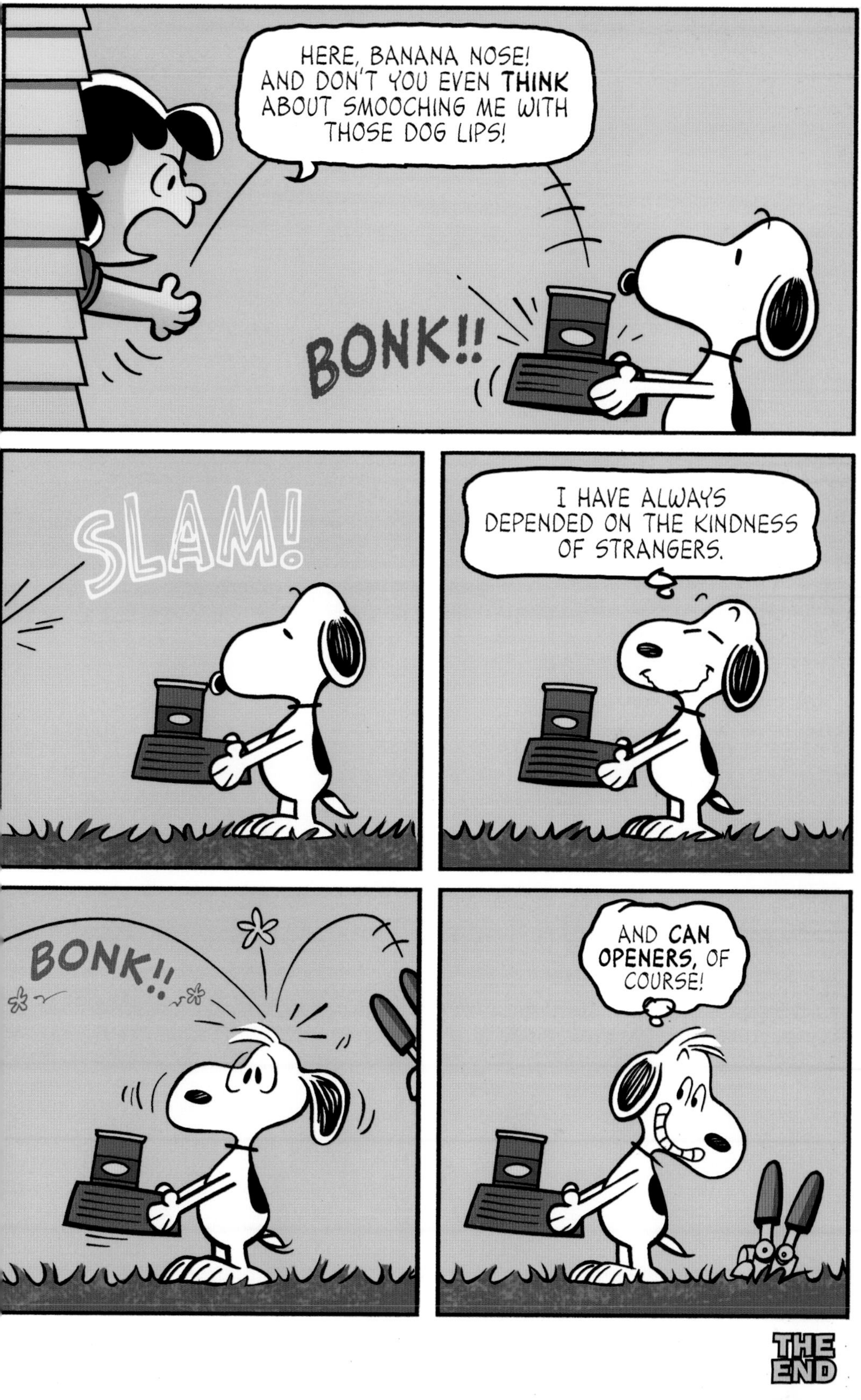
HERE, BANANA NOSE! AND DON'T YOU EVEN **THINK** ABOUT SMOOCHING ME WITH THOSE DOG LIPS!
BONK!!
SLAM!
I HAVE ALWAYS DEPENDED ON THE KINDNESS OF STRANGERS.
BONK!!
AND **CAN OPENERS,** OF COURSE!
THE END

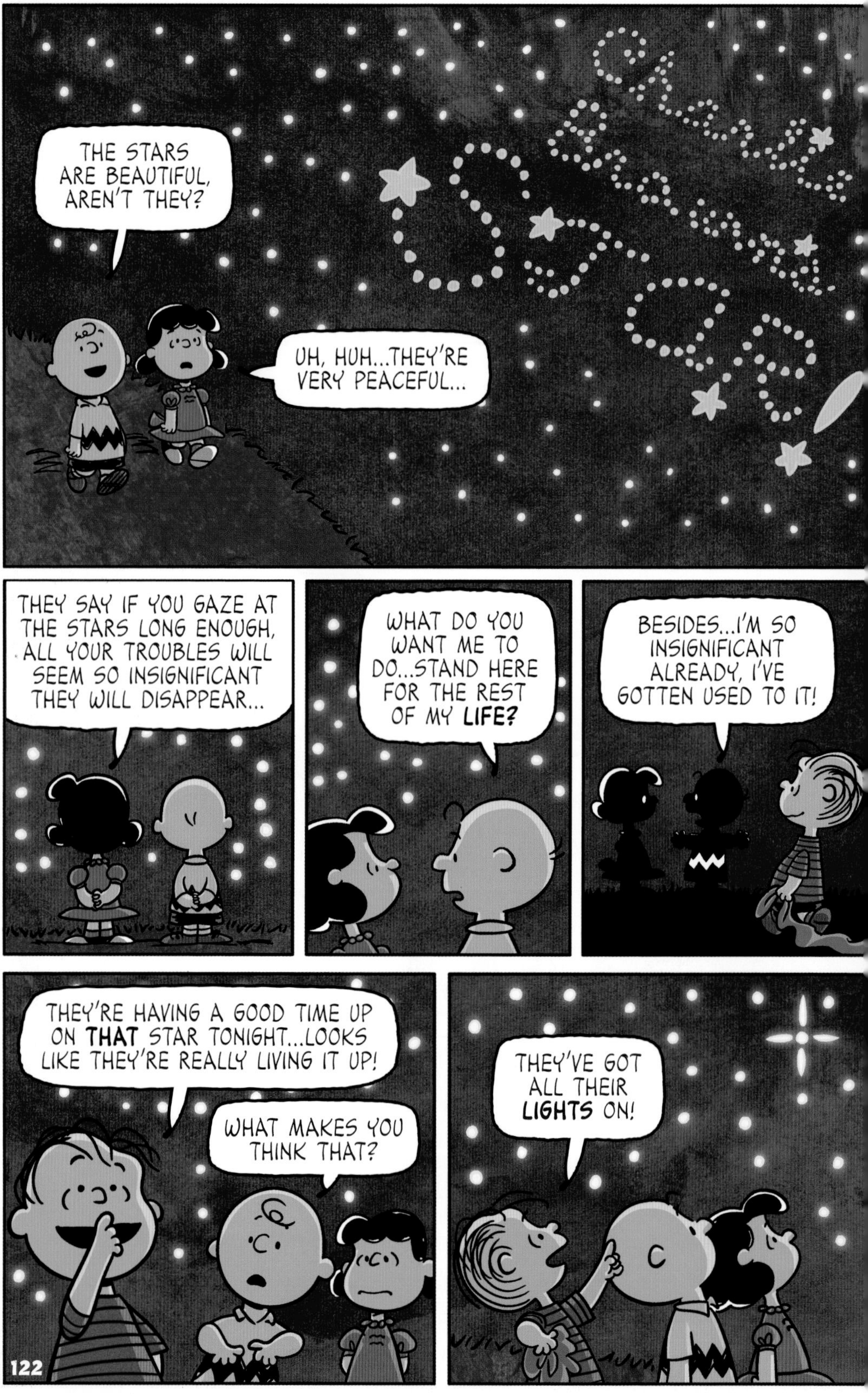
THE STARS ARE BEAUTIFUL, AREN'T THEY?
UH, HUH...THEY'RE VERY PEACEFUL...
THEY SAY IF YOU GAZE AT THE STARS LONG ENOUGH, ALL YOUR TROUBLES WILL SEEM SO INSIGNIFICANT THEY WILL DISAPPEAR...
WHAT DO YOU WANT ME TO DO...STAND HERE FOR THE REST OF MY **LIFE?**
BESIDES...I'M SO INSIGNIFICANT ALREADY, I'VE GOTTEN USED TO IT!
THEY'RE HAVING A GOOD TIME UP ON **THAT** STAR TONIGHT...LOOKS LIKE THEY'RE REALLY LIVING IT UP!
WHAT MAKES YOU THINK THAT?
THEY'VE GOT ALL THEIR **LIGHTS** ON!

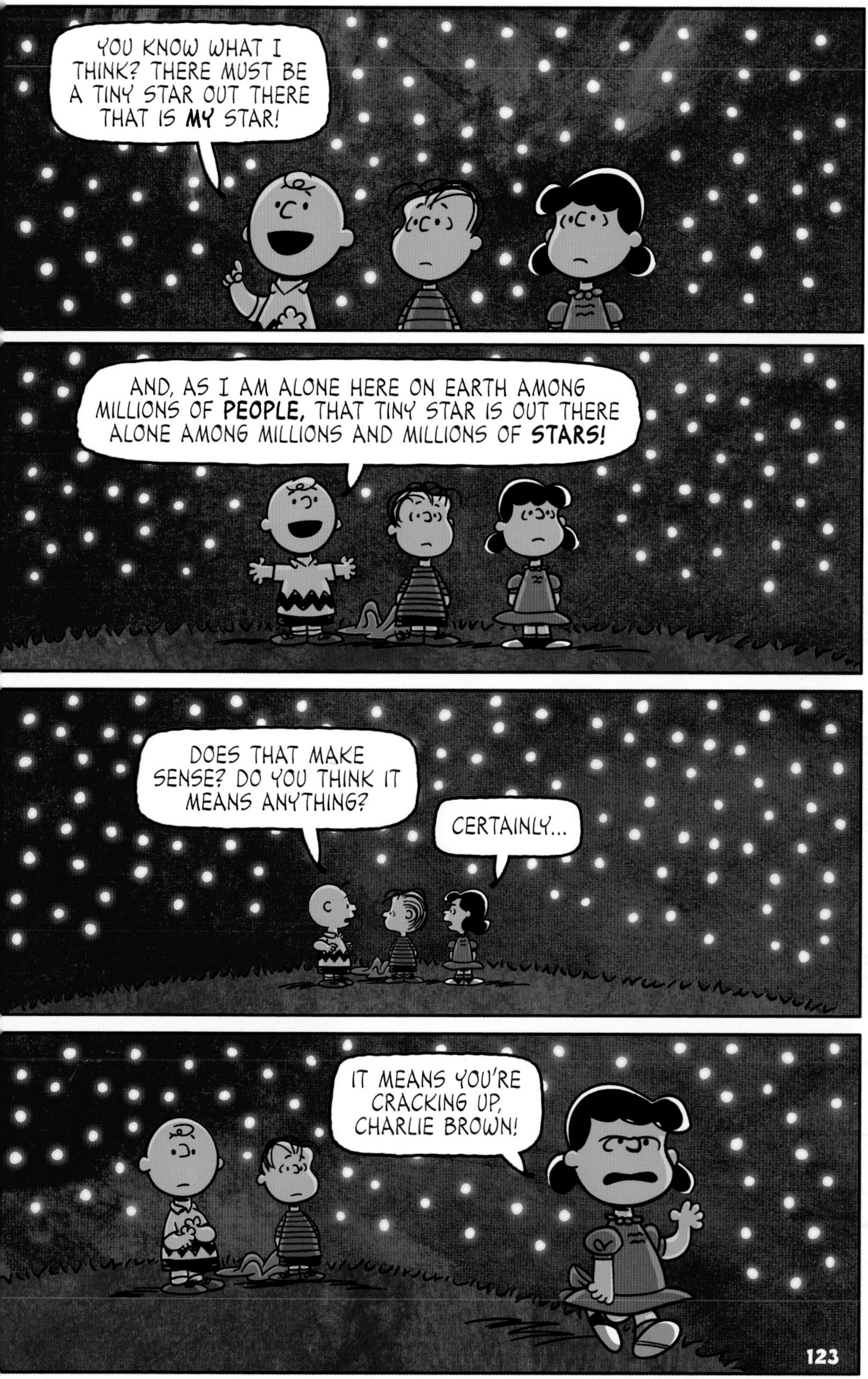
YOU KNOW WHAT I THINK? THERE MUST BE A TINY STAR OUT THERE THAT IS **MY** STAR!
AND, AS I AM ALONE HERE ON EARTH AMONG MILLIONS OF **PEOPLE,** THAT TINY STAR IS OUT THERE ALONE AMONG MILLIONS AND MILLIONS OF **STARS!**
DOES THAT MAKE SENSE? DO YOU THINK IT MEANS ANYTHING?
CERTAINLY...
IT MEANS YOU'RE CRACKING UP, CHARLIE BROWN!

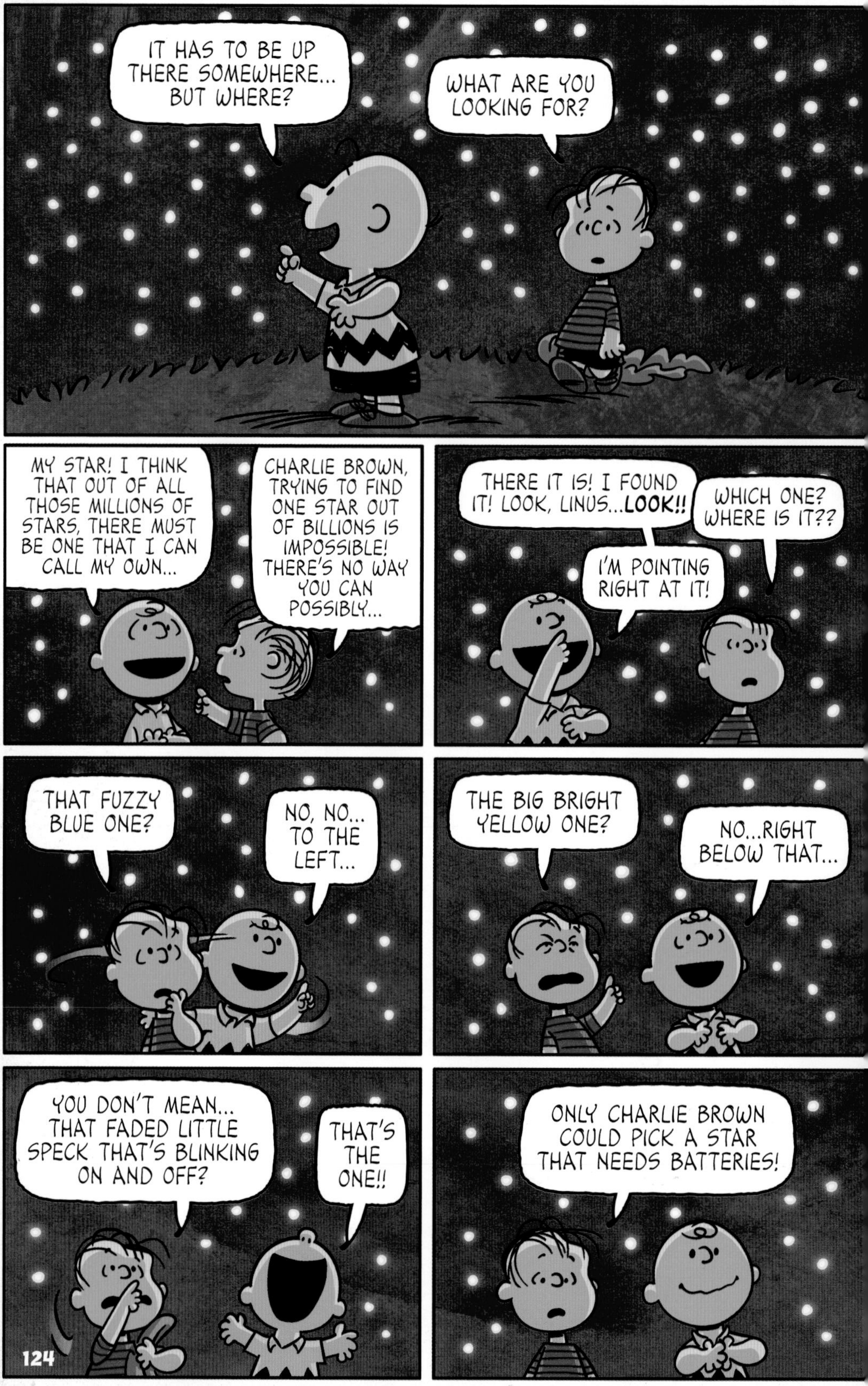
IT HAS TO BE UP THERE SOMEWHERE... BUT WHERE?
WHAT ARE YOU LOOKING FOR?
MY STAR! I THINK THAT OUT OF ALL THOSE MILLIONS OF STARS, THERE MUST BE ONE THAT I CAN CALL MY OWN...
CHARLIE BROWN, TRYING TO FIND ONE STAR OUT OF BILLIONS IS IMPOSSIBLE! THERE'S NO WAY YOU CAN POSSIBLY...
THERE IT IS! I FOUND IT! LOOK, LINUS...**LOOK!!**
WHICH ONE? WHERE IS IT??
I'M POINTING RIGHT AT IT!
THAT FUZZY BLUE ONE?
NO, NO... TO THE LEFT...
THE BIG BRIGHT YELLOW ONE?
NO...RIGHT BELOW THAT...
YOU DON'T MEAN... THAT FADED LITTLE SPECK THAT'S BLINKING ON AND OFF?
THAT'S THE ONE!!
ONLY CHARLIE BROWN COULD PICK A STAR THAT NEEDS BATTERIES!

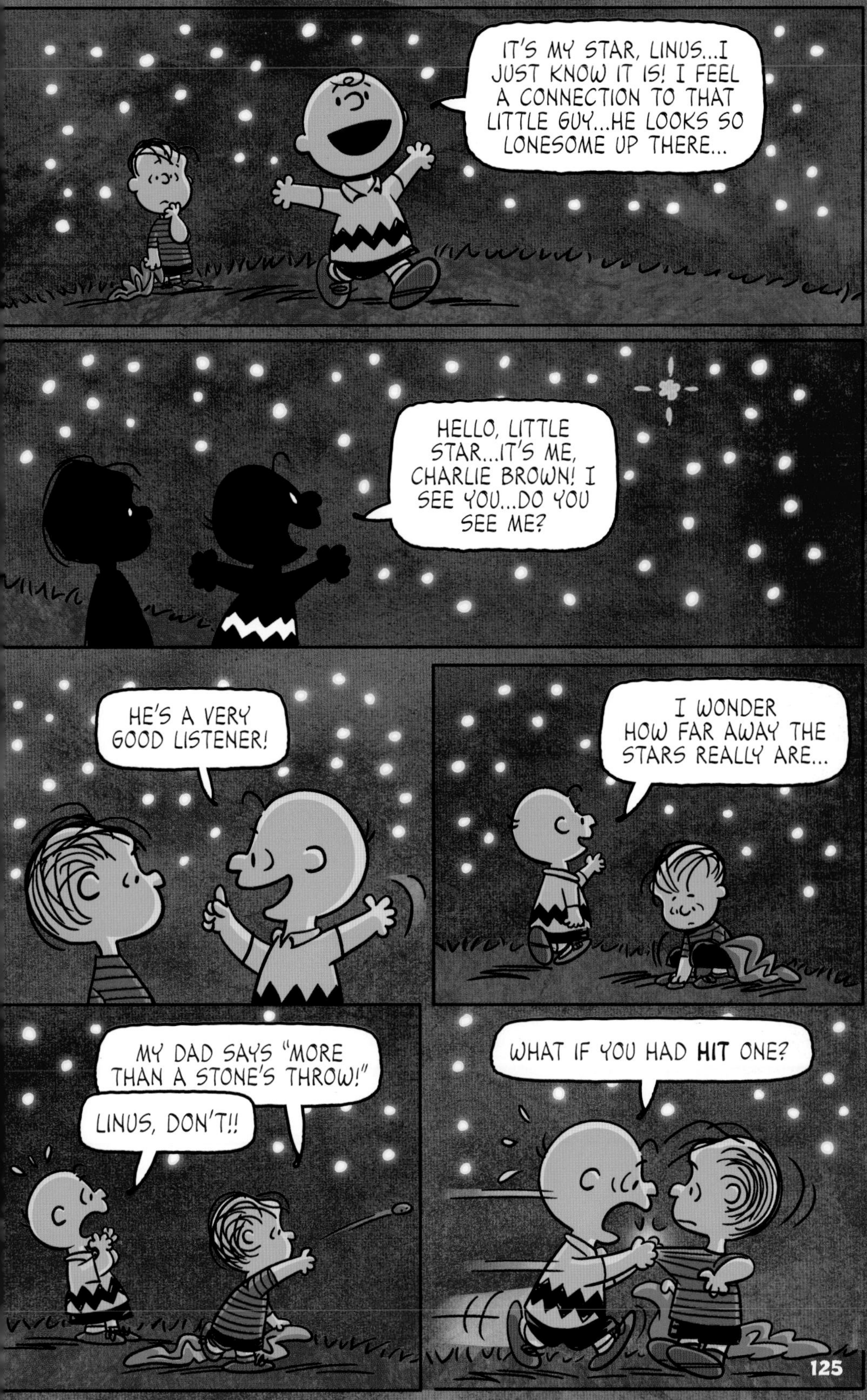
IT'S MY STAR, LINUS...I JUST KNOW IT IS! I FEEL A CONNECTION TO THAT LITTLE GUY...HE LOOKS SO LONESOME UP THERE...
HELLO, LITTLE STAR...IT'S ME, CHARLIE BROWN! I SEE YOU...DO YOU SEE ME?
HE'S A VERY GOOD LISTENER!
I WONDER HOW FAR AWAY THE STARS REALLY ARE...
MY DAD SAYS "MORE THAN A STONE'S THROW!"
LINUS, DON'T!!
WHAT IF YOU HAD HIT ONE?

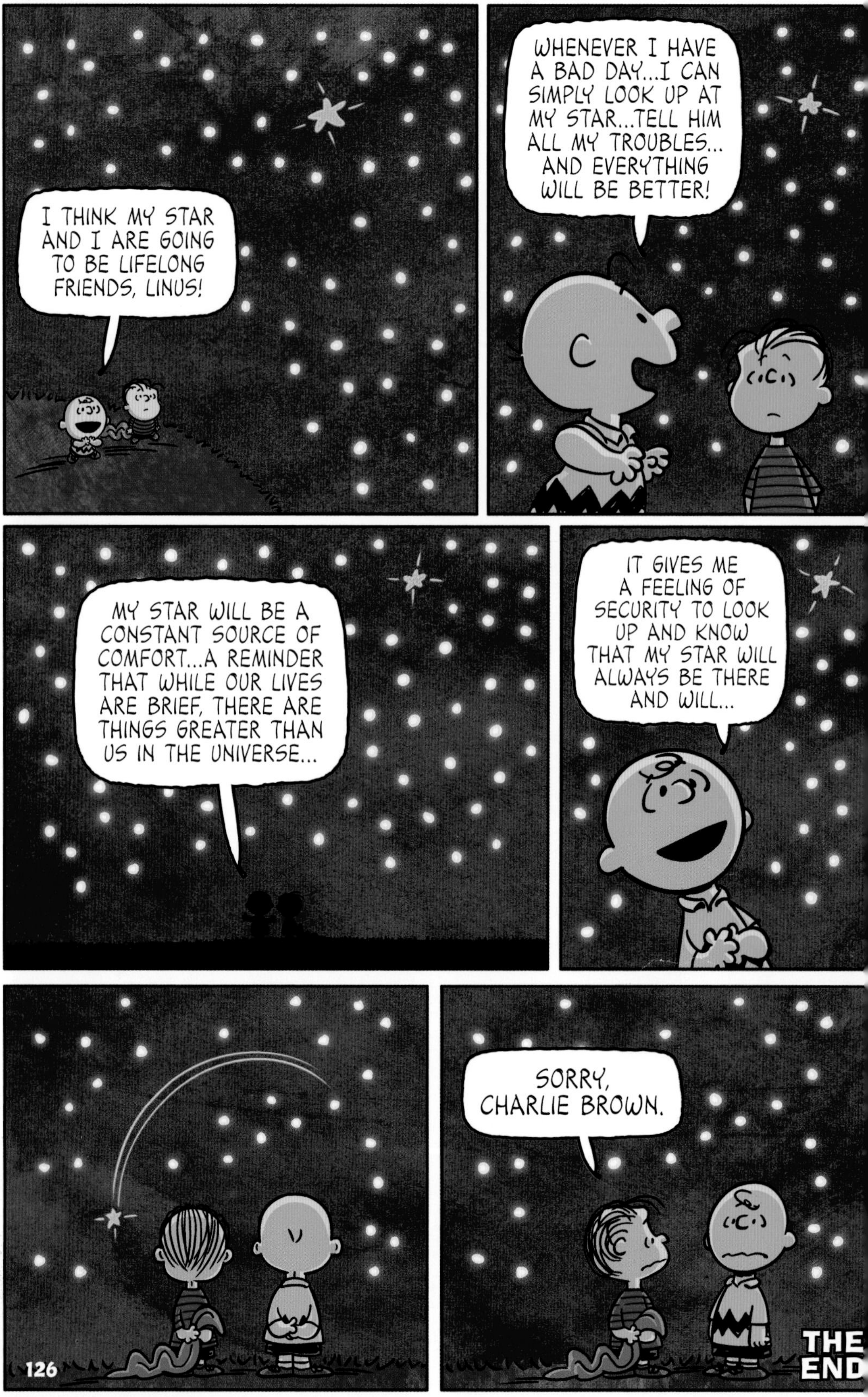
I THINK MY STAR AND I ARE GOING TO BE LIFELONG FRIENDS, LINUS!
WHENEVER I HAVE A BAD DAY...I CAN SIMPLY LOOK UP AT MY STAR...TELL HIM ALL MY TROUBLES... AND EVERYTHING WILL BE BETTER!
MY STAR WILL BE A CONSTANT SOURCE OF COMFORT...A REMINDER THAT WHILE OUR LIVES ARE BRIEF, THERE ARE THINGS GREATER THAN US IN THE UNIVERSE...
IT GIVES ME A FEELING OF SECURITY TO LOOK UP AND KNOW THAT MY STAR WILL ALWAYS BE THERE AND WILL...
SORRY, CHARLIE BROWN.
THE END

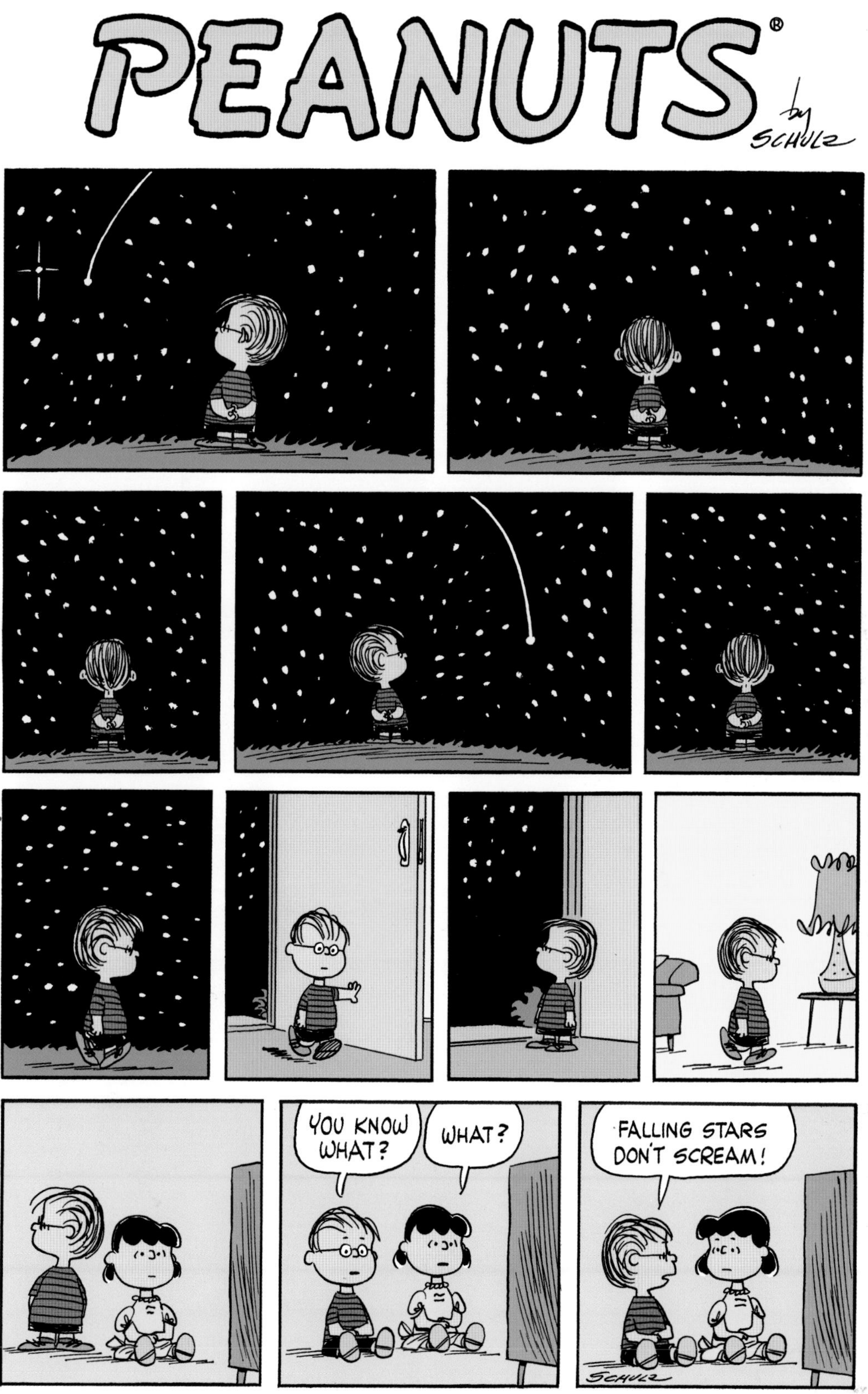
PEANUTS®
by SCHULZ
YOU KNOW WHAT?
WHAT?
FALLING STARS DON'T SCREAM!
SCHULZ

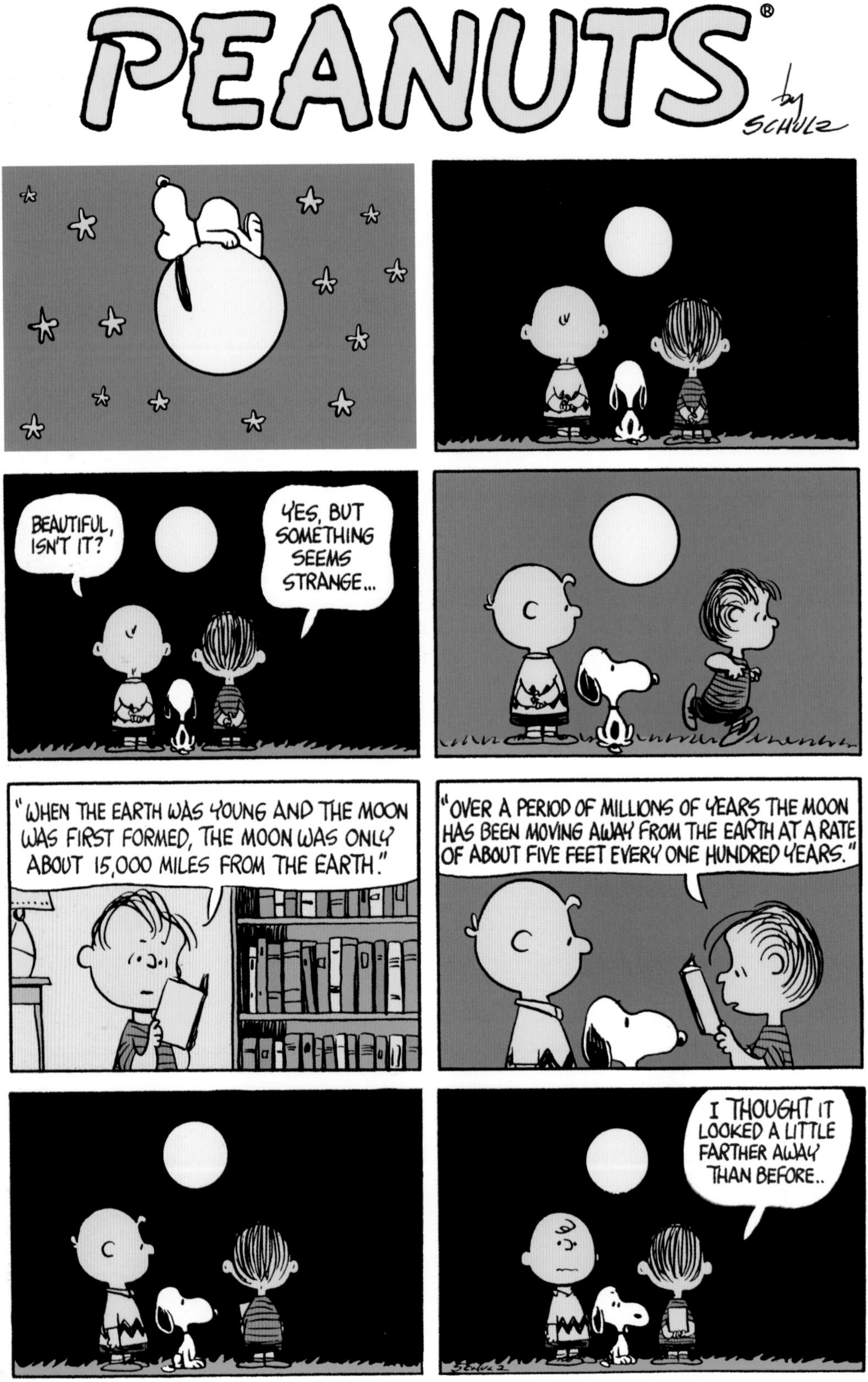
PEANUTS®
by SCHULZ
BEAUTIFUL, ISN'T IT?
YES, BUT SOMETHING SEEMS STRANGE...
"WHEN THE EARTH WAS YOUNG AND THE MOON WAS FIRST FORMED, THE MOON WAS ONLY ABOUT 15,000 MILES FROM THE EARTH."
"OVER A PERIOD OF MILLIONS OF YEARS THE MOON HAS BEEN MOVING AWAY FROM THE EARTH AT A RATE OF ABOUT FIVE FEET EVERY ONE HUNDRED YEARS."
I THOUGHT IT LOOKED A LITTLE FARTHER AWAY THAN BEFORE..
SCHULZ

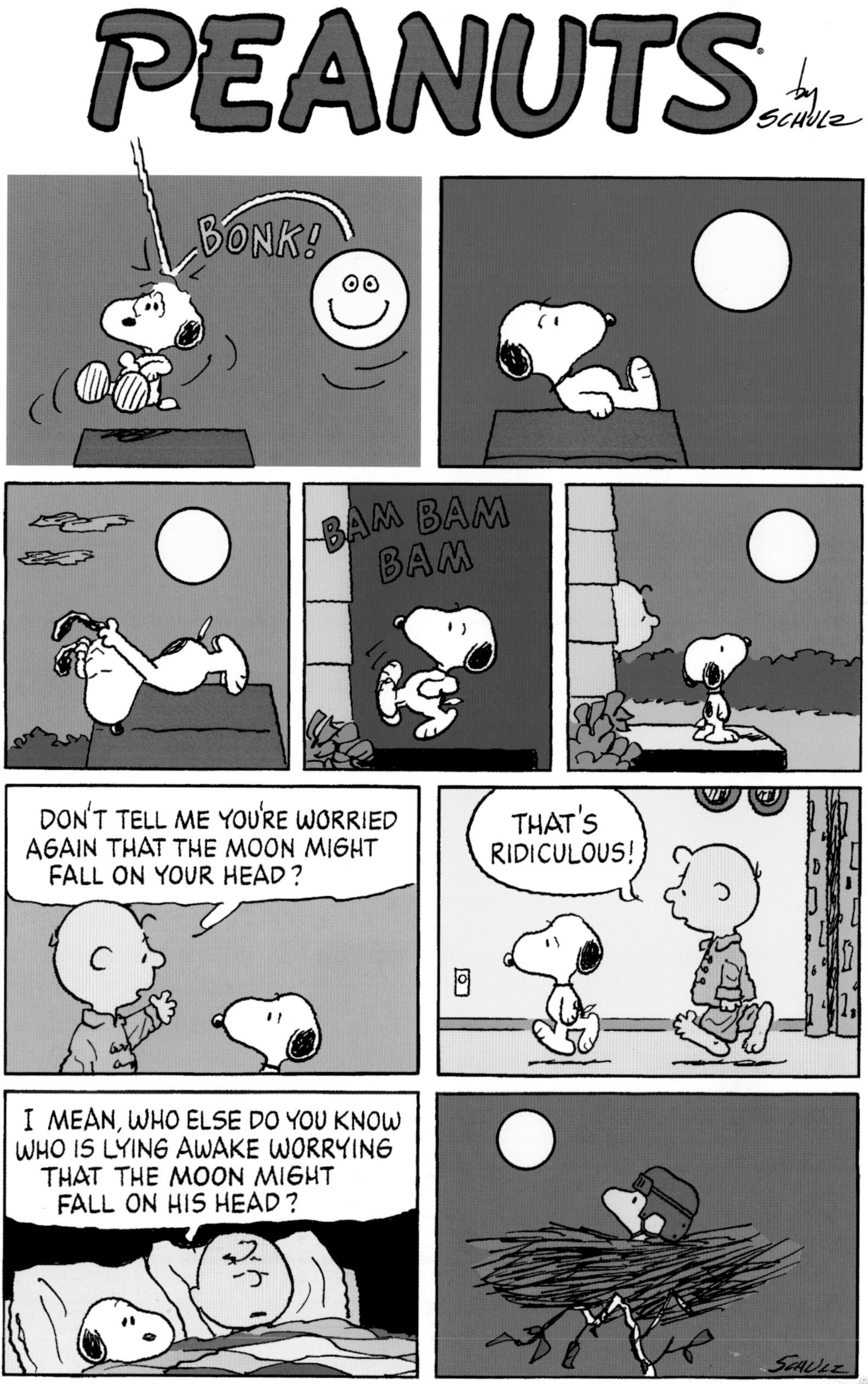
PEANUTS
by SCHULZ
BONK!
BAM BAM
BAM
DON'T TELL ME YOU'RE WORRIED AGAIN THAT THE MOON MIGHT FALL ON YOUR HEAD?
THAT'S RIDICULOUS!
I MEAN, WHO ELSE DO YOU KNOW WHO IS LYING AWAKE WORRYING THAT THE MOON MIGHT FALL ON HIS HEAD?
SCHULZ

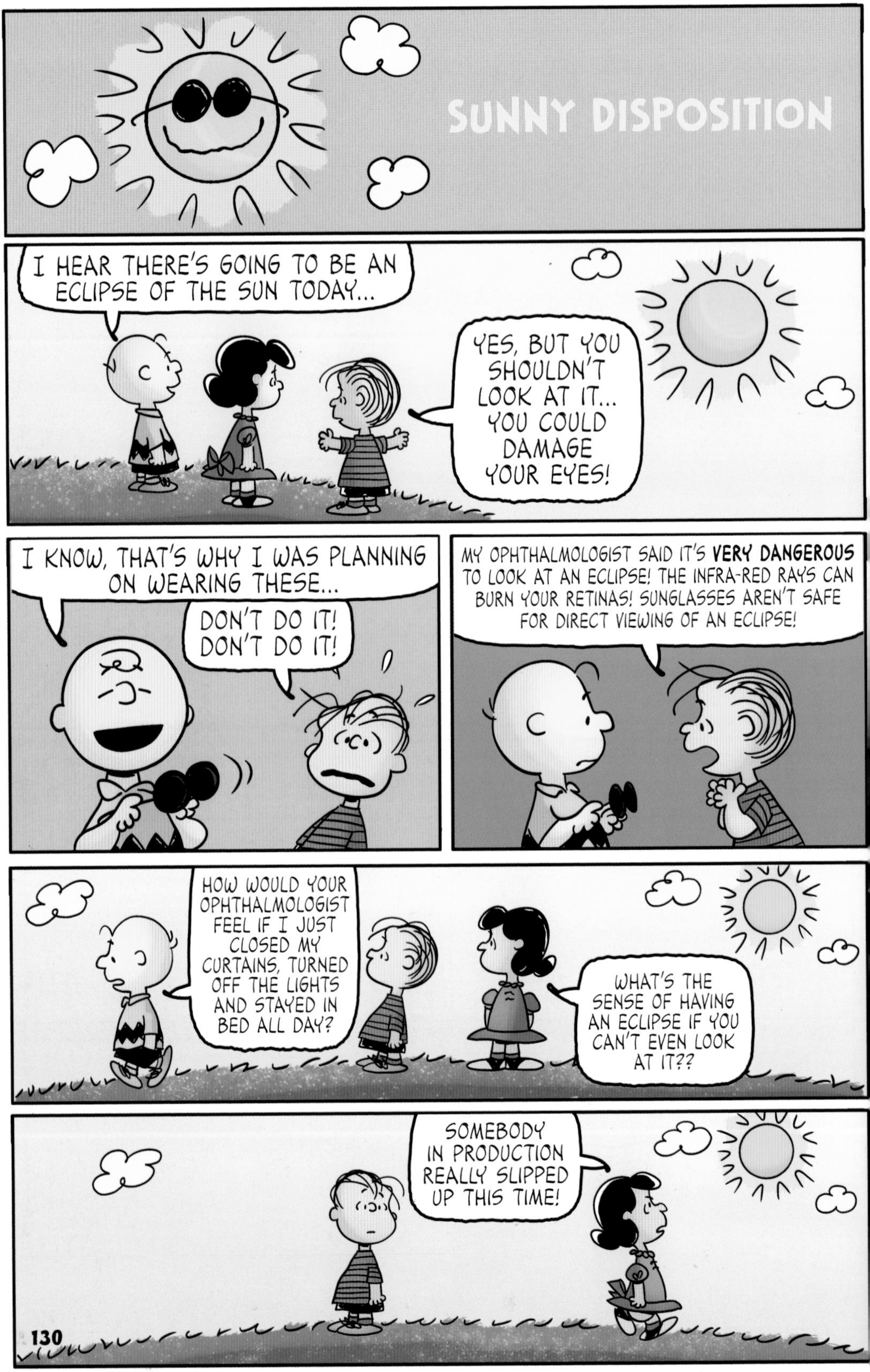
SUNNY DISPOSITION
I HEAR THERE'S GOING TO BE AN ECLIPSE OF THE SUN TODAY...
YES, BUT YOU SHOULDN'T LOOK AT IT... YOU COULD DAMAGE YOUR EYES!
I KNOW, THAT'S WHY I WAS PLANNING ON WEARING THESE...
DON'T DO IT! DON'T DO IT!
MY OPHTHALMOLOGIST SAID IT'S VERY DANGEROUS TO LOOK AT AN ECLIPSE! THE INFRA-RED RAYS CAN BURN YOUR RETINAS! SUNGLASSES AREN'T SAFE FOR DIRECT VIEWING OF AN ECLIPSE!
HOW WOULD YOUR OPHTHALMOLOGIST FEEL IF I JUST CLOSED MY CURTAINS, TURNED OFF THE LIGHTS AND STAYED IN BED ALL DAY?
WHAT'S THE SENSE OF HAVING AN ECLIPSE IF YOU CAN'T EVEN LOOK AT IT??
SOMEBODY IN PRODUCTION REALLY SLIPPED UP THIS TIME!

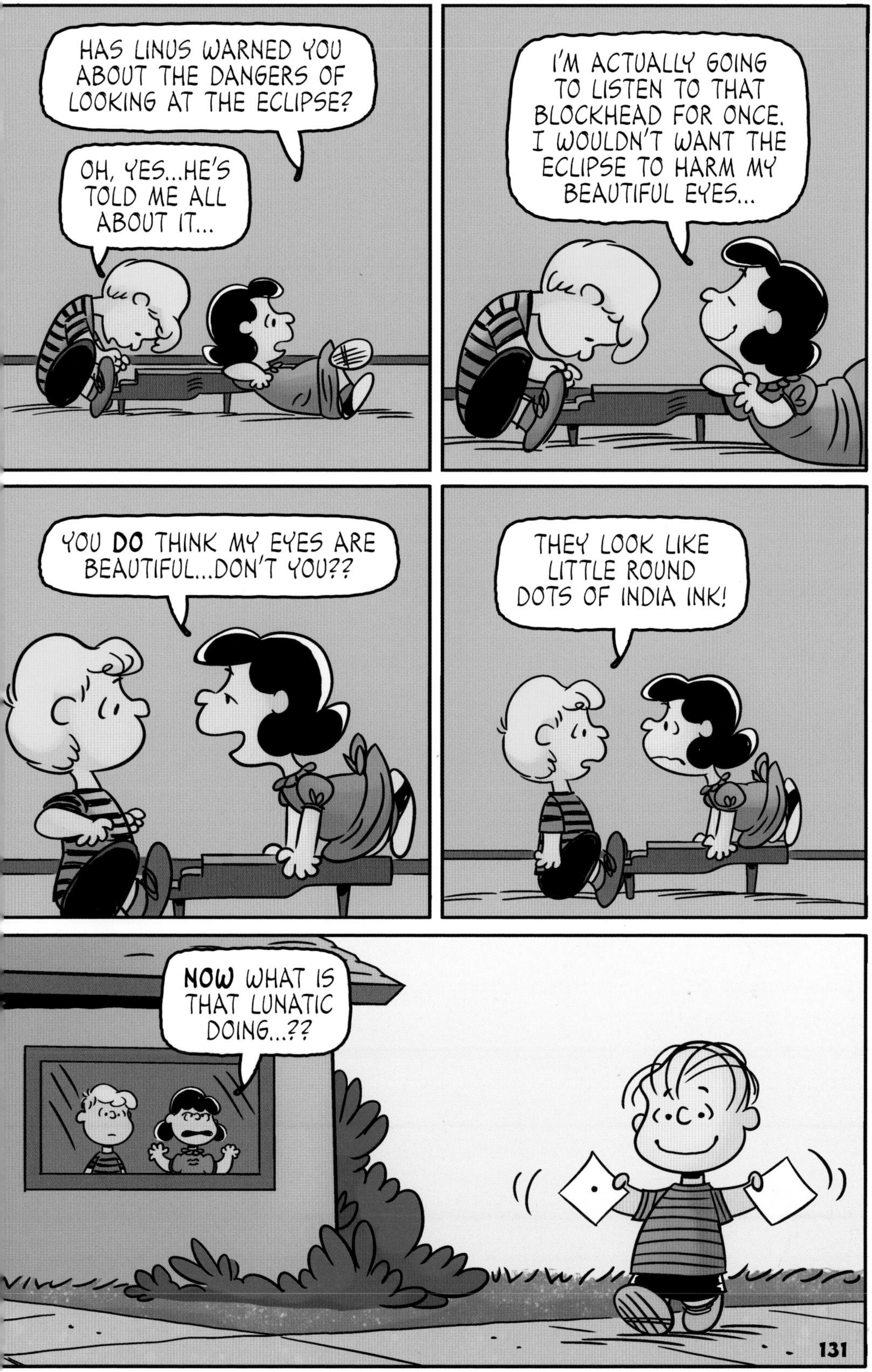
HAS LINUS WARNED YOU ABOUT THE DANGERS OF LOOKING AT THE ECLIPSE?
OH, YES...HE'S TOLD ME ALL ABOUT IT...
I'M ACTUALLY GOING TO LISTEN TO THAT BLOCKHEAD FOR ONCE. I WOULDN'T WANT THE ECLIPSE TO HARM MY BEAUTIFUL EYES...
YOU DO THINK MY EYES ARE BEAUTIFUL...DON'T YOU??
THEY LOOK LIKE LITTLE ROUND DOTS OF INDIA INK!
NOW WHAT IS THAT LUNATIC DOING...??

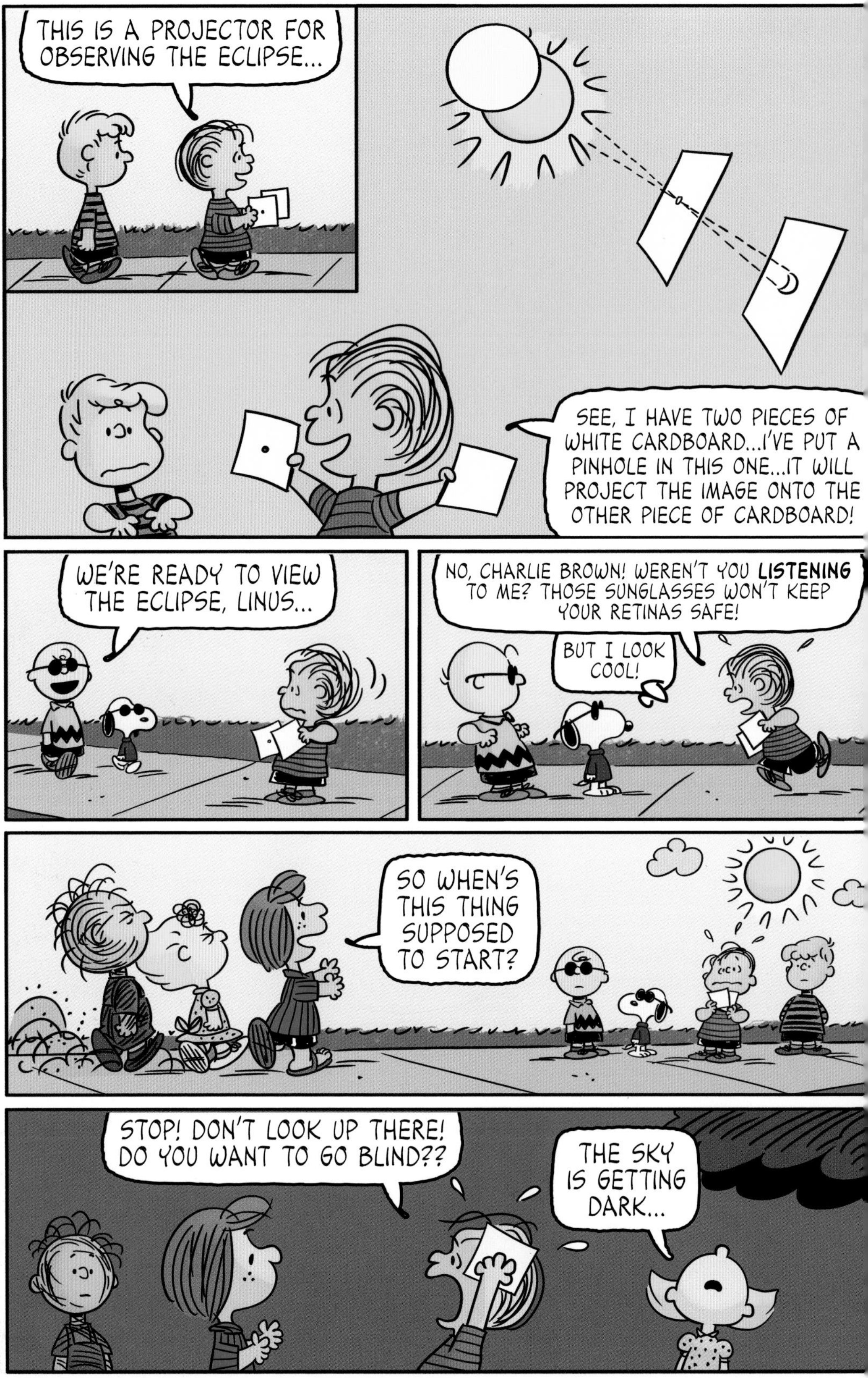
THIS IS A PROJECTOR FOR OBSERVING THE ECLIPSE...
SEE, I HAVE TWO PIECES OF WHITE CARDBOARD...I'VE PUT A PINHOLE IN THIS ONE...IT WILL PROJECT THE IMAGE ONTO THE OTHER PIECE OF CARDBOARD!
WE'RE READY TO VIEW THE ECLIPSE, LINUS...
NO, CHARLIE BROWN! WEREN'T YOU **LISTENING** TO ME? THOSE SUNGLASSES WON'T KEEP YOUR RETINAS SAFE!
BUT I LOOK COOL!
SO WHEN'S THIS THING SUPPOSED TO START?
STOP! DON'T LOOK UP THERE! DO YOU WANT TO GO BLIND??
THE SKY IS GETTING DARK...

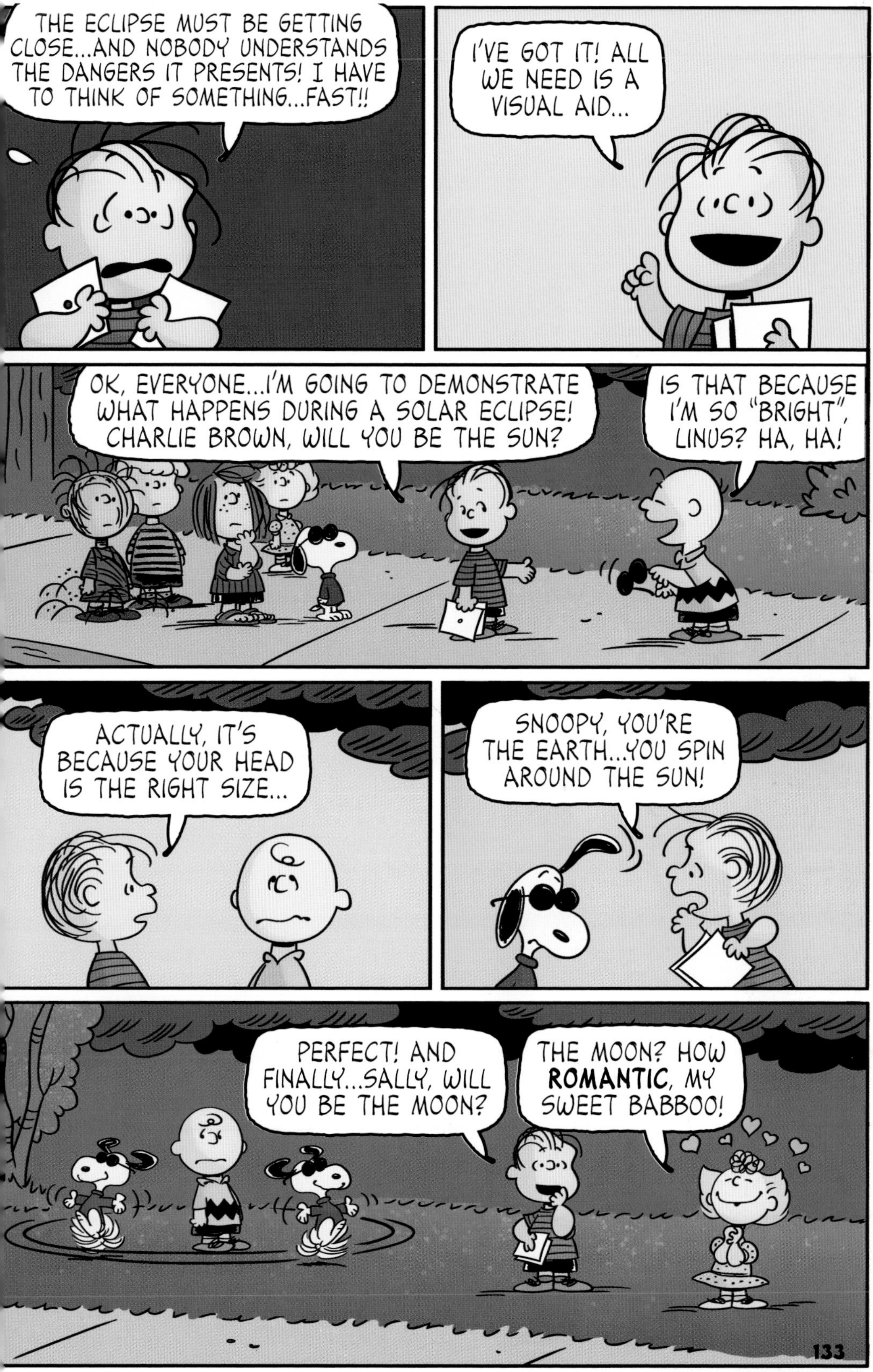
THE ECLIPSE MUST BE GETTING CLOSE...AND NOBODY UNDERSTANDS THE DANGERS IT PRESENTS! I HAVE TO THINK OF SOMETHING...FAST!!
I'VE GOT IT! ALL WE NEED IS A VISUAL AID...
OK, EVERYONE...I'M GOING TO DEMONSTRATE WHAT HAPPENS DURING A SOLAR ECLIPSE! CHARLIE BROWN, WILL YOU BE THE SUN?
IS THAT BECAUSE I'M SO "BRIGHT", LINUS? HA, HA!
ACTUALLY, IT'S BECAUSE YOUR HEAD IS THE RIGHT SIZE...
SNOOPY, YOU'RE THE EARTH...YOU SPIN AROUND THE SUN!
PERFECT! AND FINALLY...SALLY, WILL YOU BE THE MOON?
THE MOON? HOW **ROMANTIC**, MY SWEET BABBOO!

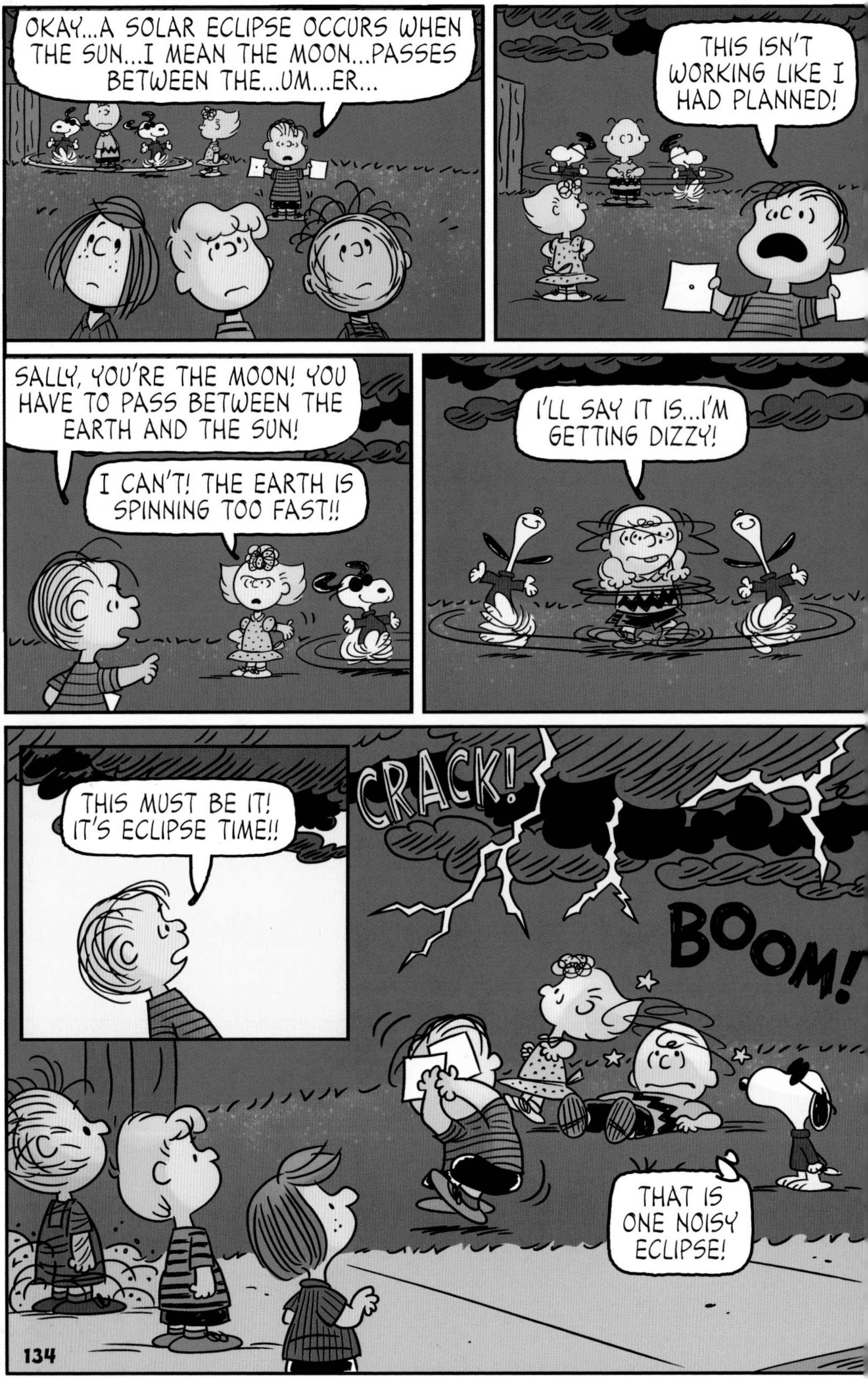
OKAY...A SOLAR ECLIPSE OCCURS WHEN THE SUN...I MEAN THE MOON...PASSES BETWEEN THE...UM...ER...
THIS ISN'T WORKING LIKE I HAD PLANNED!
SALLY, YOU'RE THE MOON! YOU HAVE TO PASS BETWEEN THE EARTH AND THE SUN!
I CAN'T! THE EARTH IS SPINNING TOO FAST!!
I'LL SAY IT IS...I'M GETTING DIZZY!
THIS MUST BE IT! IT'S ECLIPSE TIME!!
CRACK!
BOOM!
THAT IS ONE NOISY ECLIPSE!

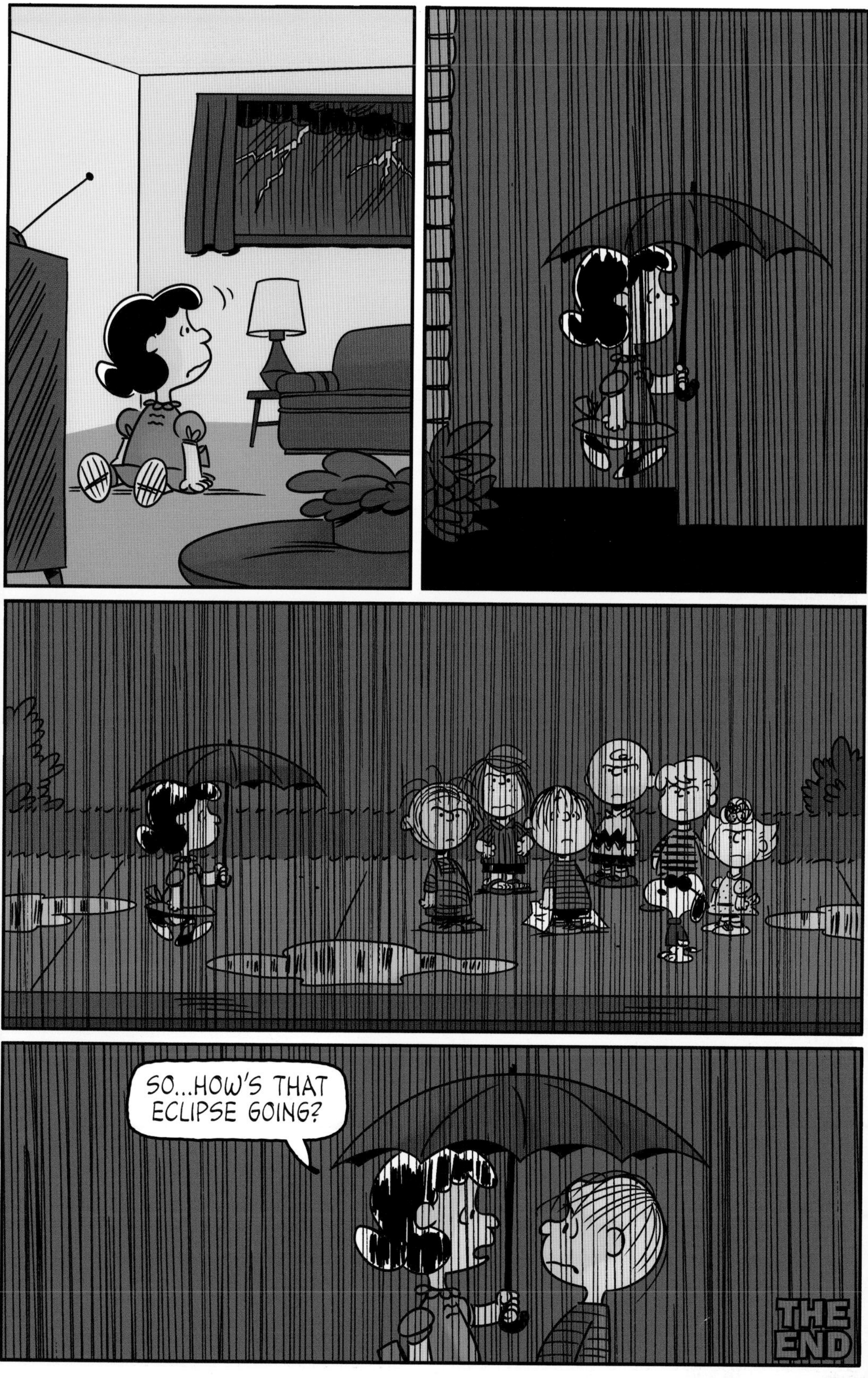
SO...HOW'S THAT ECLIPSE GOING?
THE END

# twinklethinkle

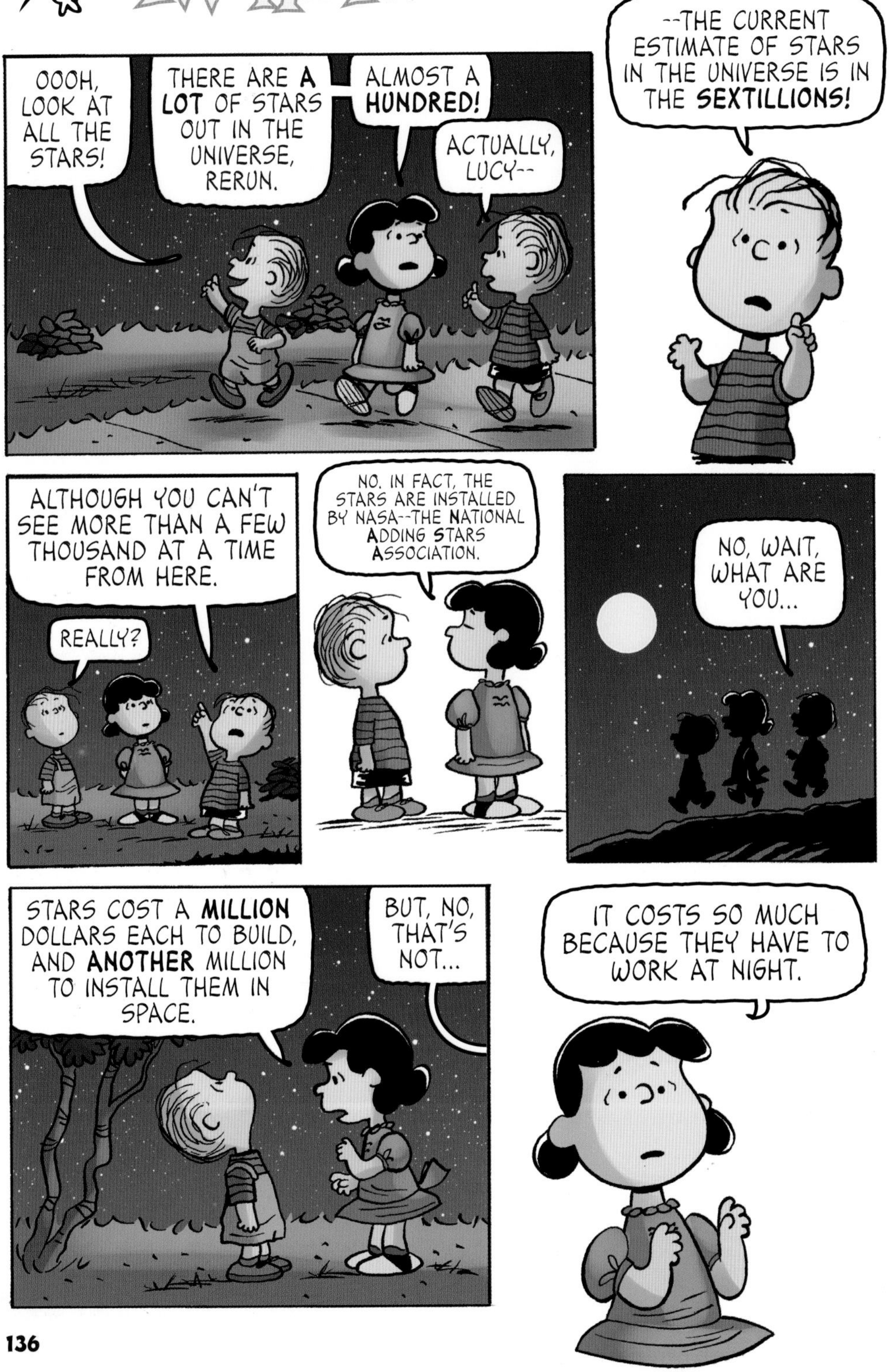

OOOH, LOOK AT ALL THE STARS!
THERE ARE A LOT OF STARS OUT IN THE UNIVERSE, RERUN.
ALMOST A HUNDRED!
ACTUALLY, LUCY--
--THE CURRENT ESTIMATE OF STARS IN THE UNIVERSE IS IN THE SEXTILLIONS!
ALTHOUGH YOU CAN'T SEE MORE THAN A FEW THOUSAND AT A TIME FROM HERE.
REALLY?
NO. IN FACT, THE STARS ARE INSTALLED BY NASA--THE NATIONAL ADDING STARS ASSOCIATION.
NO, WAIT, WHAT ARE YOU...
STARS COST A MILLION DOLLARS EACH TO BUILD, AND ANOTHER MILLION TO INSTALL THEM IN SPACE.
BUT, NO, THAT'S NOT...
IT COSTS SO MUCH BECAUSE THEY HAVE TO WORK AT NIGHT.

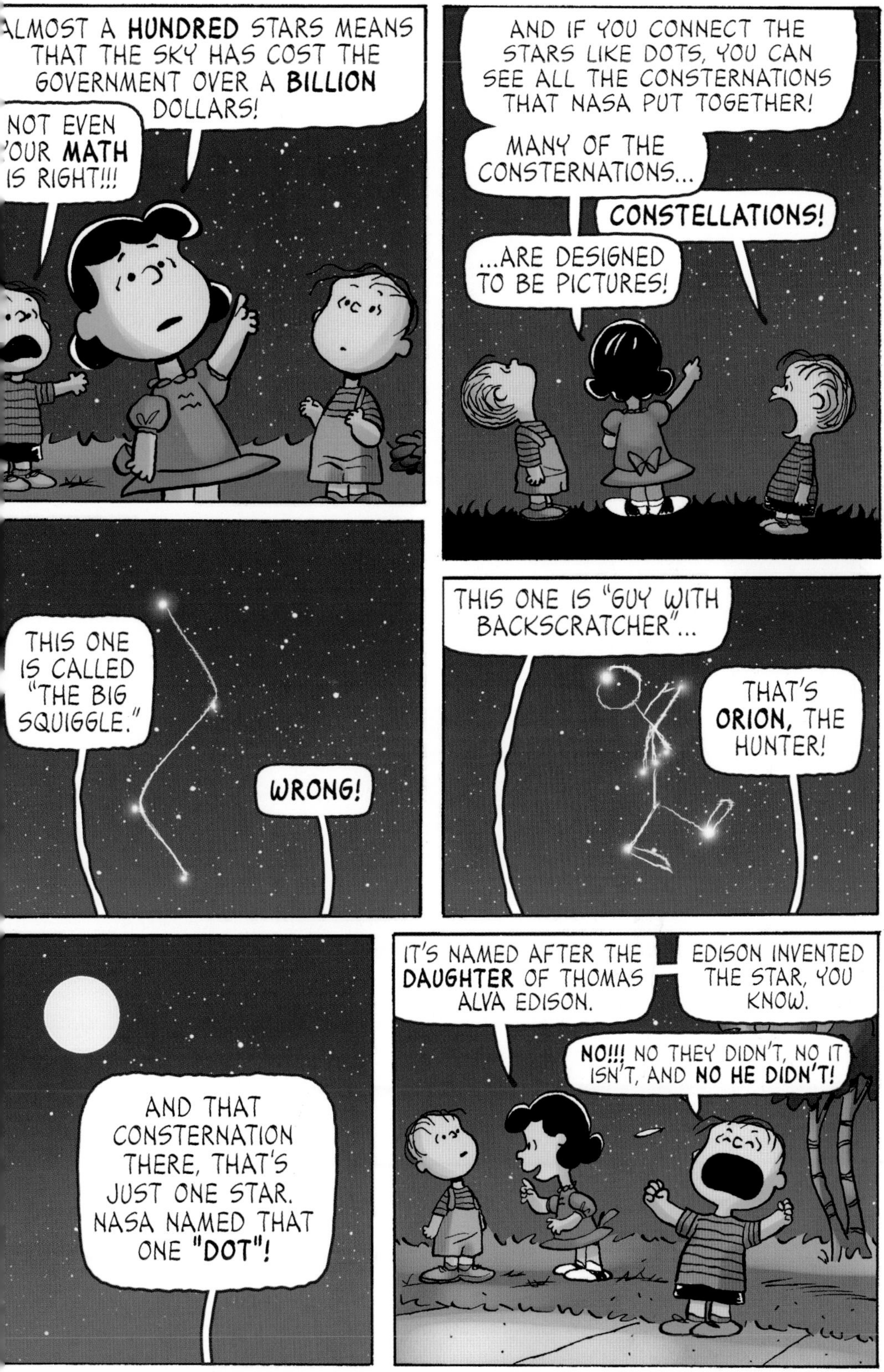

ALMOST A HUNDRED STARS MEANS THAT THE SKY HAS COST THE GOVERNMENT OVER A BILLION DOLLARS!
NOT EVEN YOUR MATH IS RIGHT!!!
AND IF YOU CONNECT THE STARS LIKE DOTS, YOU CAN SEE ALL THE CONSTERNATIONS THAT NASA PUT TOGETHER!
MANY OF THE CONSTERNATIONS...
CONSTELLATIONS!
...ARE DESIGNED TO BE PICTURES!
THIS ONE IS CALLED "THE BIG SQUIGGLE."
WRONG!
THIS ONE IS "GUY WITH BACKSCRATCHER"...
THAT'S ORION, THE HUNTER!
AND THAT CONSTERNATION THERE, THAT'S JUST ONE STAR. NASA NAMED THAT ONE "DOT"!
IT'S NAMED AFTER THE DAUGHTER OF THOMAS ALVA EDISON.
EDISON INVENTED THE STAR, YOU KNOW.
NO!!! NO THEY DIDN'T, NO IT ISN'T, AND NO HE DIDN'T!

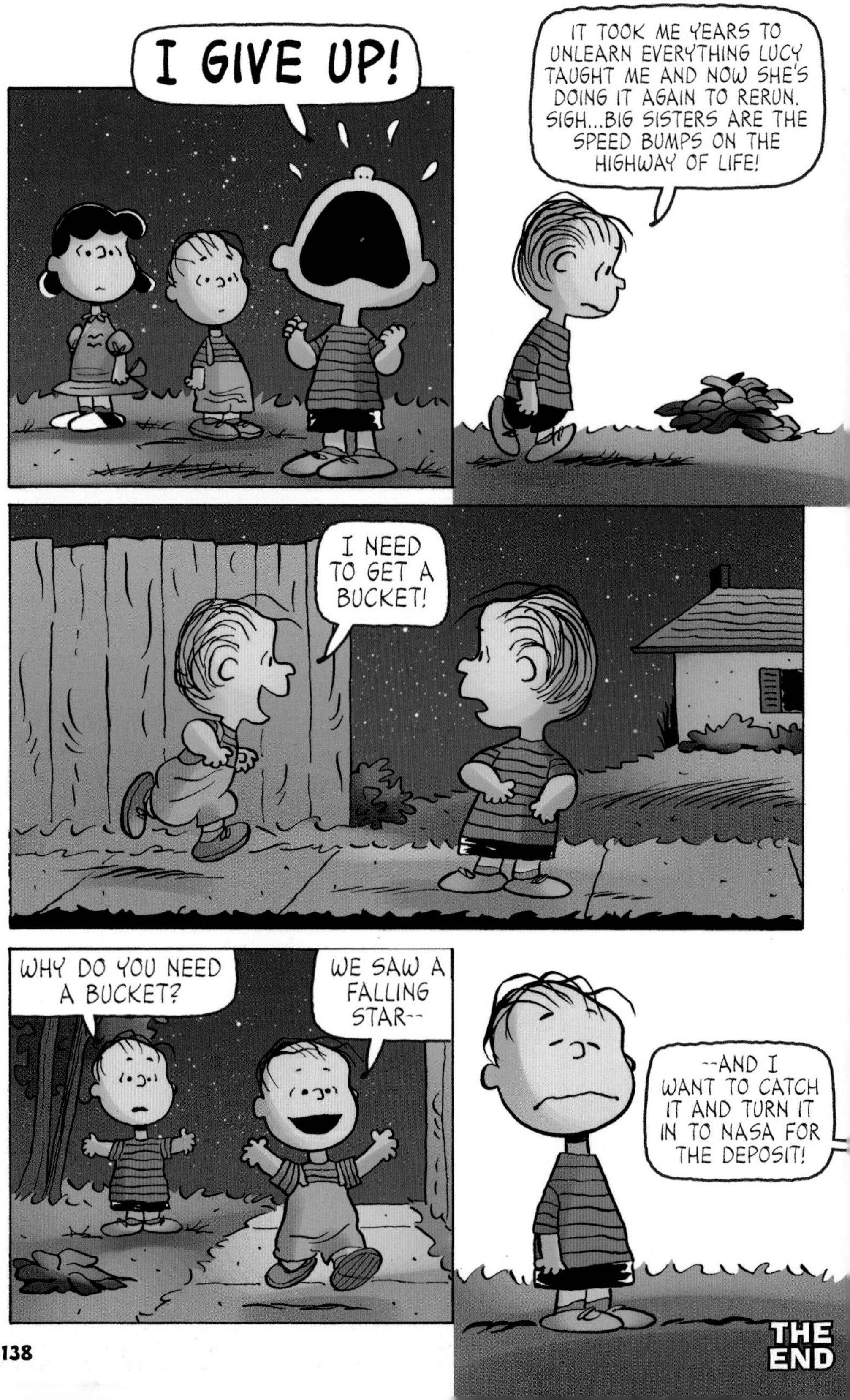
I GIVE UP!
IT TOOK ME YEARS TO UNLEARN EVERYTHING LUCY TAUGHT ME AND NOW SHE'S DOING IT AGAIN TO RERUN. SIGH...BIG SISTERS ARE THE SPEED BUMPS ON THE HIGHWAY OF LIFE!
I NEED TO GET A BUCKET!
WHY DO YOU NEED A BUCKET?
WE SAW A FALLING STAR--
--AND I WANT TO CATCH IT AND TURN IT IN TO NASA FOR THE DEPOSIT!
THE END

LOOK WHAT I JUST FOUND IN THE BASEMENT! IT'S MY ROCK COLLECTION!

KICKOFF TO THE MOON

OH, SURE. I LOVE ALL KINDS OF ROCK. IGNEOUS. METAMORPHIC... THE ONES YOU GET ON HALLOWEEN...

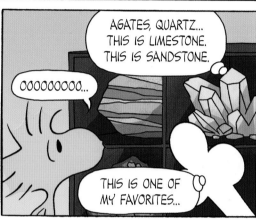

AGATES, QUARTZ... THIS IS LIMESTONE. THIS IS SANDSTONE.

OOOOOOOOO...

THIS IS ONE OF MY FAVORITES...

A ROLLING STONE!

AS YOU CAN SEE, IT GATHERS NO MOSS...

/ ¹\¹¹¹!?

YES. A MOON ROCK. I WAS NEVER ABLE TO GET ONE.

/¹¹¹¹!?

139

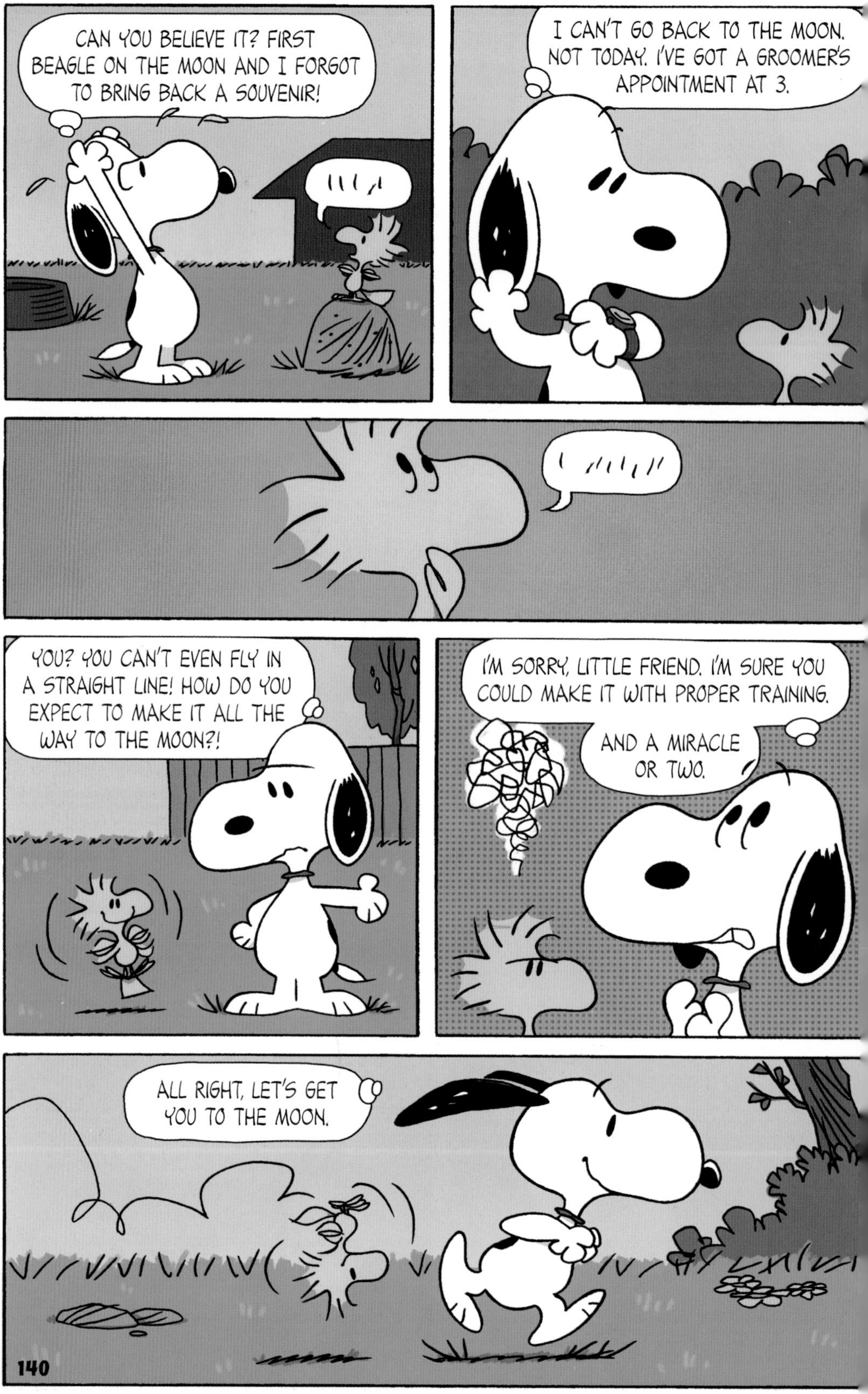
CAN YOU BELIEVE IT? FIRST BEAGLE ON THE MOON AND I FORGOT TO BRING BACK A SOUVENIR!
I CAN'T GO BACK TO THE MOON. NOT TODAY. I'VE GOT A GROOMER'S APPOINTMENT AT 3.
YOU? YOU CAN'T EVEN FLY IN A STRAIGHT LINE! HOW DO YOU EXPECT TO MAKE IT ALL THE WAY TO THE MOON?!
I'M SORRY, LITTLE FRIEND. I'M SURE YOU COULD MAKE IT WITH PROPER TRAINING.
AND A MIRACLE OR TWO.
ALL RIGHT, LET'S GET YOU TO THE MOON.

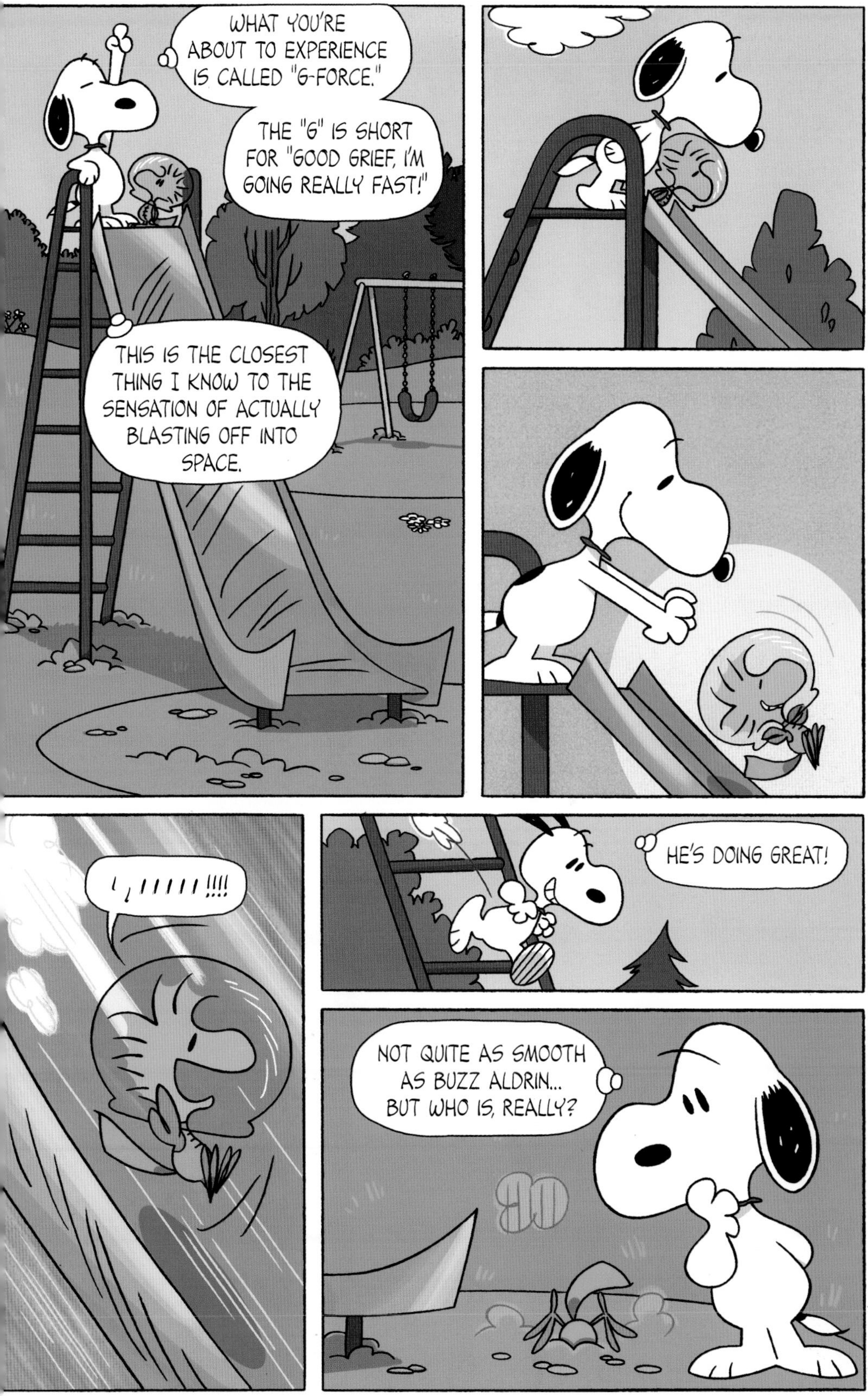
WHAT YOU'RE ABOUT TO EXPERIENCE IS CALLED "G-FORCE."
THE "G" IS SHORT FOR "GOOD GRIEF, I'M GOING REALLY FAST!"
THIS IS THE CLOSEST THING I KNOW TO THE SENSATION OF ACTUALLY BLASTING OFF INTO SPACE.
!!!!
HE'S DOING GREAT!
NOT QUITE AS SMOOTH AS BUZZ ALDRIN... BUT WHO IS, REALLY?

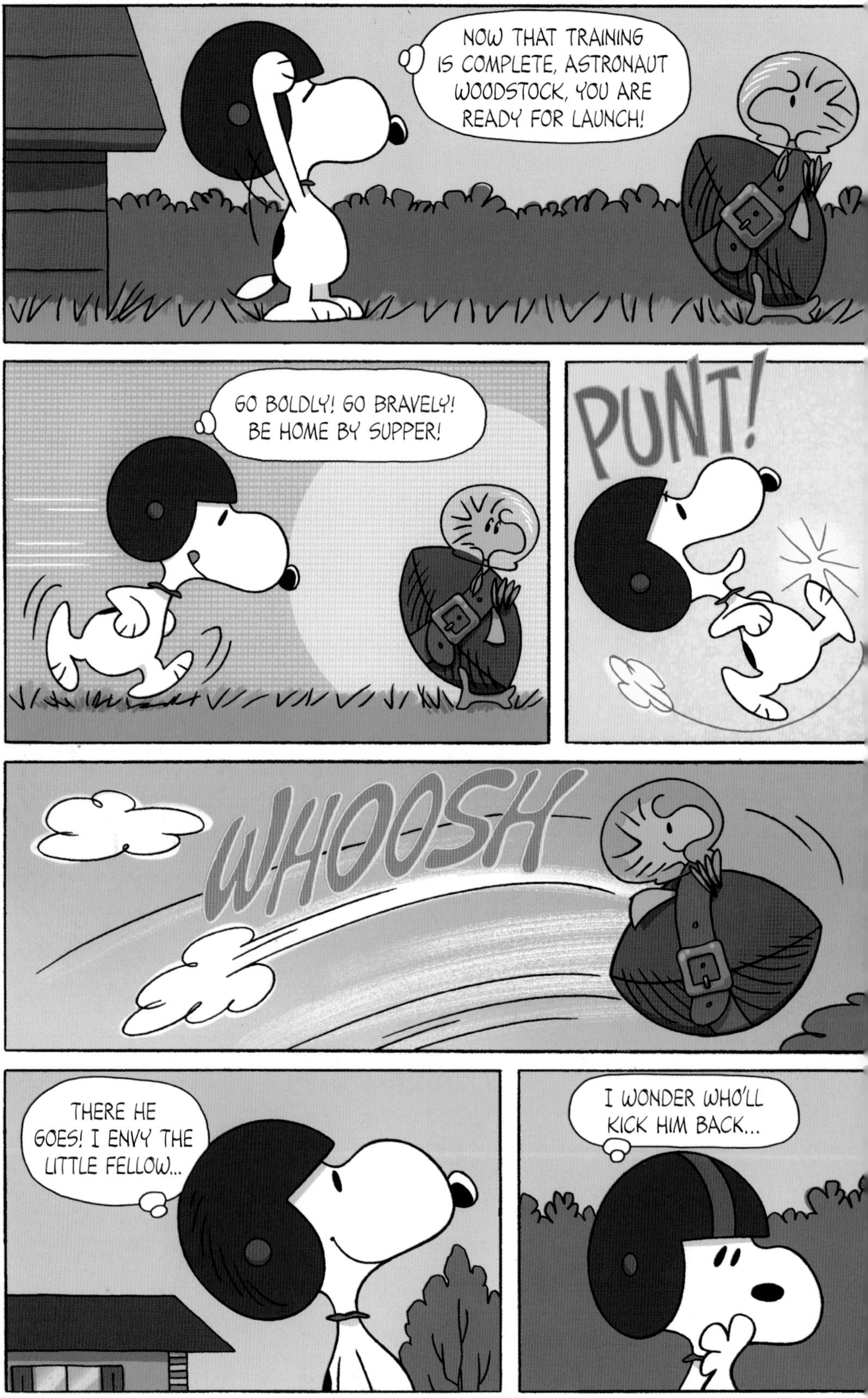
NOW THAT TRAINING IS COMPLETE, ASTRONAUT WOODSTOCK, YOU ARE READY FOR LAUNCH!
GO BOLDLY! GO BRAVELY! BE HOME BY SUPPER!
PUNT!
WHOOSH
THERE HE GOES! I ENVY THE LITTLE FELLOW...
I WONDER WHO'LL KICK HIM BACK...

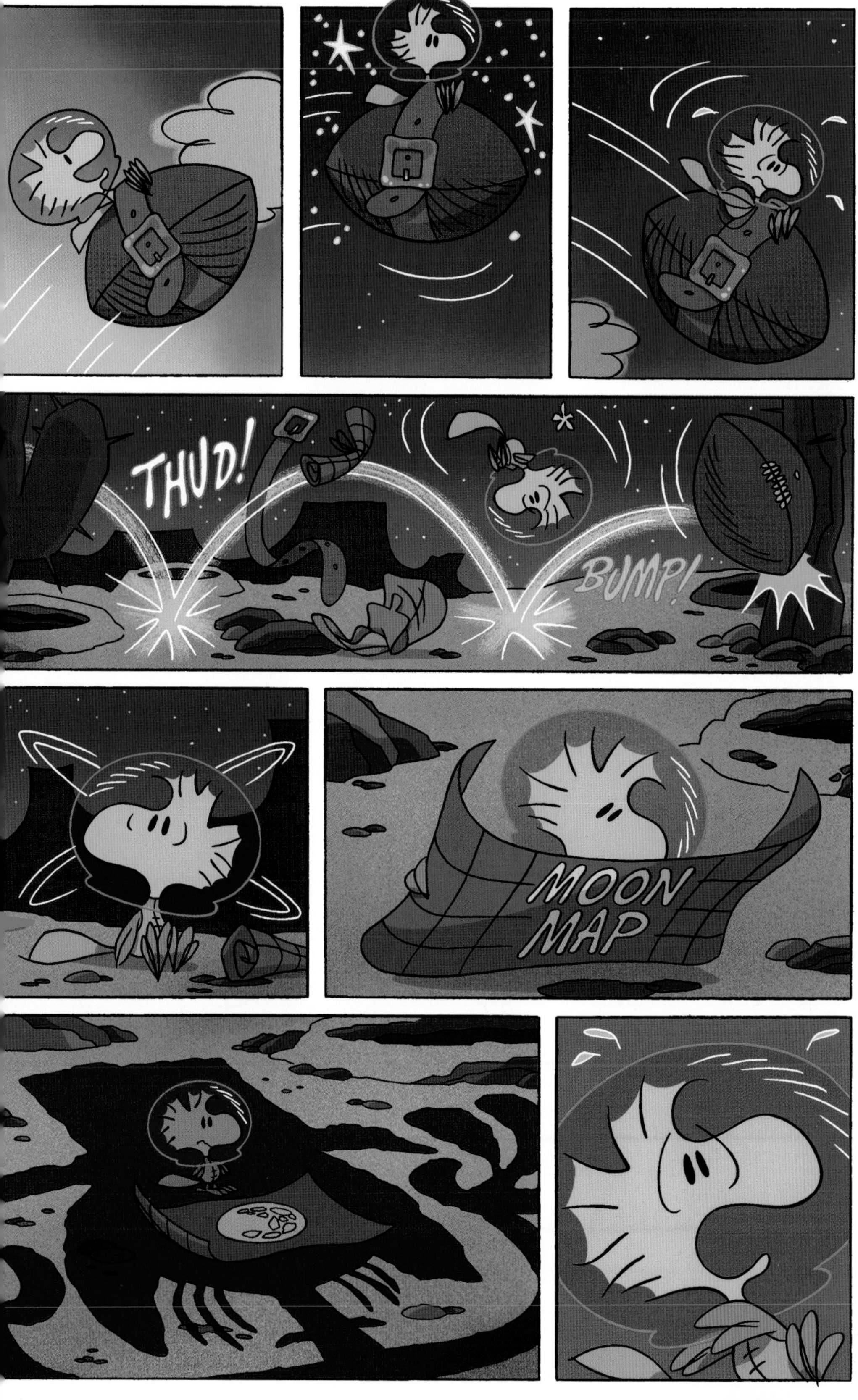
THUD!
BUMP!
MOON
MAP

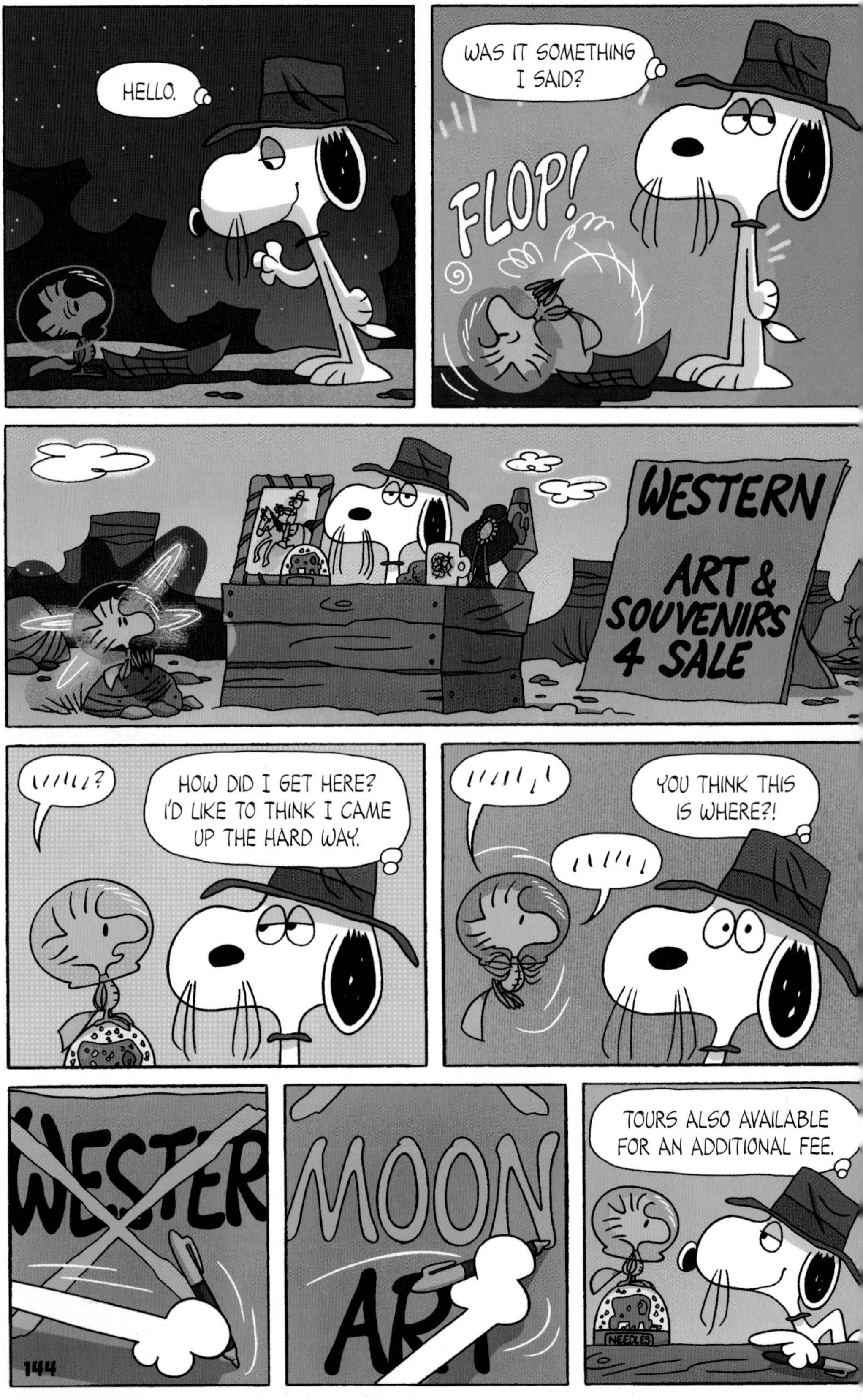
HELLO.
WAS IT SOMETHING I SAID?
FLOP!
WESTERN ART & SOUVENIRS 4 SALE
HOW DID I GET HERE? I'D LIKE TO THINK I CAME UP THE HARD WAY.
YOU THINK THIS IS WHERE?!
WESTER
MOON
AR
TOURS ALSO AVAILABLE FOR AN ADDITIONAL FEE.
NEEDLES

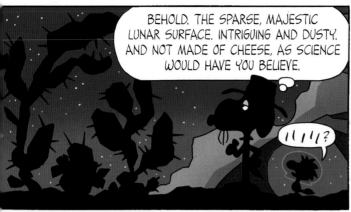

BEHOLD. THE SPARSE, MAJESTIC LUNAR SURFACE. INTRIGUING AND DUSTY. AND NOT MADE OF CHEESE, AS SCIENCE WOULD HAVE YOU BELIEVE.

ALIENS? SURE, WHY NOT.

THEY PREFER TO KEEP TO THEMSELVES, MOSTLY.

THE MOON ALSO HAS SOME INTERESTING REAL-ESTATE INVESTMENT OPPORTUNITIES IF YOU'RE INTERESTED...

SCREEE

SCREE!

IT ALSO HAS BATS! FEISTY MOON BATS!

145

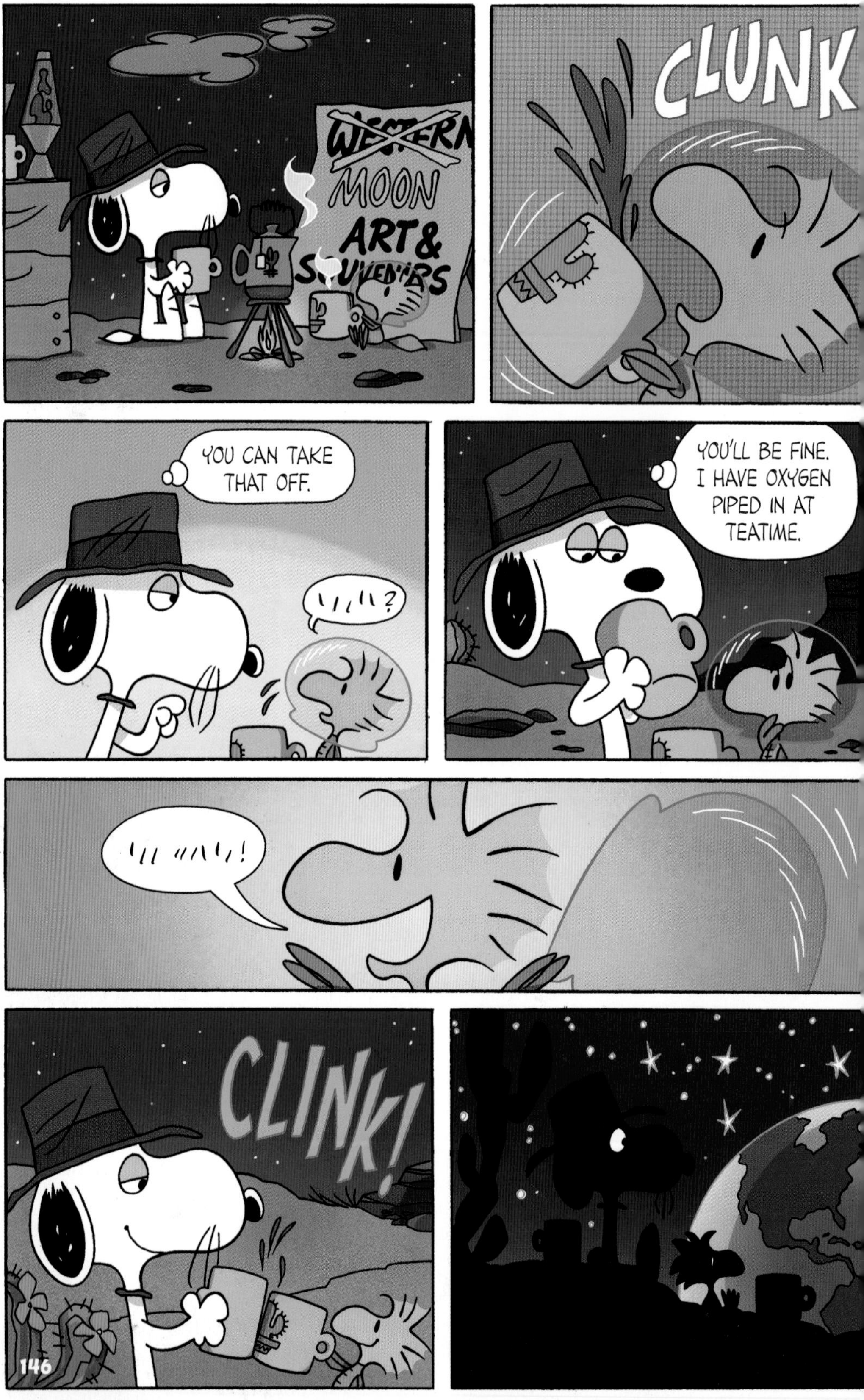
WESTERN
MOON
ART &
SOUVENIRS
CLUNK
YOU CAN TAKE THAT OFF.
YOU'LL BE FINE. I HAVE OXYGEN PIPED IN AT TEATIME.
CLINK!

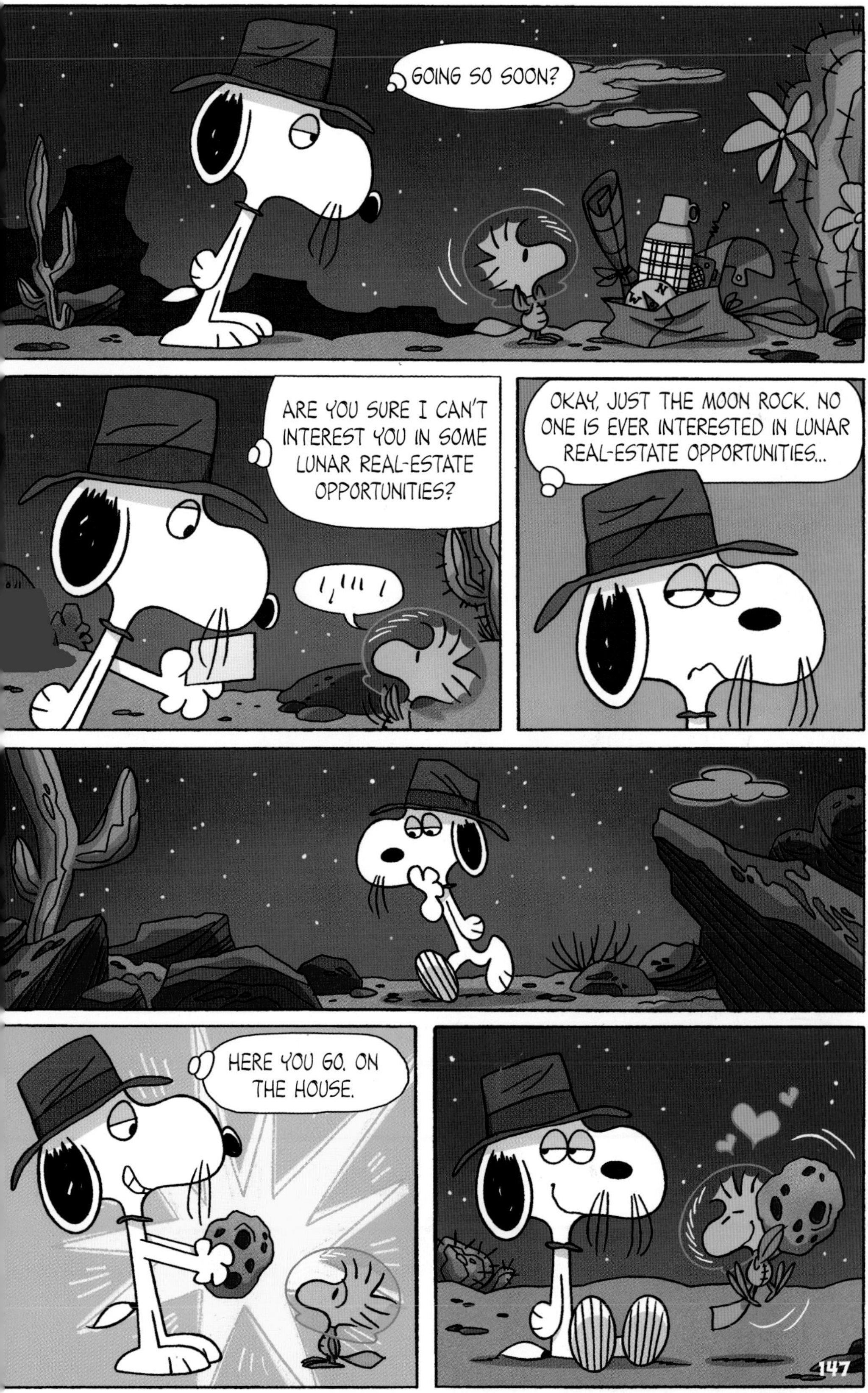
GOING SO SOON?
ARE YOU SURE I CAN'T INTEREST YOU IN SOME LUNAR REAL-ESTATE OPPORTUNITIES?
OKAY, JUST THE MOON ROCK. NO ONE IS EVER INTERESTED IN LUNAR REAL-ESTATE OPPORTUNITIES...
HERE YOU GO. ON THE HOUSE.

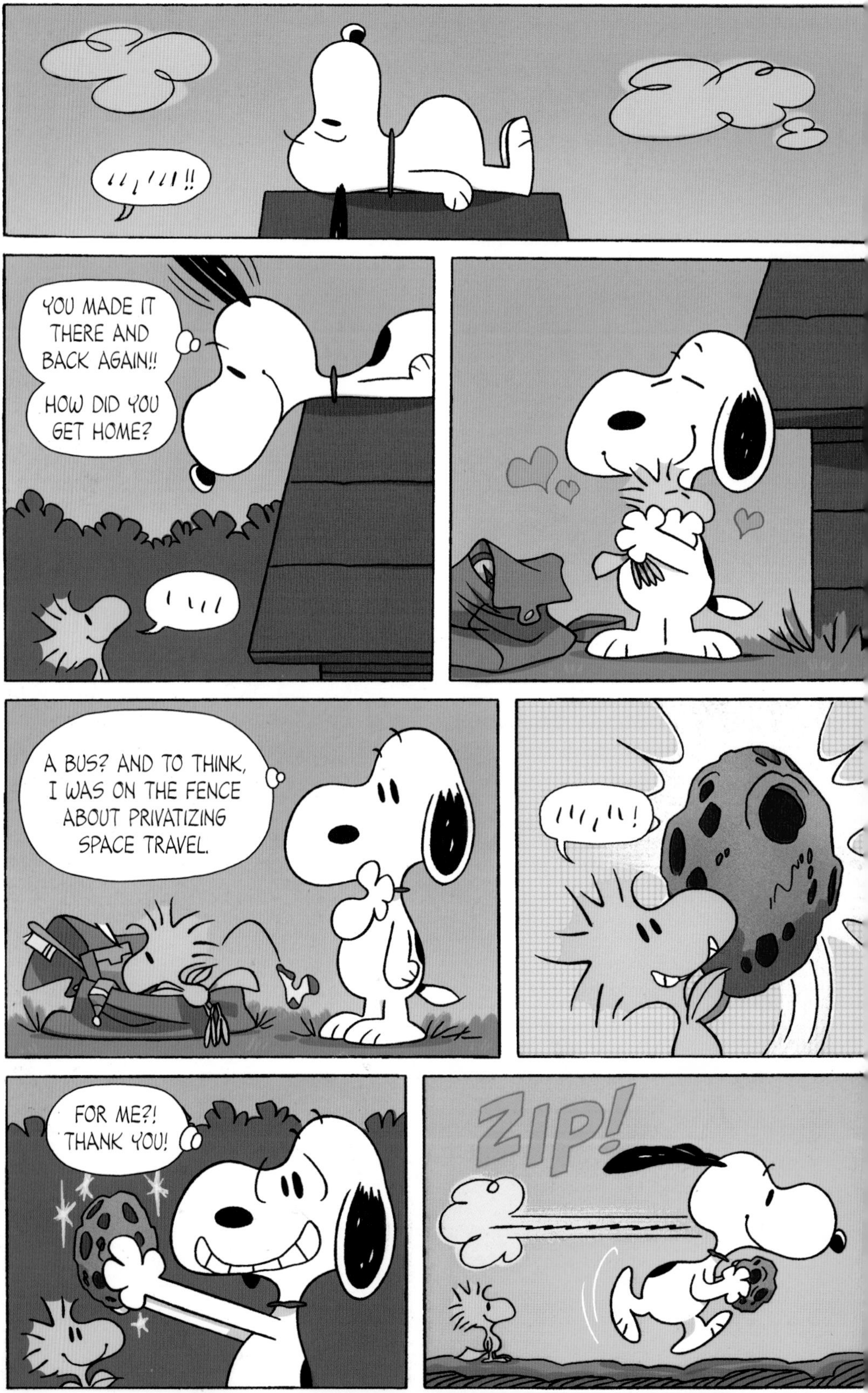
YOU MADE IT THERE AND BACK AGAIN!!
HOW DID YOU GET HOME?
A BUS? AND TO THINK, I WAS ON THE FENCE ABOUT PRIVATIZING SPACE TRAVEL.
FOR ME?! THANK YOU!
ZIP!

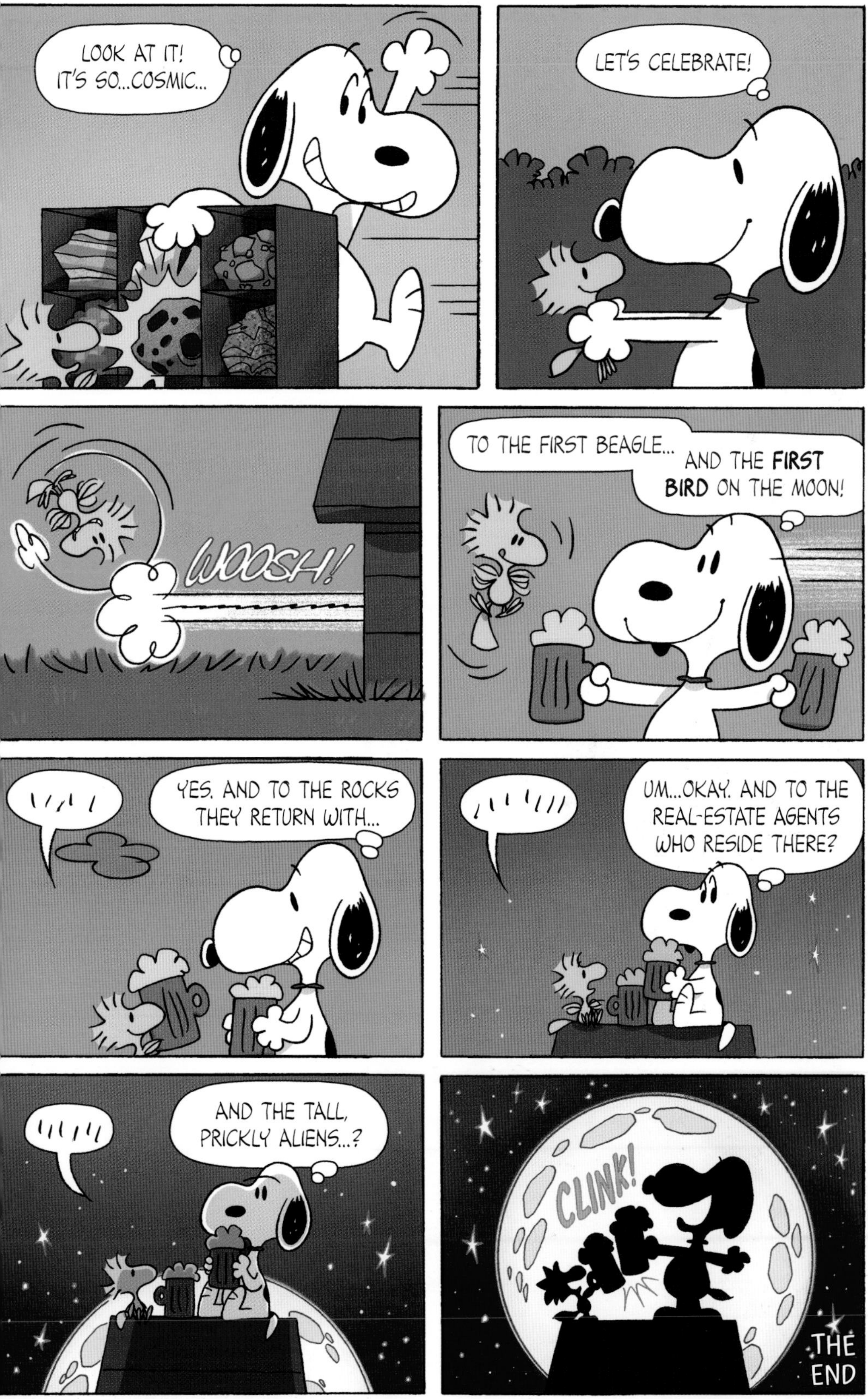
LOOK AT IT! IT'S SO...COSMIC...
LET'S CELEBRATE!
WOOSH!
TO THE FIRST BEAGLE...
AND THE FIRST BIRD ON THE MOON!
YES. AND TO THE ROCKS THEY RETURN WITH...
UM...OKAY. AND TO THE REAL-ESTATE AGENTS WHO RESIDE THERE?
AND THE TALL, PRICKLY ALIENS...?
CLINK!
THE END

# FROM THE
# DRAWING BOARD

## "Snoopy, literally, is the first character to go to the moon."

PEANUTS

"[NASA] wanted to start a new safety program around a cartoon character and they asked me if Snoopy could be the character...

I'M GLAD YOU'RE GOING TO THE MOON

"...They made beautiful little metal things...and if a person had a good safety record, one of the astronauts would present him or her with the pin and of course, those pins were taken to the moon landing. So Snoopy, literally, is the first character to go to the moon."

- Charles M. Schulz

THAT MEANS I WON'T HAVE TO FEED YOU TONIGHT..

REPORT THAT MAN TO MISSION CONTROL!!

* Sketches and pin images courtesy of the Charles M. Schulz Museum

# Behind-the-Scenes
## The Beagle Has Landed, Charlie Brown!

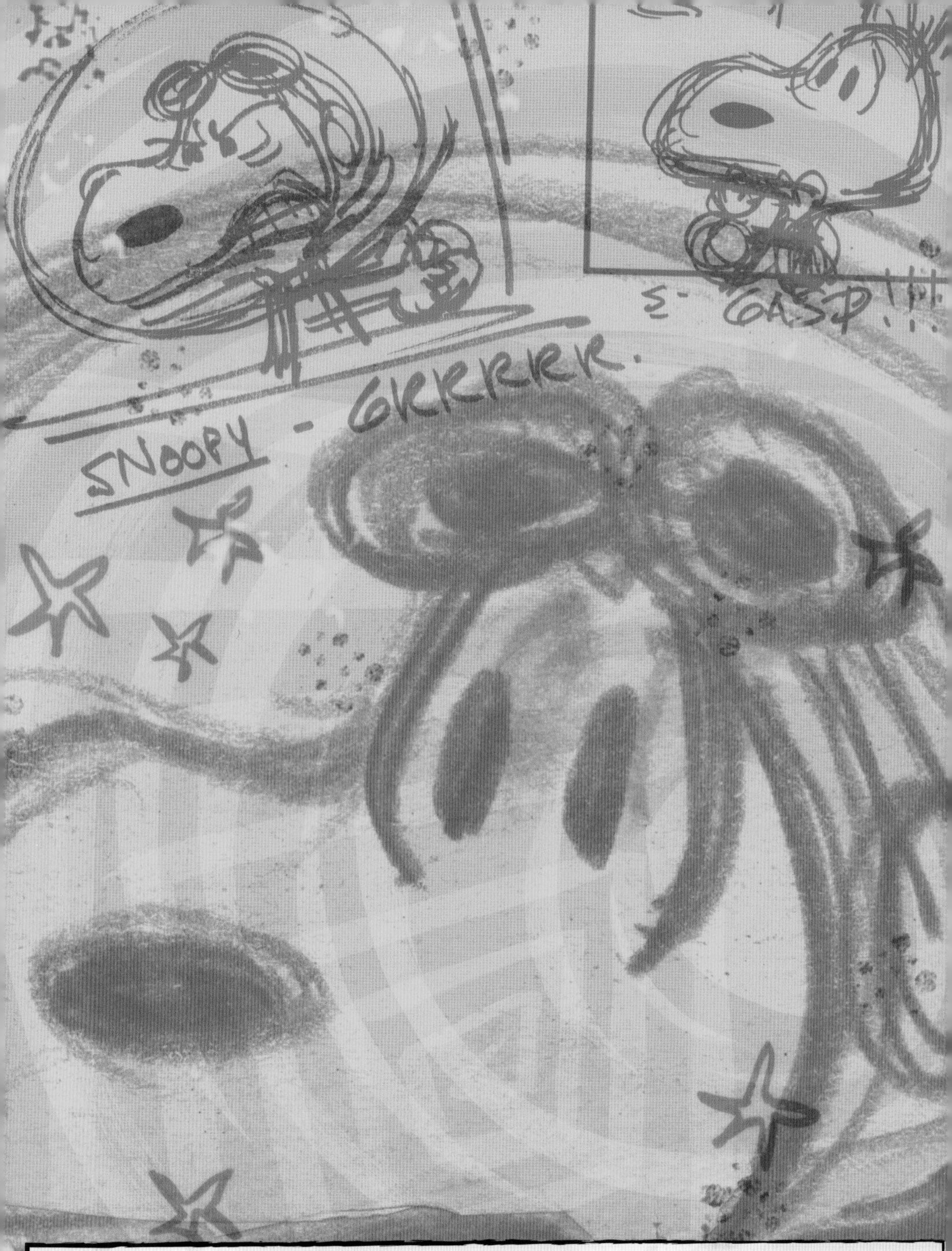
GASP!!!
SNOOPY - GRRRRR.

These are some of the developmental sketches and story ideas that went into writing *The Beagle Has Landed, Charlie Brown!* Art by Andy Beall and Bob Scott.

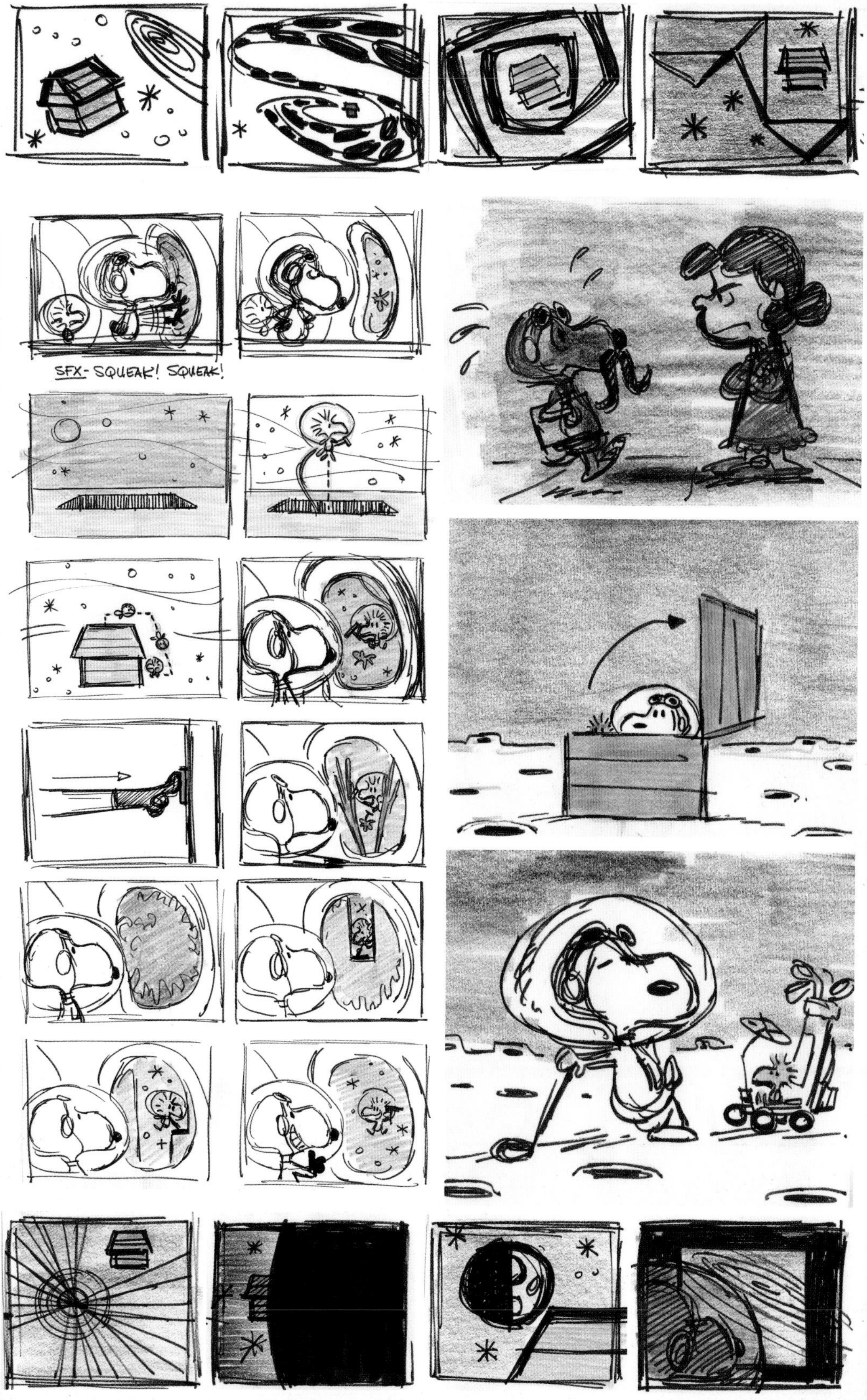
SFX- SQUEAK! SQUEAK!

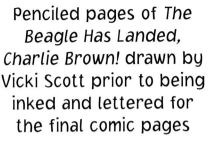

Penciled pages of *The Beagle Has Landed, Charlie Brown!* drawn by Vicki Scott prior to being inked and lettered for the final comic pages

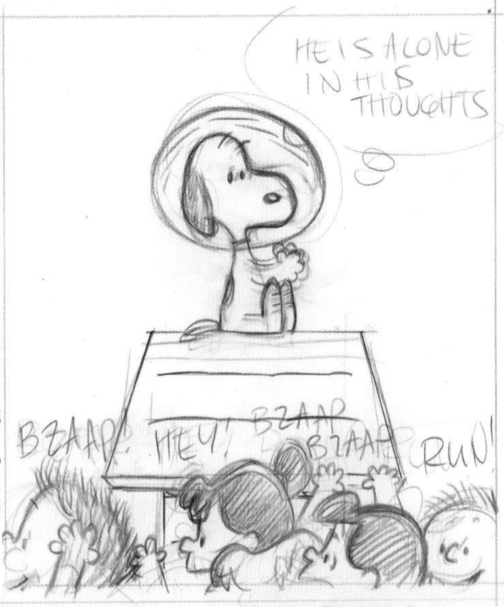
HE IS ALONE IN HIS THOUGHTS
BZAAP!
HEY!
BZAAP
BZAAP
RUN!

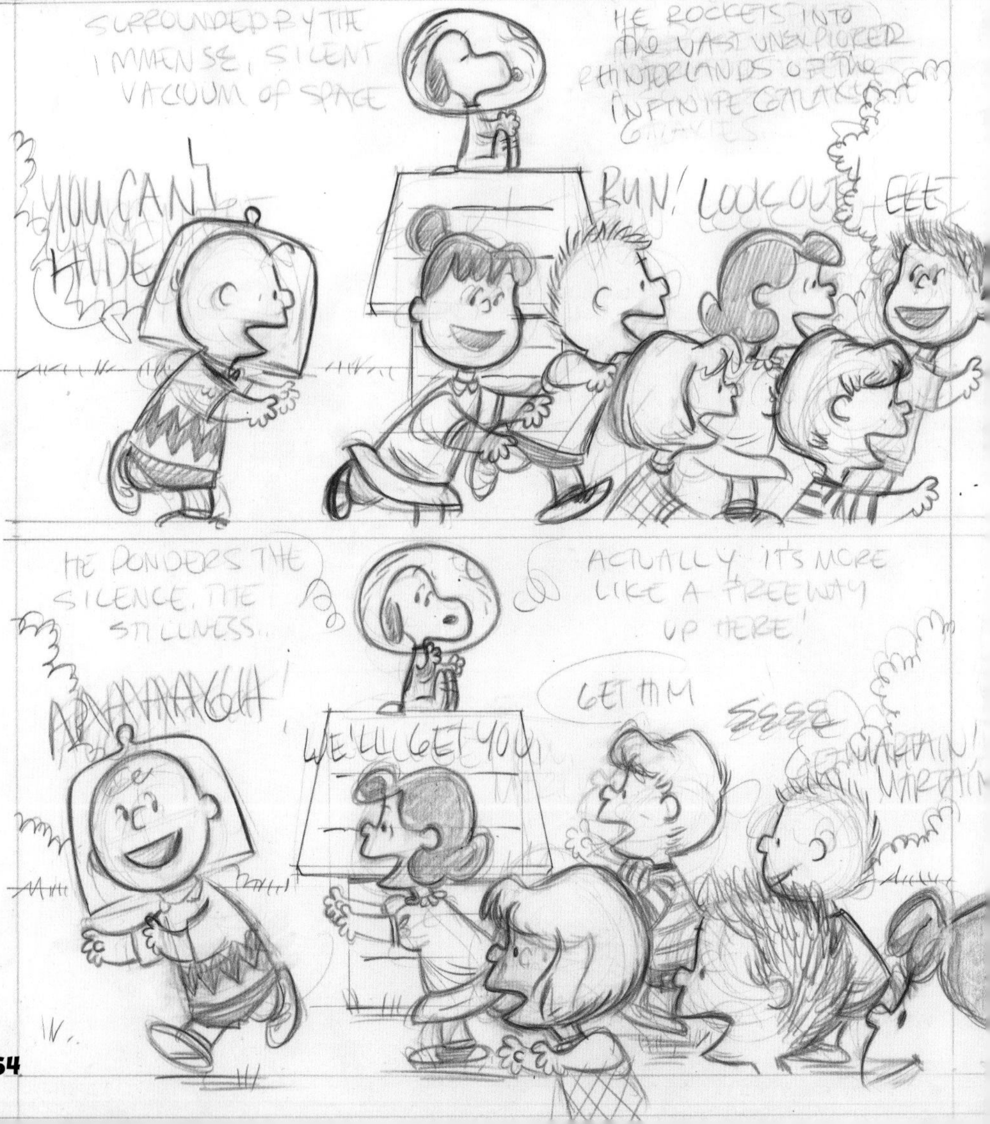
SURROUNDED BY THE IMMENSE, SILENT VACUUM OF SPACE
HE ROCKETS INTO THE VAST UNEXPLORED HINTERLANDS OF THE INFINITE GALAXY GALAXIES
YOU CAN'T HIDE
RUN!
LOOKOUT!
EEE
HE PONDERS THE SILENCE, THE STILLNESS...
ACTUALLY, IT'S MORE LIKE A FREEWAY UP HERE!
AAAAAAGH!
WE'LL GET YOU
GET HIM
EEEE
MARTIAN! MARTIAN!

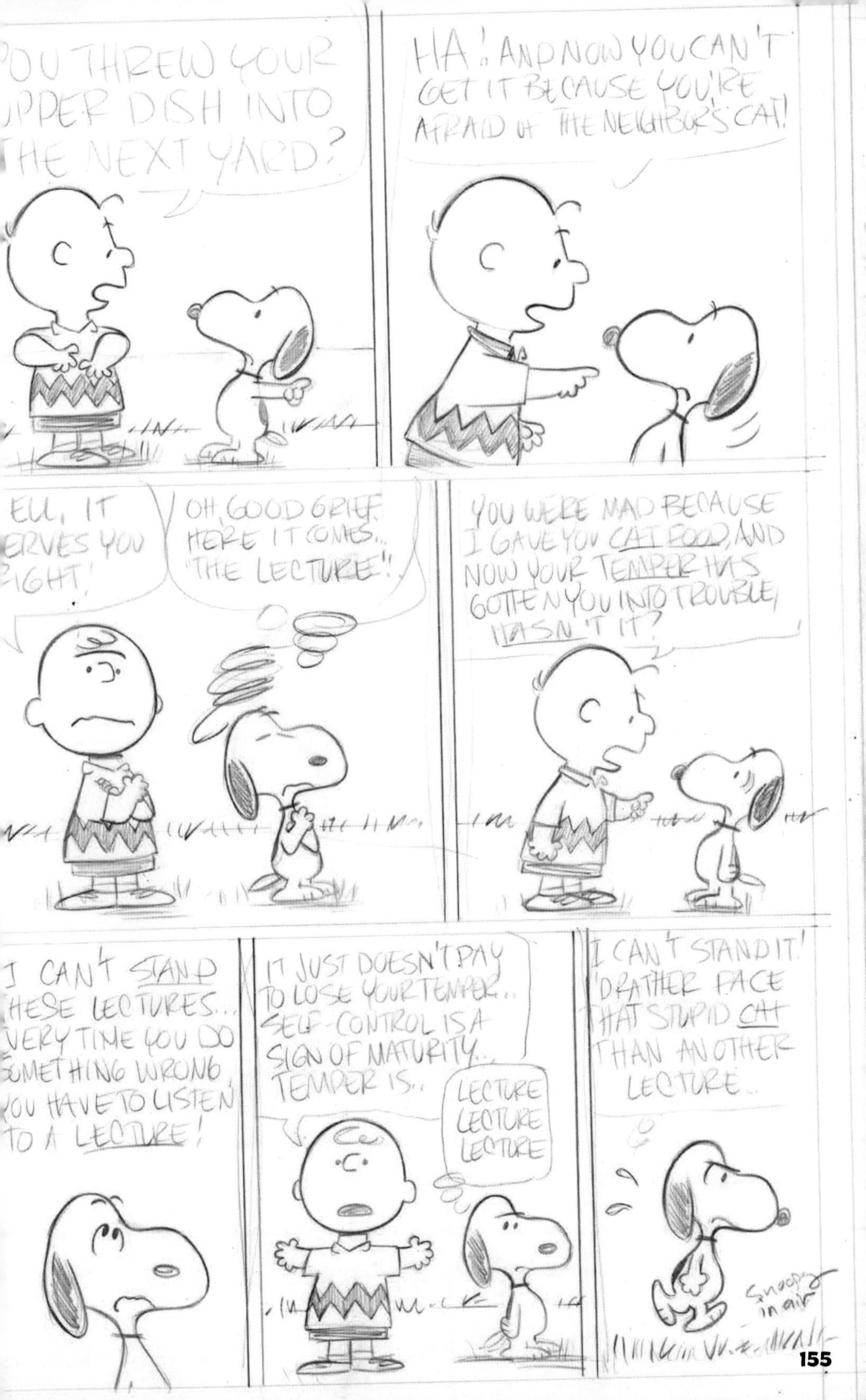
OU THREW YOUR PPER DISH INTO THE NEXT YARD?
HA! AND NOW YOU CAN'T GET IT BECAUSE YOU'RE AFRAID OF THE NEIGHBOR'S CAT!
ELL, IT ERVES YOU IGHT!
OH, GOOD GRIEF, HERE IT COMES... "THE LECTURE"!
YOU WERE MAD BECAUSE I GAVE YOU CAT FOOD, AND NOW YOUR TEMPER HAS GOTTEN YOU INTO TROUBLE, HASN'T IT?
I CAN'T STAND THESE LECTURES... VERY TIME YOU DO OMETHING WRONG OU HAVE TO LISTEN TO A LECTURE!
IT JUST DOESN'T PAY TO LOSE YOUR TEMPER.. SELF-CONTROL IS A SIGN OF MATURITY.. TEMPER IS..
LECTURE LECTURE LECTURE
I CAN'T STAND IT! 'D RATHER FACE THAT STUPID CAT THAN ANOTHER LECTURE..
Snoopy in air

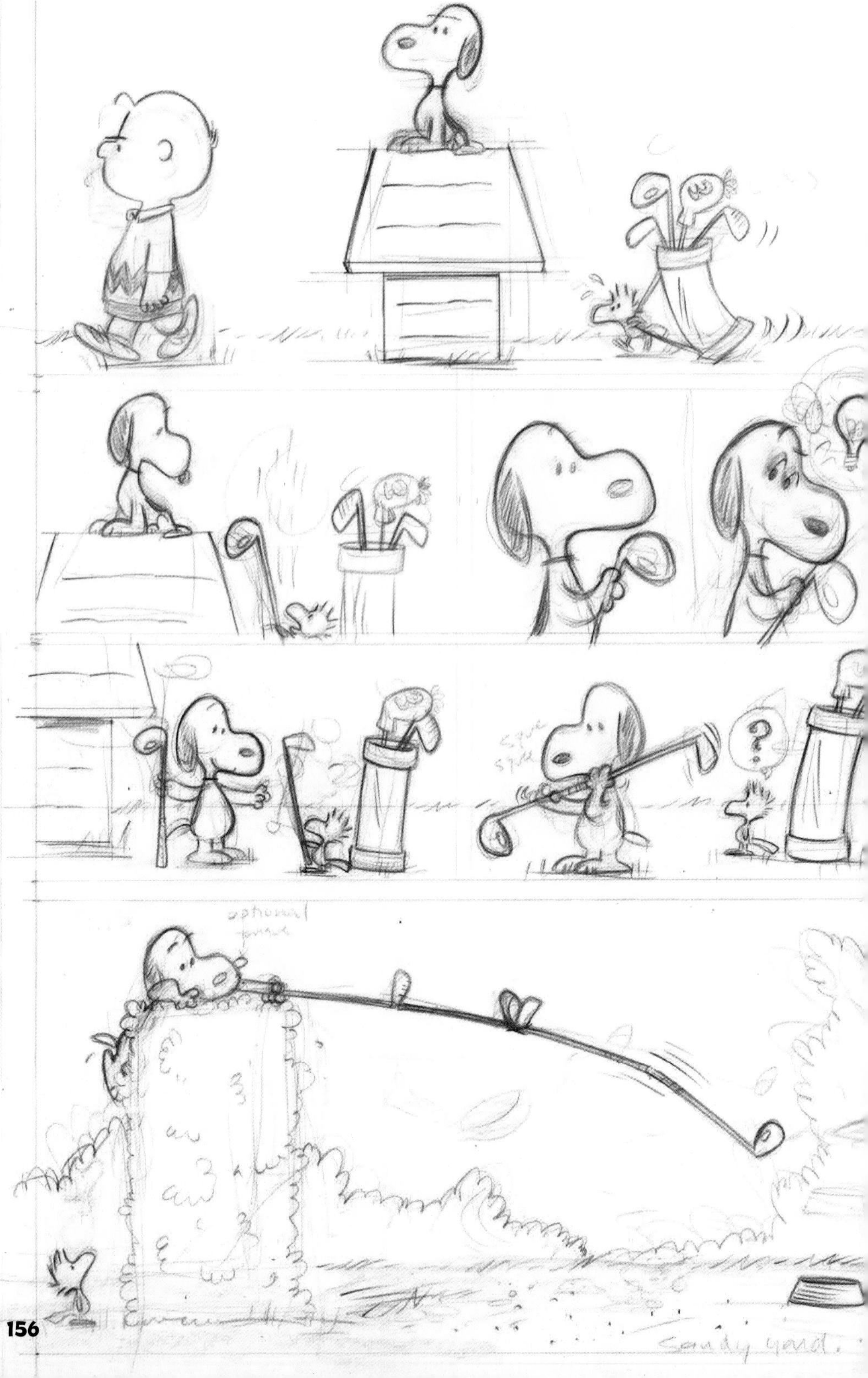
swing
swing
optional
tongue
Sandy yard.

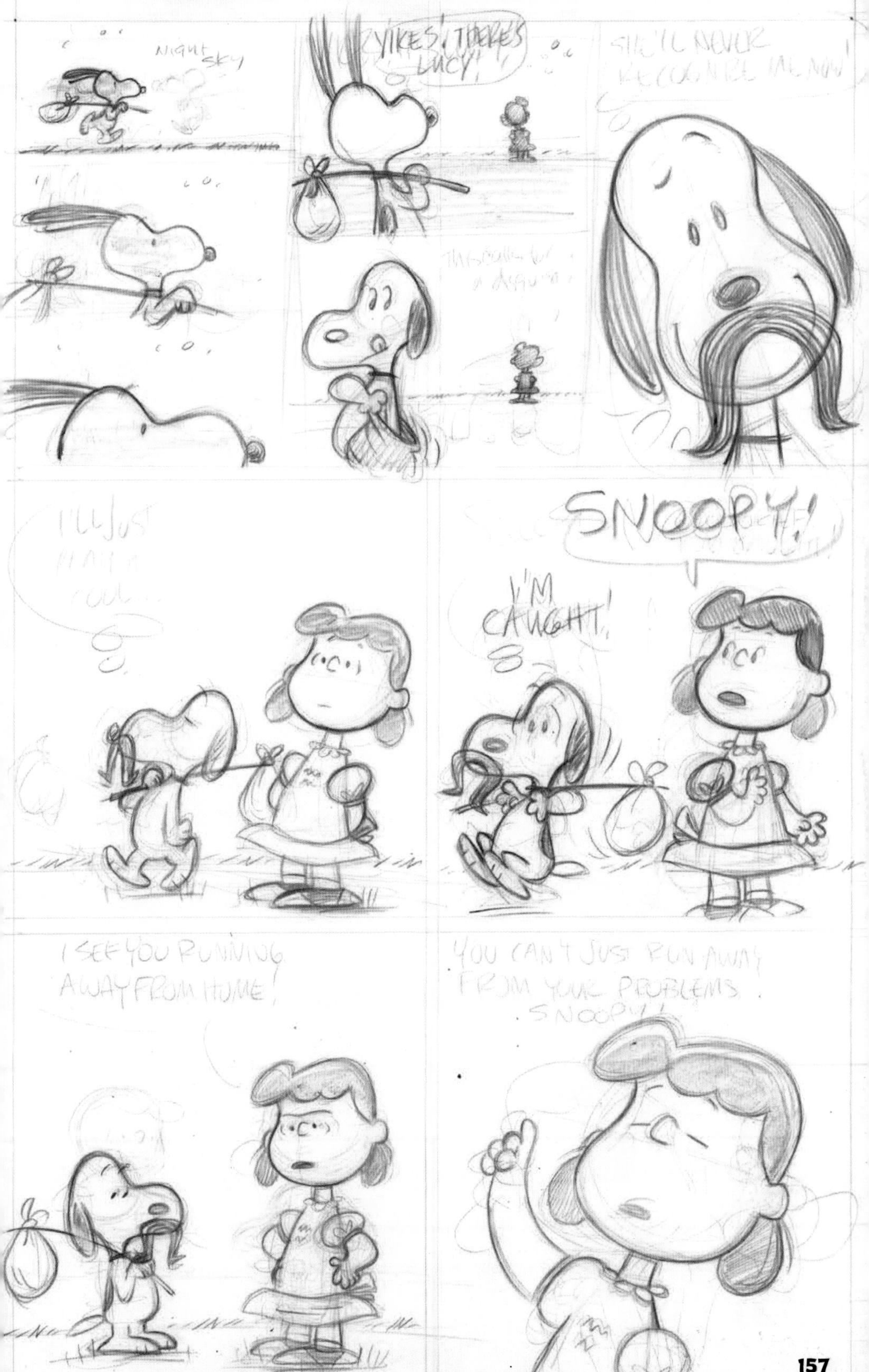
NIGHT SKY
YIKES! THERE'S LUCY!
SHE'LL NEVER RECOGNIZE ME NOW!
SNOOPY!!
I'M CAUGHT!
I SEE YOU RUNNING AWAY FROM HOME!
YOU CAN'T JUST RUN AWAY FROM YOUR PROBLEMS, SNOOPY!

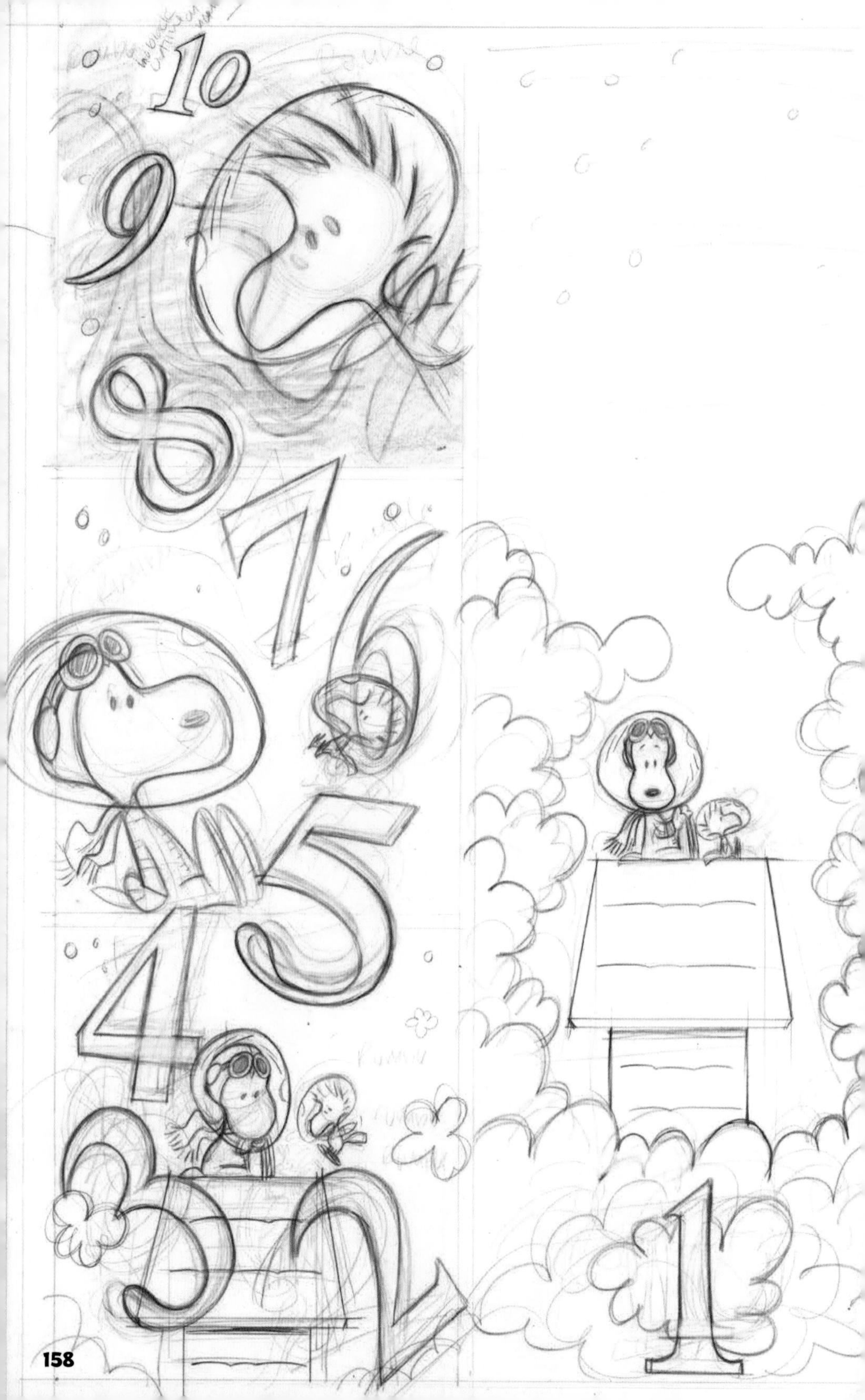
10
9
8
7
6
5
4
3
2
1

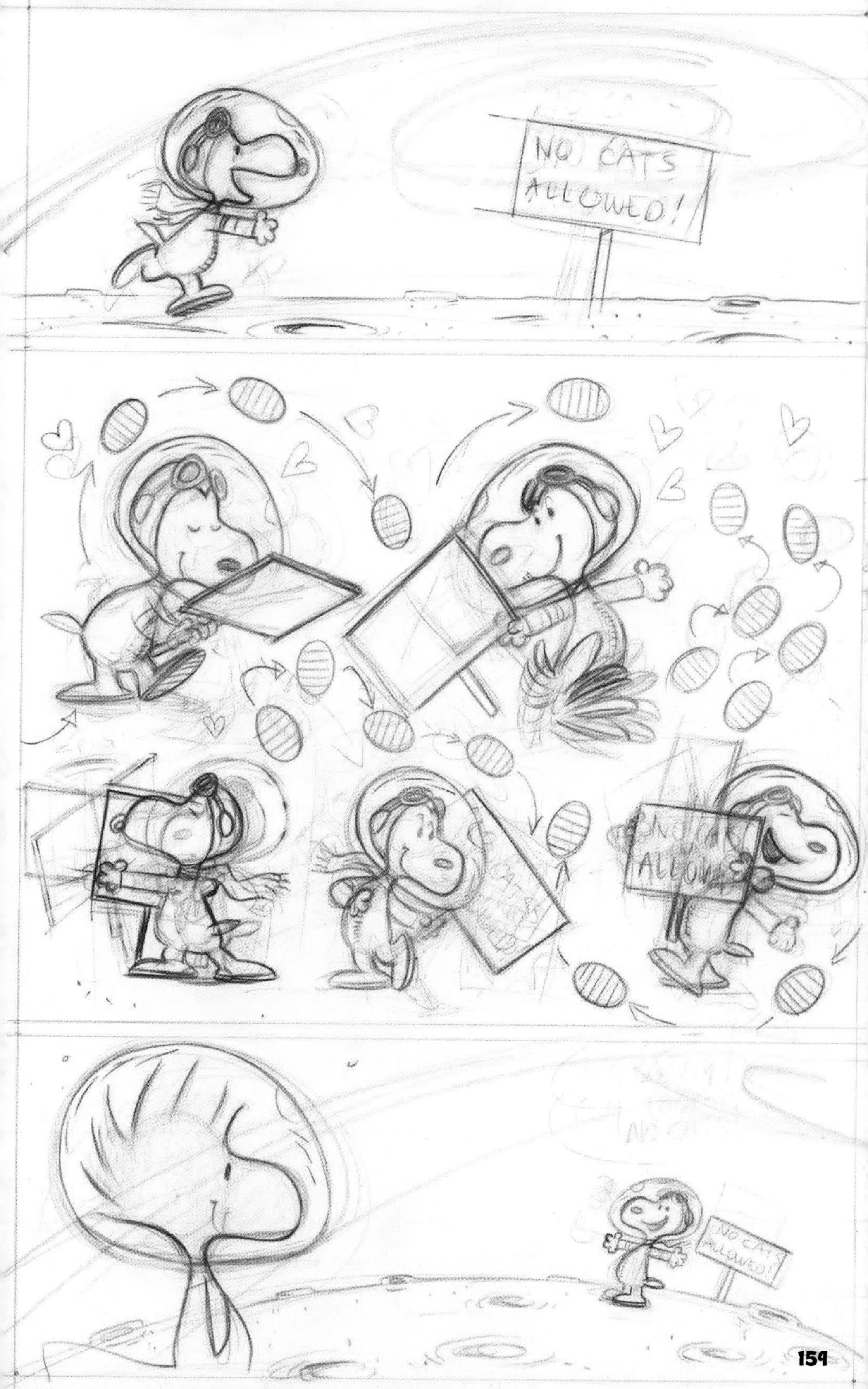
NO CATS
ALLOWED!
NO CATS
ALLOWED!

**Charles M. Schulz** once described himself as "born to draw comic strips." He was born in Minneapolis, and at just two days old, an uncle nicknamed him "Sparky" after the cartoon horse Spark Plug from the *Barney Google* comic strip. Throughout his youth, Schulz and his father shared a Sunday morning ritual reading newspaper comics. After serving in the army during World War II, Schulz's first big break came in 1947 when he sold a cartoon feature called *Li'l Folks* to the St. Paul *Pioneer Press*. In 1950, Schulz met with United Feature Syndicate, and on October 2 of that year Schulz's comic strip *Peanuts* debuted in seven newspapers. Schulz would go on to write and draw *Peanuts* for the next fifty years, and create cultural icons in Snoopy, Charlie Brown, and the rest of the Peanuts gang. At its height, *Peanuts* appeared in 2,600 newspapers across 75 countries and in 21 languages. Charles Schulz died in Santa Rosa, California, in February 2000—just hours before his last original strip was to appear in the Sunday papers.